Blow Row

Published by Burnham Publishing
Low Burnham Hall, Low Burnham, DN9 1DB

ISBN - 13 : 978-1508769545
ISBN - 10 : 1508769540

Blow Row

Si Kholmaimo may pachivalo sar o chachimo
There are lies more believable than truth

Dedicated to our Baltic Princess, Agnese
You inspire and support as both a wife and a best
friend

Publishing

Blow Row

Chapter 1 – His first day

Robert stepped out of the black cab on the corner of Harley Street and Blow Row. He pulled the thin fabric of his grey suit jacket tighter against the cold autumnal wind, regretting the decision to leave his old coat back at the apartment his uncle had rented to him.

"Ten fifty," the taxi driver snapped impatiently.

Robert fumbled in the jacket pocket of his brand new suit for his wallet.

"Keep the change," he replied, handing the driver fifteen pounds.

The driver sneered. "Yorkshire generosity." The window was still down as he drove away, chuntering to himself about short-arsed northerners having no business in London when they couldn't speak properly.

Robert pushed his brown, curly hair out of his face wishing for the third time that morning he hadn't let the barber talk him into a fashionable haircut. The floppy fringe hung over his hazel eyes regardless of the quantity of product he daubed through it. Robert straightened his shoulders. Picked up the briefcase his Aunt Carole had insisted he buy for his first day at his new job and walked purposefully towards the doors of the building on the corner of Blow Row. Its old-fashioned name belied the contemporary glass and metal exterior of The Fitzroy Clinic. Robert paused, taking a deep breath to steady his nerve. He wiped his sweaty palms on the legs of his trousers, took a steadying breath, grasped the oversized modern handle and pushed.

Robert knew something was wrong the moment he opened the highly polished front doors. The expected hustle and bustle of a busy cosmetic surgery seemed muted. He'd expected to see nurses in crisp white uniforms escorting patients to and from treatment suites and consultants in pinstripe suits flattering clients with champagne while pretending they weren't glorified sales reps. Instead, a gaggle of elegant ladies sat quietly flicking through the latest Cosmo. A few appeared nervous, others impatient at the delay. Robert thought he recognised the blonde with the large sunglasses and oversized hat from photographs he'd seen in glossy magazines. But he couldn't be sure with a cursory glance, and he didn't want to be caught ogling the clients. The attractive green eyed receptionist acknowledged him with a forced smile as he walked into the plush cream-coloured room.

"I'll let Mr Harrington know you have arrived," she said nervously, "If you'll just take a seat."

"Ah, Mr Sutherland, you've arrived," a plain mousy woman greeted as she entered the reception from the corridor. "Mr Harrington requests you scrub in." Her anxious tone confirmed Robert's suspicions. Something was definitely wrong.

Handing his briefcase to the still smiling receptionist, Robert followed the woman down the surgically white corridor, passing the modern minimalistic consultation and treatment suites he'd admired at his interview for junior surgeon.

"Where is Mr Fitzroy?" Robert stuttered, his Leeds accent even more pronounced with his nervousness.

The woman didn't answer. Instead she pushed open the heavy soundproof fire door and ushered him into chaos.

"Leave the drunk bastard," an exotic East Asian nurse shouted, "and help me get her off the floor!"

Robert couldn't hear the response over the metallic noise of surgical equipment being moved.

"Where's McGregor?" She paused. "I don't fucking care if he's being shagged by the Queen, get the bastard on the phone."

Robert pushed open the door to the surgical suite

and froze. The white tiled walls were covered in bloody spray, equipment and surgical tools were scattered across the floor next to something half-concealed by a blue surgical gown. Robert blinked as he recognised the body for what it was, a woman. Robert prayed she was still under the effects of the anaesthetic because the I.V. line had been torn from her arm, causing spurting arterial blood to mix with the growing red pool around her waist.

"Shit!" he exclaimed.

"No kidding, genius," the nurse he'd heard from the corridor snapped. "Now stop standing there gawping and help me get her onto the table.

Robert and the hulking anaesthetist helped the nurse lift the woman back onto the blood-covered table. Now that she was prone, Robert could see the origin of the bloody mess. Her gluteus maximus muscle had been cut so deeply the scalpel had sliced through fat and tissue to show the white of the bone beneath.

"The bugger didn't wait until the epinephrine kicked in," the anaesthetist said. "It looks like it's up to you to save the day."

"What do you want me to do?" Robert asked, unable to take his eyes off the pool of congealing blood.

"Stem the bleed!" the nurse shouted, pushing gauze into his bare hands.

"Gloves?" he requested, realising he had little option but to take the lead in this operation. "Where's Mr Fitzroy?"

The anaesthetist pointed to a chair in the corner of the room where an unconscious red-faced, plump man slumped, his head lolling backwards and saliva dribbling from his slack mouth.

"Too much fucking brandy at lunch," the anaesthetist spat. "Got the shakes while making an incision and cut too deep. Then he passed out, pulling this bitch with him," he gestured dismissively at the woman on the table.

Robert pulled on the surgical gloves and stared at the woman's buttocks.

"It's an arse. I'm sure you've seen one before," the nurse snapped. "For god's sake, stop her bleeding out."

An incision had been made between the cheeks of her buttocks, and while the scar would be hidden, the risk of infection increased tenfold. If he didn't get the bleed under control, she'd have serious post-operative complications. The nurse handed Robert a suture kit and surgical instinct took over.

"What procedure?" he asked when the bleeding was under control and the anaesthetist had reinserted the I.V.

"A B.I.G.," the nurse said.

Robert looked blankly at the anaesthetist.

"Butt Implant Gluteoplasty, Fitzroy's little joke. 'I like big butt, and I just can't lie,'" the anaesthetist explained, dancing as he rapped.

It was the most ridiculous thing Robert had heard and, for a moment, he had an inappropriate urge to laugh at the shaven-headed, blue-eyed anaesthetist.

"What result was she aiming for?" he asked.

"As usual, 'make me look like Beyoncé,'" the nurse said in a poor imitation of a teenage wannabe.

"So the bigger, the better," Robert replied as he cleaned the wound. "Was he intending to use lipo to enhance the shape?"

The anaesthetist shrugged his shoulders. "You can if you think it's needed, but you need to do it before you insert the implant. Last thing we need is silicone leaking everywhere."

Robert frowned, semi-solid silicone was notorious for migrating if left under the skin, and he'd rather not risk bursting the implant. He looked imploringly at the nurse, hoping she had some insight into the wishes of the lead surgeon.

"Don't ask me. I'm just the hired help," she

sighed, absolving herself of all responsibility.

Robert massaged the woman's buttocks, trying to make sense of the black surgical marks underneath the blood.

"Pass me the cannula," he said reluctantly as he made out three parallel lines on the outside of her cheeks. "Has the epinephrine taken effect?"

The anaesthetist looked at the swollen tissue of the woman's bottom. "Hard to tell with all the bruising," he said. "You'll just have to cut into her and see if she bleeds. If she does, I'll push some more drugs through."

Robert steadied his hand and made a small incision. A bubble of blood formed on the surface.

"Looks good," the anaesthetist said. "That's just the underlying bruising. You're good to go."

Robert pushed the cannula inside the small incision, forcing it backwards and forward to loosen and suction out the adipose tissue. He repeated the procedure with two other incisions, following Mr Fitzroy's surgical marks. Moving to the other buttock, he replicated the process, checking every few minutes to see that he was creating, as best he could with all the swelling, a symmetrical bottom for his first client. Passing the large cannula back to the nurse, he requested the implant and was amazed at the 600ml bag of silicon she handed him.

"Beyoncé!" the nurse repeated, raising an eyebrow.

Robert carefully double-checked the pocket he'd created, then pushed the implant underneath the gluteus maximus muscle before suturing the wound closed. Efficiently, the nurse passed Robert tape to cover the wound and then a scalpel to make the next incision.

Three hours after he'd walked into The Fitzroy Clinic, Robert made the last suture and taped the wound closed. Inserting the two drains he straightened his shoulders and stretched his back. The anaesthetist checked the patient's vitals, and the nurse removed the blood-soaked gown and bandaged the woman from her waist down to the middle of her thighs.

"Best if she doesn't see the bruising," she explained.

"Congrats Mr Sutherland," the anaesthetist said, holding out his ungloved hand to Robert. "Will," he introduced himself. "And the goddess of a woman in scrubs is Dylees." He gestured at the beautifully exotic nurse with dark eyes that slanted slightly, showing her Eastern heritage. "And you know our commander in chief, the esteemed Fitzroy." He waved at the still-unconscious man.

"Robert," Robert replied automatically, removing his gloves and shaking the man's hand.

Will was tall and attractive, somewhere in his mid-forties. His head was shaved, probably to hide the thinning, but the man worked out. His arms bulged out of the blue scrub top as he grasped Robert's hand.

"Well, Rob," Will said. "Not bad for your first day. Looks like you saved our commander in chief. Trust the old bastard to get pissed before an op."

"This has happened before?" Robert asked, dumbfounded.

"Yep, but usually McGregor's here to clean up any mistakes. He's arsing about on breakfast TV this morning, promoting ThreadLift and wooing the nation. So we get stuck with the incompetent drunk. Dylees, when you've taken our valued patient here to the recovery suite, could you get Claire to clean up in here. Rob and I will move the commander into the staff room before the clients see him passed out."

Dylees bowed her head in greeting as she pushed the now blood-free patient out of the surgical suite and down the long corridor.

"Give us a hand," Will grunted as he put his shoulder underneath one of Mr Fitzroy arms. "Shit, he stinks."

Robert approached cautiously, wrinkling his nose at the overwhelming stench of stale alcohol and sweat. He nearly dropped the dead weight back onto the floor when his hand came into contact with the damp, sweaty fabric under Fitzroy's armpits.

"Are you sure this is just alcohol?" Robert asked, noticing the red sheen on Fitzroy's face.

"Usually, but with Fitzroy you can never be sure," Will laughed.

Robert looked enviously at the flawless six pack, clearly visible even through the thick scrubs. He bet Will was never drunk, no one with such dedication to his abdomen and biceps would choose to poison his body with a million alcoholic calories. Growth hormones might be a different matter. Robert wasn't tanned or toned. Years of studying and long hours spent in the hospital wet lab had given his skin a decidedly sallow appearance. The diet of unhealthy cheap food and sugary, caffeinated drinks had gathered around his middle, so even the expensively cut suit his Aunt Carole had bought him didn't hide the flab.

"You go to the gym?" Will asked hopefully as the pair heaved Fitzroy's dead weight down the white corridor and into the sparsely furnished staff room.

"I'm not really the gym sort," Robert answered.

"Shame, I was going to suggest we bugger off to the gym until McGregor gets back from his media gig. I'll have to get Claire to work out with me instead." Will raised his eyebrows, suggesting the workout he had in mind for Claire wasn't the same as the one he'd had for Robert.

"Shouldn't we call for an ambulance?" Robert asked, concerned at the colour of Fitzroy's face.

"Nah, we've the press camped outside to take snaps of Lady Elizabeth when she leaves. Last thing we need is them seeing our esteemed commander stretchered out of here."

"But…"

"Leave it, new boy," Will barked. "We're all on a good thing here. Don't ruin it. The drunken sod will come round soon enough."

"Anywhere I can get a shower?" Robert asked to change the subject. "I'm not sure Mr Fitzroy would appreciate me leaving the building looking like this." He gestured at his blood-stained shirt.

"End of the corridor to your left. And seeing as you're not coming to the gym, you can explain to Lady Elizabeth why her surgery is delayed. Give her any reason other than the truth."

Will left, leaving Robert alone with his unconscious boss.

"Not the start I imagined," he said to himself as he bent down to check the vital signs of Mr Carl Fitzroy. Will was right, whatever combination of drugs and alcohol the portly, white-haired surgeon had taken didn't seem to be life-threatening. While his heart was beating a little faster than normal, he'd live. The sheen of sweat on his face, combined with the dilated pupils and rapid heart rate, pointed to cocaine, the red bulbous nose and yellowing skin indicated chronic alcoholism.

Robert took a clean tea towel and wet it under the tap. He wiped the sweaty round face and loosened the man's damp clothing. There was nothing else he could think of doing to assist his new boss. A cough at the doorway made him jump.

"Thought you might need these," Dylees said, holding out a neatly folded fluffy white towel and a blue scrub top. "It won't go with your suit, but at least it's not covered in blood."

"Thanks."

"You did well in there today. I think we'd have lost her if you hadn't arrived."

Robert nodded, not sure what he should say.

"This business has a way of changing you," she paused, looking like she wanted to say something more,

12

her expression softened. "You have a shower. I've cancelled afternoon surgery for everyone but Lady Elizabeth. McGregor is on his way from Elstree Studios, so if you can just drag out the pre-op with Lady Liz, we'll weather the storm."

Robert nodded again.

"Man of few words. I wonder if you're full of action." Dylees laughed as she looked him up and down in an appraising manner, bringing a blush to his cheeks. Dylees laughed even louder as she patted him on the shoulder and left. Robert watched her strut down the corridor as if she owned the building, her long, black hair tied in a loose ponytail and her small frame confirming Robert's suspicions of a mixed Eastern heritage. He was sure the ladies attending the surgery were jealous of Dylees' high cheekbones and exotic dark eyes. Just like they'd be envious of the receptionist's flame-red hair, green eyes and slim figure. The anomaly in the group was the young girl who had escorted him to the surgical suite. Her mousy, slightly overweight appearance seemed too ordinary for the enhanced beauty of the clinic.

Robert stood under the gushing water, the hot shower a welcome comfort to his tired muscles. The utilitarian stainless steel tray under his feet heated up as the steaming water ran from the powerful showerhead. Like everything in the staff bathroom, it was designed for practicality. Nothing luxurious invaded the room, other than the soft, oversized towel that seemed awkwardly out of place over the metal chair. Robert rubbed the surgical soap vigorously over his body. The patient's blood had soaked through the fabric of his shirt to mat in the small swirls of hair on his chest. He tried not to think about the number of rules he had broken by operating on a patient without the correct supervision. Technically, Fitzroy had been in the room, but those thin semantics wouldn't save him if the case were investigated by the FOBPS.

The air was icy against his warm skin. He quickly rubbed himself dry and pulled on the blue scrub top and his immaculately tailored trousers. He thought about putting on his jacket but decided it would only add to the ridiculousness of the outfit. Looking into a small hole he'd rubbed in the steamed-over bathroom mirror, he smoothed back his unruly brown hair and decided he looked as presentable as he could. Robert straightened his posture, took a deep breath and walked back into the madness. He passed the staff room where Fitzroy's prone body still lay and poked his head around the door to check on the old surgeon. The sweaty sheen had faded, and faint snores bubbled from Fitzroy's mouth in a rhythmic, reassuring regularity. Robert lengthened his stride past the surgical suite, now spotlessly clean as if nothing had ever happened, and strode towards the recovery suites. Two of the three recovery suites had blue occupied notices on the doors, and on impulse, he decided to check on the Big Butt patient.

"Do you mind!" Will snapped when Robert opened the door to the recovery suite nearest to him. "This aint a fucking orgy."

Will leant against the bed, his blue scrub trousers around his ankles and a very naked woman on her knees in front of him. Robert tried not to stare at the large breasts and ample bottom of the mousy woman kneeling metres away.

"Did I tell you to stop?" Will growled pulling her face back towards his dick.

Robert watched as she wrapped her mouth around the erect penis and started rocking. Will grabbed hold of her hair with both hands and arched his back.

"Hey, mate, if you want to watch, it'll cost you," he laughed as he thrust forward. "Claire doesn't mind, do you?"

Claire couldn't reply with a mouthful of cum. Will stretched indulgently before reaching down and picking up

Claire's white blouse. He wiped himself clean on the fabric and discarded it back on the floor before pulling up his trousers.

"Go clean yourself up. That's a good girl," Will said, spanking her playfully on the bottom. "A bit of an overweight plain Jane," Will said as she left the room, "but the plain ones always tend to be goers. McGregor encourages the homely staff to have a little bit of surgery at cost when we aren't busy, she'll improve in time. What did you want?"

"Nothing, I was just looking…"

"I know you were looking," Will interrupted.

"Looking for the buttock augmentation patient," Robert finished lamely.

"Ah, she's in suite three, across the corridor. Didn't you read the name on the door?"

"I don't know her name."

"Janet Kershaw. She's the wife of the IT billionaire. Yes, the one that's just floated his company. Don't look so worried. If anything goes wrong, we'll tell her she caused the damage by not taking things easy enough. Hint that taking it up the arse from billionaire boy dislodged the implant."

Robert looked horrified, and Will laughed again.

"For fuck's sake, Rob, where's your sense of humour?"

Will put his arm around his shorter colleague's shoulder and guided him out of the room towards Recovery Suite Three. Inside the surgically austere room lay Robert's still-unconscious patient. Her skin was an ashen grey against the white of the bed linen, and her bandaged bottom looked even bigger than when she'd left the operating suite.

"I thought it best to keep her sedated until the swelling goes down a little," Dylees said from the simple armchair in the corner of the room. "I'll get Will to bring her round in an hour, but for now, I'll need to keep her under observation. We'll transfer her to Re Vive, the recovery spa later today."

"Whatever you think best," Robert said when what he wanted to scream was, 'Wake her up now and check she's not going to sue!'

"Best if Fitzroy is awake before her," Dylees said as if reading his mind, "We wouldn't want to have to explain why her surgeon isn't available to check on her. Run along now and see Lady Elizabeth."

Dylees' tone and gestures so accurately mirrored those of his dead mother, when she dismissed him as a child in favour of a gentleman friend, he automatically obeyed.

"Lady Elizabeth?" he asked the slim red-headed receptionist.

"I'm Kate," she introduced herself before waving behind him to the only person who sat in the waiting room. Robert turned to look at the woman in large sunglasses and an oversized hat.

"Notes?" Robert asked as he stared at the beautifully familiar face of Lady Elizabeth. Now he knew her name, he wondered how he hadn't recognised her immediately. The trademark pout, high cheekbones, the long blonde wavy hair the gossip columns kept comparing to golden flax, her slim waist and pert bust shown to full advantage in the figure-hugging cerise suit.

"Notes," Kate said, pushing the file forward. "Robert, the notes."

Robert turned back to her. "Did you say something?"

"The notes you asked for!"

Robert turned his back on the goddess of his fantasies and opened the manila file. Inside were pages and pages of medical notes. Liposuction, tummy tuck, Botox, dermal fillers. Pre-op drawings scribbled with notes, drug dosages, expected outcomes and technical details. A comprehensive medical history showing a past of drug abuse, mental health problems, and emergency visits to A&E. Robert flicked to the page with today's date.

"Breast augmentation," Robert whispered, turning to look at the patient's soft pink breasts gently pushing out of the cerise fabric.

Lady Elizabeth looked up from her magazine and appraised the man who openly stared at her breasts. Dismissing the sallow, slightly overweight man in mismatched clothing as not worth her attention, she returned her interest to the catty article written about her friend Laura Philips. Perplexed, Robert frowned. What worried him wasn't the fact this beautiful goddess was having her pert breasts changed to something more buxom, but more that at the bottom of her notes were the words, 'Next – Rhinoplasty.' Robert looked carefully at Lady Elizabeth's face. Her nose was perfect, just like the rest of her. It must be a mistake or did her ladyship suffer from Body Dysmorphic Disorder. A surgeon as busy as Mr Fitzroy must have missed the signs of Lady Elizabeth's surgical addiction.

"Lady Elizabeth," Robert said, trying to disguise his Yorkshire accent. "My name is Mr Sutherland. I'm going to be looking after you until Mr McGregor is ready to take you into surgery."

"McGregor?" Lady Elizabeth asked, her rounded vowels emphasising her aristocracy and making Robert's knees weaken and other parts of him stiffen. "My dear man, my surgeon is Mr Fitzroy."

"Mr McGregor specialises in breasts," he blurted, "Mr Fitzroy wanted you to have the best and has asked Mr McGregor, as the leading surgeon in breast augmentation, to carry out your surgery. Mr Fitzroy will, of course, be supervising, but Mr McGregor will be leading your surgery." Robert knew he was waffling, but he couldn't help it under her intense gaze. Something about this woman made even stringing a sentence together challenging.

"Well, as long as Mr Fitzroy has approved the decision, I guess I'm satisfied." She paused. "However, one wrong move, and I will sue the lot of you. You've already kept me waiting. I would have left but for the horde of paparazzi outside."

"Would you like me to get rid of them before you leave?"

"Why ever would you do that?" she laughed. "Laura Philips is getting far too much coverage as it is."

Robert frowned in confusion.

"Press coverage," she said as if Robert were stupid.

Lady Elizabeth was twenty-eight, the darling of the society pages and the only daughter of Lord Mowbray, a highly respected judge. She was known for her ability to party and show off a variety of high fashion designer clothing. Robert had always felt sympathy for the young heiress hounded by a relentless press even as he devoured the articles splashed over the internet and newspapers. He had often been troubled by the invasion of her privacy as she appeared in various compromising situations on the front cover of the glossy magazines. He'd assumed she was a victim of the paparazzi, yet here she sat courting the very media that tried to embarrass and demonise her actions.

"Let's get you into pre-op," Robert said, confused by the reality of the woman before him.

Chapter 2 – Jelly beans

"It is all about choosing the right treatment," David McGregor continued. "If you only need a minor lift in the muscle tissue, then the new ThreadLift treatment is definitely the best solution. However, if it is a more drastic change, then I'm afraid it's back to the good, old, proven facelift."

"Very interesting, David," Hazel Woods agreed, placing her hand casually on the handsome McGregor's knee. "Could we persuade you to tell our viewers which of our volunteers are suitable for the ThreadLift treatment?"

Hazel gazed longingly at the tall surgeon. His dark, brooding eyes seemed to analyse the depth of her soul. She imagined her manicured fingers running through his almost-black hair, highlighted by flashes of distinguishing grey. Her eyes travelled from his clean-shaven face to his tanned neck, which hinted at an athletic physique. The top button of his crisp white shirt was left open under the expensively tailored black suit jacket, implying relaxed confidence.

"Of course, Hazel," McGregor said, flashing his flawless white teeth at the camera. "By all means, let's go and say hello to our audience volunteers."

McGregor flashed the same smile at the attractive woman sitting on the red couch next to him. Her pale blue eyes, blonde hair, petite figure and charismatic, chatty personality made her the perfect front woman for Morning Wake-up, but McGregor knew better. Her small, slim frame belied her ruthless nature. Hazel was a calculating, twisted monster who ruled daytime television with an iron fist.

"After you, Hazel," he said courteously, holding his hand out to help the five-foot-five dictator from the comfortable couch.

Across the studio, perched on high steel stools,

were four women over forty and one very attractive twenty-something. McGregor strutted across the studio, his eyes focused on the younger model. If he could just manage to get away from Hazel's clutches, he could slip his number and maybe something else to the twenty-something. The camera crew followed David McGregor's movements, his stride and posture designed to show masculinity without arrogance. Well, that was what the acting coach had told him when he'd started appearing on TV. David McGregor was concerned with appearance. He craved the limelight almost as much as his patients, but his need was more narcissistic. He not only needed people to see him, he needed them to admire him. His psychiatrist thought it stemmed from a neglectful mother, but McGregor knew it came from watching his father fuck the household staff. McGregor didn't need counselling. The shrink was just part of the celebrity lifestyle McGregor coveted. Doctor Smith-Jones was the trusted advisor and spiritual guide to London's elite, so regardless of the expense, he eagerly attended the unnecessary monthly appointment to talk about his favourite topic, himself.

"This is Fran. She's from Doncaster, and I'm sure she won't mind me telling you she's forty-two," Hazel said, smiling into the camera before turning to Fran. "You look splendid for forty-two."

"Thank you," Fran said, slightly confused by the half-compliment.

"What do you think, David? ThreadLift or facelift?"

"Well, Hazel," David smiled, "Fran is an ideal candidate for the ThreadLift." He touched the slightly loose skin under her chin. "You can see here that this skin has just lost a little of its elastin, the compound which makes the skin firm. Using the ThreadLift, we could lift here and here." He lifted the skin at either side to show the effect the treatment would have. "It would take about five years off Fran."

Hazel and David moved on to the next audience member. Hazel consulted her information cards.

"This is Sarah. She's fifty-four and from Kent."

"Good morning, Sarah," David said, resting his hand on the slightly plump shoulder. "I'm afraid Sarah here would need a full facelift. The loss of elastin and collagen occurred pre-fifty and has resulted in the skin stretching. A facelift would remove this excess and give Sarah a youthful look."

Sarah turned visibly red underneath the glare of the studio lights, and McGregor heard the sympathetic groan from the rest of the audience.

Hazel moved on quickly to the brunette. "This is Jane, from Salford. She's just turned thirty-nine."

David looked appraisingly at Jane. Her green eyes narrowed slightly as he stared at her large boobs underneath the pale blue jumper. She wasn't much to look at, David thought, but he'd love to nuzzle between those ample breasts.

"Jane is very lucky," David said, tearing his eyes away from the nipples he could see just poking through the wool. "She has excellent skin structure. The only problem is a little excessive adipose, or fat, around the cheek area. If we used the ThreadLift, it would give her back her cheekbones and help to destroy the fat cells. Jane is an ideal patient for this treatment."

"Last but not least, Candice from Sheffield. She's 25 and wants to be a model," Hazel introduced. "Maybe David will introduce you to some of his celebrity clientele."

"Now I couldn't do that. At The Fitzroy Clinic, we're very strict about client confidentiality." David ran his hand over Candice's soft face, his hand lingering over the wet plumpness of her lips. "Candice wouldn't be suitable for the ThreadLift. In fact, at the moment, I wouldn't recommend any treatment. Anyone who looks like Candice should invest in a good face cream and just keep looking after their skin. Candice is perfect the way she is."

Candice opened her mouth slightly and wet her lips with the tip of her tongue. Her hazel eyes challenged him to take her pink tongue inside his mouth. She tilted her head backwards a little to give him a better view of her long white neck and her honey-blonde hair which bounced around her heart-shaped face.

"As always, when people volunteer to be guinea pigs, The Fitzroy Clinic extends an invitation for a free consultation to further discuss anything we have talked about on the show," David said.

"That's very generous of you, David," Hazel added as the camera focused on a close-up of her face. "Now I think it's time for the news and weather. Mark, over to you."

"Did you see the shocked expression on the Witch-Hazel's face when our beloved David offered a free consultation to the young one?" the sound engineer laughed as the news took over the air.

"Why'd you think I pulled in so close? Old Witch-Hazel should remember who makes her look good when she barges me out of the way in the morning," the camera man chortled.

"So which fanny do you think David will be getting wet during the commercial break?"

"My money's on Candice," the cameraman replied.

"Witch-Hazel has claws!"

"Candice has nipples like jelly beans. Here, have a look." The camera man zoomed in on Candice's breasts.

"I'd sure like to suckle on those beans."

Unaware of the conversation, Candice twisted her shoulders and thrust her jelly bean nipples at David McGregor.

"Did you really mean it?" she asked in a husky half-whisper, her lower lip trembling.

David tore his eyes away from her chest and

looked at her lovely lips. "Mean what?" he asked.

"That I'm perfect the way I am?" She bit her lip invitingly and leant towards him.

"Yes, in my professional opinion, you are perfectly perfect," David said before lowering his voice. "In fact, Candice, I would love to take some photographs of you as an example of perfection."

Candice licked her lips and leant in even closer, brushing her mouth softly against his ear. "I'd let you."

"David!" Hazel's shrill voice broke through McGregor's wandering fantasies of a tied-up Candice posing for him through a camera lens. "David," she repeated, "we've gone to commercial break. I was hoping you'd discuss next week's slot with the researchers."

David gritted his teeth. Hazel was truly awful sometimes. The darling of daytime television was a bitch when she thought someone was treading too close to her toes. Her imperious dominance was a turn-off, and he'd have to resort to taking her from behind or beating the arrogance from the wicked witch. At least she had a good arse. He'd enjoy slapping the soft white skin until it turned red, but not as much as he'd enjoy corrupting the delicious Candice.

"Coming, Hazel!" he shouted over his shoulder. "Sorry, darling," he purred to Candice, "I'm afraid duty calls, and work must come first. Could we pick up this conversation later on this evening? Maybe at my hotel?"

McGregor never took women back to his West End apartment. It was too difficult to get rid of them in the morning. And once they knew where you lived, it made it all the harder to prevent them turning up unannounced. He'd had a stalker once and, while flattered by the attention, it gave him the creeps to think about some psycho bitch going through his rubbish.

"I'll think about it," Candice said, running her hand down his firm chest and resting one delicate manicured finger on his trouser belt.

David felt himself harden; he coughed and took out a business card from his wallet. "So will I." He passed her the card and regretfully turned his back on the tall, sexy Candice. At least he'd be able to think about her pert nipples while shagging Hazel.

"The witch defeated the kitten," the camera man said.

"Ah, but I think the kitten is playing a longer game, and McGregor is the mouse," the sound engineer replied

"Coffee?"

"Yeah, but let's go for a pint after we wrap."

David left the set and followed the trail of Chanel Number 5 to Hazel's dressing room. He knocked on the door and waited until he heard her invite him inside. He opened the door and took a step backwards as the overpowering perfume assailed his eyes, and he had to blink to stop them stinging.

"My darling," David said as he managed to stop himself from gagging and closed the door. "You look ravishing."

Hazel looked at his reflection in the dressing table mirror. She had removed the smart suit which shouted daytime presenter, instead displaying her slim figure in a lacy red bodystocking. The fabric cupped her large breasts in diaphanous red chiffon, and when she stood up from her chair, David could clearly see the high-legged thong exposing her best asset.

"Ah, David," Hazel purred, "you've caught me while I was getting changed."

David McGregor strode purposefully over to the semi-naked presenter and grabbed her breasts from behind, pinching them so hard she gasped.

"No, now I've caught you," he growled.

"So you have," she whimpered.

McGregor nibbled on the back of her neck and

trailed his tongue down the pale skin of her shoulder. He pushed her with his muscled forearm, forcing her forward over the dressing table. Keeping hold of one of her breasts, he used the other hand to pull at the thin lace string of her thong. She was already wet as he rammed his fingers inside her.

"Oh, David," she gasped.

"Quiet," he growled, pulling his fingers out before pushing them back inside her.

Hazel bit her lip to stop herself crying out in pleasure, and David laughed. "Much better."

David forced her legs further apart, pushing deeper and deeper inside her until she tensed and began to shake. "I don't think so," David hissed, pulling his finger from her and slapping her hard across her bottom. The slap left a red handprint on the pale white skin, and David felt himself stiffen. There was nothing quite as magnificent as the redness of pain. He slapped her again and again, bringing a rosy red glow to her cheeks, until he felt he could no longer stand the pressure building in his groin. Slowly, so she could hear each and every metal click, David unzipped his trousers. Then with a torturous lingering thrust, he slid his cock inside her warm, moist body. He smiled, appreciating every millimetre of entry as his quarry quivered in anticipation. His cold skin met the hot flesh of her beaten buttocks, and he shuddered in anticipation of the orgasm to come. Slowly, he pulled away and then pushed back forcefully deep inside her. She bucked against him as he knew she would. His phone vibrated in his pocket and then started the operatic ringtone signalling the clinic was calling.

"Still," he growled, fishing the phone out of his pocket. "McGregor," he snapped as he pressed the accept call button. "The bastard's done what?"

Hazel could hear a muffled voice on the other end of the phone. "Can't you wake the bastard up?"

More muffled conversation. "Okay, I'm on my

fucking way. But you tell the bastard from me, this is the last time I cover his incompetent arse."

David McGregor ended the phone call. Pushing the phone back into his pocket and pulled out of Hazel.

"Emergency at the clinic," he spat. "I have to go."

"Can I see you tonight?" Hazel whimpered.

"No," David said. "But if you're a good girl," he paused and pushed his fingers back inside her, "I might let you blow me next time I'm in the studio."

Hazel tensed and exploded in a world of pleasure as David allowed her to orgasm. She looked down at his marvellous cock. "I can blow you now," she whispered, taking hold of him in her warm hands.

"Don't have the time," David snapped, removing her hands and pushing his dick back inside his trousers. At least the sexual tension would make fucking Candice all the more enjoyable. Delayed gratification really was a carnal innovation.

Hazel looked at the departing back of David McGregor. He was a cruel lover, but he was hers. It was only a matter of time before he proposed and they became the next celebrity power couple. His brooding good looks and commanding manner combined with her feminine likeability and media contacts guaranteed success. They would control daytime television and one day make the transfer to the states.

"Hazel McGregor," she whispered to her reflection, picturing herself in a cream satin wedding gown. How much would Ok! Magazine pay for the rights to photograph the ceremony, she wondered blissfully.

The buzzer bleeped on the wall above the mirror. In five minutes, she was due back in the studio. Hazel smoothed her hair, applied powder to her reddened cheeks and slinked back into her blue suit.

"Two minute call!" a voice shouted from the corridor, followed by a polite knock on her door. "Two minutes, Miss Wood."

"I heard you!" she shouted at the underling.

David McGregor was not a happy man as he stormed towards his Jaguar. Not only had Fitzroy ruined a good fuck, he'd left Lady Elizabeth in the waiting room for over an hour and endangered the health of a good friend's wife. If Fitzroy's name hadn't been on the plaque above the surgery, McGregor would have kicked the alcoholic bastard out years ago. As it was, The Fitzroy Clinic couldn't survive without Fitzroy.

"Just hurry up and fucking die," McGregor whispered as he yanked open the door to his Jag.

At least the Sutherland chap had started today. If he'd managed to successfully cover for Fitzroy's fuck up, McGregor decided he would take the newbie to Bankers as a reward. It wouldn't hurt to corrupt the new surgeon, besides the best way to ensure someone's loyalty was to have a little bit of blackmail ammunition. Pushing the keys into the ignition and linking his mobile to the car's hands-free system, David decided he'd take Candice out for dinner as a prelude to taking her to bed.

"Clarmile," he said to the smartphone. After a few rings, a voice answered.

"It's David McGregor," McGregor said, "I'd like my usual suite for this evening."

"Good morning, Mr McGregor. Would you like champagne left in your room?"

"Yes," McGregor replied. "But make it a cheap bottle. Cristal should be okay."

"What time shall we expect you?"

"About eight thirty. Can you reserve me a table for two at nine?"

"Will that be all, sir?"

McGregor hung up, feeling confident in the delights of his evening entertainment. Candice would be impressed, and impressed young women were always so very grateful.

"Clinic," he said in a clear voice, and the phone started ringing again.

"The Fitzroy Clinic," Kate answered. "How can I help you?"

"It's McGregor," McGregor snapped. "What the fuck is going on?"

When he hung up the phone, he was surprisingly pleased with Fitzroy's choice for junior surgeon. It appeared Robert Sutherland had a little more going for him than McGregor had expected. He'd opposed Fitzroy's choice for the express reason that Sutherland was somehow related to the shark Sharp from the NuYu clinic. But Sutherland, it seemed, had come through and was competently carrying out the buttock augmentation surgery on Janet Kershaw. If he could charm Lady Elizabeth for half an hour or so, McGregor would be at the clinic in time to carry out her breast enlargement surgery. His journey Elstree to Harley Street would take at least an hour in this traffic. Turning up the classical music so it reverberated outside the car, McGregor drove.

Chapter 3 – Patty Cake

"Gwen, come look at this fool," Patrick Sharp laughed, his Irish twang still noticeable even after forty years in London. "Gwen quick, or you'll miss it."

The small auburn-haired nurse rushed into the comfortable staff room of NuYu and looked at her boss spread-eagled across the oversized couch and waving his doughnut at the big flat screen TV.

"Gwen, have you ever seen such a tit? And I'm not talking about the two melons on the front of Hazel Woods!" Patrick looked over his shoulder at the diminutive Gwen Charles, her heart-shaped face and high cheekbones never having a need for cosmetic enhancements.

Gwen glanced quickly at the screen. David McGregor was on his weekly style slot on Morning Wakeup. His sharp, black, tailored suit and dark, wavy hair with a smattering of grey, contrasted so much with Patrick Sharp's large white T-shirt, green surgical scrubs and balding head she had to laugh.

"What's the dick talking about this morning?" she asked, her hazel eyes crinkling mischievously as she laughed

"Well, in between slobbering over Hazel's melons and eyeing up the audience victims, he's telling the general public about the new ThreadLift treatments. You'd better let Sasha know to expect the ladies-that-lack will all be phoning for ThreadLift consultations. It doesn't take much for crowd mentality to kick in. I could kiss his hairy backside if I weren't so sure he waxed it."

Gwen laughed. "I'll get Andrew to check we have plenty of ThreadLifts in stock."

Patrick slumped back onto the sofa and rested his hands on his belly. He smiled to himself. It was going to be a good day. He'd an hour before treatments, and the new bubbly receptionist Sasha had turned out to be something of a saleswoman. She only needed to mention a treatment to potential clients, and the bookings came rolling in. His wife had forgiven him for his affair with the young glamour model, and he'd had a big win at the boxing. Life was indeed magnificent. He decided he deserved a cigar, a nice fat Cuban cigar, and a glass of Irish whisky.

Patrick stood and walked over to the tabletop humidor. He opened the cedar wood box and let the aroma of fine tobacco assail his senses. He ran his fingers over the crisp outer leaves. Why did the texture always remind him of his wife? Dry and brittle, but a complexity of richness underneath that could leave you feeling dizzy. Patrick sloshed a measure of Midleton's whisky into a glass, tucked the racing pages under his arm and headed out of the staff room into a small garden at the back of his clinic. He'd built the garden as somewhere for patients to sit and relax after treatments, but more and more he'd been escaping to this little green scrap of paradise. He sucked on the cigar, bringing a hot flame to the delicate end until the tip glowed red. He rolled the smoke around his mouth, enjoying the eucalyptus, chamomile and hint of creaminess that developed. He exhaled slowly, making small puffs of smoke on the cold air. Patrick sat underneath the willow arch and sipped his Midleton's whisky. He spread the race pages out in front of him and started studying form. It was due to be a cold, wet weekend in York, and the weather favoured Lady Red and Dom's-in-ator in the three-thirty. The odds were better for Lady Red. Patrick quickly circled Lady Red and five other horses, scribbling amounts at the sides of their names. He pulled out his phone from the pocket of his green surgical scrubs and called his bookie.

By the time he'd hung up, he'd placed over £1000 worth of bets on the horse races and, as an afterthought, had gambled yesterday's winnings on another underground boxing match. It was a good bet. If Azim Nyoni won, Patrick stood to quadruple his money. And if he didn't, well, it was only money.

"Patrick," Gwen called from inside, "your wife is on the phone."

"What does she want this time?" he mumbled under his breath. "Tell her I'll be right in!" he shouted over his shoulder before downing the last of the whisky in one throat-burning gulp.

"Patty Cake," his wife's syrupy voice purred on the other end of the line.

"Yes, Cupcake," Patrick replied. The pet names had been sweet when they were in the first flush of marriage. But after twenty years of being called Patty Cake in front of some of his closest friends, the sweetness had given him a cavity.

"Are you going to be home this evening?"

"Yes, Carole, I'll be home after surgery. Can Mae have dinner ready for eight?"

"Of course, Patty Cake. I was just wondering if you needed me. The girls are planning to go to the spa this afternoon and stay overnight..." Carole's voice trailed off.

"That sounds marvellous, Cupcake," Patrick smirked. "You have a fantastic time with the girls. Treat them to a champagne lunch on me."

Things had worked out excellently. He'd be able to rush home, have a bite to eat and then go watch the boxing. In fact, he could skip going home and have a liquid lunch at The Wellington Club. He made a mental note to call Mae after Carole had left and tell her not to expect him home until late in the evening. He also dropped Mr Green a text to put him on the door list for the boxing. The saying 'if your name isn't down you aint coming in' was taken to extremes by Trae La Muerte, the Bolivian cartel, running the underground bare knuckle boxing matches.

"Patrick," Gwen said, standing at the doorway of

Patrick's office, "your client is here. Do you want me to prep her for theatre?"

"No, I'll do it," Patrick replied. "She's in for a tummy tuck?"

"Yes, but Sasha's been talking to her about a buttock augmentation, so it might be worth having a quick chat about using the liposuction to extract adipose and re-injecting it today."

Patrick grimaced. It wasn't that he was opposed to some last minute additions to surgery. It was, after all, another three grand in his pocket and saved on surgical disposal costs. It was more the fact it would add another two hours on to his day. Greed won over. Three grand would cover his gambling on the bouts tonight.

Straightening his scrub shirt and smoothing back his thinning, black hair, Patrick marched into the waiting lounge with the authority of a surgeon at the top of his game.

"Mrs De-Costa, how delightful to see you again," Patrick said, offering his hand to the tanned twenty-five year old sitting in the plush armchair. "I see you've managed to get rid of your minder for the day."

The attractive lady laughed, throwing her head back, so the mane of dark brown curls bouncing around her lovely face. "Mr Sharp, you wicked. You know well Luis in car."

Patrick grinned. "Ah, but it would be more wicked if I whisked you away for lunch."

Mrs De-Costa giggled. "You know Luis is watching door."

"Ah, but he cannot watch the back door as well."

"You are rogue, Mr Sharp. I tell my husband."

"No, you won't." Patrick smiled and ran his fingers gently over her hand. "Now," he said, his voice turning from melting honey to professional courteousness. "Sasha tells me you've been considering a buttock augmentation. Should we have a chat in the consultation room and discuss the possibilities?"

"Wonderful, wonderful, Mr Sharp. My husband like large bottom, mine too small."

Patrick looked at Mrs De-Costa's ample and round bottom. "I can see what you mean, my dear, but with just a little bit of work, I'm positive we can make a difference."

Mrs De-Costa smiled, showing her white veneered teeth. "I knew you'd fix me perfect."

Patrick took the lead and ushered her into the luxurious consultation room. No expense had been spared to make NuYu look as far from a medical centre as possible. The walls were covered with regal flocked wallpaper, the windows tinted and hung with burgundy brocade curtains. The furniture was antique, leather Chesterfield armchairs around a walnut coffee table. The usual trappings of a doctor's consultation room had been discarded in favour of a cosy opulence to put clients at ease and make them forget they were about to have an invasive medical procedure. Patrick Sharp realised a long time ago if a customer considered plastic surgery in the same way as a facial or Botox injection, they relaxed. Take away the fear, and you took away the inhibition, after that, clients automatically spent more.

Patrick left the room while Mrs De-Costa changed into the luxurious white dressing gown. He buzzed Gwen to chaperone and checked the diary for the rest of the day's appointments. His finger moved down the paper diary. Botox, fillers, more Botox, nothing challenging. If he was delayed in surgery, Sasha would be able to smooth any ruffled feathers. Then, noticing a note on the page from Gwen, he sent his annoying nephew a 'good luck on your first day' text message. It wasn't that Patrick felt any particular warmth towards his newly qualified nephew, but more that his useless nephew might come in handy for a bit of insider information now he worked for the arse,

McGregor. Patrick Sharp was greedy, and if he could poach a few of McGregor's richer clients to the other end of Blow Row, he'd be a happy chappie. What was it his Yorkshire mother-in-law used to say? 'Appy as a pig in muck.'

"Andrew," Patrick said as he knocked on the anaesthetist's office door, "Mrs De-Costa will be having fat injections with her vaser liposuction. If you can make sure we are set up for the treatment."

Andrew nodded and went back to reading his car magazine. Patrick stood silently in the doorway, staring at the curly brown hair of the anaesthetist until he closed the magazine and stood up.

"I was just reading up on the new Porsche. Can't decide whether to trade in the Merc and get something a bit more...you know, grr."

"You live in London, you hardly drive and from what I've heard, your penis is of average proportions. I'm not sure a Porsche will make that much difference to your 'grr.'"

Andrew slapped Patrick on the back as he went past.

"Get a haircut," Patrick ordered. Andrew was an amazing anaesthetist, but a childhood spent surfing in Cornwall had affected his outlook on life as well as his appearance.

Patrick waited and watched the anaesthetist until his tall, lean frame entered the surgical suite, safely away from distractions.

"What are you looking at?" Gwen asked, tapping her small foot impatiently. "Mrs De-Costa is this way."

"Just making sure Andrew is away from surfing magazines and car brochures," Patrick said, wrapping his arm around her slim shoulders.

Mrs De-Costa sat in the plush dressing gown on the leather armchair. Patrick glimpsed red underwear as she fidgeted in the chair.

"Sasha tells me you've been thinking about buttock augmentation," Gwen said repeating Patrick.

"Yes," Mrs De-Costa answered. "I think I might as well. Suck it out of tummy and push it in bottom. Seems good idea, don't you think?"

"Before we decide if you're having the treatment, I need to explain the procedure," Patrick said. "First, we carry out the vaser liposuction. We make a small incision here and here." Patrick demonstrated on Gwen's stomach. "Then we take out the adipose tissue. This gets stored and purified, and we inject this adipose back into your buttocks, here and here." Patrick turned Gwen around and pointed to four places on her bottom. "We keep the injections small and evenly spaced to get the best shape. The benefit of this type of procedure is that we are using your own tissue, so there is no risk of rejection or of an implant rupturing. The downside is that it's fat, so if you exercise a lot, the effects will not be as long-lasting."

"But I just have it done again?" Mrs De-Costa asked.

"Why of course, this is the advantage of adipose injections. They can be done as and when needed."

"Perfect, let do it. Franco will be so surprised when he return Bolivia, and I have big bottom."

"I'll make the necessary changes to your account. Would you like a copy for your records?"

"No, no, I not deal with money. This is man's job."

It was always the same with his female Bolivian clients. They liked to spend money, but they never wanted to sully themselves with questions like how much. In fact, even knowing how much things cost seemed to suggest their families weren't wealthy, a characteristic he'd often taken advantage of. Bolivian women didn't want to know how much and Bolivian men didn't want to know what their women spent money on. You'd never catch a Bolivian gentleman exclaiming, 'You spent how much on shoes?' A man granted, expecting his wife to spend to excess, and a woman knew that whatever she wanted would be provided for. Conversations were not degraded with things such as amounts or value for money. It was their way, and Patrick played on that fact.

"I shall see to it," Patrick responded. "Now if you can just stand up and drop your gown, I will mark up for your treatments."

Mrs De-Costa stood up, dropping her robe to the floor so she stood tall and slim in her red thong and bra. Patrick consulted his notes and then took a large black marker and started to draw on her delicate tanned skin, two oblongs on each side of her waist and a small circle around her belly button.

"If you can turn round, my dear," Patrick instructed.

Mrs De-Costa pirouetted on her tiptoes, and Patrick started making black marks on her bottom. "This is where we shall inject the adipose," he explained, pressing gently on the underneath of her buttocks. "If we inject here and here, it will provide a fuller shape without widening."

"Wonderful."

"All done. Now if you can just go with Gwen, she will get you into your surgical gown and take you through to see Andrew. Is everything the same as last time? No change to your overall health? No medication you're currently taking? No chance of pregnancy?"

"Everything same as always. One day I will have baby, but you know Franco. Always tomorrow."

Gwen smiled at Mrs De-Costa, but Patrick knew she was thinking the same as him. Would Mrs Maria Lopez-de-Costa give up her incredible life and figure to be a mother? He didn't think so.

"This way, Mrs De-Costa," Gwen said, showing her out of the room. "Let's get you ready and comfortable. You remember Andrew, don't you? He's just going to take your blood pressure and ask a few questions."

Patrick could hear the two women chatting as they walked down the corridor. If he was quick, he had time to call Mr Green and his housekeeper, Mae, and maybe even the blonde he'd met last week. What was her name? Candy or something?

"All set, boss," Andrew said, poking his head around Patrick's office door. "We putting her to sleep?"

Patrick thought about it for a while. Unconscious patients were easy patients, awake ones tended to ask questions. "Keep her awake," he said after a pause. It meant she would be ready to leave the clinic a few hours earlier, and he would have more time at the club for a whisky and a bite to eat before the boxing.

Andrew headed to the pre-op room to chat with Mrs De-Costa before administer the local anaesthetic and drug concoction to enable Patrick to carry out the treatment. Andrew would be explaining how Vaser liposuction was much more refined, gave better results and produced less bruising. 'You'll be in your bikini in no time' was one of his favourite phrases as he placed a reassuring hand on the patient's arm. Many a client had fallen for the soft brown eyes and warm smile of the charming anaesthetist. Patrick wondered if the bachelor would ever take up the plentiful offers to be a kept man. He guessed it would depend if those offers included a surfboard and a Porsche.

Patrick wandered along the hall of the clinic he'd started eight years ago at the height of the recession. He'd not been able to afford a property on Harley Street and had to settle on this building on Blow Row, a small narrow street just off the famous road. Number thirty-seven had once housed an old boys club which had closed with the implementation of the smoking ban and sexual discrimination laws. The Victorian building had just enough period features for Patrick to fall in love with, and he signed the lease on the first viewing. Patrick Sharp had decided to keep the oak panelling and rose cornices as they added an old world charm to his new business. When contracts had been signed and he accepted the keys, the building had been full of old furniture and documents dating back to the 1800s. After throwing out the crap, he'd been left with some highly collectable antiques he could never have afforded. The décor gave the clinic a feeling of stability and age, as if NuYu had always been there. He smiled to himself. It might not have been his first choice for a clinic, but fate had smiled on him. While Harley Street might have the reputation and fame, clients who wished not to be seen visiting a plastics clinic chose NuYu. The very thing that had put others off had been the making of his business. NuYu was for only those rich enough to know it was there. Unlike The Fitzroy clinic at the other end of the row, with its highly polished glass door and reporters camped outside to photograph the latest celebrity nose job, NuYu represented discretion. Patrick shook his head. When would McGregor realise true wealth hid from the limelight. Only those who needed money courted the press.

Patrick ran his fingers along the mahogany frame of an oil painting, still amazed someone had left such an inspiring work of art behind in an abandoned building. The dedication of the artist to his craft was unmistakable, and at times Patrick compared his skills as a surgeon to the unknown artist of this inspiring landscape.

"Patrick," Gwen said quietly to avoid startling him, "time to scrub in."

"On my way, Gwen."

"Ah, Mrs De-Costa, do you want me to explain what I am doing?" Patrick asked as Andrew wheeled the patient into the surgical suite.

"Definitely not," she laughed. "Just put up curtain, and I chat to Gwen until you finish."

Patrick laughed, placing one hand on her shoulder

and smiling reassuringly. "We'll have you all done before you can even finish telling her about your cruise."

Patrick turned while Gwen lifted the small green surgical curtain that obscured the procedure from the client. Andrew injected another 5ml of epinephrine into the soft tissue of Mrs De-Costa's abdomen and then sat down to monitor the machines beeping softly and regularly in the background.

"Scalpel," Patrick said, holding out his hand.

First, he made a small incision on the right-hand side of the abdomen, just below the panty line he'd marked earlier.

"Probe."

Gwen passed Patrick the ultrasonic probe that transmitted a small sonic energy into the body, breaking down the membranes surrounding the fat cells and effectively melting the adipose. Patrick moved the probe around while Gwen and Mrs De-Costa chatted aimlessly about the South of France.

"2.2 cannula."

Gwen passed him the large cannula, and he pushed it forcefully into the incision. It took a bit of strength to get it beneath the skin, and sweat beaded on Patrick's forehead. Gwen wiped it away with a white cloth before turning on the suction. The cannula sucked out the liquefied fat, depositing it in a large closed tube. The fat was transferred through a purifying processor to another sterilised closed container ready for re-injection.

"Suture."

Gwen handed Patrick the curved suture needle. Two and a half hours had passed, and Mrs De-Costa had finished telling them about the South of France and started gossiping about the wives of her husband's business associates. Gwen grinned at Patrick as she handed him the scalpel for the next incision. Many of the people Mrs De-Costa was gossiping about were clients at NuYu. Mrs De-Costa knew she was breaking confidences as she prattled on. Freda had a new pool boy, Casandra's philandering husband had strayed again and Roberta had built a gaudy new summer house to show her wealth to the new neighbours.

"Probe," Patrick said as he continued the surgery.

Three hours in, and Patrick was happy with the sculpted abdomen of Mrs De-Costa.

"You'll have a stomach like a sixteen-year-old when the swelling settles. I'm very pleased with the outcome," Patrick said, leaning over the surgical curtain. "Let's get you turned over and give you a bottom to match."

Gwen bandaged Mrs De-Costa's abdomen and padded the stomach area with breathable foam avoiding placing pressure on the drains. Carefully, with Andrew's help, he rolled the woman onto her side.

"We'll have this done in no time," Patrick assured.

Patrick prepared for the lipo-injections, checking the quantity of adipose in the sealed glass jar and the number of syringes Gwen had made up. Andrew passed Patrick the local anaesthetic, which he injected into the upper outer quadrant of gluteal, avoiding the neurovascular structure. He carefully made a small incision in the crease of Mrs De-Costa's bottom and pushed the long 1mm cannula under the skin. Gwen filled the syringes with the adipose and passed them one by one to Patrick. It was important that the two litres of fat was injected slowly by hand in 2cc strips to ensure a smooth round appearance. Keeping the cannula moving, Patrick sculpted Maria De-Costa's bottom cheek into a beautiful round peach.

"Halfway there Mrs De-Costa," Gwen reassured as they turned her onto her other side.

When he was finished, Patrick laid down the cannula. "Gwen, can you make sure Mrs De-Costa is comfortable and Luis knows she is out of surgery and will be ready to go to Re Vive in an hour." He turned to his patient. "Gwen will take you through your post-op medication and explain what you need to do and what you need to avoid for a few weeks. I'll see you before you go to Re Vive and then again in two weeks. Do you have any questions?"

"You book me private suite?" Mrs De-Costa asked.

"Of course and a complimentary manicure and pedicure," Gwen reassured.

Patrick snapped off the latex gloves and removed the green gown he'd been wearing, throwing them in the surgical waste bin. He left Andrew to supervise the cleaning and rushed off to get ready for the four Botox patients he'd kept waiting. The curvaceous Sasha had kept them happy with a smile, a glass of champagne and rich Belgium chocolates. She'd even quietly suggested Patrick would put a little extra Botox into each client's forehead for the inconvenience. He must remember to give the Latin goddess a bonus or treat her to a table for two at Beckwoods.

Chapter 4 – What the doctor ordered

"What the fuck is going on here?" McGregor shouted, marching into the minimalistic staff room where Fitzroy was slumped on the beige Ikea couch.

"Has the bastard been at the lidocaine?" he hollered down the corridor before remembering Lady Elizabeth was somewhere in the building. "Dylees, can you tell me what the fuck has happened while I've been at the studio."

"Calm down, David, " Dylees said placing a calming hand on McGregor's shoulder. "Yelling isn't going to change anything."

"You pissing sure about that?" McGregor barked.

"I'm damn sure that if you keep yelling at me, I'm going to walk out of that door, and you can wake the commander up yourself."

McGregor swallowed his acidic retort and laughed at his senior nurse. She was stubborn enough to follow through on her threats, and David McGregor needed her soothing presence in his chaotic life. Dylees had been McGregor's nurse for fifteen years. The two professionals had formed an immediate partnership at the Bristol clinic where McGregor had served his residency. Dylees had been exotic and unobtainable, McGregor determined and ruthless. He'd needed her loyalty, and she saw in him a chance to provide for her new family. McGregor had rewarded her allegiance, demanding a senior position for his nurse each time the rising star had been headhunted. Dylees was the only person he showed any loyalty or affection towards. The shrink Doctor Smith-Jones had suggested McGregor was in love with the surrogate mother figure Dylees represented. McGregor thought the shrink was full of shit. He liked Dylees because she didn't put up with his crap.

"Get an I.V. in him, and tell Claire to clean the bastard up. He needs to be in surgery even if he's not performing surgery."

"Please!" Dylees said, her tone mirroring the one she used when talking to her children.

"Please," McGregor said meaning it. "How's the boy shark working out?"

"Surprisingly well. He pulled our arses out of the fire this morning. I've just checked on Mrs Kershaw, and she's recovering satisfactorily. The ambulance has been ordered to take her to Re Vive."

McGregor grinned. It seemed Robert Sutherland was just what the doctor ordered, straight after taking 5mg of lidocaine and passing out.

"Where's Lady Elizabeth?"

"She's in a consultation suite with Sutherland. He's talking her through her procedure and then through the pre-op checklist. I told him to draw things out as long as possible."

"Good, means I have a chance to get this fucking makeup off my face before I meet her. Claire," he hollered. "Get me a coffee and a fag while I wash up."

Claire almost bowed as she rushed away to get McGregor a large espresso and a cigarette. Dutifully, she placed a mint on the tray with the drink then rushed back to set it all down in McGregor's office.

"Cheers," he smiled around the door of his private bathroom.

He'd removed his shirt to avoid getting make-up on the white fabric, and the sight of McGregor's tanned stomach made Claire blush. While Will was attractive and muscled, David McGregor, with his chiselled features, slightly greying hair and toned body, was the perfect older gentleman girls dreamed about. The fact he seemed not to realise how attractive he was made him all the more irresistible to most women. Claire wished she was in love with the kindly, charismatic McGregor instead of Will. The anaesthetist just used her for sex when he couldn't find anyone else.

McGregor dried his face and pulled his shirt back on. Claire was such a plain, funny thing. She practically wet herself every time he looked at her. He sipped his dark coffee and leant against the frame of the window so he could blow the cigarette smoke outside. Claire had a little too much padding around the middle, but her ample breasts and willingness to engage in any sexual game made McGregor annoyed that Will had bedded her first. McGregor stubbed out the end of his cigarette and gulped down the dregs of the hot coffee before sticking the mint in his mouth to disguise the smell. He glanced in the mirror and ran his fingers through his hair. He didn't waste time inspecting himself. He knew he was flawless, so why spend time checking. McGregor marched out of his office at the same time as Dylees walked out of the staff room.

"He's awake, but he's not making much sense. It would be best if Lady Elizabeth didn't have a chance to actually talk to him," Dylees said.

"Splendid, could this day get any better?"

"You could have had Fitzroy in his pants being papped by the press outside."

McGregor gave Dylees a playful slap on her bottom. "But you wouldn't let that happen, would you!"

"Lady Elizabeth is waiting," she said, sidestepping to avoid his groping hands.

David McGregor knocked politely and waited for Robert to open the consultation suite door.

"Robert," he greeted the younger man as if the two of them had been working together for years. "Have you explained the procedure to Lady Elizabeth?"

"I have."

"Good, good. Do you have any questions?" David hesitated only a moment before continuing, "Wonderful, wonderful, I didn't think you would have. We'll get you into a surgical gown and into pre-op right now. Mr Fitzroy will be joining us in a minute. I trust Mr Sutherland has explained my taking the lead?" Again, he didn't wait for an answer but opened the door. "That will be Dylees with your gown. If you'll excuse us, we will scrub in while you get changed. The next time you talk to our dashing Mr Sutherland, you'll be in recovery."

Robert took his cue. He tilted his head reassuringly towards Lady Elizabeth, picked up her notes and followed the senior surgeon out of the room. Dylees took their place and closed the door so Lady Elizabeth could change into the blue gown.

"I hear congratulations are in order," McGregor said, slapping Robert on the back.

Robert looked confused.

"Your first B.I.G. I've been informed it went very well, all things considered."

Robert acknowledged the compliment, "It's not a procedure I've done unsupervised, but I didn't have much choice. I hope it won't affect my position with you, but I understand if you have to terminate my employment."

McGregor laughed at the short northerner. "Far from it, Sutherland, flying by the seat of your pants makes you part of the family. And as such, I think I should take you out to celebrate your first, first. You're one of the big boys now, and I think it's time you were introduced to the world of big boys' toys."

"Thank you, sir," Robert answered, not sure what else to say.

"Don't call me sir. McGregor will do. Has Dylees ordered the implants from stocks?"

"I don't know."

"Well, you should know," McGregor said, his voice turning acidic. It didn't do for a junior to get too comfortable. Carrot and stick or, in this case, women and intimidation, worked best.

"I'll go check, sir. I mean, McGregor," Robert

said, hurrying down to the surgical suite to see if the implants had been ordered.

McGregor smiled smugly. He knew Dylees would have had Will fetch the implants from stores and seen to it they were ready for surgery, but it didn't pay to let Sutherland get too comfortable. He turned his back on the fleeing Robert and walked into the staff room. Fitzroy was on his back, an I.V. inserted into his arm with Claire standing next to him, pushing the clear fluid into him as quickly as his body would accept the saline.

"He's starting to come round," she apologised as McGregor walked in.

"Not fucking fast enough," McGregor growled, walking up to Fitzroy and striking him across the face. The hollow slap reverberated in the room, and a large red welt formed instantly on Fitzroy's cheek.

"Hey, fuckwit, wake up," McGregor screamed into Fitzroy's face. "If you don't get your arse in surgery, I'm going to bury you in a breach of contract suit."

Fitzroy opened his eyes and tried to focus on the blurry man in front of him. "McGregor, old boy, what're you doing here? You're not due in until lunch," he slurred.

"It's one fucking o'clock," McGregor fumed, spittle flying into the pale face of Fitzroy as he tried to rise from the sofa. "Lady pissing Elizabeth is refusing to have surgery unless your incompetent drunken arse is in there. Claire will get you cleaned up. You will stand up straight and nod until she's under." McGregor grabbed hold of Fitzroy's shirt, hauling him upright. "Do you fucking understand?" he roared, emphasising each word by twisting the fabric in his fist until Fitzroy stood on his tiptoes.

Fitzroy nodded. McGregor let go of his shirt, and Fitzroy thumped back onto the sofa, his head crashing against the wall.

"You've five minutes," McGregor said without turning back to face him.

"We're ready, boss," Will said from the corridor. "Lady Liz is all prepped and just waiting for you and the commander."

McGregor frowned. The nickname Will had coined for the incompetent bastard when he first joined the Fitzroy clinic seemed even more ironic today.

"Perfect," he spat.

If Robert hadn't seen him unconscious hours before, he'd never have known anything had been amiss. The strong black coffee Claire had somehow poured into Fitzroy seemed to have brought him back from the dead. The man was full of old world charm as he greeted the aristocratic lady.

"Lady Elizabeth," he purred as he bent over and placed a delicate kiss on her cheek, "I'm so sorry I wasn't available earlier. I'm afraid I had a rather complicated reconstruction procedure. You know, one of those we do pro bono for the police. Mr McGregor has very kindly offered to assist me in your surgery. It's a two for the price of one, a B.O.G.O. F. if you like."

Fitzroy was the only person laughing at the lame attempt at a joke, and Robert doubted a person as wealthy as Lady Elizabeth would ever have bought one, got one free. She looked more like the sort of lady who would throw something away if she thought it might have been reduced in the sales.

Fitzroy continued. "How's his Lordship? Still being overworked by the courts?"

"Daddy's fine," she answered, "although I hardly see him some weeks, especially when he is overseeing a difficult trial." She lowered her voice slightly. "At the moment, he's presiding over a horrible case, the one with those Bolivian people traffickers the news keeps talking about."

Fitzroy feigned interest. "Oh, that's terrible, my dear. He must make sure you are looked after."

Lady Elizabeth reached out her delicate manicured

hand to Fitzroy's arm and looked deep into his eyes. "He does, but thank you," she said, smiling. As the anaesthetic took effect, her eyes glazed, and she slipped into unconsciousness.

"Right, wheel her into the surgical suite," McGregor commanded the moment her eyes closed. "Fitzroy, sit," he barked in the same tone one used with a dog. Fitzroy blinked and then sat down on the chair McGregor had gestured to.

"Sutherland," McGregor snapped.

"Yes."

"Stand here and pretend you know what you're doing. Dylees, let's have some Mozart. Die Entfuhrug, I think."

Dylees tried to hide her dislike of his choice and failed.

McGregor laughed. "Ah, our Dylees is not an opera lover. She is an Emperor Joseph complaining there are too many notes. Like Mozart, I say there are just as many notes as there should be. Get over it."

"I'd just prefer something written in the last year. Hey, the last decade would be an improvement on Connie's lament."

Robert didn't know much about opera. It all sounded the same to him. Women grabbing their buxom chests and men in tights warbling incomprehensible words to complex notes he couldn't follow. The music blasted out of the surgical suite's speakers, the opera loud and hostile as if McGregor was trying to drown them in sound. Robert resisted the urge to cover his ears with his hands and instead attempted to discern meaning from the jumble of noise and words.

"Scalpel," McGregor said in a booming voice, and Robert handed him the knife.

The surgery progressed quickly. McGregor was efficient and skilled. His hands moved in quick, deliberate motions with McGregor barely concentrating on his actions. When his hands were not in direct contact with the patient, they swayed backwards and forwards in time with the music as if McGregor were directing the piece as well as the procedure.

"Ah, this is my favourite part," McGregor said when the music had quietened and the only sound was the pure and tortured voice of the fair Konstanze. "She begs not to be tortured, throws herself at the feet of a man pleading for mercy. Wahl ich jede pein und not. I accept every pain and grief," McGregor translated, listening to the heartrending pain in the voice of the soloist. "Death will liberate."

"He likes to forget the opera has a happy ending," Will laughed as he twisted the dials on one of the monitoring machines and checked Lady Elizabeth's vitals.

McGregor scowled. "Scalpel," he demanded.

Until today, Robert could not imagine a breast augmentation could be carried out so quickly and yet so exceptionally. The small incision on each breast was almost invisible thanks to his skilful positioning and while there was bound to be a little bruising, the speed with McGregor had performed the procedure had minimised the swelling. Lady Elizabeth was now the proud recipient of two perfectly round double Ds.

"You want to cop a feel?" McGregor said, noticing Robert staring at Elizabeth Mowbray's boobs.

"If he don't, I do," Will replied.

Robert shook his head. "Ha ha, very funny," he said as Will reached over and grabbed both breasts in his large hands.

"Feels like the real thing. McGregor, you are a genius, and now I can say, I've felt up a Lady."

Dylees sighed and quickly pulled the blue surgical sheet over Lady Elizabeth. "Enough fun, boys. If you rupture those sutures, you'll have her back in surgery, and you'll not be able to blame faulty French implants this time."

"But Robert didn't get a grope," Will sulked on Robert's behalf.

"You'll have to let him fondle yours," Dylees replied. "But I get the feeling you would probably like that."

"Want to cop a feel?" Will asked, thrusting his muscled pectorals out towards Robert. "Go on, Robbie, I don't bite…unless you ask me to." Will struck a provocative pose and winked.

McGregor laughed. "Maybe he's a virgin."

"Take him to Bankers and cure him."

"I'm taking him tonight as a thank you for cleaning up the fuckwit's mess. Just as soon as Lady Elizabeth awakens to appreciate her McGregor-given boobs, and we pack her off to Re Vive for a few days of luxury recovery. You up for it?" he asked Will.

"I could do with a few days at a luxury retreat, a personal chef and a massage therapist while nurses in pink, striped uniforms check my temperature."

"I meant Bankers, but I can book you in for a little lipo, save you having to do all those crunches if you like," McGregor laughed.

"Think I'll stick to the exercises, boss," Will grinned. "You want a little ketamine to get you in the mood?"

"Why not? I'll get Sutherland to join us."

Chapter 5 - A sub or a dom?

"Is she the last?" Patrick asked as he walked out of the treatment room.

"One more," Gwen replied, pointing to a mature lady sat in the corner, "She's a newbie, one of Mistress Lovelash's recommendations."

Patrick raised his eyebrows as he looked at the woman. "You can never tell," he said under his breath. "Do you think she's a sub or a dom?"

Patrick appraised her auburn hair cascading in gentle curls onto her shoulders. Her small upturned nose and full lips were very attractive, and when she smiled, laughter lines creased the corners of her eyes. She had a fuller figure, which was attractively displayed in a 1950s style cinched waist dress. Patrick let his eyes follow her curves past her naturally full breasts to her ample bottom and long slim legs in black stockings. He studied her high-heeled black shoes with the telltale red soles. "Dom," he said. "No submissive would ever be able to wear those heels. They're designed for standing on a man's cock, no doubt about it."

Gwen looked down at the plain white trainers on her feet and screwed up her face. "What does that make me then?" she asked.

"The cleaner," Patrick laughed.

Gwen picked up the nearest thing, the heavily bound appointment book, and hit him solidly on the shoulder.

"I'm docking your pay."

"Try it," she warned. "Ms Law, Mr Sharp is ready for you now."

Ms Law was one of those clients Patrick hated. She niggled at the last remaining shred of his conscience. Like a fine wine, she'd matured over the years into a rich, full-bodied vintage. Instead of leading her into the plush treatment room, he really wanted to escort her out of the building and to the nearest hotel. Sometimes nature didn't need any assistance. But as he shut the door and invited her to sit down, greed overtook his appreciation for natural beauty, and he started cataloguing the treatments he could sell her.

"Gwen tells me the clinic has been recommended."

"Yes, by a very close friend of mine. We move in the same circles," Ms Law purred, lifting her dress slightly as she sat exposing an inch of white flesh at the top of her stockings. "You are a highly respected surgeon. I was hoping after we get to know each other, we might have a chat about potential business."

The musky, intoxicating perfume she radiated brought a lump to Patrick Sharp's throat. He was right. No way in hell this woman had ever been dominated.

"Shall we concentrate on the Botox and then arrange a suitable time for a discussion?" he replied, intrigued by her brazen sexuality and curious about the potential business.

"Wonderful, Mr Sharp. I will book an appointment with your luscious Sasha. She would make a wonderful mistress with that dark hair and those exotic features of hers. You won't be offended if I try to woo her away from you?"

Patrick thought about Sasha's long brown legs in heeled boots, her voluptuous body encased in leather, her short pixie haircut offset by dark eyeliner and fake lashes. "You can try."

"And I will!" In three words, she'd delivered a challenge. The contest was about more than the employment of Sasha Haia, it was about the balance of power.

"Shall we get started? Tell me what areas concern you most, Ms Law?" Patrick said, trying to regain supremacy over the consultation.

"Call me Andrea," Ms Law purred, resting her manicured hand on his knee.

Patrick gulped the last of his coffee before showing Ms Law to the lounge. He'd spent the entire consultation trying to salvage his nerves and act professionally around the provocative woman.

"So?" Gwen asked counting out the £500 in cash Ms Law had just paid for her Botox treatment. "What's her deal?"

"I have no idea, but I guess I'm going to find out. She's booked an appointment to discuss her needs."

"Maybe she's looking for a new submissive," Gwen giggled.

Patrick picked up the appointment book in a threatening manner.

"You wouldn't dare!"

He raised an eyebrow, and Gwen backed away. "I think I'll go and re-stock the treatment rooms."

"Good idea. Can you lock up?" Patrick asked, leaning over the counter and removing the £500 in fifty pound notes and stuffing them in his pocket.

"Of course," Gwen replied, taking back the diary and rubbing out Ms Law's name. Poor recordkeeping and bad handwriting weren't the only tools Patrick Sharp used to avoid tax, but they were the most efficient.

Patrick walked back into his office. He couldn't shake the feeling of tension, a knotting in the pit of his stomach when he thought about Ms Law. Something about her blatant sexuality knocked him off balance, and he didn't like it. He looked at his watch. He didn't have time for a shower, but the cloying scent of the woman wafted from his clothes and skin. He yanked open the door to his private bathroom and resolved to put Andrea Law out of his mind.

"Patrick!" Andrew shouted from the doorway. "Phone call!"

"Take a message," Patrick yelled from the shower

as his hands wandered down to his hard cock. "I'm busy."

Patrick dressed and walked out of his office. The cleaners had started on the surgical suite, and Gwen was preparing Mrs De-costa for her transfer to the Re Vive Spa. It was easier and more cost-effective to send his patients to the luxury recovery spa than applying for a licence for overnight care with FOBPS. Patrick popped his head around the door.

"Mrs De-Costa, how are you feeling?" Patrick asked.

"Fine, thank you, a little sore," Mrs De-Costa answered.

"Ah, it's to be expected. Gwen can you make sure you prescribe some Percodan."

Gwen nodded. "Your messages are on the reception desk."

"Thank you. Can you let Luis know to come round in ten minutes?"

Patrick checked Mrs De-Costa's bandages before leaving the room and picked up the handwritten messages from his desk on his way out. Hazel Woods wanted to know if he could do a guest appearance while David McGregor was on holiday. His accountant urgently needed him to call, and Miss Connelly would love to have dinner. He crumbled the first two notes and threw them in the bin, the third he shoved into his jacket pocket. It was only five o'clock. He had plenty of time to have a whisky and cigar at the Boot Room before phoning the blonde Candy. He had no intention of seeming keen.

The Boot Room was the nickname of The Wellington Club in Belgravia. While the constitution allowed for female members in line with the equalities act of 1975, no woman had ever stepped through the doors of Wellington's. In fact, until ten years ago, even the likes of Patrick Sharp would have been refused entry on the basis of heraldry. But new blood meant new money, and the committee of Wellington's had to accept that businessmen like Patrick Sharp knew how to make money, while hereditary peers knew only how to spend it. Patrick pulled his car up to the kerb outside the white five-story building and smiled. What would his separatist father think of him socialising with the very people he'd fought against. Patrick knew if his father were alive today he wouldn't be patting his son on the back for his success, but turning his back on a turncoat who had forgotten his Catholic roots. Luckily, the old bastard was dead, and Patrick didn't have to deal with his sniping comments or black moods anymore. Absently, he rubbed his hand over his scarred shoulder, feeling the bumpy gathering of skin where his father had beaten him repeatedly with his belt.

The valet knocked politely on the window. "Do you need my services, sir?"

Patrick looked at the young, attractive boy dressed in a smart black suit with grey tie and shiny shoes. He smirked as he thought about the answers the young man was likely to receive to that question from some of the other patrons. He nearly warned the young man, but thought better of it. Perhaps the lad welcomed the consideration of an older wealthy gentleman and if he didn't? Patrick opened the door to his black Merc and handed his keys and a tenner to the boy. The ornate steps in front of him led to a large oak door with a plaque announcing that Wellington's was a private members club. As Patrick walked into the Boot Room, he was immediately surrounded by a fog of smoke. He breathed deeply and smiled. The Boot Room now had its own cigar sampling room and specialist tobacconists. It had been a costly but necessary addition to the club to avoid the government's ban on smoking. And after the initial checks and spot visits had finished, the patrons of the Boot Room had casually moved smoking from the sampling room to the rest of the club just as it had been before. The waiters were paid well to turn a blind eye to the breach of their human rights.

"Hey, Sharp," a loud voice boomed from the other side of the room. "Come over here, my good chap, and settle a bet for us."

Patrick Sharp turned and looked over at the two gentlemen in the high-backed leather chairs. The overweight, balding gentleman in his later years sipped a fine brandy and puffed on a Churchill cigar. His decadent lifestyle was written across his face in the wrinkled forehead and red bulbous nose, his traditionally styled suit straining over his potbelly as he waved Patrick over. The second man was slight, almost feminine in dress and looks. While Patrick had never treated him, he could clearly see the signs of skilled surgery. An eye lift, a nose job, possibly some liposuction around the neck area.

"Danny boy, here." The older man gestured to the younger man perched on his chair, holding an almost forgotten glass of port and sucking delicately on a mini cigar as if it was a roll of weed. "Danny here reckons Hazel Woods and your pal McGregor are heading for the aisle. I told him McGregor's too tight to purchase a diamond. Besides, her tits are a national treasure. She'd have to petition the Queen to remove them from public ownership."

Patrick sneered. "That bastard isn't a friend of mine. I have no idea if he's getting hitched, and Miss Woods' tits aren't natural, they're McGregor's work."

"Damn fine work," the older gentleman coughed. "Wonder if I should send the wife to see him."

"Wife number four," Danny added. "Latvian."

"Bring her to the clinic tomorrow," Patrick said. "I'll make sure I guide her towards making the right decisions."

"Discounted?"

"Yes, with a friends and family discount," Patrick replied. This was, after all, the whole point of the conversation. Sir James was one of the wealthiest men in

Britain, but like most wealthy men, he didn't like spending his unearned money.

"Marvellous, old boy," Sir James said, patting Patrick on the back. "Care to join us for a drink?"

Patrick looked at Sir James' nearly empty glass. "Just the one. I've an engagement I can't get out of." He waved his hand in the air. "Jones," he said when the waiter walked over. "Can I have a Brora, the thirty-five-year-old? Sir James, can I get you another Frapin Cuvee 88? And Danny, what port are you drinking?"

Patrick knew the brandy Sir James was currently drinking would not be the £200 a shot Frapin, but it didn't hurt to flatter the old goat a little. Especially when wife number four would be a ready source of cash come Tuesday morning.

"Very courteous of you, old boy," Sir James mumbled. "Better make it a double."

Patrick smirked and nodded his agreement. Danny asked for another Warre port.

"I'll just go and get a cigar," Patrick said. "It would be rude not to."

He stood up and walked across the threadbare carpet and into a wood-lined room. The smell of cedar wood and Havana cigars assailed his senses. He stood for a moment in the doorway and breathed in the heady scent. Collecting his key from the cigar host, Fredrick, he walked slowly and deliberately across the walnut floor to the small humidity-controlled cedar lockers. Reverently, he inserted the little key in the lock and turned delicately to the left. He listened for the rewarding click as the lock slipped and the door opened. For Patrick, this was as near to heaven as you could get without the company of a willing young woman. He reached out one of his hands and stroked the delicate box inside. Removing the box with the dexterity of a surgeon, he placed the small precious contents on a velvet-covered table. Several boxes of Cohibas, six tubed Partagas for when he wanted to feel lightheaded, a box of

Bolivar Cornonas Extra and his rare Cohiba Behike. He'd only been able to find one so far, but his dealer was looking for more of the scarce £150 cigars for Patrick's collection. With gloved hands, he took out the Cohiba Behike and held it gently under his nose. Inhaling the delicious coffee smell, and then returned it to its home nestled in gold tissue paper in a hidden compartment. Patrick selected one of the Cohiba H2s and returned the box to his locker. Glancing at his watch he decided to find a quiet place to call Candy. Patrick sucked on the cigar, pulling the satisfying smoke into his mouth and rolling it around his tongue while he waited for his call to be answered. The phone rang five times before he heard the sensual voice on the other end.

"Hello, this is Candice. I'm afraid I'm a little tied up at the moment. But leave me a few words, and I'll call you back as soon as I get free."

Patrick growled under his breath and nearly hung up, but the image of Candy's bouncy breasts filled his mind. "Patrick Sharp," he said in a professional manner. "Call when you have time." He hung up frustrated. Not only did he have a raging hard-on, he now had two hours to kill before the boxing.

"Jones," he said as he walked back into the room. "Grab me a bite to eat and another double."

Jones bowed. "Anything in particular, sir?"

"Whatever special cook has prepared will be fine."

"I'll bring it to your table shortly. Will you be dining with Sir James and his friend?"

Patrick thought. If he dined with them, he'd have to pay, but if he didn't, he'd be drinking alone. "Yes," he answered after a considerable pause. "Make sure the drink keeps flowing, but stick the old goat on the Martell."

"Very good, sir."

Patrick reached into his coat pocket and pulled out a fifty pound note. He handed it to Jones who bowed slightly and walked away. The evening was going to be expensive, Patrick reflected, but Sir James had connections, and if he was drunk enough, he might let a few business confidences slip. It always helped to have a little insider information, besides he would just stick the additional cost on top of the price of the wife's surgery.

Chapter 6 – Like a lollipop

McGregor poured three shots of vodka while Will carefully measured out 65mg of ketamine into each glass.

"Alice," he said, handing Robert the shot glass, "down the K-hole."

Robert had no idea what Will was talking about but downed the shot anyway.

McGregor slapped the junior surgeon's shoulder and laughed. "Best get comfortable before the K takes effect."

Robert slumped into the comfortable armchair in McGregor's office. Nothing to it, he thought, as he watched McGregor and Will knock back their shots. Then his vision started to blur, and his eyes felt heavy. He had a sickening feeling in the pit of his stomach like he was about to throw up and a warm feeling in his trousers as if he was about to orgasm. A strange sensation of pleasure and pain dulled his ability to coherently process his thoughts. His legs felt heavy, and he couldn't move them. He looked down sleepily, to where his legs should have been, but all he could see was two wooden logs. He panicked, frantically pulling off his shoes. He wiggled his wooden toes through the hole in his socks and laughed.

"I'm made of wood," he giggled.

"He has wood," Will tittered. "McGregor look at Robbie's wood. It's sticking out of his trousers like a lollipop. Shall we lick it?"

"Just as soon as I can get off the ceiling," McGregor answered, clinging to the floor as if he was about to fall off.

Robert's head rolled backwards. Pink lights twirled in front of his eyes, the pirouetting lights turning into the enlarged breasts of Lady Elizabeth. He reached out a hand to touch the dancing boobs, but each time he reached up, they darted away, only to return moments later to torment him. He grinned and felt drool dribbling down his chin. It was nice, a wet and warm trickle of spit. Then it became a torrent of water gushing from him so fast his dry mouth hurt. Each time he sucked the water back in, his bulbous lips couldn't hold the treasured liquid. The more he tried to close his mouth to protect the precious water, the quicker the water seemed to escape. Robert grunted and forced his head against the wall, tilting his chin backwards until he felt like he was upside down. He clamped his lips shut, his teeth crashing together on his tongue. The pain felt good. He could hear the pulsing of the blood in his tongue, a steady, comforting rhythm. He followed the rhythm back along his tongue and down his throat, straight into his heart. The beating stopped for a moment, and Robert felt like he was floating inside his own heart. Then the valves contracted, and he whooshed out of the left ventricle and into the aorta. He picked up speed in the descending aorta until he reached the common iliac artery. Here his body slowed to drift lazily, his body bobbing in the gentle current while he swished his arms around in the sticky red fluid. He floated towards the artery wall and was caught in the bloody rapids, down the internal iliac, rushing into the internal pudendal artery and crashing into the wall of the dorsal artery of the penis. Robert felt himself harden, a strange feeling of being in two places at once, inside and outside of his body. Terror gripped at his throat as he realised there was no way out. His dead body would float inside his dick forever while his corpse would be buried with a raging hard-on. He pictured the church congregation trying not to laugh as the embarrassed Reverend stared at Robert's dick. He had to do something, anything to prevent the embarrassment of being taken to the mortuary with his cock pushing through the fabric of his trousers. Frantically, he pulled at the zip, knowing the only way to get out was to ejaculate. Out of the mist of his drug-induced coma, he could make out the giggling Will and McGregor.

"Guess he wants us to lick his lollipop."

"Can we?"

"You can if you like. I want to watch."

Robert wrapped his hands around his penis, tugging his hand back and forth. The sensation was erotic and wrong and fantastic and intense. It wasn't his body, yet it was. His back arched in ecstasy as the sticky wet fluid shot across the room. Robert collapsed, his energy spent. He closed his eyes and curled into a ball of warm, sticky wetness.

When he finally opened his eyes, he had no idea how much time had passed. McGregor and Will were curled up fast asleep, their bodies entwined together like two lovers. Robert yawned and unsuccessfully tried to push himself upright. His body felt weak, his legs shaky and unable to hold his weight. His mouth was dry, and his eyes felt like he'd rubbed his face in a sandpit. He crawled on his hands and knees towards the sink using McGregor's desk to pull himself onto his unsteady feet. He attempted to fill a glass with water three times before giving up and pushing his head under the gushing water. The water woke him, his senses snapping back into focus as if someone had let go of an elastic band. Immediately, he felt the wet sensation in his groin.

"Shit, I pissed myself," he whispered, but when he looked down, he saw the residue of sticky, white cum. He pushed his dick back inside his trousers and pulled up the wet zip, hoping McGregor and Will hadn't witnessed his humiliation.

"Go get a shower," McGregor said, placing a reassuring hand on Robert's shoulder. "One hell of a show you put on, Sutherland."

Robert closed his eyes and tried to remember.

"Will was very excited and wanted to help."

Robert shuddered, and McGregor laughed. "Go

have a shower, and I'll leave a suit out for you to borrow. It'll be a little tight, so don't fasten the jacket. Should I send Will in to help you wash up?"

Robert tried to form one word, one simple word, but his mind failed, and instead he vigorously shook his head.

McGregor laughed again. "Ah well, I guess Will is going to have to wait until later to get you naked."

Robert fled into McGregor's private bathroom.

McGregor walked over to Will and kicked him in the back. "Wakey, wakey sleepyhead. It's time to corrupt the shark's nephew."

Will groaned and held his head in his hands. "After that trip, I need to find Claire."

McGregor kicked him again. "You don't have time, and besides, she's gone home. You'll have to wait until you get to Bankers."

Will groaned again but managed to push himself to his feet. "I'll grab a quick shower and meet you out front. I need a fag."

McGregor smirked, wondering if Robert was the fag Will was referring to. While McGregor and Will both preferred the company of women, there was something irresistibly taboo about corrupting a fellow. McGregor grinned. It had nothing to do with attraction and everything to do with the act of domination. Robert wasn't attractive in the slightest, but the thought of imposing his will over the relative of a rival had McGregor tingling with excitement. But not tonight. Tonight was about pert breasts and nipples you could hang your coat on. Tonight was about a particular sexy blonde with wet lips and a name as sweet as she would taste.

"Sutherland!" McGregor hollered. "Get your arse out of my shower."

Robert couldn't believe he'd taken drugs. He couldn't believe he'd masturbated in front of his boss and co-worker. He couldn't believe how good and yet disturbing it had felt to ejaculate while high. The feeling of being out of control was terrifying, and he didn't like the disconcerting knowledge that anything could have happened, and he'd have let it. He remembered Will and McGregor suggesting they lick his lollipop and knew he'd have willingly submitted to their attention if they tried. He pushed the thought aside. It was the drugs and nothing more. He grabbed the soap and washed himself clean, rubbing his skin until it was red. He vowed then and there that while an interesting experiment, he was not a drug addict and intended never to use the stuff again.

"Sutherland!" McGregor shouted. "I need a shower. If you don't get your arse out now, I'll send Will in there to drag you out."

Robert heard the toilet flush in the next room. He gasped as the water went from a nice warm, comforting temperature to icy cold. He jumped out of the shower, grabbing the fluffy white towel, and heard the cruel laughter of his boss.

"One minute," he called back as the door burst open, and McGregor strode into the room.

"I've already seen it, boy," McGregor said, shedding his clothing to show off his tanned, toned body. Robert looked down at his pale feet and blushed. McGregor stepped into the shower, leaving the glass door ajar for Robert to admire his rippling muscles. Robert turned and fled to the sound of McGregor's laughter.

Robert dressed quickly checking his appearance in the mirror. McGregor was right. Will's shirt was a little large, while McGregor's suit felt just a little too tight across the middle. How was it that a man nearly two decades older had a better physique? He heard a slight squeak as the shower was turned off and fled McGregor's office before a muscled, naked McGregor appeared in the doorway to embarrass him further.

Robert discovered Will outside The Fitzroy Clinic,

leaning casually against the wall next to the shiny brass plaque identifying the two resident surgeons.

"Are you ready?"

"Ready for what?" Robert asked nervously.

"You'll soon find out," Will answered, offering Robert a small hand-rolled cigarette from a silver case.

"My own blend," Will boasted. "I've a mate who imports the stuff. It's called Harrington Herbal High, Triple H for short."

Robert took one of the small white cigarettes. It smelt of tobacco, cinnamon and something Robert couldn't place.

"Clover," Will said. "It gives the tobacco a sweet fruity taste and hides the telltale smell of satvia."

Robert nodded as if he knew what satvia was. Will smiled and lit Robert's cigarette.

It must be the lack of food, Robert thought halfway through smoking the cig. His head started to spin, and he had to lean heavily against the wall to stop himself from collapsing to the floor.

"Will," McGregor boomed from the steps. "What the fuck have I told you about smoking weed outside my clinic?"

Will shrugged his shoulders and put out the offending cigarette. "Sorry boss, I just needed something to take the edge off."

"Wait until Bankers," McGregor ordered, snatching the offending roll-up from Robert. He took one deep inhalation and then stubbed it out on the engraved nameplate of his partner, Carl Fitzroy. "Taxi will be here in fifteen, and they won't take drugged-up bastards."

Will took hold of Robert's shoulders. "Let's walk it off a little, Robbie. There's a sandwich deli at the end of Blow Row. We'll go grab some calories and chat up the waitresses."

Will and Robert left a fuming McGregor to wait for the taxi and swayed arm in arm down Blow Row, away from the busy Harley Street traffic.

"My uncle owns that," Robert slurred as he and Will stumbled past the NuYu Clinic. "He never thought I would pass my finals. He said I'd never make it as a surgeon and had better find a nice girl and become a GP." Robert spat the last word. "He even said if I made the top ten percent of my class, he'd give me a job with a six-figure salary. I came first in my year and turned the bastard's job down."

Will's mouth opened wide. At the Fitzroy Clinic, Robert would be on less than half the money his uncle had offered. "Why didn't you take the job?"

"Old bastard's in with some dodgy individuals. He's bent. If he's not shagging the help, he's gambling. Couldn't work for a man who treated my Aunt Carole so badly."

Will sympathetically patted Robert on the shoulder. "I really need a slash. You want to pee on his doorstep?"

Robert untangled himself from Will and unzipped his fly. "Good idea," he slurred, spraying urine all over the potted plants at the base of the steps of NuYu. Will joined in, and soon both sets of splendid pruned topiary rose trees were covered in a vile-smelling yellow fluid that pooled around the base of the red pots. Will and Robert giggled hysterically like two mischievous children.

"I think I've run out," Will giggled, shaking his penis at a white rose as a large black Lexus 4x4 with blacked-out windows pulled up in front of them. Two large muscle bound men dressed in identical black suits stepped out of the front.

"Move it," the larger of the two men growled. "Cojudo run allqu run."

The slightly smaller man grabbed Will by the shirt and practically hurled him away from the NuYu clinic. Will righted himself, his cheeks red with anger and his chest puffed out, ready to fight. Robert reacted as quickly as he could in his drug-induced stupor. He threw himself in between the angry anaesthetist and the two menacing men.

"Leave it, Will," he hissed under his breath. "They'd think nothing of shoving you in the back of that thing and beating the shit out of you."

Will pulled away from Robert's restraining arm. "This is London!" he exclaimed incredulously. "No foreign fucker's going to mess with me in my own country."

"Luis," the slightly smaller man called.

"Warmi cojudo, run now!" Luis ordered.

Robert did the only thing he could think of. He grabbed hold of Will's tricep and pinched hard, propelling the stoned Will away from the danger.

"What the fuck?" Will growled, bending Robert's fingers backwards so he was forced to let go.

"Trust me, it's not worth it," Robert winced. "Didn't you notice the accents? My uncle is involved in some pretty messed-up shit."

The effects of the Triple-H had started to fade, allowing Will to focus on the burly men he had been about to challenge. The black jackets of their suits bulged with more than their muscles, and he could clearly recognise the outline of a handgun on their hips as they strode purposefully up the whitewashed steps of the NuYu Clinic.

Will and Robert backed away slowly, neither of them able to turn away from the danger these men posed. The larger man looked back and noticed they were still close. He turned purposefully and took one menacing step towards them, his hand resting casually on his hip near the concealed weapon. Will and Robert turned and ran, the guttural laughing of the two thugs chasing them up Blow Row.

Chapter 7 – Buy on Friday

Patrick Sharp stumbled down the steps of the Boot Room. He'd given his keys to Jones so the attractive valet could drive his car to NuYu the next morning. He hadn't intended to drink so much, but the problem with Sir James was a propensity to overindulge, especially when he wasn't paying. The three men had spent a pleasant hour getting merry, and before Patrick's mind had turned into a jumbled mess he was sure Sir James had talked about a merger between two of the leading pharmaceutical companies. Patrick squinted, trying to remember the details of the hostile takeover bid for the British firm Faunaceutical, by the large Chinese giant, Beijing Biochemistry Laboratories. The offer was close to ten billion sterling, but Sir James had said the board of Faunaceutical was holding out for the proposal to be increased to fifteen billion before they approved the sale to their shareholders. Anyone with this inside knowledge could clean up after the company's announcement on Wednesday that the two boards had not been able to reach an agreement. The shares in Faunaceutical would plummet only to double or in value when BBL increased their offer.

"Buy on Friday," he mumbled to himself as he lurched down Belgrave Square and onto Chesham Place, heading for the tube station. "Easy money."

Patrick took the overcrowded tube from Piccadilly and changed onto the Northern line. The crowds lessened a little after the train crossed the river. He stumbled up the steep steps of the broken escalator and emerged back on the street in Kennington. He shouldn't have drunk so much, he thought as the orange glow of the street lights caused him to squint. He tried to look less drunk by straightening his shoulders and carefully placing one foot in front of the other rather than adopting the lurching gait of an impaired mind. Patrick walked past the leafy trees and terrace housing. As he progressed, more and more houses were empty and boarded up, scrawled with red and yellow graffiti signatures. Even the houses still occupied had old sofas and black bin bags overflowing with human waste in the gardens instead of flowers. An estate agent had put up a 'For Sale' sign on one of the large empty retail units. The company's purple boarding futilely covering up broken windows had been tagged with black spray paint. What a waste of effort. Nothing would sell in this area unless sanctioned by Trae La Muerte. Keeping the area derelict preserved the status quo. The police hardly even bothered driving down the street these days. Patrick walked past a strategically placed burnt out car serving as an unofficial boundary, a do not cross for the locals unfortunate enough to live nearby. Patrick strode past, safe in the knowledge the unseen lookout would recognise his face and alert the thugs waiting in the rundown café. As he walked past the cafe's dirty window, the two overweight men with greasy, stained T-shirts looked up and nodded. Patrick nodded back, and they held up three fingers. Three fingers signalled the door under the rusty railway bridge was the entrance for tonight's bouts. Two fingers informed the punter that the gate behind the old warehouse was in use, and one finger meant keep walking because the police were surveilling the area.

Patrick knocked at the battered green door, then pushed it open forcefully. Anyone who didn't knock or waited after knocking would be greeted inhospitably by the four armed men who stood in a small darkened room on the other side of the door.

"You started?" Patrick asked.

"No," grunted one of the security team. "You have time to bet."

Patrick grinned and walked through the room and out into the main warehouse. The uneven floor had green moss growing in the corners and saplings creeping out of the cracks in the concrete. He looked up to see the broken panes of glass in the roof that accounted for the vast quantities of bird guano splattered on the floor. In the middle of the warehouse, surrounded by a dozen or so men, stood the obligatory boxing ring. While the ring had seen better days, it was serviceable with professionally replaced ropes. It would be bad for business to have a punter knocked out by a boxer landing on top of him. To the side of the ring stood two gentlemen, one of them scrawny and shifty-looking with greasy hair and a dark, narrow moustache. Behind him stood a man who seemed to prove the link between man and monkey. Nature's generosity had provided him with a wild beard and wilder hair. More hair sprouted out of nose, ears and chest, leaving only his prehistoric cranium visible. Muscle competed with fat to bulge out of his dirty, white T-shirt as he lumbered menacingly behind his slight companion. Patrick knew neither man was what he appeared; the unkempt giant was physically fitter than any of the boxers, with a mind as sharp as one of Patrick's scalpels. The thin, wiry man was a mean fighter, and Patrick had witnessed many men brought down by one of his strategically aimed blows. Neither man could be accused of following the gentlemanly rules of Queensbury Boxing, and Patrick knew he had a better chance of surviving a bout with a heavyweight champion than either of them.

"Mr Sharp," the wiry chap greeted.

"Mr Green," Patrick replied. "How goes the day?"

"Very well, we have excellent odds on the fourth fight," Mr Green informed. Mr Green wasn't his name, but what you didn't know, you couldn't tell the police.

Patrick looked at the scrawled writing on the chalkboard. "I'll have £200 on the first fight, Marcello to win, £200 on the second, Little Tyson to win, and I've a grand on the forth, Nyoni to win."

"You cash now or credit."

"Credit. I've a few outstanding bets for tonight

and tomorrow. I'll settle this weekend."

"Good," Mr Green said, a sneer crossing his face. He knew Patrick Sharp was good for the debt. His boss, Mr Costa, had sent strict instructions to extend as much credit as Patrick Sharp required. In fact, he was to be encouraged to bet big. Mr Green checked his black book. Sharp was already down four and a half K today, and fifteen grand from last month. Whatever plan Mr Costa had for the upstart plastic surgeon, Mr Green didn't want to know.

Patrick took the offered betting slips and moved towards the makeshift bar. Drinks were free, and while the illegally imported booze tasted like piss when sober, it tasted just fine after a bottle of Brora.

"Whisky?" the barman asked as Patrick approached.

"Is it drinkable?"

"Not really, but the brandy is," the barman laughed.

"Brandy it is then."

The barman poured a triple into a tea-stained mug and handed it over. "Ran out of glasses," he shrugged.

Patrick laughed and let the eager gentleman to his left push through to the bar. Even in his semi-drunken state, he could see the man had the shakes, worrying over large gambling debts or needing a fix of alcohol. Patrick didn't think about it long enough to come to a conclusion because a sexy brunette holding a large card above her head had just entered the ring.

As she strutted her way around the boxing ring in six-inch heels, Patrick appreciated her slim waist and surgically enhanced chest in the shocking pink bikini. Absently, he wondered where she'd had her work done until she bent over, exposing her pert bottom to the crowd. All talk hushed as the mass of men admired the sight of her soft pink skin. The referee then stepped into the ring and announced the first fight was to start, three rounds of five minutes each with only one rule, don't kill your opponent. The two fighters entered the ring. Marcelo, a typical athletic Bolivian with tanned skin and straight black hair, faced off against Liam, a rather scruffy and overweight Irish lad covered in tattoos. The two opponents shook hands before retreating to their corners. Neither man had a trainer or support, just a bucket of cold water and a small wooden stool to sit on between rounds. The referee checked the fists of each boxer, making sure that while their hands were strapped, neither competitor had hidden anything inside the bandages. When he was satisfied a fair if brutal fight was about to take place, he signalled for the brunette to enter the ring. Carrying the first round placard to the appreciative wolf whistles of the crowd, she walked the ring, stopping to kiss each boxer for luck as she passed. The fighters stood and faced each other. The Irish lad smiled, showing missing teeth beneath his lopsided grin. The Bolivian's face showcased stony concentration as the referee stepped backwards and the bell rang.

The Irish fighter reacted first, his left arm windmilling towards the head of Marcelo, who leant back out of the way. The movement forced Marcelo to lower his guard in order to retain his balance. The Irishman's right hand raised in a lightening uppercut that caught his opponent under the chin, slamming his teeth together with such noise it could be heard at the back of the warehouse. The crowd groaned in sympathy as Marcelo's head snapped back. The Paddy, Liam, hadn't finished. Stepping forward, he used his weight advantage to push the Bolivian against the ropes, pummelling his fists into the man's ribs. All the Bolivian could do was bring his arms in front of his face, hunch down and take the beating. It seemed as if the fight would be over in the first round, but Patrick knew better. The wild, swinging punches were slowing as the Irish fighter tired. What he needed to do was step back and use the weight of his body to rain down pain on the slighter man. But in such tight confines, only strength of muscle counted, and that was something the pub brawler didn't have. Marcelo waited until first one and then another blow missed its mark, then he responded. His right hand pulled out to the side for a roundhouse blow. But instead of trying to hit his attacker with his knuckled fist, he lifted his thumb upwards and half-slapped, half-punched the Paddy's ear and cheekbone. The effect was immediate. Liam stepped to the side, his balance and hearing momentarily gone. Marcelo stepped to the right, positioning himself behind the larger man, and punched him in the kidney. The crowd cheered as the Irish fighter was forced to one knee in pain. Marcelo raised his arm, ready to deliver an elbow to his opponent shoulder. His arm came down, but Liam had anticipated the movement and thrown himself to the left. It seemed both fighters were more equally matched than Patrick had thought. The men appeared to have gained respect for each other. They circled the ring, each feigning a thrust before stepping back. Liam dropped his guard, making obscene gestures at the Bolivian, trying to entice him into a foolish rush. The Bolivian's lip twitched into an evil smile that bespoke of death and pain and contempt, but he didn't move. His mouth moved, but Patrick couldn't hear what he said. The colour drained from the Paddy's face, and he howled in anger, stepping forward and barrelling into the smaller man. His arms windmilled, catching Marcelo off guard. It was one thing to defend against a skilled opponent, another to stop a man who seemed to no longer care if he was injured. It no longer mattered how many blows Marcello landed, the Irishman just wouldn't stop. Spittle and blood sprayed across the first rows of the crowd as the bout turned into a brawl. The Irishman had taken a cut to the eyebrow, and Patrick doubted he could see anything through the red haze. But it didn't seem to matter as the street brawler relied on instinct, not thought, to batter his opponent to the floor. Before the crowd could comprehend the violence, Liam had Marcello pinned to the floor with his knees. His fists contacted one after another with the face of the Bolivian until it was impossible to see the features of the man through the blood. The referee stood back in shocked silence until Mr Green shouted for security. Two giant men barrelled through the crowd and pushed under the ropes. Each one grabbed an arm and physically hauled the Paddy from the semi-conscious man. Inch by inch, with Liam fighting each step, they forced the fighter to his corner and restrained him on a wooden stool until Marcello could be removed from the ring.

"What did the Bolivian say?" Patrick heard a man ask.

"He told the Paddy he was going to celebrate his victory by fucking his sister."

"Does Liam have a sister?"

"Fucked if I know."

Patrick downed the last of the brandy from the chipped, stained mug and ripped up his betting slip. He hoped the next two fights went his way. Otherwise, Cupcake wouldn't be getting the interior design fairy to redecorate the morning room and he would have to bear the sound of her nagging voice. 'But the McCoy's have had their whole house done by Freddy. His designs are to die for, and you promised.'

Patrick turned and headed back towards the makeshift bar.

"We're out of brandy," the barman said, filling Patrick's mug with the undrinkable whisky, "But if you bet on Marcello, you'll need this. What a fight, who'd have thought Liam McGrady would have made such a comeback?"

The name rang warning bells. McGrady had been a world class boxer until he'd started believing his own hype. He'd been thrown out of BBBC for attacking another fighter outside the ring five years ago. How the hell had Costa found the drunk and persuaded him to fight?

"Better luck on the next match."

"I'll need it," Patrick grimaced, emptying his mug of whisky in one gulp. "Put another one in there."

The second fight lasted the full three rounds. The two North London lads were equally matched, knowing each other's weaknesses and strengths, so it should have been an exciting bout. Instead, the bloody heap that was Marcello, being treated by the medics at the corner of the warehouse, seemed to have put a damper on their bloodlust. They danced around the ring, barely laying a hand on each other, to the increasing agitation of the crowd.

Patrick decided to go for a smoke and wait for the last match. He reached into his coat pocket for his cigars and instead pulled out his mobile phone. Might as well try calling Candy again while he was outside. The phone rang three times before being answered.

"Hello," purred a young female voice.

"Patrick Sharp," Patrick slurred. "Dinner?"

"Oh yes please," she responded. "Let me just get my diary."

"I meant now."

"Right, I've grabbed my diary. When were you thinking?"

"Now."

"Oh, Patrick," she giggled seductively. "You are a one. Next week? Maybe Friday?"

"Why wait so long?" Patrick garbled.

"Good things come to those who wait," she breathed into the phone. "You do think I'm worth waiting for, don't you?"

Patrick thought about her long slim legs. "I hope you aren't too good."

"Even good girls can be naughty," she whispered conspiratorially into the telephone.

Next week, he was supposed to be speaking at some Federation of British Plastic Surgeons conference about the ethics of plastic surgery in regard to body dysmorphic disorder. His wife was due to attend with him, but if he could arrange a meeting with Fairy Freddy for that evening, she'd be forced to cancel.

"Next Friday. I'll have someone pick you up at nine." He should be able to sneak away by then.

"Looking forward to it," Candice replied. "Oh, Patrick?" she whispered.

"Yes."

"Do you want me to tell you what I'm wearing?"

Patrick hung up the phone. He'd missed the last boxing match, but he didn't care. His body trembled with arousal as he thought about Candy's illicit commentary.

"Mr Green," Patrick said heading out of the warehouse, "can you arrange for a girl to be at my hotel in say, thirty minutes?"

Mr Green nodded. "Would you like a car?"

"Yes and in that case, have the girl meet me in the lobby in fifteen." The quicker he arrived at the hotel, the faster he could relive his conversation with Candy.

Chapter 8 – Pissing up Sharp's roses

"Where the fuck have you two been?"

"Pissing up Sharp's roses," Will replied, trying to keep a straight face.

"Is that a euphemism for something?" McGregor asked.

"No," Robert giggled. "We actually pissed into the rose bushes at NuYu before Willy here decided he wanted a fight with a South American bodyguard."

McGregor shook his head. Obviously he wasn't going to get any sense out of the two pricks while they were high on Triple H.

"Did you get something to eat?"

Will and Robert looked at each other and burst into laughter. "We forgot," they chorused.

"Fucking idiots! The taxi's here. Try to look like you aren't stoned."

Will and Robert pulled themselves up to their full height and tried unsuccessfully to wipe the daft grins off their faces, but each time they looked at each other they couldn't contain their giggles.

"Fuckwits!" McGregor spat, turning his back on his stoned colleagues.

The bored cab driver barely looked at the three men as they piled into the black taxi. The combination of an affluent area and the ability to overcharge drunken passengers outweighed any hindrance his passengers throwing up in his car might pose.

"15 Kings Street, The Bank Club," McGregor said, leaning towards the driver from the back seat.

"Okay, governor," the cabbie replied, inputting the address into his sat nav while pulling out into the road.

A horn blasted behind them, and the rear window was filled with the view of a shiny black Lexus. The cabby put his hand out of the window to wave an apology as the doors of the black vehicle opened and two large men stepped out, their hands casually placed on the bulges in their jackets.

"Time to move," McGregor prompted as the driver sat open-mouthed, watching the intimidating men stride purposefully towards his car.

"Fucking hell," the cabby gasped, pressing his foot down on the accelerator. The car wheels screeched as they rocketed up the narrow road. "What the hell? Who the hell were they?" he stammered as he rounded the corner onto Harley Street and sped towards Kings Street.

"You think they're still pissed we pissed?" Will joked.

"Glad they haven't got my number plate," Robert commented unhelpfully.

"Do you think I ought to go to the police?" the cabby asked, clearly shaken.

"Definitely not," McGregor answered, immediately thinking about the questions he'd didn't want to be asked if the police became involved. "I'll give you the number of a superintendent I know. You can give him a call off the record, and he'll look into it. The last thing you need is to end up with them claiming against your insurance or worse, being the star witness in a criminal case against a drug cartel."

McGregor had no idea who the men were or what their business had been on Blow Row, but he was sure the cabby hadn't either. If the man contacted Superintendent Hayes, McGregor knew Haysie, as a fellow member of Bankers, would keep the whole thing under the radar and, more importantly, out of the papers.

"Cheers mate," the cabby said. "I owe you one. Bastards came out of nowhere."

McGregor gave the cabby a fifty pound note when they arrived at The Bank Club. "Keep the change."

"Cheers mate," the cabby repeated, pushing the

note into his jeans pocket.

The effects of the Triple H had dissipated by the time Will and Robert walked up to the stately oak doors of The Bank Club, usually referred to by members as Bankers. In the past, the building had housed a respectable English bank. The four stone columns surrounding the massive, oak double doors spoke of age, resolve and conservatism. Ornate carved stonework reliefs led the eye upwards towards the imposing peaked stone balanced expertly on the vast columns. The faded brickwork still showed craftsmanship long lost to modern methods of architecture. Tall, original leaded windows were now tinted to make it impossible for passers-by to see inside the grand, aged building that had stood on this spot for hundreds of years.

McGregor turned to Robert. "Whatever you do, don't fucking embarrass me. You are here as my guest, and what you do or don't do reflects on me. Do you understand?"

Robert nodded, having no idea what McGregor was talking about. He'd assumed they were going to a private members club to grab a couple of celebratory drinks. What damage could he possibly do to McGregor's reputation?

"Keep your mouth shut and follow my lead," Will said, slapping Robert on the back as McGregor tapped three times on the door, waited a moment and then rang the doorbell.

Both oak doors swung open, and it wasn't until Robert was through the doors that he realised they were held by two shirtless black men. The men bowed as Will, McGregor and Robert walked into Bankers. Robert gazed back at the bewildering sight of the doormen's naked torsos, oiled in a sweet-smelling musky lotion that gave off a heady, intoxicating scent. The contrast of the pinstriped trousers and highly polished shoes of the doormen's outfit added to his feeling of disorientation and excitement.

Their dark skin rippled as they pushed the heavy doors closed, imprisoning Robert in a world of the unknown. Two slim ladies dressed in identical diaphanous corporate suits stepped out of the shadows. They emanated the same enchanting aroma as the men as they glided forwards. Robert reached out to touch one of the magical creatures, convinced his hand would pass straight through this obvious hallucination. A vice-like grip closed around his wrist, and he looked down to see a black hand grasping his arm.

"No touch," the doorman growled.

"It's his first time," Will explained.

The doorman looked Robert up and down in an appraising manner before releasing his arm. "Take him to vault," he laughed, his voice heavy with a South African accent. "Miss Lovelash would like reprimanding him for breaking the rules."

McGregor's twisted laughter erupted behind the petrified Robert. Will placed a reassuring hand on Robert's back and pushed him forward. "You need a drink?"

"Damn, yes!" Robert answered. "What was all that about?"

"You're not allowed to touch the staff," Will explained. "Fraternizing with them is strictly forbidden."

"You could have told me. I nearly shit my pants."

"And spoil Limukani's fun?" McGregor sniggered.

Robert looked back at the perverted humour glinting in McGregor's eyes. Something about David McGregor's countenance unnerved him, and he knew for certain he was in way over his head. He felt like he was standing on the railings of a bridge with McGregor shouting, 'Jump, jump, jump!' Whatever happened after this, there was no escape. He'd taken the first step onto the ledge, and now all that remained was the exhilarating fall.

Will steered the party across the slate floor towards a repurposed bank counter. Robert gawked at the strange sights. Everywhere he looked, he could see the skeleton of the respectable bank corrupted by warped minds into a hedonistic retreat for the wealthy. Velvet ropes strung between brass poles guided the guests to the tellers' counter, where beautiful women dressed in transformed bank uniforms served expensive drinks to the wanton willing. The chairman's portrait had been replaced by an erotic oil of a curvaceous Latin woman, her hands caressing her olive skin while her expression clearly dared you to touch. The stonework ceiling relief of weights and measures had been replaced with a detailed carving of the Kama Sutra. All sixty-four sexual positions painstakingly sculpted by talented hands to leave the spectator inspired and aroused. In groups of threes and fours, men and women in opulent clothing chatted and drank from heavy crystal glasses. But what intrigued Robert the most out of all the wonders was the noise of orchestral music coming from somewhere in the heart of the building.

"You're not in Kansas anymore," Will laughed as he noticed Robert's astonished face. "Through those doors lies a wondrous world of debauchery and sin."

Robert looked in the direction Will pointed to a heavy security door with a porthole and electronic lock. When the building had been a bank, this had clearly been the staff entrance to the offices. Now it was guarded by two strong, attractive men in warped security uniforms. Their trousers were cut low to expose abdomen and groin while their open shirts displayed smooth, muscular chests. On their duty belts hung handcuffs, whip, TASER and some metal objects Robert couldn't identify by name but could hazard a guess to their perverted use.

"While they may look pretty, those muscles are not just for show," Will warned.

Robert watched as a sexy woman dressed in a sheer pinstriped business suit that left nothing to the imagination approached a group of people who were raucously drinking around one of the tall tables. She consulted the clipboard she held, asked a few quiet questions and then escorted them to the guarded door. She inputted a four-digit PIN into the keypad and the door clicked open. As the celebrants filed through the doorway, the woman presented each guest with a small, elegantly wrapped package.

McGregor returned from the tellers counter with three glasses of brandy. Robert gulped his back. "Hey, slow down Sutherland, you'll pass out before the fun starts."

"How long?" Will asked.

"About twenty minutes," McGregor replied. "Miss Adventure is performing with the orchestra tonight, so there's a bit of a backlog getting people in."

"Time for another round then," Will said, walking towards the tellers counter. "Come on, Robbie, you can have a closer look at the boobs."

Robert didn't need to be asked twice and eagerly rushed after Will. The bar ladies wore bank teller uniforms comprised of skirt and blouse, complete with little red scarves tied around their necks. However, the fabric of their clothing was so sheer the dark pink of their nipples could clearly be seen. When the woman serving Will stood up from the tall stool, Robert felt his manhood harden. Through the translucent pencil skirt, he could see the thin line of curly hair that ran across her pubis and when she turned round, the round curve of her voluptuous bottom.

"I prefer my conquests clean shaven," Will said, nodding towards Robert's hard penis.

Robert flushed. "I just thought..." He left the sentence unfinished. He wasn't sure what he had thought, but he hadn't expected the first day at his new job to end with him staring at some woman's Brazilian.

Will smirked. "The best is yet to come, just you wait and see."

The two made their way back to McGregor, who was engaged in conversation with an attractive black lady in a bright red dress that hugged her small chest and hips until it flowed seductively across her voluptuous bottom. Her dark eyes flashed mischievously as Robert and Will approached.

"Is that…" Robert started to say.

"Yes, our illustrious Secretary of State for Health," Will agreed. "You'll find this club caters to all kinds. Even those as perverted as government MPs can find something to tempt them at Bankers."

McGregor turned towards Will and Robert. "Sarah, I'd like to introduce you to our newest surgeon, Robert Sutherland."

Sarah Wilson held out a delicate hand to Robert, her long red nails matching perfectly with her vibrant lipstick and dress. "Pleased to meet you," she said in a deep husky voice. Robert shook her hand, and she laughed playfully, "So formal, Mr Sutherland."

She turned to Will. "And Willy, always a pleasure."

Will took her hand and kissed her gently on her smooth dark skin. "The pleasure's all mine, or at least I hope it will be if your husband hasn't accompanied you."

"He has, but we won't let that stop our fun, will we, Willy?"

"He can always watch."

Robert choked as the fiery liquid he'd inadvertently swallowed burnt his throat.

"So can you, mate," Will laughed, slapping him on the back. "After all, you put on such an incredible show this afternoon, it would seem rude not to reciprocate. Sarah wouldn't mind. In fact, I think it would heighten her pleasure."

Sarah licked her lips seductively and smiled at Robert, looking him up and down appraisingly like someone about to buy a new dress. "I'd need something in return," she whispered, running a long finger down Robert's cheek, under his chin and along his neck before resting it on his chest.

"Anything," he replied, his erection threatening to push its way out of the confines of his trousers.

Sarah laughed joyfully. "So eager to please. I'll think of something while Miss Adventure performs. But for now, tell me all about this performance I missed."

Robert blushed as Will tantalised the MP with the erotic exploits at Fitzroy's.

"I demand an encore from you, Mr Sutherland," she laughed. "Oh, Clara's waving at me. My party is entering," she murmured huskily, kissing the three men. "I'll see you inside."

McGregor smiled and slapped her bottom as she walked away. Robert stared, horrified. "What?" McGregor asked innocently.

"Fuck," Will exclaimed, darting behind the stone pillar and pulling Robert in front of him.

"Which woman are you avoiding now?" McGregor sneered.

"Not one of mine this time. Lord Mowbray's over there. His right honourable has been trying to get me to have a look at some page three girl's lips."

"Which set?"

"Don't know, and I don't want to. Just stay still until the shady bastard's gone in with his party. After he's taken Bankers dust off that pair of tits he's fondling, I'll be the last person he's thinking about."

McGregor laughed. "You'd be the last person I was thinking about."

It wasn't long before the three men were approached by the semi-naked, clipboard-wielding hostess.

"McGregor, party of three," she said in a professional manner, unaware or unaffected by her near nakedness.

"Yes," McGregor said.

"If you'll follow me," she instructed, ticking off their names on the clipboard and walking away.

McGregor glared at Robert. "No matter what you

see or what you do, remember one thing." Robert stood waiting for the one important piece of information that would help him navigate this strange new world. "Don't come to work with an eyebrow piercing."

"He gave me the same advice," Will laughed. "I got my dick done instead. It fucking killed, so I don't advise it."

They reached the key-coded door, and their hostess handed them a small elaborately wrapped parcel. "Enjoy," she said, opening the door and stepping out of the way to let them enter.

Chapter 9 – Lead the way girly

The black Town Car pulled up just as Patrick left
the warehouse. The cold evening air made his head swim,
and he stumbled into the back seat.

"Mr Green has suggested we pick Layla up on the
way to your hotel. Is that acceptable, sir?"

Patrick closed his eyes and tried to force away the
feeling of swimming in honey. "Sure," he mumbled before
slumping back into his seat.

Jerry glanced back at the unconscious overweight
man. He'd seen him many times before. In fact, he had
taken him to his hotel at least a dozen times in the last
year. Jerry knew better than to ask for a name or even
speculate about what the man did for a living. Jerry's job
was to drop off girls, drive punters from one place to
another and not ask any questions when suddenly and
mysteriously they went missing. He looked forward at the
road and set off to collect Layla. He liked Layla. She was a
fun South American girl, Bolivian maybe or Columbian.
She spoke with a perceptible accent from voluptuous lips
that made Jerry want to kiss her, but he never had and
never would. It paid not to get too close to the working
girls, they never lasted long. Layla had once told him about
a sister living back home to whom she sent money to pay
for a future that didn't involve spreading her legs. She'd
confided she was only whoring until her sister finished her
degree, then she planned to quit and go home. Jerry knew
she'd never get to follow that dream, but he guessed
holding the conviction that prostituting her body was only
a temporary measure helped her to do the things she
needed to do to stay alive. Checking to see if the middle-
aged man was still asleep in the back of the vehicle, he
picked up his mobile and dialled.

"Old fart's passed out," he said into the phone.
"I'll pick you up outside the house, save you having to

walk to Queen's Street."

"Thank you, Jerry, you so thoughtful," Layla said.

Trae La Muerte punters were never allowed to see where the girls lived. In part to prevent them from being able to tell the police and in part to prevent them from contracting with the girls privately. The three-story building presently housed seven girls. All from South America, abducted and trafficked to England by the cartel. Layla pulled down her white dress to expose another inch of her tanned breasts and checked her red lipstick in the mirror. She slid her feet into the six-inch heeled shoes that killed her feet and checked for condoms and lubricant in her handbag. Mr Green had called. Her client wanted straightforward sex, no games, no submissive bondage. Layla liked those jobs. The appointments were quicker and less painful. Most of the cartel's punters were twisted. One guy liked her to hit him and call him names before he could get it up, another wanted her to change his nappy and breastfeed him. Some just wanted to tie her up or beat her before sex. Layla had seen girls deformed by sadistic johns. If Mr Costa prized a girl enough, she was taken to a plastic surgeon to be fixed. If not, she was thrown on the streets to fend for herself. Layla looked out of the window as the black Town Car pulled up. Jerry was breaking the rules. She ran down the stairs and rushed out to meet him before the house madam noticed. Her dark hair bounced around her shoulders as she hurried out of the door making her seem even more adorable to the smitten driver.

"Mr Green asked me to give you this," Jerry said, handing her a large brown envelope. Layla's heart sank. Brown envelopes meant special instructions, and special instructions meant a weird request or fetish.

"What now?" she sighed. "More dress up as furry animal or change man's diapers?"

Jerry cringed. "You really have to do that?"

"Yes, and other things. One guy wanted to piss on me. Lots want to tie up girls." She opened the envelope and started to read. "Mr Green want me to spend full night. He say get man to spend money in hotel and on me." She stared at the white sheet of paper. "I not understand, but it easier than pretending to be horse for judge." Pushing the note back into the envelope, she noticed the small bag of white powder. "For me or him?" she wondered aloud.

"The cocaine's for him," Jerry growled. "You just got clean."

"With help from Jerry." She smiled. "I will not take. I mix it with drink for him. Hopefully after sex he pass out, and I can watch films and order room service."

"Bring me a bottle of champagne if you do."

Jerry pulled the car up a few streets away from the hotel. "You'd best get in the back and wake him up. The hotel is discreet, but I think even they would have a problem if we tried to carry him in."

Layla clambered through the middle of the car into the back seat, giving Jerry a very pleasing view of her naked thighs and lace panties.

"Mr Sharp," Layla said, shaking Patrick by the shoulders. "Mr Sharp," she repeated when he didn't wake.

"Slap him," Jerry advised.

Layla slapped Patrick hard across the face, causing his head to bang against the window of the Town Car. "Mr Sharp, wake up," Layla pleaded.

Patrick murmured something neither Layla nor Jerry could make out. Layla pulled her hand back and slapped him again, leaving a red welt on his cheek.

"What?" Patrick mumbled, half-opening his eyes. "Where am I?"

"Mr Sharp," Layla said, "we are at hotel. You need to open eyes, and we go to room."

Patrick opened his eyes and looked at Layla's lovely face and beautiful boobs. "You're very attractive," he said, lifting his hand to touch her cheek. "You'll look after me tonight, won't you?"

"I'll look after you good," Layla said, "but first hotel need signature."

Patrick shook himself, closed his eyes and slapped his hands against his cheeks. He opened his eyes and looked at Layla again. His eyes focused, the pain temporarily combating the effects of the alcohol.

"Sniff here," Layla said, pouring a little of the white powder onto the back of her hand. Patrick leant forward and snorted the drug. His eyes opened wide, his pupils dilated and he sat up straight.

"Lead the way, girly," he said, slapping Layla on the bottom as she exited the car.

"Call when you're finished," Jerry said through the open window.

Layla looked back and nodded.

The bored hotel receptionist barely looked up from her computer monitor as she checked the two guests into their suite. She didn't notice the way the older gentleman leant on the slim South American girl in tight clothing or the worried expression on the girl's face as the older gentleman tried twice to sign his name. She failed to register the lack of luggage or the way the man's hand slipped up the girl's skirt before they entered the elevator. It wasn't that she was paid to ignore these guests, it was that she wasn't paid enough to notice.

"Mr Sharp," Layla pleaded as they entered the elevator. "Wait until the room. I make sure you very happy, but wait moment."

Patrick couldn't understand her reluctance. He had a raging hard-on, and all he wanted to do was thrust his dick between those luscious boobs and into her pouting mouth. He grabbed hold of her shoulders, forcing her to her knees.

"Mr Sharp," she squealed, trying to stand. "If I let go, you fall over. You too heavy for me to lift."

Patrick stopped pushing and let her stand. She propped her shoulder underneath his arm and guided him out of the elevator and to the room. Hindered by Patrick's wandering hands, it took her three swipes with the key card to get the door to open.

"Mr Sharp, we have all night," she giggled as the pair fell through the door and onto the plush carpet.

On her hands and knees, she crawled forward and pushed the door closed just as Patrick grabbed her legs and pulled her back towards him. His hands slipped up the outside of her thighs, his fingers curling around her lace panties to pull them down. Layla gasped, first in shock and then in pleasure, as his hands retraced their path, and he pushed his fingers gently inside her.

"You like that, don't you," he grinned as she squirmed against his pressure.

"Yes," she said and meant it.

Patrick laughed as he massaged inside her, the wet heat making his penis throb. With his other arm, he pulled her onto her knees so her bottom bounced playfully in front of his face. Ever so slowly, he pushed her dress up so he could see the tanned flesh of her round cheeks and just a hint of hair around her red lips. Layla moaned and pushed herself backwards onto his fingers. Patrick leant forward and nibbled on the fleshy part of her thighs and bottom before snaking his tongue out to lap at the wetness his fingers had created. She tasted wonderful. He removed his fingers and sucked. His hands wandered upward to grab and twist her hard nipples. Layla threw her head back, tensed and shuddered as she exploded in an eruption of orgasmic pleasure. Patrick drank as she shook.

"Stand up," he growled huskily, fumbling with the zip on his trousers. Layla stood and turned, ready and willing to get on her knees.

"No," Patrick growled. "Turn round."

Layla did as she was told and faced the door. Patrick pushed against her, his warm body heating her skin through their clothes. She heard the zipper pulled down and then felt the warmth of him against her bottom. She clenched her teeth, waiting for the pain. "Lubricate, please."

"I think I've already done that," Patrick rasped and grabbed her hands, pulling them up over her head.

Layla tried not to tense and closed her eyes. Then she opened them wide and in pleasure as Patrick pushed his throbbing cock inside her wet vagina. His breath was laboured in her ear, and she found her own breathing matching his. He thrust deep inside her, his strong rhythmical strokes rubbing in all the right places. She pushed her bottom into his crotch and opened her legs slightly to let him deeper inside. Patrick moaned in pleasure, he tensed and his rhythm broke. Layla knew he was close to orgasming. She untangled her hands from his grasp and pushed them against the door. She lifted herself onto her tiptoes and tilted her hips backwards and forwards drawing herself on and off his erection. The angle of her hips meant the full shaft of his penis rubbed deliciously against her clitoris, causing her to moan in pleasure. Patrick tensed, shook and came. The pressure of his orgasm came in a pulsating wave that pushed Layla into her second orgasm. Her nails clawed down the door as she cried out. The two of them stayed locked together, panting in exhausted pleasure. Patrick nibbled on her perfect earlobe and ran his tongue down her tanned slim neck. He had never seen such a beautiful creature as the woman he had his arms wrapped around.

"Mr Sharp," Layla whispered.

"Call me Patrick," he said.

"Layla."

"Pleased to meet you, Layla. Would you care to join me for a shower?"

Layla nodded.

Patrick stood up and walked towards the bathroom. Layla stood still for a moment, listening to the sound of water splashing against the tiles. She'd never orgasmed with a client before. She'd never experienced anything like it before with any of the hundreds of men Mr Costa had forced her to have sex with. She wondered if it meant anything and then shook her head. What it meant was some men were nicer than others. Nothing more. It was only as she pulled her dress down she realised in the heat of passion neither she nor Mr Sharp had thought to use a condom.

"Layla," Patrick called from the bathroom. "I think it's time for you to get nice and clean. While I watch."

Layla giggled. Something about the idea of Patrick Sharp watching as she rubbed soap on her naked body made her tingle delightfully.

"I coming, Patrick," she said, the name feeling strange and exciting on her lips. "Patrick," she whispered again.

Patrick stared at the beautiful woman in front of him, her long dark hair curled around her slim shoulders, the ends brushing the top of her magnificent natural breasts. He let his eyes wander across her tanned stomach and down to the thin strip of hair between her legs. He felt his body reacting to her nakedness as she stepped into the shower. The water washed over her body, leaving her skin glistening and her hair clinging to her smooth back. She bent over to reach the soap, and Patrick groaned in appreciation at her rounded bottom. She looked over her shoulder and smiled, almost shyly as if this was the first time a man had seen her naked.

"I wash now?" she asked.

Patrick nodded, unable to speak around the lump of desire in his throat. Layla rubbed the soap in her hands, making a white lather of bubbles. As Patrick watched, her hands moved slowly up her arms, covering them in the white foam. Her hands circled her breasts and ran sensually across her collarbone before descending down. Patrick felt the heat rise in his body. The way this woman moved had a primal effect on him. He stood and shed his clothing on the floor before striding towards her. His mouth clamped down on hers, his tongue forcing its way into her mouth. Layla collapsed against him, her wet soapy body quivering with desire. Her hands moved to his shoulders, her nails digging into his skin as she clung to him. Then they moved, hesitantly at first, then with growing confidence. Her nails grazed his back, following the curve of his hipbone before encasing his erection. Patrick closed his eyes and moaned in pleasure as her hands massaged, her fingers tickling yet firm. Without needing to be asked, she moved her lips from his and knelt. Her mouth replaced her hands. Patrick opened his eyes and watched as she rocked, her tongue dancing over his skin bringing involuntary cries of joy from his body. He wanted to be inside her, yet he couldn't move as she drew him ever closer to orgasmic pleasure. His hands dug into her shoulders, as she pushed her finger deep inside him. Patrick tensed and came, his body shuddering at the intensity. Layla stood slowly.

"Did I do good?" she asked.

Patrick couldn't speak. Instead, he kissed her.

Chapter 10 – Jacket on

Robert looked in the small parcel he'd been given. "What are these for?" he gasped, pulling out three ribbed condoms and a small, clear packet of white powder.

"Bankers has a strict jacket-on policy," McGregor explained. "Anyone caught not using protection is immediately thrown out of the club."

Robert remained quiet. He had no idea what sort of club McGregor had brought him to, but he got the feeling it wasn't going to be urban chic city types sipping expensive wine and talking about the day's FTSE. Robert held up the little packet and shook it at Will.

"Bankers' dust. It's a performance enhancer," Will answered. "Quality controlled cocaine, so don't worry."

"Willie," Sarah squealed, rushing up and grabbing hold of his bottom, her red nails digging in as she pulled him towards her and planted a sensuous kiss on his lips. "Miss Adventure is about to perform. Come and watch with me."

Will untangled himself from her wandering hands and stepped backwards, "Just let me take this," he said, holding out the performance enhancing white powder, "and I'm all yours."

Sarah licked her lips and pouted. "Am I not enough?" she sulked.

"You're too much," Will answered. "And that's why I need this." He touched her cheek then ran his hand down to rest his fingers between her cleavage. Sarah wriggled and giggled like a school girl caught behind the bike sheds.

McGregor shook his head and whispered to Robert. "And that's the woman who's supposed to sort out the NHS."

Will looked over his shoulder at his two

companions and winked. Then he sprinkled the white powder onto Sarah Wilson's black breasts before pushing his head in between them and snorting the drug.

"Now I'm all yours," Will said, slapping her on the bottom. "Lead the way to adventure."

McGregor and Robert followed the cavorting pair along an oak-panelled hallway and into a large, ostentatious board room. The room was dominated by an imposing mahogany table, and on the table stood a naked statue of a beautiful exotic woman. Her pale, almost translucent skin gleamed under the soft candlelight surrounding her. Her eyes were closed, but the look of desire in her crooked smile showed the skill of exquisite craftsmanship. Every twist of hair entwined into a crown of curls seeming so real Robert expected it would be soft if you reached out to touch it. The statue was naked apart from a string of pearls coiled around its waist and neck.

Thirty or so people gathered around the table, looking at the sensual statue. The tension perceptibly built as they waited for something or someone. The orchestra played an evocative piece from a balcony above the table, their skilled performance adding to the atmosphere of suspense and anticipation. A chord struck, the unnerving sound of a violinist pulling the bow across the exceptional instrument in a violent manner. Deafening silence followed. The audience held their breath. No one moved, no one made a sound. Robert stood frozen with apprehension. Should he run? Before he could make his feet move, the violinist took up a haunting slow solo melody. The statue moved. So minutely at first that if Robert hadn't been staring at her graceful fingers, he would have missed the slight movement. Her hand inched up her thigh, leaving a blue tinge on the flawless alabaster skin. The hand stroked sensually across her flat stomach and out to the side, where it twisted in rhythm with the soloist. Robert held his breath, transfixed on the long elegant fingers. The hand froze in a classic ballet position, the fingers cupped and relaxed. Robert swallowed. How could something so diminutive be so erotic? Her other hand moved, tracing a red line across her body. The red intersected with the blue, creating a purple smear. Again the hand left her breast to be thrust outwards. After a moment of stillness, the statue's hips began to sway. Her hands moved upwards to cross above her head, and she opened her piercing blue eyes and looked directly at Robert. The audience gasped in delight as she delicately lifted herself onto her tiptoes and gracefully arched one smooth leg behind her. Her fingers clasped her foot, and she pirouetted to give the gathered crowd a sensual view of her curvaceous body. With muscle control Robert didn't think possible, the living statue lowered her leg and arms to stand in a traditional Greek pose, hands open to welcome them. Her fingers curled, and she brought her hands to her neck before tracing a trail of red and blue across her collarbone and down between her breasts and stomach, creating an intricate pattern of colourful swirls. Robert's cock throbbed as he watched her fingers slip between her legs, and she threw her head back in delight at her own erotic attention. The music changed to a more urgent tempo, the rest of the orchestra joining in to bring a crescendo of sound into the room. The living statue moved rapidly, her head swaying from side to side, her legs trembling in an erotic dance that spoke of pleasure and release. The enchanted audience watched transfixed as the statue dropped to her knees, arched her back, and cried out once as an exploding orgasm convulsed through her body. Then there was silence, broken only by the heavy breathing of the living statue. A flute sounded a sad tone of regret, changing to a tune of hope and naivety. The living statue stood, a small flame held in her cupped hand. She brought her hands together, and they caught fire. Her expression changed to one of wonder as she offered the audience the flames and then touched them to her skin. The fragile paths of red and blue caught, turning the living statue into a living flame. Her body encased in fire, the heat was so fierce Robert needed to step back. The flute blew a wrong note, and the flames distinguished. The statue fell. The audience burst into loud applause and shouts of 'Miss Adventure, Miss Adventure' resounded around the room.

McGregor slapped Robert on the back. "You need to get rid of that hard-on?" Robert swallowed. He didn't know if McGregor was joking or not. "Come on, I'll introduce you to a friend of mine. Mistress Law will make sure your needs are provided for."

McGregor guided Robert out of the room, leaving Will with the horny politician. Her legs were already wrapped around Will's waist as she forced him back towards the boardroom table.

"I think Willie and Sarah are about to rival Miss Adventure's performance," McGregor laughed as the crowd made way for the entwined couple.

"They…" Robert spluttered.

"Nothing a politician likes more than being centre of attention."

Robert and McGregor retraced their steps along the oak-lined corridor. McGregor greeted several beautiful ladies, leaving them with promises of sexual adventure later in the evening. Out of nowhere, a muscled man forced McGregor against the wall. A bulging forearm pressed against McGregor's throat before the man lowered his head and kissed McGregor with such passion Robert looked away. McGregor growled and bit the man's lip, drawing blood.

"Piss off, Holden," he spat. "If you want me to fuck you, you have to ask nicely."

The muscled man took a step away and looked suggestively at McGregor. He flexed the toned forearm still pressed against McGregor's neck. "Please," he said in an aggressive grunt, his green eyes sparkling with a challenge.

"Not good enough," McGregor spat in Holden's face. "Shouldn't you be abstaining before a bout?"

"When I win the belt, I'm coming for you."

"When you win!" McGregor laughed. There was a hint of promise in his voice, as if the day Holden won, McGregor would submit to the man's advances.

McGregor pushed himself off the wall, turning his back on his male suitor. He wrapped his arm around Robert and shoved the junior surgeon in the direction of the vault.

"Be careful," Holden warned. "He bites in all the right places."

McGregor smiled and blew a kiss at the man over his shoulder.

"Was that the boxer, Scott Holden?"

McGregor cuffed Robert on the back of the head. "Mind your own business."

They arrived at a heavy, reinforced metal door with a large steel wheel in the middle.

"The vault," McGregor announced, turning the wheel clockwise and pulling the door open.

Robert stared in open-mouthed amazement at the room beyond the door. The walls were lined with small metal security deposit boxes while the smooth floor showed the faded crest of the former bank. The lighting had been amplified to provide a blinding whiteness that added to the sense of disorientation. Robert blinked, trying to see further into the unreal world of Bankers. McGregor strode up to one of the security deposit boxes. Taking a key from his pocket he opened a safety box.

"Who'd think to look here?" he justified, pulling a wad of fifties from his jacket and pushing them into the already crammed box. Robert quickly estimated the box contained about half a million in cash. "It's all declared, so don't get any ideas. I just like to keep it away from Witch-Hazel."

McGregor led Robert deeper into the vault. A lattice of bars formed another door that obstructed their way. Robert peered through the crosspieces at the hedonistic paradise beyond while McGregor spoke quietly to the shirtless security guard. The guard stepped aside, a sadistic smile crossing his face as he looked at Robert.

""Come on," McGregor said, "Mistress Law is waiting for us."

Robert stepped into a land of debauchery. The aroma of lust and sex and that heady perfume prevalent in Bankers wafted around the vault. The bright light changed to one of flickering candle flame bewildering the uninitiated Robert. Along the walls, men and women were chained while their partners, dressed in tight leather and high heels, punished them for imagined wrongdoings. Others cowered at the feet of their masters, showing off their nudity with collars and restraints.

"Mistress Law," McGregor introduced the beautiful woman who stood in front of them.

Mistress Law was stunning. There really was no other way of describing her. Her long auburn hair was tied up in an intricate topknot, and her slim figure was shown to perfection in nothing but a loose chainmail dress. She turned and smiled at McGregor, laughter lines creasing at the corners of her hazel eyes.

"When are you going to let me get rid of those lines?" McGregor asked.

Andrea Law walked up to McGregor, her high-heeled boots clicking seductively on the tiled floor. Robert followed the sensual sway of her hips, the curve of her waist and the swing of her surprisingly muscled arm as she slapped McGregor across the face.

"Mistress," she snapped.

"Mistress Law, forgive me," he replied, his head lowered in submission. "I've brought a friend for you and Miss Lovelash to play with."

"Then you are forgiven."

Andrea Law turned her attention to Robert, appraising the young man trembling in front of her. He looked out of his depth, confused and excited. He wasn't what she expected from an acolyte of McGregor's.

"Come," she ordered.

Robert followed the older woman, his brain on fire with the possibilities. "Aren't you coming?" he asked McGregor.

"No, I'm off to find my own entertainment. Say hello to Miss Lovelash and her friends."

McGregor left the vault. That bitch Law had recently had Botox. He could see the faint needle marks on her forehead. Had she seen the shark Sharp? McGregor scowled, his lips forming an unattractive sneer. If she was prepared to pay for second-class treatment by a working class surgeon, that was her luck out, but Patrick Sharp was starting to affect his bottom line. The sneer turned into a smirk as he wondered if Sarah Wilson had any connections at FOBPS.

Robert followed Mistress Law deeper into the unknown. He walked past fornicating couples and into the darkness of the furthest corner of the vault. The faint candlelight didn't reach here. Robert heard a noise behind him and twisted to look. When he turned back, Mistress Law had vanished. His body trembled with anticipation and fear.

"Mistress Law?" he whispered into the gloom.

His hands were grabbed from behind and a blindfold pulled over his eyes. He tried to run away, but something had hold of his legs, and he fell forwards. He tensed, preparing for his face to crash against the solid floor. Instead, he landed on the softness of warm skin.

"Slave," a woman's voice purred. "I am your mistress, and you will do as you are told. Is that understood?"

"Yes." Robert trembled.

"Good."

Strong hands stood him upright, and his clothes were torn from his body to leave him naked and vulnerable.

"Drink."

A glass of cold, bitter liquid was forced to his lips, and Robert drank. Underneath the blindfold, lights danced in front of his eyes, and his other senses snapped into sharp focus so that every touch, every sound was heightened beyond reality. Robert felt hands stroking his hot skin, tongues and lips tasting his flesh. The gentle touch of long hair and the sharp crack of a whip on his legs and bottom mingled to provide a pleasurable pain. His mind couldn't catch up with the sensations. He tried to concentrate on the number of hands, lips, and breasts that caressed and aroused him. Lips pressed against his, a mouth wrapped around his dick, teeth nibbled his bottom, a tongue teased his nipples until they hurt.

"Stand still."

Robert tried to remain still as he listened to the unknown, attempting to ascertain the future. He felt the warmth of a wet pussy encasing his dick, the muscles clenching around his pulsating cock. He tasted the salty moisture of a woman's arousal against his lips and felt the tickle of pubic hair on his face. He opened his mouth to suck and instead groaned as something entered his anus, pushing him beyond his own limits and into a world of carnality he hadn't known possible.

McGregor stalked the hallways of Bankers, looking for a victim. The stuck up bitch Candice hadn't called. His frustration, heightened by Miss Adventure's performance and the sounds of rutting couples, bubbled over, and he rammed his fist into the wall. Clara Huntington, wearing nothing but a pair of white cotton pants and a cowboy hat, ran into him. Her pigtails bounced playfully on her naked breasts as she jiggled.

"I seem to have lost my mustang," she giggled.

"Have you seen him?"

McGregor scowled.

"Mowbray, Mowbray," she called, running down the hallway. "Come here, boy, I've some sugar for you."

So this was the page three girl Will was avoiding. Maybe if he'd seen the wobbling bottom of Clare Huntington, he'd be more willing to entertain the judge's request.

"Fuck, even the judiciary are having more fun than me," he spat, storming back towards the bar. A couple of shots of vodka and he'd call it an evening. The idea of Lord Mowbray playing horsey with the pouting Clara Cuntington had dulled his ardour.

Chapter 11 – Something bad

Patrick woke up slowly. The first thing he sensed was the oppressive weight across his chest, followed quickly by a skull-shattering headache. He tried to open his eyes, but pain exploded through his brain as the shafts of weak morning light stabbed into his corneas. He groaned painfully, and the weight across his body moved. Gingerly, he moved his hand upwards and touched the warm skin of a slim arm. Layla snuggled into him, making small noises in sleep. Patrick ran his hand down her arm and gently lifted her hand. Carefully, he placed the arm next to her and slipped out of bed. He stumbled to the bathroom over the empty bottles of champagne and discarded clothes. The smell of sex and the lobster they ordered from room service mixed together in a cloying fishy aroma. Patrick's stomach lurched. He sank heavily and painfully to his knees in front of the toilet as the retching took hold. Wave after wave of vomit splashed into the bowl, the orange bile burning the back of his throat. Everything hurt as he gasped for air between the spasms. He felt the warm, wet feeling of urine dribbling down his thighs as his body heaved again, and then through the haze of pain and confusion, a reassuring hand on his shoulder.

"I help," Layla whispered, pushing the wisps of sweat-soaked hair from his face.

Patrick managed a weak smile. "Water," he croaked.

Layla turned on the cold water tap. The sound of rushing water hitting the porcelain sink caused Patrick's face to contort. How could the noise possibly be so loud? Layla held the glass to Patrick's lips. He drank, the water sloshing down his chest in cold rivulets. He shivered, and Layla covered his naked body with a heavy towel, stroking his head reassuringly.

"Worst is over. You rest."

Patrick turned his head to look at the naked woman beside him. Her full lips broke into a smile, but her face showed concern.

"Thank you," he croaked. "Can you help me into the shower?"

Somehow the two of them managed to get Patrick's bulk off the floor and into the shower. The tepid water cascaded onto his head, washing away the stench of vomit and sweat. He remembered the night time pleasure of being with Layla, and couldn't help but compare his sorry state this morning to his prowess of the evening before. For the first time, he felt every one of his fifty-six years. His body ached, and he felt old, bone-weary old, next to the youthful girl he'd spent the night with. The telephone rang, and Layla answered. He could hear her voice but couldn't make out the words. She walked back into the bathroom.

"Mr Costa say it time I leave," she apologised. "He downstairs and needs to talk with you." She tried to hide her fear. Mr Costa was here in the hotel, and that couldn't be a good thing. Had she done something wrong? Was she going to be punished for not getting Mr Sharp to spend enough money? She knew she had screwed up, fallen asleep in Patrick's arms rather than encouraging him to order more champagne or take more of the stash of drugs she'd been given to push. Layla grabbed her clothes and dressed. She splashed a little water on her face and pulled her long hair back into a ponytail. "Did I do bad?" she asked.

"No," he replied. "Layla, last night was magnificent."

"You not complain with me?"

"No, Layla, why would I when you gave me everything and more?"

Layla closed her eyes. If she wasn't in trouble then, Patrick Sharp was. Suddenly everything made sense. The note to get him to spend big, the alcoholic blackout after gambling at the warehouse. Comprehension smashed into her like a sledgehammer. She tried not to let her panic show on her face as she walked towards the tired, overweight man. She kissed him gently on the forehead and leant close, her face pressed against his cheek. Afraid of being heard, even in a locked hotel suite, she whispered into his ear. "Patrick, something bad happen. Be careful and no trust Mr Costa. He bad man and he hurt you if you do wrong."

A ripple of fear ran down Patrick's spine. He grabbed hold of Layla's arms and pushed her away from him. His fingers dug into her delicate skin as he searched her face for deception. Her face showed nothing but her fear.

"Patrick," she cried. "You hurting."

"Sorry," Patrick muttered, letting go and stepping out of the shower.

Layla straightened her dress and rushed for the door, tears gathering in her eyes. She slammed the door shut on the first man she'd ever liked. Would she ever see Patrick Sharp again?

Mr Costa waited downstairs in the hotel lobby, two muscled and tattooed bodyguards standing protectively at either side of him. His tanned skin and oiled hair could not be mistaken for European, the white suit over his bulky frame and snakeskin shoes shouted South American. The exotic group looked out of place in the conservative Clarmile Hotel, but not one of the staff questioned their right to be there. The security personnel noticeably ignored the presence of these thuggish intruders, finding urgent tasks in other parts of the hotel instead of challenging the invaders. The reception staff tried to busy themselves with menial chores to avoid staring. The elevator doors opened, and Layla stepped out. Mr Costa motioned for her to approach. Nervously, she walked forward, the sound of her stiletto heels the only noise echoing around the vast lobby.

"Is he happy?" Mr Costa asked.

Layla nodded, unable to speak around the knot of fear.

"Did he spend?"

"I stay all night and keep him awake."

Mr Costa slapped her on her bottom. "I bet you did," he laughed. "Go. Jerry is waiting outside. He take you home."

Layla placed a kiss on Mr Costa's hand and, with as much confidence as she could muster turned and strutted towards the door.

Mr Costa beckoned one of his bodyguards. "Have little Layla available for afternoon. Put her in one of our apartments at St James."

"Sir," the bodyguard replied, drawing a mobile from his pocket.

Mr Costa leant forward and sipped the espresso he'd ordered. He was in no rush to meet the Irish surgeon. Besides, for Patrick Sharp, the waiting would be worse than the meeting.

Patrick threw on his clothes. His crumpled shirt smelt of tobacco and alcohol, his stomach retched at the cloying smell of it against his skin. He dragged a hand through his thinning hair and stared at the red-faced old man in the mirror. His bloodshot eyes focused on the wrinkles and dark circles, the sallow skin and the extra weight. He had to be in surgery in a few hours, and yet the hands he looked at shook uncontrollably. He picked up his phone and dialled the clinic, cursing when he realised no one would be there so early in the morning. Gwen would be up. Her children made sure a lie-in was a luxury she never received. He dialled her home number, gritting his teeth at the loud sound of the ring tone.

"Gwen, it's Patrick," he coughed. "I'm at the Clarmile Hotel. Can you arrange for a car to pick me up?"

"Patrick? Are you okay?" she asked, alarmed at his calling so early.

"Heavy night and a few bad choices," he explained. "Just get the car here as quick as you can and make sure the hotel rings up to my suite when it arrives. 247."

"Patrick," Gwen repeated, his anxiety transmitting to her, "do I need to call someone?"

"No," he replied. "Just a car ASAP."

He pressed the red key on his phone just as the hotel door opened.

"I hope you don't mind," Mr Costa said, holding out a key card. "But I took liberty of asking reception for key."

"Quite alright," Patrick replied. "Layla's already left. Quite the gal you have there."

"I'm glad she met your needs," Mr Costa smirked. "But it other matters I wanted to discuss. Sit, please."

Patrick sat on the end of the large bed on top of the mound of jumbled sheets while Mr Costa sank into a comfortable chair and folded his hands across his chest. Costa stared until Patrick's skin started to itch, and he couldn't sit still.

"I think," Mr Costa began, "we need to look at repayment of debts. You had expensive night with little Layla and big loss at boxing. Added to horse races and drugs, and we have bit of problem."

"I always pay," Patrick blustered.

"But it never been this much before," Mr Costa said, leaning in so he could speak in a threatening whisper. "Your debt standing thirty-four thousand pounds, sterling, as of morning. With interest, that will be well over forty thousand by end of week. I do not want to see you in financial difficulty, Patrick."

Patrick closed his eyes and swayed, the lack of sleep and after effects of the drugs slowing his thought process. Could he really owe thirty-four thousand pounds?

"Is it that much?" he asked.

"I afraid so, and I must ask you pay at least some today."

Patrick tried to think. He could go to the bank and draw out a couple of grand, the clinic was bound to have some cash lying about and maybe he could raise more over the next couple of days. His bank balance wasn't great thanks to Carole spending ten grand on Mediterranean plants for the garden, and it had cost him fifty thousand to get his mistress to disappear. Something Mr Costa was well aware of because he'd help set up the transaction.

"I'm a bit short this month," Patrick said. "The payoff to that bitch cleaned me out. I can raise 4K for this afternoon, but the rest…" He shrugged apologetically.

"This not good, Patrick," Mr Costa hissed. "I cannot let our friendship get in way of good business. If I give you time, I have to give everyone time, and then chaos."

Patrick looked at Mr Costa. "I don't have more."

"Maybe you work off your debt."

"I can't provide you with drugs," Patrick stammered. "The Federation of British Plastic Surgeons keeps track of our orders. It wouldn't be safe for either of us."

"Patrick, you are far more useful than drug source. I am offended by suggestion."

"I didn't mean…" Patrick began to apologise.

"Think nothing of it. I meant you could do some surgery here and there…"

Something clicked in Patrick's mind as he half-listened to Mr Costa. "What about a merger tip," he blurted out before thinking. "BBL is positioning itself for a hostile takeover of Faunaceutical. The current deal will fall through, but I have it on good authority BBL is prepared to offer fifteen billion."

"Is information solid?"

Patrick nodded. "It came from Sir James."

"If you are sure." Mr Costa's tone became menacing. "If the tip is good, debt is gone. If tip is bad, my loss is your loss."

"It's from the horse's mouth, so to speak."

Mr Costa waved one of the bodyguards forward and spoke rapidly in Quechan, a Bolivian dialect. The man bowed then left the room.

"I trust you in this, Patrick, old friend. Now I leave you to shower." Mr Costa wrinkled his nose. "Maybe change of clothes before you leave."

Mr Costa and the remaining bodyguard turned and left. Patrick waited until the door closed behind them and then fell forward onto his knees, vomiting yellow bile onto the carpet.

Mr Costa stepped into the highly polished black Bentley. It was a car he'd always wanted to own, and now he had three. He leant forward to speak to his driver.

"Take me to St James apartment and then take afternoon off."

He leant back into his leather seat and poured himself a glass of La Concepcion, a Bolivian wine made from grapes grown in the mountains of Tarija. The red wine had a robust acidic flavour Costa liked. Importing the stuff was damned expensive, but he decided a touch of home was well worth the added hassle of including a case in his shipments of drugs and people. His phone rang, and he answered.

"The tip is good," Costa's man said in a heavily accented voice. "We have investigated the matter with a client."

"The Sopla?" Costa asked.

"Yes, he very close to Sir James. He remembers conversation with Mr Sharp."

"Good," Costa replied, swirling the dark red liquid around his glass. "I think it time we get into medical research. Tell Vargas what we know and get him to act according."

"Si, sir."

Costa sipped on the red wine. He had no intention of letting Patrick Sharp out of his debt so easily. He had plans for the NuYu clinic which involved the upstart plastic surgeon. But if he had a chance to make some money, he'd be foolish not to take up the offer of insider trading. Patrick Sharp would soon build his debt back up. He'd have Layla and Mr Green see to it.

"Get Green to call at five, and have my Maria meet me for dinner. It time I get benefit of ass. I pay for it."

The driver grinned through the mirror at his boss and nodded. Costa was a twisted man, but he paid well. Riky knew his place. Drive, keep his mouth shut and pass on messages when needed. The book of times and dates and people and venues he was compiling was an insurance policy against the day Costa decided he had seen too much. Riky never intended to use it, but it was better to have just in case.

Chapter 12 – Who are you?

Robert felt he was suffocating. The weight of a heavy arm lay across his chest, long pink nails digging painfully into his hairy chest. He pushed the arm off his torso and tried to sit up. His shoulders resisted his effort as if his neck just wasn't strong enough to lift his cumbersome head. Panic struck as he realised his immobility wasn't the effect of a hangover but that he was tied to the bed with a leather studded collar. His numb fingers groped at the offending collar, trying unsuccessfully to release himself from the restraint. He clawed at the buckle locked with a small metal padlock. He twisted his head to the right then the left, trying not to let panic build into hysteria. To his right, all he could see was a pale cream wall. To his left, he could see a mass of blonde hair and the tanned skin of shoulders and arms, a fluffy pillow hiding the unknown face. He reached over and shook the shoulder, and the person moaned but didn't wake. Robert held his breath. He could hear the sound of water running in the bathroom and someone moving about. He strained his head, trying to see over the body slumped next to him. He wanted to shout out but couldn't make his vocal cords work above a hoarse whisper.

"Ah, you are awake," a masculine voice said from beyond the blonde. "I thought I was going to have to call boss to come give you something."

"Who are you?" Robert croaked, his throat painfully dry.

"You mean you not remember? I hurt. You not remember the pleasures of the vault and after?"

"I don't," Robert began weakly and then stopped, realising he couldn't remember anything. "Can you take this off, please?" he asked, pointing at the collar. "I need to sit up. I think I'm going to be sick."

Footsteps sounded. The tip-tap of high stiletto heels on the wooden floor. "Let me see if I can find the key."

Robert heard a drawer being opened and the rattle of objects being moved. "Ah, here it is," the voice said triumphantly.

The body next to him stirred slightly in sleep and snuggled deeper into the covers. Robert could now see the back of a curvaceous lady in a low-cut black dress who stood a few steps away from his confinement. The fabric clung enticingly to her hips and round voluptuous bottom. Her long, slender legs were bare, showing off her bronze colouring and as she stood up, Robert could see a slim waist and long dark hair. The woman turned, her fingers tangling in black curls. "You mind if I take this off?" she asked, pulling the black wig from her head. "It itches."

Robert couldn't speak. Beneath the wig was a round shaved head, but this revelation wasn't the one that caused the room to spin nauseatingly. The statuesque figure wearing a tight-fitting sexy dress had not only large breasts pushing out of the fabric, but also a huge penis encased in black Lycra.

"I had fun last night," he said, leaning over Robert to unlock the collar.

Robert stared at the soft, perfect breasts bouncing in front of his face and panicked. He heard the click of the lock and sat up, pushing the man-woman out of the way as he dashed unsteadily for the bathroom.

"Are you okay?" the man asked sympathetically from the doorway. "Bankers' dust affect people sometime."

Robert's naked skin was covered in a sheen of sweat, and bruising had started to form in purple bands on his wrists, ankles and neck. He sank to the floor, his heart hammering so hard in his chest he thought he was having a heart attack.

"Robert? Are you okay?"

Robert gagged, vomit spewing from his mouth in a fountain of bile and bloody fluid. He tried to stand but fell forward into the vile mess and passed out.

He woke up with three distorted faces looming over him and a stinging sensation across his cheek.

"Slap him again," the blonde said.

"Juan, this isn't S&M session. You give him concussion."

"Idiot," Juan replied. "Why he take so much bankers' dust if can't handle drug."

"It was his first time," Will said. "I think maybe McGregor pushed him too far. How was he in the sack?"

"Gave as good as he got, didn't he Bobby?" Juan laughed. "Miss Lovelash is a genius in vault, but we prove to him lady-boys are better."

Robert's eyes slowly focused on Will's face and the two transvestites who stood leaning over him.

He licked his lips and tried to talk.

"What did he say, Juan?" the bald she-man asked, her impeccable make-up expertly in place on her heart-shaped face as she leant forward to listen.

"I don't think he said anything, Bobby," the blonde replied, her mascara and eyeliner smeared across her chiselled face, a definite stubble growing on her top lip.

Both strangely erotic lady-boys spoke with South American accents, their near-perfect English sounding exotic in their lilting musical voices.

"He's awake," Will said with a certain amount of relief. "Hey, man, you gave us a scare. What the fuck did McGregor give you?"

Robert shrugged his shoulders helplessly. "Drink," he managed to gasp around the tightness in his throat.

"I think you've had enough." Will shook his head.

"Water," Robert rasped.

Juan headed to the mini bar while Will and Bobby helped Robert off the floor and onto the toilet seat to sit.

The mirror opposite showed Robert a puke-covered, slightly overweight, sallow naked man with red eyes and a purple welt forming on his neck. He shuddered, trying to remember how he'd ended up in a hotel suite with two transvestites. Flashes came back to him. Bare legs and arms, thrusting passions. A blindfold and a mistress. His hands holding a woman's head. The pleasure of something inside him. Being smothered in wonderfully warm breasts. He held his face in his hands as tears of frustration ran unashamedly down his face.

"It's the temazepam," Bobby said. "We took them to help us sleep around five this morning."

"Get him in the shower and hose him down," Will ordered. "I have to phone McGregor and tell him Robbie here isn't fit for clinic. Fucked if I know what he'll say."

"McGregor promise me and Juan Botox if we loosen Robert up a bit. If he doesn't go in, who going to inject us?"

"You want him injecting you?" Will said pointing at Robert slumped on the toilet, his mouth open and drool dribbling down his chin.

"It is free," Bobby answered as if this was a good enough reason. "Give him coffee, and if it doesn't work, I've uppers in my purse."

"I think he's had enough."

Robert wanted to agree, no more drugs, but the effort of lifting his head from his chest was taking all his energy and concentration. Bobby's strong arms wrapped themselves under his arms, and he felt the transvestite lift him as effortlessly as if he were a small child.

"I have to go to work," Robert pleaded. He couldn't call in sick on his second day. McGregor would sack him for gross misconduct and his Uncle would ridicule and belittle him until he ran back to Leeds. His dreams of a new life would end in his luxurious hotel suite, vomit-covered and confused all because he couldn't handle the big boys' toys McGregor had supplied. He needed this job, needed to prove to himself that he could fit in and succeed.

"Grab his legs," Bobby said.

Will lifted Robert's legs into the bath. Bobby stood back and turned on the shower. Cold water splattered on Robert's head and face, the icy drops making him shiver. Then torrents of freezing water gushed over his goose-bumpy skin. He opened his mouth and let the stream of water surge into his throat.

Robert wasn't sure how much time had passed. It could have been two minutes or two hours. He sat staring at the white tiles while the water drenched his body. He didn't focus or try to think, but every so often flashes of memory burst in vivid colour in front of his face. A fingernail trailing down his chest, a tongue lapping softly at his dick then sucking with a pleasurable force, a round bottom impaling itself on his erection. The images were frightening and erotic. A forbidden pleasure he had enjoyed and knew he shouldn't have. Had he willingly left the vault with Juan and Bobby? Had he known they were transvestites? Why had he taken the white powder when he'd resolved never to touch drugs again? Each time he tried to concentrate on a thought, it twirled away from him like a leaf on an autumnal wind. The water stopped suddenly, and the shaking began. It started in his toes and moved upwards until his whole body shuddered uncontrollably. His jaw knocked together with such force he thought his teeth would shatter. He tensed his muscles and squeezed his eyes shut trying to regain control.

"Drink this," Will said, forcing a hot cup against Robert's trembling lip. "It's strong and hot. It'll help."

Robert sipped at the dark bitter coffee, the fluid burning away the congestion in his throat and the fuzziness in his head. "Thanks," he managed to say as the caffeine flooded his body. "I think I can cope now." He grasped the hot cup like a lifeline pulling him back from the brink of insanity.

"Here," Will said, passing Robert the soap. "Clean yourself up. You stink worse than Fitzroy."

Robert looked down and blushed with the realisation he was naked in the shower with three men watching him. "Thanks," he muttered, pulling the opaque shower door closed and conveniently forgetting he'd awakened naked in bed with at least one of the men.

Will laughed, remembering his own initiation to Bankers. Robert had gotten off relatively lightly by comparison. While he might be disorientated, at least he had nothing pierced. Will rubbed his bruised nipple thoughtfully. He'd spent the night with Sarah Wilson, and he bore the bruising and bite marks to prove it. Her lovemaking was always violent, exciting and satisfying. Which of her loyal constituents would have thought the right honourable Mrs Wilson would be into such an exhibitionistic, twisted fetish? Will imagined the tall black woman knocking on doors and kissing babies or discussing reforms to the health service, while secretly enjoying the vibrating beads her secretary unwittingly controlled by her computer's mouse. The thought made Will horny.

"Where are my clothes?" Robert asked, his skinny legs sticking out of the huge white towel he'd wrapped around his shoulders.

"McGregor's suit is at the hotel's dry cleaners, and my shirt is in the bin. I don't want it back!"

"What will I wear?" Robert panicked.

"Relax, Cinders, you will go to the ball," Will smirked. "I picked you up a pair of jeans and T-shirt from the supermarket down the street. They might not be the best fit, but hey, they'll get you to the clinic, and you can change into scrubs."

"Where are we?"

"The Clarmile Hotel. You're in McGregor's suite. He took a taxi home."

Robert looked round the unfamiliar suite while he pulled on the ill-fitting jeans and baggy white T-shirt. The rooms were opulent. White and cream shades mixed tastefully, highlighted by the odd accent of burgundy. The huge, messy bed seemed to float on its transparent base in the centre of the room as if the only reason to stay was to cavort in its luxurious sheets. Contemporary sofa and chairs nestled around a wide screen smart TV, boasting 3D adult entertainment from the open magazine next to it. White roses graced the artistic coffee table along with scattered chocolates and an empty bottle of Cristal champagne.

"McGregor got stood up," Will answered Robert's unasked question. "He decided you and your friends could use the suite more entertainingly than he could."

Robert shivered as he tried to remember any of the things that had happened.

"You'll need to cover those bruises when we get to the clinic," Will said, pointing at Robert's neck and wrists. "Get Dylees to give you some of the make-up stash we keep for clients and lead surgeons when they have to face the paparazzi."

The two lady-boys appeared from the bathroom. They had showered, styled their Louis Ferre wigs and reapplied the heavy make-up. Respectfully, they had chosen their clothing to flatter their feminine curves and hide the added extras for their excursion to the Fitzroy clinic.

"They look..." Robert started to say until he noticed Will's warning glare.

"Did you enjoy your dive into the depravity of the Vault?" Will asked to fill the awkward silence.

"I can't remember," Robert whined, "but I hurt everywhere, even my…"

"Been there and done that. Just don't have a shit for a few days, and you'll be fine."

Robert felt tears forming in his eyes. What had he done? It was the not knowing that made it worse. I am never doing drugs again, Robert promised himself.

"Ladies," Will said, taking Juan's hand and placing a gentlemanly kiss on her fingertips, "it's been lovely to meet you. If you would like to stay for breakfast and then get a taxi to the clinic, Robert here can wow you with his skills with a syringe."

The lady-boys giggled and lowered their eyes as if flattered and embarrassed by Will's courteous attention.

"Come on you, man whore," Will said, placing a friendly hand on Robert's shoulder and steering him towards the door. "It's time you and I were at the clinic. McGregor said nine, and you don't want to be late on your second day."

Chapter 13 – She has a dick

"Dylees, where the fuck is my list?" McGregor shouted from his office. He'd woken alone and in a foul mood. The slut Candice hadn't called, so he'd wasted five hundred quid on a hotel suite and not had the pleasure of fucking in it. He'd been so sure of the evening he'd even laid out for flowers and champagne to impress the little whore.

Miss Adventure had gotten him so revved up with her erotic fire dance he could have exploded at the mere touch of a manicured finger. Instead, he'd been home alone with his hand and a bondage magazine, nowhere near as satisfying as tying Candice up in intricate knots and forcing her to submit to his desires. She owed him, and in the very near future, she'd have to pay.

"Dylees," he shouted again. "I asked you for my fucking list."

Dylees stood with her hands on her hips at the door of the reception. She looked straight at her uptight boss and smiled. "And I told you, David," she yelled, "it's on your desk!"

McGregor turned and slammed the door. He stomped back to his chair and picked up the manila file placed neatly in the middle of the near empty desk. He opened the cardboard folder to see a neatly typed list of names and procedures, times and medical notes. 11.00 Faye Smith – Rhinoplasty. 1.00 James Dunway – Liposuction on stomach and chest. 4.00 Candice Connelly – Consultation. McGregor stopped reading and sat down. He folded his hands over his chest and smiled wickedly.

Pressing the reception button on the phone's intercom. "Move my five o'clock to Mr Sutherland," he said.

"Are you sure?" Dylees asked incredulously. "It's Hazel Woods."

"I'm sure. Let's put the bitch in her place."

McGregor rubbed his hands together. Maybe he had misunderstood Candice, maybe the sweet girl wanted something for her time, perhaps a free treatment. McGregor remembered the curve of the tight jumper over her pert breasts and slim waist, the bounce of her bottom as she walked away. He couldn't think what treatment someone so young would want, but if it resulted in her being more pliable, he'd cut her up as often as she liked. He looked at his list again. Faye Smith's beakectomy would be time-consuming. He looked at the notes and the pre-op photos. The woman really did have a beak. He'd need to shave the nasal bone aggressively and remove the majority of the cartilage. He'd have to be careful so as to maintain her airways. Such an aggressive procedure could easily impair her natural breathing. The lipo on James Dunway MP needed to be subtle. It would be bad PR for his right honourable to be accused of spending taxpayer money on plastic surgery. Sutherland could assist with both procedures to save time. McGregor had every confidence the young surgeon would be in work today, battered and bruised but definitely in work.

David McGregor studied the revenue forecast on his computer. Business was booming. The publicity from being on TV had pushed this year's profits into the millions. The clinic had always been recognised for providing an excellent service to the elite and wealthy, but now it was also known for providing treatments to the famous. McGregor had been accepted into the elite circle of the red carpet crowd, mixing with film stars and musicians who understood the benefits of having a talented surgeon as a friend. He signed a few forms approving purchases of equipment and drugs before proofreading an interview he had been sent by the celebrity magazine Haut Monde. The interviewer had been a middle-aged woman well past her sell-by date, her face so full of fillers and Botox it hardly moved. The tight jeans and fitted blouse showed her slim but aging figure in an unflattering way as she clumsily flirted with the TV star. McGregor had found it difficult to turn on his renowned charms in the face of such an unpleasant appearance. He carefully read and re-read the piece. He came off aloof but professional. While the article wouldn't win him TV personality of the year, it definitely presented him as an expert in his field. He made a few quick changes in red pen and stuffed the papers into the prepaid envelope. He returned to his computer and started to write next week's Morning Wake-up slot. The broadcasters wanted him to talk about the dangers of Botox. A bandwagon reaction to the photographs of Clara Huntington, the page three model had been pictured with a deformed eyebrow and lips swollen past a trout pout into a lump-sucker pucker. The model claimed her distorted lips were the result of an allergic reaction, but McGregor suspected negligence on her surgeon's part. McGregor sighed. The problem with highlighting dangers wasn't that it affected his bottom line, actually just the opposite. If pitched correctly, the segment would see the clinic injecting patients from the moment they opened the doors until they pushed them closed at night. People were gullible. Tell them about the dangers of cheap Botox and under-qualified practitioners and they worried. Bring the Botox onto Harley Street with a surgeon holding the syringe, and they handed over their three hundred quid like children buying sweets, eagerly and without thought to the consequences. McGregor made a note to order more Botox serum and remind the staff to dilute it with 5cc of saline, not 2cc. He tapped his fingers on his desk, trying to remember a conversation he'd had last night about Botox, before remembering the drug-fuelled pact. He'd invited two transvestites to the clinic if they fucked Sutherland.

McGregor smiled. "Splendid."

Dylees and Sutherland could have a quick training session on the lady-boys before the actress Faye Smith arrived for her pre-op appointment. With the extra capacity, they'd be able to cope with the influx of patients from this Wake-Up slot. McGregor's fingers started to type, the words flowing onto the screen. He expressed concern for the poor glamour model and reminded people how Botox wasn't the problem, but the way it was injected was. He emphasised that Botox was like anything else, you only got what you paid for. Use a reputable clinic, and the treatment was safe. McGregor enjoyed quoting the phrase, 'If a deal sounds too good, it usually is.' He added, 'Avoid any cosmetic clinics offering two for one deals or massive discounts.' He ran through the piece, making a few notes in the margins for himself, smile into the camera here, mention Fitzroy's here. He added the final paragraph about the use of Botox to treat medical conditions and the benefits of early intervention to prevent wrinkles. 'At The Fitzroy clinic, like other reputable clinics, Botox is administered by qualified medical professionals. Professionals who have trained for years to ensure they understand the human body and the way we as surgeons can best enhance your appearance. You must remember the dedication and professionalism of our staff and compare that to the two-day training courses some people have undertaken. Do not trust an advert on Facebook or other social media sites. Don't be the next Clara Huntington.'

McGregor scribbled a note for Dylees. Get a hold of Clara Cuntington's PR manager and offer her a freebie in exchange for press coverage of her correctional surgery. If this was the model Will was avoiding, treating her would keep Lord Mowbray happy and get the clinic some free advertising. Satisfied with his morning productivity, he decided it was time to yell at someone.

"Sutherland!" he yelled into his phone. "Why the fuck aren't you at work?"

"Just outside," Robert rasped into his mobile. "I'm with Will." Robert felt sick, and he was sure his whole face was green, or white, or maybe green and white, or whitish-green? His head hurt even trying to think about it. He was sure he was going to be sick again, but Will had warned him not to 'be a baby and swallow.' Heeding Will's instructions, Robert swallowed the fiery liquid each time the acidic bile entered his mouth, praying it was the last time.

"Well, you're late," McGregor barked, enjoying the role play. "I told you to be here by nine. What time do you call this?"

Robert tried to focus on the digital clock on the dashboard of Will's car, but the numbers jumped around, preventing him from making sense of the blur. "I don't know."

"Your second fucking day, and you don't know what time it is."

"McGregor, I don't know what happened," Robert whimpered. "I was with you and Will at Bankers, and then I woke up in a hotel room with two..."

"If you can't keep it in your pants during work hours, I'm going to take your contract and shove it up your arse."

"I'm sorry." Robert slumped into his seat. "I think I'm going to be sick."

Will reached over, opened the door and pushed Robert out onto the street. "I warned you," he said as Robert looked up pitifully from the pavement.

"Get in here!" McGregor's voice boomed from the back door of the clinic. Robert crawled towards the sound, unable to stand with the cramps churning in his stomach. "What the fuck?" McGregor bellowed. "How am I supposed to teach you how to inject when you can barely stand?"

Robert groaned and tried to get his feet under him. His legs buckled, and Will only just caught him in time to stop his face hitting the tarmacked car park.

"Get him inside!" McGregor barked, glaring at the

junior surgeon. But when Robert turned away, Will saw the scowl transform into a sly smirk of enjoyment. Sometimes Will hated his boss. His cruel, twisted side had grown since he'd met Witch-Hazel. It was as if his darkness fed off her corrupting lustful energy.

"The trannies will be here at ten," Will said as he carried the now unconscious Robert into the staff room. "What do you want me to do with Robbie?"

"Give him a shot of vodka and a fluid I.V. He should be able to assist with Beakface by eleven."

Will nodded and dumped Robert on the couch Fitzroy had occupied only 24 hours earlier.

"Get Dylees and Kate to meet me in treatment suite one. They can learn how to inject and Claire can cover reception. Hey, if it goes wrong, who's going to notice on two lady-boys?"

Will raised his eyebrows in disbelief. Dylees had been pestering McGregor for months to train her to use Botox and fillers, but at least she was a qualified nurse. Kate was a receptionist with no anatomy training at all. How McGregor expected her to be able to treat patients was anyone's guess. But which was worse, an under-trained and nervous Kate or a drugged up, hung over Sutherland.

"Is the commander in chief in agreement?" Will asked.

"Fuck Fitzroy," McGregor spat. "The pissed-up arsehole hasn't even made it to work yet."

Will attached the I.V. to Robert's arm and left. He had plenty of work to do, and with McGregor's foul humour, it seemed wise to make himself scarce. He poked his head around the reception door to inform Dylees and Kate of McGregor's decision. Dylees beamed with delight while Kate turned an odd shade of puce.

It was ten o'clock on the dot when the two glamorous lady-boys graced the reception of the Fitzroy clinic.

"We're here to see our Robbie," Bobby cooed in the reception. "Such a nice boy. He promised to do us if we did him."

"We did him real good," Juan giggled. "And he's not a small boy. Under all those neuroses, he's quite kinky."

"Enough detail," Dylees said in a voice that brooked no argument. "This is a respected clinic."

Bobby put her fingers to her pursed lips and tilted her head. "And who are you? Morality police?"

"No, I'm the person who will be ejecting rather than injecting you if you don't keep it down."

"Oooww," Juan said, placing her hands on her hips provocatively. "That told Bobby."

"So it did," Bobby said, his shoulders wiggling to give Dylees the full effect of his large fake breasts.

"Not impressed," Dylees said, looking pointedly at the tanned boobs. "We do a much better job here."

"This girl," Bobby said, "is a darling. We must take her out one night. You'd have a scream, Dilly."

Dylees smiled. It was always the same whether they were ladies or lady-boys. All you needed to do with a diva was show them you weren't intimidated, and you immediately became their bestie.

"Can I get you a coffee while you wait?" Claire asked meekly from behind the reception desk. "And Kate asked if you could just fill in these forms?"

"Coffee, black, three sugars for me, sweetie," Bobby said, taking the offered clipboard and pen from the shy, mousy girl.

"I like my coffee like my man," Juan said.

"Weak and milky," Dylees added.

"How did you know?" Juan laughed.

It was as Claire returned with the coffees that Carl Fitzroy decided to honour the clinic with his esteemed presence. The portly surgeon walked into reception in a blue pinstriped suit with a purple shirt and orange tie. His orange and purple striped socks peeked out from his slightly short trousers, creating a comical appearance.

"What you ladies laughing about?" he said, grabbing Juan's bottom and squeezing it in his big hands. "And with an arse like yours, why are you here?"

Juan turned and slapped Fitzroy across the face. "Keep your dirty hands to yourself, old man. Don't touch what you not afford."

"Who says I can't afford?" Fitzroy blustered. "I'll have you know, young lady, it's my name above the door."

Bobby placed a restraining hand on Juan's arm and the other gently on Fitzroy's face. She leant into him, providing an ideal opportunity for him to ogle her breasts.

"What my girlfriend meant to say was we have long night with your young surgeon friend, and the goods need a little rest in one of your delightful treatment suites. Dylees was just about to take us through now we have drinks. But if you be gentleman, we'd prefer your company." She flashed a dazzling smile at him and lowered her head to look at him through long, fake eyelashes.

"Well, you should have said so in the first place. Allow me." Carl Fitzroy held out his elbows to the two lady-boys. The transvestites linked their arms through his and sauntered from reception, their hips swaying provocatively.

"Do you think…" Kate started to ask.

"I guess we'll find out," Dylees interrupted.

Dylees and Kate were in treatment suite two, listening to McGregor's lecture on the finer points of facial anatomy when Fitzroy burst into the room. Kate was gingerly holding a needle and nearly stabbed it into Dylees as she jumped.

"She's has a dick!" Fitzroy yelled his red face even redder than normal.

"And?" McGregor said. "Most men do."

"But I thought…" blustered Fitzroy.

"We all knew what you thought! Now go and apologise to the sweet lady-boys and tell them we're ready to go through the consultation."

"I will not!"

McGregor's expression darkened, and his mouth soured into a scowl. "You will go and apologise to the ladies and offer to take them for lunch. Tell them we will be with them shortly," McGregor hissed.

Fitzroy's shoulders slumped, and he looked at the floor like a schoolboy who had been reprimanded by the principal. Without a word, he turned and lumbered back down the corridor.

"Don't even," McGregor warned as Dylees lips twisted into a smile.

"I wouldn't dream of it, David."

The two lady-boys were happily chatting to Fitzroy when McGregor entered the treatment suite. It appeared the offer of lunch had eased the social embarrassment of Fitzroy sticking his hand up Bobby's skirt and finding something he hadn't expected. In fact, the animated conversation was currently revolving around the ins and outs of sex with a transsexual.

"I've very tight bottom," Juan was confiding. "It's the anal exercises, keep everything snug."

McGregor coughed from the doorway. The two lady-boys giggled, and Juan placed a hand on Fitzroy's leg. "We were just getting to know one another," Juan giggled.

"He's such a sweetie when you get to know him," Bobby added.

Fitzroy beamed.

McGregor sat down in the chair behind the desk and waved Dylees and Kate into the room.

"Ladies," he began, "our young Sutherland is out of sorts this morning, as you know. So I've asked Kate and Dylees to provide your treatment. I'll be talking them through it as we go along in order to assess their skills." He made it sound so commonplace and routine that both lady-boys shrugged their shoulders.

"Who's first?" McGregor asked.

"Me, me!" Bobby screamed, giddily jumping onto the couch. "Can you stay and hold my hand, Carl?"

"I'm afraid Mr Fitzroy has clients in the clinic this morning," McGregor replied before Fitzroy could answer. The room was crowded already, and he didn't need a second chair, so to speak. "Dylees," he continued, handing her the consultation form, "why don't you take Bobby through this medical information form."

Dylees stood next to Bobby and proceeded to question him. Bobby's name was Alberto Alekseev, age 36. He had no drug allergies he knew of and had tried enough meds he was sure he'd be fine with anything. He was nearly positive he'd taken no amikacin, gentamicin or tobramycin in the last week. The contraindicated drugs were antibiotics and had no hallucinogenic or sedative effects, so McGregor was almost sure he agreed.

Robert Sutherland woke dazed and confused for the second time that morning. He looked around the austere room, trying to remember where he was and how he'd got there. He pulled the I.V. from his arm and attempted to sit up. He swayed and retched, but there was nothing left in his stomach to vomit. In the last twenty-four hours, he'd taken ketamine, cocaine, weed and temazepam, and those were the ones he could remember. His head felt as if three thousand little hammers were chipping away at his brain and a family of voles had taken up residence in his mouth. If he opened his eyes, the world shook violently from one side to the other, yet if he kept them closed the room spun until he was sure he was going to be sick.

"It's awake," Fitzroy said from the doorway. "Not sure we should have taken on someone who turns up to work looking like that."

McGregor pushed passed the over-weight surgeon, "Like you can talk," McGregor growled pushing a glass underneath Robert's nose and forcing the clear liquid into his mouth. "Drink this Sutherland."

Robert gulped the liquid and choked as the neat vodka washed down his throat.

"It will stop your hands shaking," McGregor explained. "Now drink."

McGregor totally agreed with the old drunk, but he wouldn't admit it. Robert had turned out to be something of a disappointment. How could anyone be affected so dramatically by a few prescription drugs? The vodka hit Robert's empty stomach and threatened to retrace its route back up his oesophagus. He clamped his jaw shut and refused to concede to the violent tearing sensations, squeezing his eyes shut until the pain passed. Slowly, he opened his eyes. The room jolted sadistically and then settled. He took the glass from McGregor and sipped the last of the vodka. It helped!

"What do you need me to do?" Robert asked in a voice that sounded steadier than he felt.

"That's my boy," Fitzroy laughed. "A quick swig of the good stuff and you're ready for surgery."

"Get a shower and meet me in consultation suite two. I want your opinion on Beakface and her nose job," McGregor snapped.

The woman waiting for Robert in the consultation suite couldn't have been more unattractive if she'd purposefully set out to look her worst. The skinny frame and skeletal facial features were dominated by a hooked nose and sunken eye sockets. She swivelled her head much like a vulture to look at the two men as they entered. Robert swallowed hard to stop himself from laughing as the feathered collar on her grey and pink cardigan accentuated her bird of prey appearance. This woman didn't need a nose job. She needed putting down as a humane act to prevent suffering. McGregor had been talking while Robert stared, introducing Faye Smith and explaining the procedure to the character actress.

"What do you think, Mr Sutherland?" McGregor asked.

"I agree totally, Mr McGregor," Robert replied, unsure as to what he had just agreed with.

"Great. So if you agree, Mrs Smith, we'll perform both surgeries at the same time. It means less time under anaesthetic, always a safer option. Mr Sutherland here will perform the breast augmentation while I carry out the rhinoplasty."

Robert was taken aback by the quick turn of events. Five minutes ago, he was assisting on a nose job, and now he was performing a boob job with a hangover and no consultation. It seemed he knew nothing about the industry he had worked for seven years to break into. These surgeons didn't want to help people improve emotionally and physically, they wanted to make as much money in as short a time as possible.

McGregor was talking again. "I'll leave you in Mr Sutherland's capable hands. He will run through the procedures, run a few tests and then mark you up for your treatments. I'll be back in a half an hour to introduce you to our anaesthetist."

Robert heard the door to the consultation suite shut, leaving him alone in the room with Faye Smith staring at him with her beady birdlike eyes.

"One moment," Robert blurted and turned to chase after McGregor.

"Can I help you?" McGregor barked when Robert knocked respectfully on his office door.

"Errm," Robert began, "is that normal?"

"Is what normal? That an ugly bitch wants us to transform her into Kate Moss?"

"No," Robert hesitated. "To change a surgical plan so close to the procedure?"

"If you can upsell, then why not?"

"Doesn't it go against the ethics of cosmetic surgery?"

"The only ethics I care about are the ethics of the bottom line. Add to my bank balance, and I'm happy. Cost me money, and you are out."

McGregor glared at Robert, challenging him to ask further questions. Robert looked at his shoes. "I'll get Dylees to help me fast-track the tests."

"Good idea," McGregor said, looking back down at the papers in front of him.

McGregor pretended not to notice Robert turn tail and leave. In truth, he was pushing it a little, both ethically and with the schedule. But money was like that. The more you had, the more you needed. Keeping Witch-Hazel happy, maintaining a penthouse apartment and the use of a suite at the Clarmile hotel required money. Christ, his membership at Bankers cost him more than two grand a month. Witch-Hazel had aspirations of cross-Atlantic fame and spent his money on PR firms, solicitors for contract negotiations and an army of stylists. How her expenses had become his expenses, McGregor wasn't sure, but each month, another few thousand seemed to disappear from his account. He made a quick memo on his phone to contact his business manager. It seemed more and more invoices were being paid without authorisation, and he wouldn't put it past Witch-Hazel to be shagging his BM's brains out. Hazel could be very persuasive when she put her butt into in.

Mercifully, the intercom buzzed, interrupting his chain of thought. Consideration of the witch's bottom always stiffened his dick, and he didn't have time for telephone sex, even with Hazel, who could get him off in moments with her filthy mouth.

"What?" he yelled at the intercom.

"Your lipo's arrived, and Lady Elizabeth is recovering well at Re Vive."

"Get Sutherland to deal with him," McGregor said. "I've a phone call to make."

"Suit yourself," Dylees replied, slamming down the receiver.

Chapter 14 – The sexy Candice

It took three attempts for Patrick to get the key into to the back door at NuYu. His hand shook violently from fear and the drugs still flooding his system. He nearly wept when the door finally succumbed, and he could fall into the clinic. He stumbled into the dark empty building, careening off the walls as he lurched towards his office. It was quiet and cold this early. The heating hadn't switched on yet, and it would be at least an hour before the staff started coming to work. The pale light from the street lamps cast eerie shadows across his desk. Shakily, he poured himself a scotch, tipping more of the golden spirit on the mahogany desk than in the glass. Cupping the glass in both hands, he forced the liquid to his lips and drank before slumping onto his chair. He felt salty tears rolling down his cheeks and tried to stop the shaking of his shoulders. It was no use. He gave into the gut-wrenching sobbing. Patrick Sharp was not a man who cried easily. He'd not cried when his IRA activist father had been killed by the British military. He'd not cried when his mother refused to talk to him for applying to Oxford. He'd not cried when his wife lost their child three weeks before she was due to give birth. Patrick Sharp had been through hell and back, and he'd faced it all with the stoic attitude of what doesn't kill you makes you stronger. Now for the first time in his fifty-six years, Patrick Sharp felt fear and dread and an overwhelming sadness. He wiped his face with the back of his sleeve, spreading the tears, mucus and saliva across the white fabric. It must be the drugs, he concluded. Whatever Layla had given him had forced an emotional reaction. When he thought of Layla, the tears started again. He felt a connection with the young prostitute, a bond of lust and passion he'd not felt in years. He needed to see her again, to hold her naked body in his arms and gently kiss the top of her silken hair. Could she feel the same way? The way she'd looked at him showed she felt something, didn't it? But maybe all she felt was fear she would be punished for something he'd done. It was self-preservation he'd seen, not concern. The girl was a whore. She had been bought and paid for. Patrick Sharp was a fool to think anything else, and yet her lips on his. Patrick closed his eyes and remembered the smell of her skin, the feel of her hair, the taste of her. His head lolled backwards, and he passed out.

"Patrick," a voice called. "Patrick, wake up."

Patrick opened his eyes. The gentle street light had been replaced by the harsh light of midday.

"We left you as long as we could," Gwen said. "Did everything work out okay?"

Patrick nodded and groaned. The small movement made him feel as if his head was about to fall off. He reached up and grabbed it with both hands.

"Jeez, boss," Andrew said from the doorway. "You sure know how to party."

Patrick didn't try to respond, his full attention focused on not throwing up all over Gwen.

"Drink," he croaked when he'd managed to get his stomach under control.

Gwen walked over to the water cooler.

"No, scotch."

"Are you sure?"

"Yes. Hair of the dog."

"It's your hangover."

"Do you want a bacon butty from Feast?" Andrew chimed in.

"Egg and bacon," Patrick answered without opening his eyes.

"No problem. Anything for you Gwen?"

"Do I look like I eat that crap? Ask Jane to make me a NuYu salad."

Andrew raised a questioning eyebrow but didn't comment. Gwen held the glass to Patrick's lips and helped him to drink the neat scotch. Then she held the glass of cold water to his lips as well.

"Don't even think about refusing," she said, giving Patrick a determined stare. "And after this pint, another, and then in the shower with you. You have clients for consultations this afternoon and a full list of procedures tomorrow. Please tell me this is the last time you're going to be in this state. You're not twenty anymore, and neither am I. No more waking me up at six." Gwen conveniently forgot to mention she'd already been awake with a pair of strong arms wrapped around her.

Patrick drank the water and didn't comment. He knew Gwen was right, but he also knew there would never be a last time until the last time. He was self-aware enough to know he would probably end up in a ditch somewhere with a Bolivian thug and a blunt object. His father had gambled with his life in service to an ideal that never made sense to a young boy who just wanted his dad at home. Patrick's addiction to gambling was the same, an overriding commitment to self-destruction. One hot shower and one large bacon and egg butty had a cathartic effect on Patrick. A change of clothes and four strong black cups of coffee completed his transformation from drunken bum to professional surgeon.

"Good morning, Miss King," he said, walking into the consultation room. "What is it I can do for you today?"

Miss Victoria King was instantly recognisable as a wannabe. Her short skirt showed fake tanned legs, and platform heels hid the deformed feet he knew she would be blessed with. He looked at her face covered in orange foundation. Her false eyelashes competed with thick eyeliner and pencilled-in eyebrows. He questioned why women felt this was beautiful. When had natural beauty given way to horrendous caricatures of femininity, and was his profession partly or wholly to blame? Did the need to conform to a twenty-first century image of beauty rob women of the ability to claim their individuality? Patrick's mood darkened. He half-turned, ready to walk out of the consultation room, but the image of the dark hair, tanned legs, flat stomach and round cheek bottoms of Layla halted his movement. He needed money to pay to see her.

"What can I do for you?" he asked, the temporary resurgence of his morals killed by thoughts of illicit sex with his South American whore.

"Aye want to 'ave bigger tits," Miss King stated in a Chelmsford twang. "Mary Beth had her tits done 'ere, and she loved em." Miss King drew out the word loved almost as if filling in for the missing consonants.

Patrick looked at Miss King's chest, her natural cleavage poking out of the tight V-neck jumper. "And how much larger do you want to go?" Patrick asked.

"Well, I'd like a G cup like Danni."

"Danni?"

"Yeah, Danni Armstrong," Miss King said in a tone which clearly showed she thought Patrick was a little bit slow. "From TOWIE," she prompted.

Patrick shrugged his shoulders. He still had no idea what the girl was talking about. Miss King tutted and rummaged through her oversized Prada handbag.

"Don't you know anyfink?" she said, handing him a glossy magazine turned to the page of an attractive blonde with pearl-white teeth. Her figure-hugging silver dress showed off an amazing cleavage. "Danni Armstrong," she said, emphasising each word as if she said it slowly enough the words would suddenly develop some meaning to a fifty-six-year-old plastic surgeon.

"Miss King," Patrick said patiently, "I'm sure we can achieve a similar result to this young lady. However, you must remember breast augmentation is only the first step along the road to perfection."

Miss King tilted her head, much like a dog did when it listened to its master's voice.

"If we increase the size of your bust, we must also

look at sculpting your waist and possibly hips to give you the hourglass figure you're looking for."

"Darren says he'll pay, as long as aye am 'appy."

"Darren sounds like the ideal man," Patrick said, mentally rubbing his hands together at the thought of the cash. "Let's get you into a gown and bring Gwen in to help with the consultation."

"Well, she was easy," Gwen said as the surgeon and nurse left Miss King in the consultation room to get dressed. "I'm surprised you didn't get her to agree to a facelift as well."

"Not sure I could have cut through the inch-thick foundation," Patrick replied. "I'm sure she must sleep in the stuff."

"It's stained the gown!"

"Bin it," Patrick said. "With the money she's fetching in, we can afford to buy her a new dressing gown every time she visits. But for god sake, don't let her lean on the walls. I don't want to have to redecorate."

Gwen laughed. "I think your next consult is here. Miss C Connelly?"

Patrick didn't utter a word, his face said it all.

"What's wrong?"

"Nothing, nothing's wrong," Patrick stammered. He'd forgotten all about the sexy Candy in the wake of the long, tanned legs of Layla.

The woman in reception was dressed in a pink, tight-fitting jumper and skin-tight, dark denim jeans. Her pale pink stilettos tapped impatiently on the wooden floor as she twisted a curl of blonde hair around a magenta nail extension. When she saw Patrick in the doorway, she stood up and strutted confidently towards him. Her stiletto shoes put her breasts in line with his reddening face. Her nipples pointed through the thin wool, challenging him to touch.

"Patrick!" she squealed, bending down to kiss his

cheek. "I hope you don't mind me dropping in for a consultation?"

Patrick's heartbeat quickened when her nipples grazed his face as she stood.

"No problem, my dear," he said, gulping back a lustful sigh before it could escape his lips. "It's a pleasure to see you so soon."

Gwen coughed disapprovingly. "Can I show you to one of our consultation rooms and get you a coffee?" she asked, opening the door from the reception.

"Thank you," Candice said without looking away from Patrick. "A coffee would be lovely. Latte if you have one."

Her eyes narrowed slightly, making Patrick feel like prey about to be eaten, before she followed Gwen along the hallway.

"Wow!" Andrew exclaimed. "I thought she was going to take her clothes off in reception and have you over the counter."

"I was hoping she was going to take her clothes off and do me in reception. Would you have watched, you dirty bastard?"

"Of course."

Patrick laughed, releasing the tension he'd been holding since Candy had looked up from her magazine.

"What does sex on legs want from this place?" Andrew asked.

"Hopefully me! But probably what every hot woman in London wants, to stay young forever. The more attractive they are, the more they worry about losing those good looks. Bread and butter, my friend, bread and butter."

Andrew smiled. "I need you to order more morphine, lidocaine, heparin, propofol, temazepam and diazepam."

"Leave a note on my desk, and I'll get Gwen to order them. Seeing as we've no patients in today, can you

138

stocktake the implants and see what else we need to order?"

"You got it, boss," Andrew replied with a salute.

"Bastard," Patrick laughed, his mind already on other matters, including the pert nipples and small waist belonging to Candy Connelly. Maybe he could persuade her to double with Layla for certain cosmetic incentives.

"Patrick," Candice purred as he entered the room. "You're wonderful Gwen here has been explaining the types of treatments you do. I had no idea the fantastic things you could do to improve a person's looks."

Her eyes lowered, and she looked at him through her long, black eyelashes. Patrick felt his heart beating faster at the promise in her expression.

"I think I'd feel a lot more comfortable if it was just you and me," she said, looking pointedly at Gwen. "I'd rather not expose myself to an audience."

Gwen started to protest, pointing out the procedure at NuYu was clear, a nurse and a doctor must be present during a consultation. Patrick looked at the toned body of Ms Connelly and waved away Gwen's concerns.

"If that is your preference, my dear," he replied, shooing Gwen out of the consultation room and firmly closing the door. He turned to face his prey and nearly choked. Candy stood in front of him, in nothing but her underwear. Her small pert breasts encased in thin, black lace while the miniscule black lace thong displayed her youthful hips and a hint of her round buttocks.

She smiled almost shyly and twirled so he could appreciate the full beauty of her body. "Well?"

"Well, what, my dear?" Patrick managed to say as he tried to prevent himself from tearing the lace from her body and burying his face in her breasts.

"Well, what do you think needs doing?" She twirled again, slowly this time. "I'm sure my hips are too big and my boobs too small. Would you like a better look?"

She reached behind and unclasped her bra, letting the small lace item fall to the floor. She took one step towards him, her high heels clipping on the tiled floor. "I think I would like them a lot bigger." She took another step so Patrick's face was in line with her pert pink nipples. "What do you think?"

"I think what the lady wants, the lady should get," Patrick stammered.

He tried to step backwards but found the door impeded his movement. He closed his eyes and took three deep breaths, the scent of her skin and hair making him dizzy. Patrick dug his fingers into the palms of his hands and reminded himself he was a well-renowned plastic surgeon at least twice her age, and he was stood in his clinic. How had she managed to get the upper hand? Patrick swallowed hard and opened his eyes. He leant back into the door pressed against his back and sidestepped away from Candy's tempting nipples. He forced himself to walk slowly and calmly back to the desk and sit in the chair. He picked up the consultation form and a pen, his fingers gripping the barrel with such force his fingertips turned white.

"If you'll take a seat," he said. "Then we can fill in this blasted consultation form and see what we can do from there."

Candice sauntered casually over to where Patrick had indicated and sensually lowered herself onto the chair, ignoring her nudity far more effectively than Patrick could.

"Let's get some details, shall we?"

"If we must," Candice replied, chewing on her bottom lip.

Chapter 15 – Yes master

"Take your fingers out of your cunt and suck them," McGregor said into the phone, his other hand grasped firmly around his erect cock.

"Yes, master," Hazel whimpered.

McGregor listened for the sound of her lips closing around her wet fingers.

"Tell me how you taste."

The sound of Hazel sucking and the thought of her tasting her own juices made McGregor pull harder on his dick.

"Tell me how you taste," he demanded.

"Salty and hot and dirty and so very, very good."

McGregor grunted in appreciation. "Now fuck yourself with your fist. I want to hear you scream."

"I've one finger inside my wet pussy," Hazel whispered, "and I'm imagining it's you pushing inside me."

"If it was me, I'd be inside your arse," McGregor growled.

"I wish you were."

"I'd be pulling on your tits while I fucked you until you pleaded for me to stop."

Hazel gasped in pleasure. "My fist is inside me. I can, I can, I can…" Hazel moaned and then screamed as she orgasmed.

McGregor listened, his hand moving in rhythm with Hazel's moaning. He tensed his thighs and came.

"I wish I was there with you," Hazel gasped. "I'd lick the cum off your dick until you were hard enough to fuck me. If you like, I can come over now rather than later."

McGregor smiled as he pictured her sated and half dressed in the car park of Elstree Studios. He'd insisted she remove her panties in the car, rather than allowing her to go into her dressing room. The thought of someone watching as she'd undone her shirt and pulled on her nipples until they stood, raw and red. Or peeping as she'd opened her legs to take a photo of her wet pussy, gawking as she wanked until she came had made McGregor even hotter. And now the cruellest, most satisfying part of the conversation almost made him stiff again.

"I'm afraid I have an important meeting at four. I have moved your appointment across to Mr Sutherland."

He hung up the phone, not waiting for a reply.

Shit, the thought of her self-pitying temper tantrum had made him hard again. He looked at his offending erect dick and smiled at his virility.

Kate buzzed on the office intercom. "Will says Faye Smith is ready to go under. He just needs you to sign off."

"Fuck," McGregor barked. "I'll just get changed into my scrubs."

"What have you been doing for the last half hour?" Dylees asked, poking her head round his door. "Or do I not want to know?"

"You don't want to know unless you fancy helping me finish," McGregor replied, indicating she was welcome to enter.

"I'd need a big pay rise," she replied, leaving him alone with his favourite toy.

He looked at his erection again. He loved the smooth skin, the straight hardness of his shaft. Just looking at himself turned him on. He gently touched the warm skin and caressed his balls, sending a tingle of delight through his body. He watched the pulsing beat in his dick as he pulled, his speed getting faster and faster as the ache increased. He ran his thumb over the head, sending electric shivers spiking upwards, culminating in the satisfying sticky explosion. McGregor wiped away the evidence in a curt practiced manner, washed quickly and changed into his blue scrubs.

Sutherland and Will were waiting for him in pre-op. Faye Smith was laid on the trolley, talking quietly to Dylees while Will did some final checks on the monitors.

"Are you ready?" McGregor asked in a professional tone. "We'll have you up and about in no time."

"I'm in your hands, Mr McGregor."

"Mr Harrington's to begin with, so I'll hand you over to him for the moment," McGregor squeezed her shoulder reassuringly and left to scrub in.

The scrub room was white with stainless steel sinks and taps. The harsh, sterile environment appealed to McGregor. Everything had a place and a purpose, an order that made sense in a chaotic world of greed, lust and excess. The ritual of scrubbing his hands and arms seemed to somehow cleanse him of his own excesses. McGregor picked up the surgical soap and starting with his hands, he washed each finger, massaging the knuckles and rubbing the palms. He stroked the lather up his forearms to his elbows, counting the strokes before rinsing in hot water. Taking the brush, he scrubbed vigorously underneath his nails, inhaling the antimicrobial smell. He scoured each side of each finger, then his hands and proceeded to his arms, keeping his hand higher than the brush to preventing contamination from the bacteria laden suds. Religiously, he passed his hands and arms through the water in one smooth movement, turning the tap off with his elbow.

"Okay, Mrs Smith," Will said, leaning over the patient, "you'll feel a sharp scratch, and then I'll ask you to recite 'Mary Had a Little Lamb.'"

Robert raised an eyebrow questioningly, and in reply, Dylees shrugged her shoulders as if to say, 'It's Will, what do you expect.'

"You'd better scrub in," she ordered. "Mrs Smith will be under in a few moments, and McGregor doesn't like to be kept waiting."

The complex and chilling opera was already blasting from the high-tech speakers as Robert entered the surgical suite.

"Luciadi di Lammermoor," McGregor said, "Points to anyone who can tell me the year or composer?"

Robert flushed under McGregor's intense gaze.

"Leave the boy alone, you bully," Dylees snapped. "He's not been unfortunate enough to experience your limited taste in music. If it doesn't involve death or a girl going mad, you're not interested."

Will wiggled his eyebrows and posed theatrically. "What is in a name? That, which we call a rose, by any other name, would smell as sweet." He paused. "The same goes for opera. That which McGregor calls Luciadi di Lammermoor, by any other name, would still end with the star-crossed lovers stabbing knives into their own hearts."

McGregor frowned. "The composer was Donizetti, for anyone who wishes to enhance their brains. Pass me the retractor, and I'll get this Beakectomy started while Robert inserts her melons."

McGregor rammed the surgical instrument into Faye Smith's nose, pulling back the nostrils to expose the soft tissue inside.

"Fucking hell, this bitch should wax in here." McGregor laughed, pointing at the plethora of dark nose hair.

He cut the septum and pulled the skin back to expose the cartilage and bone. Taking the small chisel and hammer from Dylees, he executed a sharp blow to the offending lump. The crack of breaking bone reverberated around the surgical suite.

"Bastard," McGregor exclaimed, pulling the surgical tools from the patient's nose. "Brittle as a chicken's leg. The fucking nasal bone has fractured." McGregor pulled the offending shard of bone out with a pair of tweezers. "We'll need to harvest some bone from her rib cage and rebuild the structure. Sutherland, you lop

144

and chop while I prepare for the implant."

Dylees pulled back Faye Smith's gown and rubbed the left lower rib area with blue sterilising fluid.

"Now, fuckwit," McGregor barked as Robert stood still, a breast implant resting in one hand. "You can finish her tits after we've fixed her nose."

Dylees passed Robert a scalpel and quietly explained what McGregor needed. "We need a cartilaginous segment from her fifth rib. Make a 5cm incision 5mm above the inframammary fold." She paused, waiting for Robert to cut. "Then divide the subcutaneous tissue with electrocautery until you can clearly see the rib."

Robert took the cauterising tool and divided the tissue until he could see the bone.

"The cartilaginous portion is off-white, where the bone is reddish grey. Can you see?"

Robert nodded.

"If you use a Bovie needle," she took the needle and pushed it into the yellowing rib, "it will penetrate cartilage, whereas the bone is too hard. All, you need to do now is harvest the cartilage." Dylees passed Robert the scalpel and rib stripper.

While Robert had been dissecting the cartilage, McGregor had been smoothing the dorsum and using silicone grafts to decide on the shape and size he needed to carve from the sliver Robert was preparing.

"Waiting," he growled, not looking up.

Robert passed him the slim piece of yellowish cartilage. "Where's the K-wire?" McGregor yelled.

"I don't know how to fit one."

"What the fuck did they teach you at Leeds? Get the tits finished."

He snatched the kidney dish from Robert and fitted the K-wire that held the graft in place before turning back to his patient. McGregor ignored his junior surgeon for the rest of the procedure and stormed out of the surgical suite the moment the surgery was finished.

In the scrub room, a nervous Robert tried to explain James Dunway's unreasonable expectations to a stony silent McGregor as they washed up from Faye Smith's surgery. The obese MP expected miracles. At ten stone overweight, he was expecting the surgery to remove the fat and expose a rippled abdomen. Robert had tried to explain to him that when the adipose was removed, the muscle underneath would be weak and probably swollen. It would take rehabilitation and a strict exercise routine to bring about the Brad Pitt definition he desired.

"For fuck's sake," McGregor barked as he removed his blood-stained blue scrubs and threw them in the clinical garments bin. "Do I have to do everything myself?"

He stormed out of the scrub room, barrelling Dylees over as she brought in fresh gowns for the next operation.

"Mrs Kershaw is doing well at Re Vive, but she isn't coping well with the discomfort. Can you sign a script for more pain medication?"

McGregor nodded. "Where's the lard arse?"

"If you mean Mr Dunway, he's in pre-op with Will."

"With me," McGregor snapped over his shoulder at Robert as he marched towards pre-op. Robert trailed miserably behind, his feet dragging on the floor. The confidence he'd felt when he started his new job had evaporated under the heat of ritual abuse, drugs and stress.

"Mr Dunway," McGregor gushed, "so sorry I wasn't able to be with you when you arrived. Mr Sutherland here tells me you're hoping to expose a little muscle once we're removed the adipose."

James Dunway frowned. "Doc tells me there's no muscle underneath the fat."

"There is muscle Mr Dunway. However, as my colleague here has explained, the muscle will not be in the condition you remember it before you put on the few extra pounds. I'm afraid it will be months before you can exercise and possibly years before you can display a six pack to the ladies."

James Dunway frowned and sat up on the surgical trolley. "At the consultation, you said…" he began until McGregor cut him off.

"If you recall, we discussed this. You can either wait six months and have a diet and exercise plan worked out for you by a nutritionist," he paused for effect. "Or we can bring you back in four weeks and insert the pectoral and abdomen implants, giving you an immediate washboard stomach."

"What will it cost?" James Dunway asked, his eyes narrowing slightly.

"This is not the time or place to be discussing money, Mr Dunway. I wouldn't feel right about it when you've already had your pre-op meds. Better to discuss this at your check-up when you are able to fully appreciate the surgery and consider all the benefits."

"I knew I chose right with you. The lads at the Boot Room wanted me to go with the Irish chap, but I said if he's on TV, he knows what he's talking about. You remember we agreed you'd invoice this procedure as medical and send it to my constituency office?"

McGregor smiled and put a reassuring hand on James Dunway's shoulder, forcing him back into a prone position. "Of course. Is there a Mrs Dunway?"

"There is."

"I'll put a signed photo on reception for when you leave."

McGregor stared at Will, prompting the silent anaesthetist to stand up and speak reassuringly to the patient about sharp scratches and Mary's little lamb.

Grabbing Robert by the shirt, McGregor pulled him from the room. "That is how you fucking handle a patient. If you ever suggest surgery can't meet the client's needs, you are out! Do you hear me? Out!"

Robert felt McGregor's spittle on his skin as the celebrity surgeon screamed in his face. The taller man loomed over him, invading his personal space in such an aggressive manner Robert shrank backwards. McGregor let go of Robert's shirt, shoving him into the wall before turning on his heels and storming away. Robert stood for a moment, taking deep breaths to steady his nerves and slow his beating heart. Dylees placed a gentle hand on Robert's shoulder, and he jumped.

"Sorry," she apologised, "I didn't mean to give you a scare. Don't pay any attention to McGregor. He's been tele-shagging the witch. It warps his mood."

Robert closed his eyes to stop the tears forming in his eyes from running down his cheeks. "I didn't expect it to be this overwhelming."

Dylees put her arms around Robert and squeezed. "Give it a bit of time. You'll be as twisted as the rest of us in no time." She turned his shoulders to face the scrub room and patted his bottom. "Quickly, go scrub in. The supreme twisted one will have forgotten all about his temper tantrum by now."

Dylees decided she needed a coffee before she could listen to anymore operatic arias by soul-torn heroines. In the staff room, Will leant over Claire, his hand casually groping her breasts through the thick fabric of her uniform.

"Are you free tonight?" he asked.

"I ..." Claire stammered.

"I thought we could get a pizza and go back to mine after work."

"I could ..."

"Wonderful," Will interrupted, "You grab the pizza and let yourself in. I'll pop to the gym and meet you back at mine."

"I don't have a key."

"You do now," Will replied, dropping a small key

into Claire's cleavage. "There's a bit of ironing and stuff. If you get bored, you could do it while you watch TV and wait for me."

It was a shame Anna had cancelled at the last minute, Will thought, but this way he got clean shirts, free pizza and an energetic fuck. It couldn't have worked out better.

Dylees noticed the smug smirk on Will's face and wondered how the men working at Fitzroy's coped. Will Harrington was a child playing with a toy doll, he didn't realise, was valuable. David McGregor was an egotistical bully who needed to be kept in line. Carl Fitzroy, a grief-stricken, drunk who needed his arse wiped, and Robert Sutherland was being eaten alive by a profession he wasn't cut out for. Dylees poured two cups of coffee and walked over to Claire. She needed to have a quiet word with the timid cleaner before it was too late.

Chapter 16 – Mr Sharp knows best

Patrick sat behind his desk, looking at the consultation form of one Miss Connelly. Breasts, buttocks, a little lipo on her thighs, a skin peel followed by dermal filler in her lips and maybe labia enhancement. Annoyingly, she'd cancelled their Friday night liaison, claiming a prior engagement she couldn't get out of. Her gentle kiss on his lips had taken away the sting and hinted at her disappointment.

"Another time soon," she breathed huskily.

An elderly relative's birthday or charitable work, Patrick Sharp concluded. His left arm tingled slightly, and he felt a heavy pressure on his chest. Was he having an attack of conscience? Why would remaking this young beautiful woman affect him? Her blatant sexuality had aroused him certainly, but there was something more to it, a sense of something being out of place and wrong. Hell, he'd never had this uncertain feeling before. He'd remodelled many young wives into the images their husbands desired. He'd worked on prostitutes beaten to within an inch of their lives so they could continue to earn for Mr Costa. He'd even removed the odd bullet to keep the victims under the radar of the MET. But something about this girl worried him. Patrick poured himself another drink and pushed the consultation form to the side. He was just tired. A good night's sleep at home would do him a world of good. He'd phone Mae to tell her he'd be home early, get her to prepare him and Carole something appetising to eat and then maybe an early night. He'd five more consultations before he could go home, and while he wanted to cancel, he needed the money. There was a card game next week at the Boot Room, and Mr Green had mentioned good odds on the boxing up in Leeds. Maybe he'd take Candy up to watch. He had a feeling the violence would make an interesting appetiser to sex. Patrick rubbed

his eyes and opened the top drawer of his desk. He
swallowed one of the little white pain killers with a glass of
Midleton's Irish and decided a quiet moment in the garden
would help clear his head.

The leaves were falling in the cold afternoon, the
rich copper and red foliage crispy and dry underfoot.
Patrick pulled his jacket tighter to keep in the warmth and
sipped on the golden whisky. The cold autumnal sun
shone weakly through the clouds, giving the garden a
desolate look. Just like my life, he thought.

"Sir James' wife has just arrived," Sasha said,
peeking through the back door. "Aren't you cold?"

Patrick smiled despondently. "Show the way."

Perplexed by her boss' sudden change in humour,
Sasha chatted aimlessly to cover the awkwardness. "Lady
Asquith is quite the character. I've never seen anyone with
such blonde hair before! It's practically white. And her
eyes are the palest blue I've ever seen. Why she's here, I
have no idea. Everything about her is beautiful. Even her
accent is glamorous. Like she is a Russian princess or
something."

"Sasha, my dear," Patrick replied, "a woman is
never satisfied with what she has. Lady Asquith is probably
looking at you and wishing she had your curves or your
rich sable hair and big brown eyes. We'd be out of
business if people liked what they saw in the mirror."

Patrick plastered a warm smile on his face as he
walked into the plush reception. Lady Asquith was every
bit the Russian princess as she sat daintily on the vintage
leather chair. Her full lips pouted slightly as she flicked
through a magazine.

"Why these English girls in paper?" she asked,
pointing at a glossy picture of Laura Philips and Lady
Elizabeth Mowbray. "I prettier, yet I not get photo taken
by paparazzi."

"Why would you want to be?" Sasha asked.
"Those girls are famous for nothing other than partying.

You are far more beautiful."

"It's about perception, my dear," Patrick interrupted. "These women are IT girls. They're in the right places and wearing the right clothes after having the right surgery."

"And I can do this, too?"

"Of course. Like Sasha says, you have a much better foundation to work with. A little tweak here and there and Sasha putting you in touch with the right people, you'll outshine the English aristocracy."

Sir James had already called Patrick, insisting his fourth wife's boobs needed to be bigger.

"Husband says Mr Sharp knows best."

"I do my dear. I do."

With four consultations down and only one to go. Patrick Sharp had not only consulted, but with Sasha's gentle persuasive powers, he had also booked in over thirty grands worth of treatment. Lady Asquith had decided on breast augmentation as well as Botox to keep the wrinkles away. Ms Law's acquaintance had booked in for buttock implants and lip enhancement as a start. The third client, a quiet, easily forgettable man in a grey suit had spent as much time in the toilet as he had in the consultation room. Had wandered accidently into Patrick's office and insisted on seeing the garden where he could be at peace with nature. After a guided tour and an hour spent discussing procedures, the man had decided to think about it. Some clients were just like that.

"Sasha, you're a beauty," Patrick declared, kissing her on the forehead as Miss Jerry left with a contract signed and a deposit paid for a facelift. "I've called Bromley's and left a couple hundred on your account."

Sasha smiled and kissed her boss on the cheek. "You're the best, Mr Sharp."

"Hey, I work here, too," Gwen mockingly complained as she walked into the waiting lounge.

"And when you get a client to part with a couple thousand, I'll put a couple hundred at the deli on the corner for you. You can eat salad until you turn green."

Gwen cuffed Patrick on the head as she walked past. "This place would fall down around your ears if it weren't for me."

"Gwen, we all know that," Patrick agreed, "now tell me something I don't know."

"Your four o'clock has just arrived."

Patrick stuck his tongue out at Gwen before turning to see the client wafting into the clinic in a mass of fur and dark glasses. The collar of her mink coat was pulled up around her face in a manner that convinced Patrick Sharp the lady was actually looking for the Fitzroy clinic. Celebrity clients were McGregor's bread and butter while NuYu was more a cosmetic service for people who wished to fly under the radar. Two burly security guards stood behind her blocking the door. While he was used to the bulges in the jackets of the Bolivian thugs, these men looked too clean cut and frankly too English to be carrying illegal concealed weapons. Patrick made a few quick assumptions. Whoever this lady was, she was powerful, British and either royalty or government. He hoped for the first and dreaded the implications of the last. The lady held out her hand to Patrick. Her grip firm and commanding, her nails manicured yet short and unpolished. Patrick couldn't see her face and yet he knew with almost certainty she wouldn't be wearing heavy make-up.

"Mr Sharp," she said and smiled.

The smile did nothing to reassure Patrick. It was the smile of a person who held all the cards and knew far too much.

"I am afraid you have me at a loss," Patrick replied, removing his hand from hers. "It seems you know me while I do not have the same advantage."

"Call me Rebecca," she said. Rebecca was not her name. It was clear she was lying and equally clear she didn't care if Patrick knew.

"Rebecca, it is!" Patrick said, his eyes narrowing just enough to impart his disbelief.

Rebecca laughed. "Mr Sharp, one name is as good as another, so for now I am Rebecca. I'm here to consult with you on a delicate matter."

Patrick closed his eyes and sighed heavily. He knew the instant she spoke this appointment had nothing to do with plastic surgery and everything to do with his connections to the Bolivian underground.

"Is it that time already?" he asked in a tone he hoped showed he couldn't be bought or intimidated. "Gwen, would you get the lady a coffee and show her goons to the garden. They can wait there."

Gwen nodded nervously, Sasha found something urgent to do in the kitchen and Patrick resignedly showed Rebecca into the consultation room.

"I think we both know why I am here?" Rebecca said as she removed her glasses and coat. Underneath the fur was a smart business suit, tight-fitting, elegant but conservative. She sat on the edge of the comfortable chair and leaned forward. Patrick looked the lady up and down. The dark blue of her suit did nothing to disguise her femininity.

"Mr Sharp, we can help you."

She was plainly trying to intimidate him by providing as little information as possible. Patrick sighed. The only way to play this was to say as little as possible and force her into revealing more.

"My answer is the same," he said.

"And what answer would that be?"

"Above your pay grade apparently."

Rebecca narrowed her eyes and frowned. "Mr Sharp, we can fool about as much as you like, but the facts remain the same. I can help you, but only if you help me."

Patrick smiled. "What sort of help were you thinking of? A free breast augmentation maybe?"

Rebecca stood up and walked over to Patrick's desk. She leant forward and whispered into his ear. "The court case starts to examine Mr Costa's dealings in trafficking and prostitution next week. We can save you the embarrassment of certain pictures coming to light if you testify as to your professional relationship with Trae La Muerte."

"I don't know who or what you're talking about," Patrick replied. "As to photographs, I can only speculate as to their content, and I've nothing to hide."

"Are you sure, Mr Sharp? Compromising photographs have a habit of ruining reputations."

"Rebecca, as I am sure you are aware, today's socialites have different standards. A person as young as you are should know that any indiscretion on my part would only strengthen my market share not damage it. Don't be such a prude." Patrick hoped she didn't call his bluff, the last thing he needed was unnecessary attention or Carole filing for divorce.

Rebecca frowned again. "Don't say you haven't been warned, Mr Sharp. The conviction of the Trae La Muerte's generals is one of this government's top priorities."

"And if I knew any of the leaders of Trae La Muerte, I would be very happy to cooperate. But as I am a plastic surgeon with very little knowledge of gangs or their activities in the UK, I will have to ask you to leave."

Patrick picked up Rebecca's fur coat and helped her into the weighty garment. "Now if that is all, I have a mountain of work and a nice Midleton's waiting for me in my office."

Rebecca frowned. "I'll leave you my card, Mr Sharp. Remember it's better to be on the side of the government than in prison with those who think you have betrayed them."

The threat was thinly veiled. Help us, or we'll let them think you did. "As I have no dealing with criminal activity of any kind, Rebecca, I think I shall have to hope your government doesn't see fit to charge an innocent man."

Rebecca raised her eyebrows and made a quick assessment of Patrick's sympathies. His statement added a whole new dimension to the current crisis. Was the Bolivian cartel working with some latent element of Irish separatists? Did she need to look more closely at Patrick Sharp as a player rather than a source? Rebecca made a mental note to have surveillance expand its current remit. The simple truth was Patrick had never thought of the British government as his government. It wasn't that he held the same views as his separatist father, but more he'd never really felt he belonged anywhere or should be governed by people he had no respect for. He'd never voted for the bastards, so he didn't see the harm in hiding his money from their greedy, grasping hands.

"We will talk again, Mr Sharp," Rebecca said as she left.

"I'm sure we will," Patrick commented to her departing back.

The two armed, plain-clothed police officers joined Rebecca at the door. "Any luck?" the taller of the two asked as they left the clinic and got into the unmarked black BMW.

"No, the tricky bastard thinks he's untouchable. Our CI tells us he's in debt to Costa. Let's get more eyes on him and see what happens. Can I leave it with you, Luke?"

"Yes, ma'am," Luke replied as the car drove away from NuYu.

Patrick stood watching the car speed up Blow Row, his nails dug into the palms of his hands as he clenched his fists in anger. He had an urge to hit the wall but knew tomorrow's surgery would be impossible with a broken hand.

"Fucking fucker," he growled, grabbing the

telephone. It wasn't the first time he'd been approached by the authorities to give evidence against his clients, but this was the first time the arrogant bastards had entered NuYu. They had no business fucking up his business. The telephone rang straight through to voicemail. "Mr Green," Patrick said, "my office has been visited by a mutual friend connected with your current legal matter. If you could ask your employer to contact me at his convenience, I would be happy to provide further details on this subject."

Patrick hung up the receiver, hoping his phone hadn't been compromised and he hadn't just handed fucking Rebecca or whatever her name was the evidence she needed to lean on him. Still, he had no choice. He was far more scared of Costa and Trae La Muerte than a few years in a minimum-security prison.

He had a keynote speech to prepare for Friday's annual FOBPS conference on 'Ethical sales techniques in modern plastics.' The half-hour presentation would be sandwiched in between James Galway's keynote address on the 'Acceptability and significance of using psychological screening before surgery in private clinics' and Michelle Delvaux's 'Bioengineering in breast augmentation – the next gen of implants.' He wrote a few words and then crossed them out. Why had he ever agreed to speak? Patrick scowled. Greed, he thought. FOBPS had offered him two grand to speak and as a bonus given him the chance to rub his respectability in the face of David McGregor, who wasn't on the list of surgeons lecturing at the conference.

He put down his pen and picked up the phone. "Cupcake," he said when Carole answered the phone. "I've had a really successful day, booked in fifteen grand."

"That's nice Patty Cake," she replied apathetically.

"It means you can book Freddy Fairy."

"He'll be busy this close to Christmas," Carole muttered. "And I really don't want the mess."

Carole had been banging on about redecorating

for months. She had begged and pleaded to have Freddy Draper consult on the design of their home, nagging Patrick until his ears bled. Now when he'd offered to pay for a session with the gay interior designer, she'd lost interest.

"Alright, Cupcake. Has he lost favour with the women's circle? Is there a new designer you'd prefer?"

"It's a lovely thought, Patrick, but I don't want the mess of dirt and dry leaves traipsed into the house."

Perplexed Patrick hung up the phone and returned unsuccessfully to writing about ethical plastic surgery, his thoughts returning to the enigmatic Rebecca and the consequences of her visit.

Chapter 17 – These things happen

McGregor sat behind his desk and looked at his watch for the fifth time in as many minutes. It was ten past four, and there was no sign of Candice Connelly. McGregor poured himself another brandy. He'd been working since eight a.m. after a night of drug-fuelled partying with no sexual release other than his own hand. He'd turned down a filthy fuck with Hazel only to be stood up twice by a fucking upstart wannabe. McGregor picked up the phone and started to dial Hazel's mobile, then slammed the receiver back down. The last thing he needed was Hazel thinking she was special. He looked at his watch again and gulped back the brandy. Candice Connelly had until a quarter past, and then he was going home. McGregor straightened his desk, checked his emails and shut down his computer. He tidied his pens and rearranged his awards in the display cabinet. Finally, at four-thirty, he could think of nothing else he needed to do urgently and picked up his coat.

"Slag," he growled as he slammed his door shut. "Dylees, I'm going home," he said as he noticed her walking towards his office.

"But your four o'clock appointment has just arrived," she told him. "I was coming to get you. Should I re-book her for another day?"

"You can re-book her for another clinic," McGregor said. "No, wait, I'll tell her myself."

McGregor stormed along the corridor towards reception and pulled the door open so forcefully it shook on it hinges.

"Miss Connelly," McGregor started, then stopped as he looked into the blue eyes of the slender Candice. Her hair bounced playfully around her shoulders and her lips twitched into a shy smile.

"I'm so sorry I'm late," she breathed. "I couldn't

159

find a taxi."

McGregor looked at her slim figure in the tight pink jumper. Her pert nipples pushed out from the thin wool. The curve of her hips in her skinny jeans and the sweet way she curled a lock of hair around a long manicured nail made him hot.

"That's quite alright, my darling," McGregor purred "These things happen sometimes. Would you like to come this way?"

Candice giggled. "I'd love to come any way with you."

Dylees and Will laughed from the safety of the corridor. "Who's playing who?"

"Not sure," Dylees answered, "but I am sure it's going to be amusing to find out."

Candice strutted into McGregor's office, her hips swaying provocatively to give McGregor the full impact of her small waist and youthful bottom in the tight jeans. She positioned herself in the comfortable modern chair and pouted.

"I was afraid I might have missed you," she sighed, her bottom lip shaking slightly in a way that made McGregor's heart melt and his manhood stiffen.

"These things happen," he repeated as soothingly as he was able. "Can I get you a drink? Tea, coffee or something a little stronger?"

A predatory smile crossed his face, and Candice smiled back. It was clear McGregor liked his women cowed and vulnerable. It wasn't a role she was used to playing, but if it got her what she wanted, then she could masquerade as a helpless girl in need of a dominant male to take charge. Candice giggled. "If you're sure it won't delay you any further."

"Not at all," McGregor purred, confident he had the upper hand. "Brandy?"

"Ohhh," Candice gulped, "I'm not sure I should

at this time of day."

McGregor poured a large glass of cognac from the decanter on his desk and pushed it towards Candice. From her position on the chair, she had to lean precariously forward to reach the glass, exposing her perfect tits beautifully. She sipped delicately on the golden spirit when really what she wanted to do was knock back the drink in three gulps. Candice smiled over the glass and lowered her face, looking at McGregor through long black eyelashes. She had never understood why this made so many men weak at the knees. When she was a teenager, her mother had taught her to use the gifts nature had given her. Silly flirting was a small price to pay if it helped her achieve her goal.

McGregor coughed and choked on his brandy. "Well, Miss Connelly, what is it that I can do for you today?"

"Lots," Candice giggled. "Or at least I hope you can do lots to me."

A Cheshire cat grin spread across McGregor's face. This was just too easy. A girl with self-image issues was excellent for business and for pleasure. The question was which to tackle first. McGregor narrowed his eyes slightly. Business first. A woman with her ego in tatters always made for a better bed companion. Self-loathing was such an attractive quality in a submissive.

"Do you mind if I take notes and maybe a few photos?"

Candice assented shyly. "Do you want me to get undressed?"

McGregor only just managed to stop himself from laughing out loud. This really was too easy. "Let's take a few details first."

McGregor drew out his pen and consultation forms. "Name?"

"Candice Connelly."

"Date of Birth?"

"I was born on the 5th December 1995."

"Address?"

McGregor scribbled away on the consultation form, his handwriting even more illegible in his heightened state of arousal. He noted her medical history and next of kin before moving on to the questions that were perverted curiosity rather than medical necessity.

"Current relationships?"

"None."

"Past relationships?"

"Why do you need to know?"

"Just to flag any possible infections or danger areas. For example, we would need to run certain tests if you were very sexually active."

"Oh," Candice replied before starting to explain her past encounters in erotic detail. "Is this the sort of information you need?" she asked innocently, pushing out her chest and chewing on a lock of hair.

McGregor coughed. "Yes, quite adequate," he said as he silently thanked Hazel's filthy mouth and perverted sexting for providing him with the ability to restrain himself. If not for this erotic tolerance, he'd have a raging need to throw Miss Connelly on the floor and fuck her brains out. "One does need to know the background of a person before recommending surgery. For example, someone who likes to be gagged during sex would not be a good candidate for lip enhancement, the pressure of the ball would likely dislodge the dermal filler."

Candice giggled. "I'd never thought about lip enhancements before. Do you think it would be a good idea?"

McGregor thought tying his silk tie around her mouth and shagging her from behind would be a better idea, but this was a consultation. The rest could wait until after dinner. A few drinks and maybe a little inhibitor suppressant, and Candice Connelly would no doubt be a girl worth bedding. But for now, lowering her self-confidence and making a little money was more important.

"If you want to put on a robe now, Candice," McGregor said, pointing to the white surgical gown. "I'll take a few measurements, and then we can see what we can do to improve your self-image."

Candice smiled radiantly and picking up the thin surgical gown, sauntered sexily over to a small dressing screen in the corner of the room. She'd already noticed the strategically placed mirror in his office and decided to play along. Patrick Sharp had needed her to play the confident lioness while McGregor seemed to like his women as shy kittens to be coaxed and then broken. Either way, as long as the results were worthwhile, life was just splendid. Candice stood in exactly the right spot for McGregor to be able to use the mirror to see the curve of her thigh and the roundness of her bottom. She smiled smugly as she imagined the letch leaning forward to try and see the flatness of her stomach or her cleanly waxed fanny as she removed her lace underwear. She casually dropped the delicate lace knickers on the floor so McGregor could see and replaced them with the paper pants McGregor had so thoughtfully provided. She wrapped the gown tightly around her body even though it was almost see through and stepped out from behind the screen.

"Where do we start?" she asked nervously.

"What is it you're trying to achieve?"

"Well, I want to work in the media, and I want to be prepared. So I need a bit of a make-over before I start. You know how the TV executives think. Natural just isn't good enough for on camera. I believe I have a good bone structure, but I don't know if my boobs are big enough. And would you recommend that I have a little extra here?" she said, patting herself on the bottom. "Maybe Botox is a good preventative to wrinkles, and maybe a bit bigger lips like you suggested. Could you take a look at my nose? I think it's a bit lopsided."

It was even better than he'd imagined. This girl

had serious issues. No wonder she'd been on the plastic surgery segment. She was even more dysmorphic than Lady Liz. McGregor managed to stop himself from rubbing his hands together as he mentally added up the cost of the treatments. Twenty thousand pounds if she had the money, or ten grand and illicit sex if she didn't.

"Is money an issue?"

"I'm happy to spend what little I have. Daddy is very keen to help, but I'm hoping we can come to some arrangement."

McGregor's ears pricked up at the word Daddy. Either she was from a wealthy family or she was banging a rich sugar daddy. From her demeanour, McGregor's money was on the former. She seemed too priggish to be a rich man's plaything.

"I'll get some measurements, and then we'll work something out."

McGregor leaned forward and pulled on the ends of the ties securing her white robe, leaving Candice naked bar the small paper pants. He ran his hands professionally over her skin, checking elasticity and tone. His finger grazed her nipple very slightly as he stood up to look at her face. The excitement he felt was mirrored in her eyes. Her pupils had dilated slightly, and he could feel the quickened pulse in her neck.

"Let me get some measurements, and then we'll mark up areas for improvement."

Candice bit her lip and nodded. McGregor stepped back. He'd measured every inch of Candice, his hands caressing her smooth skin until she trembled at his touch. Then, when he was sure of her arousal, he'd pulled out a thick black marker and drew lines on her pale, rose-pink skin. His marker had circled the small amount of flesh on her hips for liposuction, drawn straight lines on her bottom to indicate lift and augmentation. He'd put crosses on each slight blemish on the skin of her legs and stomach to be removed by laser. Made a couple of deft marks on her breasts to signify implants and suggested work on her triceps. None of the work was necessary, but if she was willing to pay.

"If you look in the mirror, please," he'd ordered.

Candice turned in her paper underwear and looked at the black scrawl across her skin. The marker pen looked permanent, and her skin was already raw from scrubbing the marks off from the NuYu clinic.

"Don't be alarmed, my darling," McGregor purred, misreading her expression for one of self-loathing. "Let me talk you through the changes we can make to give you more confidence."

McGregor was in his element by the time he reached her face. He had total control over her self-esteem. He could build her up or crush her fragile ego between his skilled fingers. He licked his lips, tasting her vulnerability. He reached out a hand, grabbing her neck to turn her face first one way and then the other. He momentarily imagined squeezing her slender neck in his firm grasp, the look of panic and then ecstasy in her eyes as she gave herself to him. He regarded her profile. The slight bump on her nose could go with a small rhinoplasty, and a touch of dermal filler in her lips would give them a fuller appearance. Botox was unwarranted, but she'd mentioned wanting the treatment.

Candice looked intently into the mirror. Last month, she'd not even thought about having plastic surgery. Her natural good looks had always helped her achieve her goals, get men, land the job she desired, receive discounts, and get served first at the pub. The small imperfections in her features had always given her a quirky look that appealed. Yet in the last twenty-four hours, each and every flaw had been highlighted and marked, and a procedure suggested to alter her looks to a uniform plastic beauty. The bump on her nose had always been there, and she'd grown up thinking it added a certain integrity to her face, giving her a Roman regalness. Now as she turned her head from one side to the other, she had to agree it did affect the symmetry of her face. McGregor was right, remove the bump, and she'd take the world of media by storm.

"When can I have the treatments done?"

"As soon as you like, my darling," McGregor replied. "It will be easy to schedule the procedures together. We prefer to get everything done in one or two sessions. It reduces the risks with anaesthetic and means you achieve your goals quicker."

"Isn't that dangerous?" Candice asked, chewing on her lip.

"Not if it's done by a professional clinician like myself," McGregor countered. "While those clinics based in the regions often recommend a more sedate pace, this is more to do with the experience of the surgeon than any safety concerns for the patient."

Candice smiled. "You're the celebrity surgeon."

McGregor missed the slight tension in her voice and the mocking undertones in her comment.

"I am," he agreed. "Now if you're happy, I can take a few bloods, run a few tests and book you in for your pre-op. Then, as my day is finished, I can take you for a cocktail and a bite."

Candice giggled. "But you haven't told me how much."

McGregor smirked. "It seems wrong to discuss money when you're standing naked in front of me, my darling. I feel my head is not on business at the moment. How about we talk money after cocktails, and you can try and persuade me to give you my friends' discount."

Candice turned away slightly to hide her revulsion behind a pretence of shy embarrassment. "That would be lovely, Mr McGregor," she whispered.

"Please call me David."

Chapter 18 – A little star struck

"Has the pretentious git saddled you with Witch-Hazel?" Carl Fitzroy asked as he lumbered into the staff room.

"Miss Woods is due in for a consultation, and McGregor is busy," Robert replied

"I bet he is. I saw the nice piece of ass he's in with when I left surgery. I'd be busy with the little tart, too. I'd be offering her the BJ discount."

Robert looked confused.

"Blow me, and I'll half the price," Will supplied helpfully.

"You're joking," Robert gasped.

"You think?"

Fitzroy laughed. "You're telling me, you wouldn't?"

Robert blushed and looked at his feet.

"Is he going to be able to handle the Witch?" Fitzroy asked Will, pointedly ignoring Robert's spluttering.

"Hey, he managed admirably with the lady-boys last night."

"Aye, but Witch-Hazel has a much bigger dick."

Will nearly fell over laughing, "And big, salty, hairy balls."

"Maybe you can suggest she have a ballectomy, Robert?"

Robert choked on his coffee. "I'm sure Miss Woods will be fine. McGregor and her are friends, aren't they?"

Will chuckled and then explained in minute detail the sort of relationship McGregor and Hazel Woods were engaged in. Robert turned red then green as he listened.

"But she seems so sweet on TV."

"Sweet?" Fitzroy chuckled. "Did you see the photographs McGregor accidental left on his desk? Black leather masks and school girl uniforms."

"Excuse me," Will said suddenly, "but all this talk has given me an erection. Have you seen Claire?" he asked Dylees as she entered the staff room.

Dylees rolled her eyes. "She's in the linen cupboard, and for goodness sake, shut the door and keep the noise down." She turned to Robert. "Miss Woods is in reception. She is not in a good mood, so the same goes for you, shut the door and try to keep the noise down."

Fitzroy laughed and Dylees turned to glare at the older man. "And you, you old sod, your patient is awake, and I need you to check her and sign off on her prescriptions so I can have her transferred to Re Vive."

Hazel stamped her foot impatiently in reception. Surely McGregor didn't intend to palm her off on his idiot junior? It was just his cruel, twisted way of keeping her in line.

"Miss Woods," Robert introduced himself, "I am Robert Sutherland, and I'm going to be your clinician today."

"The fuck you are!" Hazel exploded. "Where's McGregor?"

"He's ..."

"Not here," Dylees interrupted. "Mr Sutherland will be carrying out your treatment, or you can book in for another time."

Dylees was not in the habit of covering for her boss, but frankly she couldn't do with a headache from Witch-Hazel's screeching. Hazel considered the matter. She wasn't going to get anywhere with McGregor's guard dog. She might as well make the most of a bad situation and woo the northern lackey. It always paid to have loyal underlings. If she flattered the unattractive man's ego, she might cultivate an accomplice to spy for her at the clinic. She pasted a smile on her flawless features and turned to the uncertain Robert.

"Lead the way then," she sighed.

Robert mouthed his thanks to Dylees before leading the glamourous Hazel to one of the treatment suites. He couldn't believe he was actually treating the goddess of daytime television. He'd always admired her gentle ability to get her guests to reveal their most personal information. Her empathy shone through the camera as she talked to them about cheating husbands, dead children or their struggle with some horrible disease. She shared her own feelings about the stories she covered in a way that made the viewer feel she was part of the narrative. Now she sat in the same room as him, her familiar face no longer a pixilated picture but real flesh and blood.

"Mr McGregor informs me you're having a little Botox?"

"David," she said, pointedly reminding this little upstart of her relationship with his boss, "usually carries out my treatments. I don't want to look like Clara Huntington." Hazel paused, considering the man in front of her. "What are you staring at?"

Robert blushed. "I am so sorry, Miss Woods. I guess I'm a little star-struck."

Hazel melted. She put her hand on the dear boy's leg and smiled. "I get that a lot. If you'll give me a moment to remove my make-up?"

Robert blushed deeper and left the room so Hazel could remove the heavy television make-up. He stood outside the door of the consultation suite, his heart pounding in his chest as he rubbed his sweaty hands on his trousers. He was talking to Hazel Woods, the Hazel Woods, and not only had she been ever so nice, she'd stroked his leg. McGregor was a lucky man to have such a beautiful, kind creature in his life. Will must believe Robert incredibly gullible to believe his tall story about Hazel being a depraved nymphomaniac. As he stood outside the suite, he imagined himself and Elizabeth Mowbray as the next McGregor-Woods. With Elizabeth's beauty and camera presence, and his surgical skills they would dominate the media, just like his mentor. He smiled happily and knocked politely on the door and waited for Miss Woods' dulcet voice to give him permission to enter. Hazel lay on the couch. She had removed her make-up and underneath the skin was as smooth and perfect as he'd imagined. But it wasn't her flawless skin that had the young surgeon spluttering, it was Hazel's lack of clothing.

"I didn't want to get my dress stained," she explained as Robert openly stared at her slim near-naked body.

He grabbed one of the gowns hung up in the treatment suite and covered Miss Woods. "How kind," she said mischievously.

"I wouldn't want you to get cold, Miss Woods."

"Call me Hazel," she purred.

Robert tried to control the shaking in his hands as he drew 2cc of saline into the 100 units of Botulinum powder. The 33 gauge needle shook in his hand. "Miss Woods, I mean Hazel," Robert stammered. "If I could get you to frown."

Hazel frowned, and Robert injected the Botox first into her procerus muscle and then the corrugator muscle. A slight bruising appeared immediately, and he nervously placed his hand on top of the injection spot.

"Don't worry," Hazel reassured, "my make-up girl Olivia will be able to cover that little bruise."

Robert smiled gratefully at her, and his nerves melted away. "Smile, please."

Hazel smiled, revealing small crow's feet at the sides of her eyes. Robert injected the Botox into the orbicularis muscle on both sides of the face, then moved on to the last injection site, the large frontalis muscle that ran across the width of her forehead. "If you could just lift your eyebrows?"

Hazel did as she was asked. With her eyes closed, Robert's voice had a pleasing, attractive Yorkshire lilt. His warm hands were still hesitant as he touched her skin, and she wondered what he would be like in bed. Maybe she would annoy McGregor and find out. Her hand casually brushed against his thigh. Robert moved away from her touch, and Hazel smiled. It would definitely be fun to corrupt McGregor's newest acolyte.

Robert escorted the gracious Hazel Woods to reception and blushed when she kissed him on the cheek.

"She's so nice," he gushed when she'd left. "Just like on TV."

Dylees and Kate raised their eyebrows but didn't comment as Robert practically skipped away. Still distracted by thoughts of the amiable TV celebrity, he opened the wrong door. Instead of filing away Hazel Woods' medical records in the filing cabinet in McGregor's office, he walked in on Claire in the consultation suite opposite.

Claire stood in white cotton bra and pants in front of a full-length mirror. With the marker pen she held in her hand, she drew a large circle across her stomach. Robert stared in horror at her graffiti-covered legs and arms patterned with irregular rings and black crosses. Claire noticed Robert standing in the doorway. Her skin developed a blotchy redness on her neck and chest as she looked down trying to cover her nakedness with her arms.

"Please don't tell anyone," she pleaded.

"What are you doing?"

Claire reached for the white dressing gown and pulled it in around her shoulders.

"Shut the door," she whispered.

Robert closed the door and moved closer to her.

"Will is always saying how plain I am. I was hoping Mr McGregor might fix me."

Comprehension sank slowly into Robert consciousness. Claire had been marking the areas she thought needed work, and thanks to the aggressive sale tactics at The Fitzroy clinic and Will's constant comments, she had come to the conclusion everything needed altering.

"Take off the robe," Robert said, picking up the surgical spirits used to remove marker pen.

Claire looked apprehensive but did as she was instructed.

"This area here," Robert explained using cotton wool soaked in surgical spirits to remove the marker from her thighs, "is just a thin layer of fat. While you could use liposuction, you would be better going to the gym. This here," he rubbed gently at her bottom. "This is perfect the way it is. No one wants a flat arse."

Robert moved across Claire's body, removing most of the black halos and carefully explaining why she shouldn't have a breast augmentation and why her nose was perfect, just a little crooked. "If you really do want to take advantage of McGregor's offer, I'd do two things. Firstly, a bit of lipo on your stomach. Once you've lost the muscle, it's very difficult to get rid of the fat. And a bit of dermal filler in your lips. With a new haircut and a make-up lesson from Kate, you'd look fabulous."

"Could you?"

"The dermal filler here and now if you'd like. I don't have any clients in. For the lipo, you need to have a consultation with McGregor."

Claire smiled shyly. "Do you think Kate will help me?"

"I'm sure she will. I'll go ask while you get dressed. Meet me in treatment suite one in five minutes."

When she smiled, Claire's face lit up. Amongst all these glamorous men and women, it was easy to miss the natural beauty of imperfection. Claire blended into the background, her white uniform and lack of make-up a camouflage of neglect.

"Robert," Claire said as he turned to leave, "thank you."

Claire fetched two coffees into the treatment suite. Robert was already preparing the dermal filler injections. He smiled at Claire as she entered.

"You better drink that before we inject," Robert laughed. "After the dental block, you won't be able to keep it in your mouth."

The comments brought a small apprehensive smile to Claire's lips.

Robert turned back to the syringes on the counter. The first contained lidocaine, the second the transparent dermal filler gel.

"Kate's on for the make-over by the way. Said it was about bloody time. Now just lie on the couch for me."

Claire lay on the paper-covered couch, biting her lips nervously. All of a sudden, the idea of remaking herself seemed vain and frivolous, a waste of Robert's valuable time and an exercise in futility. How would bigger lips or a new haircut help her win Will's affections? The only reason he'd asked her to his apartment tonight was because some bimbo had cancelled.

"Just relax. I'll make sure the effect is subtle. We can always inject more if needed," Robert reassured, placing his hand gently on her shoulder. "I promise, no trout pout." Robert picked up the syringe containing the lidocaine anaesthetic and lifted Claire's top lip. "Just a little scratch," he lied, pushing the needle into the inside of her mouth. Robert made three injections of the dental block into the top lip and two into the bottom. Claire's face felt numb almost instantly. "Now for the good bit," Robert said. "You won't feel a thing."

He picked up the syringe of dermal filler and attached the disposable needle, pushing the rod gently until droplets of the gel appeared at the end. Stretching the lip with his left hand and holding the needle flat against the edge of the lip line with his right, he pushed until he could see a centimetre of the metal shaft underneath the skin. Slowly, he depressed the rod while gently pulling the needle out. A thin, round seam rose on Claire's lip line. Robert removed the needle and moved a centimetre up the lip, repeating the process until he reached the Cupid's bow. He then started at the other side, repeating the injections until Claire's top lip looked full and attractive.

"Halfway there," he said. The lower lip needed less treatment, and Robert used less than the recommended 2 ml of dermal filler. "You'll have a little swelling for an hour or so and maybe a small bruise. Go and grab a break, and I'll cover for you."

Claire tried to smile, but the lidocaine made the action lopsided and comical. "Can I look?" she slurred.

Robert passed her the small mirror. "Remember, you've seen enough women walk out of these rooms to know you'll be a little swollen."

Tears gathered in Claire's eyes as she looked at herself. Her face looked balanced for the first time in her twenty-nine years. The thin, pinched lips had been replaced by a full, bountiful pout.

"Thank you," she mumbled, hugging a shocked Robert.

"No worries," he managed to say as she fled from the treatment suite to hide her tears.

Chapter 19 – The odds were promising

Patrick walked out of his last consultation. The pain in his chest had worsened. A cold sweat ran down his face, and he tried to take deep slow breaths to slow the hammering of his heart.

"Too fucking old," he muttered to himself as a wave of fear gripped him.

He staggered into his office and collapsed onto the chair. His phone vibrated on the oak desk, he grabbed at the black plastic and swiped across the screen, his hand shaking so badly it had taken three goes before he managed to get the screen unlocked. Three text messages flashed on the screen. One was from Carole, informing him she was staying at a girlfriend's for the evening so not to rush home. One was from Mr Green, listing odds for various boxing matches and racing events. Patrick took that as a good sign. If Mr Green was still sending odds, then the chance of ending up with concrete shoes had lessened slightly. The third message was from an unknown number. Patrick's hand shook as he accessed the text.

'Thank you for the information. It confirms our suspicions. If we require more details, we will be in touch.'

The shaking that had started in his hand vibrated up his arm and into his shoulder until his whole body was trembling uncontrollably. One meeting with Costa was scary. The possibility of having to meet with him twice terrified Patrick. People didn't survive meetings with Mr Costa. And while Patrick hoped he would be the exception to the rule, the feeling of dread gripped his heart in its cold fingers and refused to let go. He looked blankly at the screen of his phone until the letters coalesced from a fuzzy blackness that made no sense into words he could understand. He read and re-read the message from Costa, trying to find a hidden meaning, a warning or some sort of threat. When he couldn't, he turned his attention to the text from Mr Green to see if perhaps these words provided more information than a quick scan had revealed. The odds were promising for the football at the weekend. Burnley v Chelsea shouldn't have such favourable odds. Was this Mr Costa's reward to Patrick for his loyalty? The boxing odds seemed standard although if he read between the lines, perhaps these had been fixed in his favour. The more Patrick considered the matter, the more convinced he became that Costa was compensating Patrick for his allegiance. He jotted a few notes on the consultation form in front of him. Five grand on Chelsea to win, five grand on Irish for the boxing at Leeds, two on Geoff King and four on Pablo the Bolivian boxer. He scribbled more notes on the racing at Doncaster and finished by totalling up the tally. All in all, he'd allocated twenty-five thousand pounds. Enough to settle his debt with Costa and a little left over to lavish on Candy. Maybe he'd book a weekend in New York, and if she wasn't free, he'd enjoy a drug-fuelled weekend with the delicious Layla. Patrick was so sure the odds were in his favour, why wait until the weekend? With Carole out, he could easily sneak out of the FOBPS conference early and spend the night with Layla. With excitement he hadn't felt in years, Patrick dialled Mr Green and placed his bets along with his request to spend the evening with Layla.

Mr Green's smirk spread from ear to ear as he took Sharp's bets. Mr Costa had been right. The fool had been taken in by the favourable football odds. He might make a few grand if Chelsea played well, but he'd lose it and more on the boxing and horses. The sopla would ensure Patrick lost at the Boot Room card game, and a few expensive nights with the whore Layla would mean Patrick Sharp would have no choice but to agree to Costa's demands. Mr Green hung up the phone and dialled his boss.

Sasha fetched Patrick a double espresso. He'd looked like he needed a hit of caffeine to bring the colour back to his face.

"Have you eaten anything?" she asked.

"Not yet."

"Should I get you a sandwich from Feast?"

"If you would," Patrick said, returning to his notes.

Sasha grabbed her coat and on impulse decided she may as well buy four sandwiches as two. She hurried back down the hallway, looking for Gwen and Andrew.

"Don't," Gwen giggled.

"No one's looking," Andrew replied as Gwen's girly scream pealed again.

"Patrick's in the next room."

"Then keep your voice down."

Sasha could hear Gwen's gentle laugh and Andrew's throaty groan.

"They'll find out about us," Gwen warned.

"And if they do, who cares? Gwen we're both single, and you've introduced me to the children. Why are you so worried about Sasha and Patrick?"

Sasha stood as still as a statue. She knew she should either skulk quietly away or make some noise so they knew she was there, but instead she stood transfixed.

"It's not Sasha." Gwen paused, trying to get her thoughts in order. "Patrick's seen me destroyed by my marriage. I just don't want him to worry."

"I'm not Eddie," Andrew snapped. "I am not your ex-husband. I don't beat you, and I don't sleep around. Patrick knows me, Gwen, and as long as I make you happy, he'll be happy." His voice trailed off, his initial anger gone.

"I'm sorry. Soon. We'll tell them soon. Just let me get my head around it." Gwen kissed him.

"Well, if you put it like that," he moaned in

pleasure, "how can I refuse?"

Sasha smiled. The sly pair had kept quiet about their relationship. She wondered how long it had been going on and how Patrick would react. He'd be happy for them, she was sure, just as soon as he regained consciousness. Sasha backtracked silently. She'd get them a sandwich and a cream cake to celebrate.

"Gwen, have you printed off my speech?" Patrick asked as he grabbed his coat and briefcase, he should have left ten minutes ago, but he'd been delayed at Re Vive. Mrs Rawson had ruptured her stitches and Miss King needed additional reassurance that the bruising would fade.

"It's on the printer," Gwen replied. "I made a few improvements."

Patrick grabbed the paper from the printer he was so late he'd have to read the alterations in the taxi. Whatever changes she'd made would improve the flow of his writing, but she had a habit of throwing in words his Irish accent just couldn't pronounce.

"Looking sharp, Mr Sharp," Sasha commented as he walked through reception in his tailored suit and shiny shoes.

"Wouldn't pay to have our competitors thinking of Blow Row as not quite Harley Street."

"In that suit, they'll be thinking Harley Street isn't quite Blow Row."

Patrick laughed. He hated these bloody FOBPS conferences. It was just a collection of overpaid windbags congratulating themselves on their achievements while downing champagne as if it was Mad Dog 20/20. The speeches would be boring, the food dry and overcooked. Pharmaceutical companies would be enticing surgeons with deals and offers. Giving demonstrations of their latest developments, and trying to coax them into attending the after-dinner parties in luxury hotel suites with enough girls and pills to put the Trae La Muerte cartel out of business.

At least he had a night with Layla to look forward to.

He stepped into the taxi Sasha had thoughtfully arranged and gave the driver the address. Then he sat back and let thoughts of Layla's smooth skin relax his tense shoulders.

"That's twenty-three quid," the taxi driver shouted over his shoulder.

Patrick flinched at the loud noise. In his dozing sleep, he'd been running his hands over the pert brown nipples of his Bolivian temptress. He fumbled in his jacket, grabbing his wallet and thrusting three ten pound notes at the driver. "Keep the change," he muttered as he stepped out of the warm taxi into the cold night air.

"Mr Sharp," Christopher Kerrigan greeted, "we were just about to send out a search party for you."

"Traffic," Patrick apologised.

"If you'll come this way, sir, Mr Galway's talk is underway. We'll sneak you onto the stage while the lights are down. When Mr Galway has finished, Sarah Wilson MP will introduce you. Do you know Mrs Wilson?"

"By reputation only," Patrick replied, thinking about the slim black politician and the rumours floating about the Boot Room about her sexual preference for public displays.

Sarah Wilson thanked James Galway for his riveting insights into psychological profiling. Pointing out that with the increase of body dysmorphia, it was even more important for clinicians to use all the tools available to them to prevent harmful surgeries taking place. Many of the doctors fidgeted in their seat at her comments, wondering if the government intended to introduce stricter guidelines or potential legislation.

"This leads perfectly to our next keynote address by Mr Patrick Sharp. Mr Sharp, a renowned surgeon, will be speaking on the ethics of modern sales techniques in an industry that should be predominantly about the good of the patient rather than the bottom line," Sarah said into the microphone.

Patrick felt the sweat prickle under his collar. Sarah Wilson had wrapped a noose around his neck, and he'd willingly stepped onto the rickety stool for a bag of fool's gold. The only choice he had was which way to jump, but neither avoided injury. If he came down in favour of caution over profit, he'd alienate his profession and risk the massive discounts he'd negotiated with the pharmaceutical companies. Advocate pressured sales, and he'd be quoted by the assembled press as an unscrupulous doctor out to cash in on a patient's insecurities.

Sarah Wilson clapped as Patrick made his way to the podium. "David McGregor says hello," Sarah Wilson whispered to Patrick as she shook his hand.

Patrick didn't have time to respond as the spotlight found him. The audience hushed, waiting for his speech. Patrick nervously laid the A4 printed paper on the stand in front of him and took a deep breath.

"We are at a momentous point in the history of plastic surgery," he began. "From the Roman surgeon's advancements in ancient times to modern medicine's progress in the trenches to bring our soldiers home whole. Plastic surgeons have always been at the cutting edge, making life a better place for our patients." Patrick paused. This wasn't the speech he had written, but the one he wished he had. He offered a silent thank you to Gwen Charles. "Today, surgery to fix a bump on a nose or remove the bulges that exercise will not touch is as commonplace as a facial and a new haircut. However, as respected clinicians, we must remember the origins of our profession. We must remember the wounded soldiers, the victims of crime and those unfortunate enough to be born with life-threatening defects. Our calling is not only to assist people in looking their very best, but to provide a service for the greater good. Plastic surgery is not all about whether we should make her breasts a little bigger or improve his jawline. It is about what we can give back to the wider community by working alongside the police, the military and the NHS."

Patrick spoke until he turned the last page of Gwen's keynote address. The gathered medical professionals listened as he detailed the ethical responsibilities they had to ensure treatments were carried out respectfully and with restraint. They murmured in agreement when he urged them to understand that the needs and wishes of the patients were paramount. That only they as doctors could decide what was and what wasn't justified. He concluded by talking about the moral imperative to give something back to the wider community, to remember the roots of their profession and treat pro bono the nation's heroes returning from war. As he finished his last sentence, the audience stood up and applauded.

"Screw you, McGregor," Patrick hissed under his breath.

Chapter 20 – Don't be foolish

The last thing Robert remembered was McGregor suggesting Will take him for a drink. He vaguely remembered vodka shots off the flat stomach of a sexy Spanish lady and puking in an alley behind a nightclub. He sort of remembered Will leaving at about two, muttering something about a booty call at Claire's. And he was almost positive he'd again broken his vow to stay away from drugs. He'd had a sensual dream about the enigmatic Lady Elizabeth and woken in the dark with a raging erection. Robert reached out and pulled the alarm clock off the table, yanking on the cable until the plug came out of the socket and the wretched bleeping stopped. His mouth felt like something had crawled inside and died. He felt the need to hold onto his head in case it rolled off his neck, and yet the dizzy sensation when he let go was almost pleasant.

The Fitzroy clinic was nothing like what he'd expected. He'd been taught professional ethics and had sworn an oath to do what was best for his patients. Yet McGregor and Fitzroy preyed on the weak and the vulnerable, persuading beautiful people that the very things that made them unique were flaws needing to be fixed. Robert hadn't been naïve enough to believe plastic surgeons were saints who helped burn victims, scar sufferers and those with unfortunate genetics, but he hadn't been prepared for this full-scale assault on his morality. Each consultation identified the client's concerns and emotional scars, holding them under a bright light to magnify their importance. Each patient was picked apart physically and mentally until they had only one choice, agree to surgery. Used car salesmen and politicians had nothing on the manipulative practices of these cutters. Was this the world he wanted to be part of? Robert had never been confident in his looks. Years of study and a bad diet had made him undesirable to the opposite sex. At university, he'd had only one girlfriend and in hindsight, he'd been more a meal ticket than a life partner. Yet since he started at the Fitzroy clinic, he'd slept with at least five different women and a couple of lady-boys. His weight had dropped drastically from not eating during the day and puking up the contents of his stomach each night. He woke with a hangover every morning and would swear it would be the last time. But each evening, when McGregor pushed a pill into his hand, Robert took it. He didn't consider himself a coward for not resisting the pressure but rather an adventurer exploring the hedonistic underworld of London. Life had never been so exciting. He wasn't about to give it up because he felt a little ill in the mornings or a tad guilty about duping some poor little rich girl into paying a couple of grand for lipo she didn't need. Was he actually hurting anyone?

Robert slowly sat up, his stomach muscles protesting at the forced movement and his vision alarmingly blurred. He took three deep breaths to steady himself and swung his legs out of bed. The sudden motion upset the contents of his stomach, and he vomited down his naked body. He managed to get to the bathroom before the next surge of puke gushed forth. Robert daren't look in the mirror as he stood gasping for breath. He clambered unsteadily into the shower. The icy water blasted away the vertiginous feelings, leaving him shaky and cold. Wrapping a large towel around his middle, he stumbled into the small kitchen of his apartment. He pulled open the fridge to find a moulding pack of bacon and a couple of slices of dry bread. The goo in the bottom of the vegetable drawer might possibly have been salad or carrot, but could equally have been a handy place to vomit last night. He gingerly smelt the half bottle of milk and decided black coffee would be an ideal breakfast.

The apartment he'd originally prided himself on keeping pristine as a surgical suite now resembled the student digs his peers called home. Cigarettes littered the floor along with used condoms and empty bottles of vodka, gin and whisky. A pair of discarded stockings poked out from under the sofa and a sticky residue burnt the polish from the coffee table. Robert took his black coffee and sank onto a decidedly wet sofa cushion. He gagged slightly and tried not to think about what the aromatic damp patch might be. What would his Uncle Patrick think of the state of the apartment he'd rented his nephew?

How long he'd been awake, he didn't know. But the clock suddenly struck 3 pm. He jolted at the intrusive noise, spilling cold coffee on his naked legs.

"Shit," he cursed, jumping up. The motion made him feel sick again, and he nearly sat down. "You are an arsehole," he muttered, gritting his teeth until the dizziness passed. He looked around the dishevelled room and resolved to do something about the mess.

Robert showered again, and this time the water revived him. He dressed in the only clean clothes remaining in his wardrobe. He stripped the bed of filthy sheets and threw discarded underwear and condoms in a large black bin liner. He pushed a load of washing into the machine and determined to tackle the pile of dirty glasses in the sink. The noise of the washing machine drove him out of the kitchen, and the unbearable sound of the juddering spin cycle forced him to grab his keys and wallet and rush out of the apartment.

He wandered aimlessly for half an hour, appreciating the quiet Sunday afternoon. The cold breeze was pleasing and brought with it a clean, refreshing smell that made him hungry. Robert meandered into a little coffee shop on the corner of the street he'd strolled onto. The delicious aroma of roasted coffee beans assailed his senses. The bustle and noise of people chatting and cups clinking together mixed soothingly as the smartly dressed barista busied herself making drinks. Robert sank gratefully into a comfortable armchair near the door and ordered a coffee and fancy bacon sandwich. He picked up a discarded newspaper nearby and started to read the Sunday news.

"Mr Sutherland, is that you hiding behind the paper?"

Robert recognised the voice and lowered the newspaper to see the astonishingly attractive Lady Elizabeth in front of his table, a latte grasped in one hand as she tried to manoeuvre the large quantity of bags in the other.

"You grabbed the last table," she chastised. "I had to get mine to go."

Robert blushed. "Will you join me?" he asked hesitantly. "Or I can eat at the counter if you prefer?"

"Don't be foolish," she giggled in a way Robert thought almost flirty. "Karen," she said over her shoulder to the barista, "I will have that panini after all. My Serenity appointment isn't for another half hour."

Robert stood up, and Lady Elizabeth handed him the shiny designer-labelled bags from Tiffany's, Burberry, Chanel and a few others Robert had never heard of. He pushed them onto the spare chair next to him and sat down.

Lady Elizabeth noticed his disapproving glance. "I know I'm not supposed to be carrying anything," she whispered, "but my driver couldn't find a parking space, and I just had to get a new outfit for the gala. Will you be attending?"

Robert shook his head. He had no idea what gala she was talking about, but she'd flattered his ego just by thinking he might be invited.

"Mr McGregor is keeping me pretty busy," he replied lamely. "I'm afraid this afternoon is the only free time I have."

"That's a shame," she said in a tone of voice Robert thought might hold a hint of disappointment.

Karen brought the food, interrupting Robert's musing over whether the attraction he felt for this aristocratic lady could possibly be mutual.

"How do you feel?" he asked, changing the subject. "You must be due to see Mr McGregor soon."

"Tuesday. I will be glad to get rid of this bandaging" she said gingerly touching her chest." I'm apprehensive about the next procedure. I'll have to stay at Re Vive for a fortnight until the splint is removed. That place can be so dull I shall look forward to the visits of my surgeons."

The tingle Robert felt in his stomach at the hinted invitation was tempered by her consideration of more surgery. Robert remembered the note about rhinoplasty on her medical records.

"Surely you should wait until…" Robert started to say until he noticed the furious look in her eyes.

"Mr Sutherland, I have shared a coffee with you, not a friendship. It is not your place to decide what treatments I can or cannot have."

Grabbing her bags, she stormed out of the coffee shop without a backward glance. Of all the absurd beings on earth, that man Sutherland was surely the most annoying. She'd only put up with his company so she could sit for a moment. Her chest under the tight bandages was agonisingly painful, and she was sure she'd ripped open a couple of stitches while trying on the Valentino dress. "Bastard," Lady Elizabeth cursed under her breath.

She wasn't sure why the little sallow man offended her so much. After all, what did she care what a nobody like him thought? Mr Fitzroy had agreed that her nose needed doing, and he was the name people respected. Why on earth had she even sat down at that table? She felt tears welling in her eyes and dashed them away with the back of her hand. She rummaged in her oversized designer handbag for her Miu Miu sunglasses and pushed them on. It would be typical for the paparazzi to take her photo when she looked her worst.

Robert sat opened mouthed at the table. What had he said? He had only meant to compliment her and suggest she didn't need surgery. Instead, he'd put his big oversized feet in his mouth and insulted her. He resolved to talk to McGregor or Fitzroy about her need for surgical intervention. Maybe it was time she had some counselling before self-improvement turned into self-harm. Robert's lighthearted mood evaporated. He pushed away the plate of untouched food in front of him and picked up his coat. As he reached for his scarf, he noticed a small bag underneath the table. The elaborate Tiffany's bag must belong to Lady Elizabeth. He grabbed the turquoise bag and rushed out of the coffee shop, looking both ways to see if he could see her. When he didn't, he despondently made his way home, stopping at the corner shop to pick up cleaning supplies and air freshener.

It wasn't until he turned the key in the door to his apartment that he realised he could return Lady Elizabeth's purchase to her when she returned to the clinic for her check-up. The thought made him smile. Even if she didn't return his feelings of admiration, just being in the same room as her was like a drug. She made his knees weak and his heart beat faster. To even imagine anything more was silly, but Sundays were made to be silly. Sundays were an opportunity for fresh starts, to make new resolutions and restyle oneself into a new person, maybe even a person Lady Elizabeth would want to spend time with.

Robert cleaned the apartment with renewed vigour. He boxed up the remnants of his old life into two large cardboard boxes. The childish mint condition plastic action figures from Marvel, inside their unopened packaging. The geeky comics and collection of vintage Superman T-shirts were lovingly and yet ruthlessly packed away. Robert binned his old and comfortable clothing, leaving his wardrobe practically empty. He even went as far as to cancel his World of Warcraft membership and close down his avatar's Facebook page. This was a fresh start, a new beginning for the new Robert. He was a surgeon at one of the top clinics in London. Thanks to his uncle, he had a two-bedroom apartment in one of the up and coming areas of London. And a bright future if he kicked the drug habit. Robert had found excuses when Will invited him to the gym, but no more. In fact, why didn't he start today? The building had a gym in the basement. Robert pulled out his pair of grubby, grey jogging bottoms and the old, smelly trainers that from the black bin bag.

The building's gym was high-tech and intimating, where people needed a degree in engineering to understand the complex weight machines. Robert clenched his fists at the doorway, refusing to be overwhelmed by metal and rubber. He could read instructions after all, and how many people would be likely to work out at two on a Sunday afternoon? Cautiously, he reached out and pushed the door open. Slowly he stepped forward and then, realising he must look a complete idiot stood half in and half out of the gym, rushed through the doors and into his personal hell.

The treadmill wasn't difficult to understand. The almost sentient machine told him exactly what to do in bold red writing on the LCD screen. It provided helpful hints about gait, speed and pulse rate. All of which, while incredibly interesting, were utterly incomprehensible to Robert. The fact he hadn't fallen over was enough of an achievement, balancing better on his instep for a more efficient run was much too complicated. Robert ran for a full ten minutes before hitting the emergency stop button and wobbling off the conveyor belt. Sweat ran into his eyes, and for a moment he wondered if you could still buy sweatbands before imagining himself in one. He stretched slightly, more because it was what you were supposed to do than for any understanding of the value of the action. He grimaced as he tried to touch his toes and gave up on the hamstring stretch when it just hurt too much. Instead, he walked over to one of the complicated machines. If he followed the diagram, this contraption was supposed to work out his biceps and triceps simultaneously. Robert read and re-read the instructions, pulled on a few levers that didn't seem to do anything and set the weight to its lowest setting. Finally, when he'd run out of delaying tactics, he sat on the shiny leather seat and placed his arms on the torture device. The concept was simple. Hold on to the rubber hand grips and push forward with your forearms. Keeping the tension, push your arms open and then close them in a controlled, slow manner. Robert pushed forward, the weight offered no resistance and he fell off the chair. He looked around self-consciously to check no one had witnessed his humiliation, he increased the weight with the primitive silver bar you pulled out of one slot and into another. This time, the armrest resisted his attempts. He pushed harder and felt satisfaction as he achieved the desired effect. Buoyed by his success, he worked out for over an hour until every muscle in his body ached.

Chapter 21 – Is that?

The door closed shut with an almost silent click as the call girl left the suite. McGregor turned over and dozed. It was six am and he had another luxurious hour of sleep before he needed to hit the gym and four hours before he had to endure brunch with Witch-Hazel. Brunch was such a stupid meal, the invention of bored, fat housewives who wanted to eat cake at eleven o'clock. Predictably, it was Hazel's favourite meal. McGregor ran his hand over his flat stomach and smiled sleepily to himself. It was no wonder women found him irresistible. Candice had been playing hard to get all weekend. She'd gone for a drink with him after her consultation then claimed a prior engagement and left just as the night was getting interesting. Thinking about the stuck-up bitch was putting a dent in his good mood. Did she really think she was special? McGregor rolled over, his sleepy self-satisfaction evaporated. He threw back the covers and ordered breakfast from room service. Fuck Candice, and fuck Hazel and her fucking stupid fucking brunch. He was going to have a fried breakfast and then hit the gym.

The cute girl on reception handed him a towel as he walked into the gym and asked if he could sign a magazine cover featuring his handsome profile. He smiled and signed the magazine, writing his phone number underneath the signature with a suggestion she should call if she wanted tickets to the show. The young girl giggled and blushed, but underneath the shy smile, he could see a wild child wanting to be tamed. He kissed her on her cheek before heading for the treadmill. McGregor refused her the reward of looking back, but he knew she'd be watching. He eased himself into a jog and then quickened his pace until he was running at the treadmill's maximum speed, his long legs loping forward with natural grace. He imagined the nubile beauty staring at his muscled back and bottom as he sprinted. He pushed himself further than he normally would, male pride dictating he outpace the twenty-year-old jogging next to him. The youth quit at 10K, wiping his face with one of the hotel towels and nodding appreciatively at McGregor as he left. McGregor grinned and ran on until the readout indicated he'd run 15K. He pressed the stop button and turned to smile at the girl on reception.

McGregor scowled. The youth and the girl had their heads together in quiet conversation, and every so often, she twisted a lock of hair in her fingers and bit her bottom lip in open invitation to her suitor. McGregor hit the weights hard, lifting dumbbells in successive reps until every muscle ached, but he didn't feel any better. In his mind, all he could picture was the young man bending the asinine girl over the reception counter and laughing at him while they fucked.

"Slut," he muttered to himself as he walked past her to the sauna.

Checking his phone as he dressed, McGregor read the increasingly agitated text messages from Hazel. Starting with, 'Where are you darling' and ending in, 'You bastard don't you fucking dare stand me up.' He seriously considered going home and letting the bitch suffer, but they had a TV slot tomorrow, and he needed her to be cooperative. If that meant he had to endure her banging on about their agent and then banging her brains out, so be it. He could always take a shot of morphine to enhance the experience and drown out her whining. He popped to the hotel bar for a quick brandy and a bottle of Krug to take to Hazel as a peace offering. When Hazel was annoyed, it was better not to face her empty-handed, and the Krug was easier than nipping to Libertine Lingerie for some erotically devious knickers.

It was past twelve when McGregor pressed the

doorbell at Hazel's house. The ornate doors buzzed, and he pushed them open to be greeted by the leather-clad TV star.

"What time do you call this?" she demanded, slapping him solidly across the face.

"Time I fucking left," McGregor yelled, turning around and heading out the door.

Hazel's wail of rejection could be heard from the street as the darling of daytime television rushed outside in nothing more than a peephole leather bra and matching G-string. Her face was covered by a leather mask, so while the onlookers were shocked by her appearance, they weren't reaching for their iPhones just yet.

"David, I just wanted you..." Hazel whimpered.

McGregor turned and growled. Her nakedness was drawing a crowd, and it was only a matter of time before someone recognised him. While he had no concern for Hazel's reputation, his own business depended on people believing he was a clean-cut professional.

"Get inside," he growled, grabbing her by the arm and pushing her towards the door.

Hazel refused to move, planting her high-heeled boots firmly on the ground. The bitch was strong when she wanted to be.

"Only if you agree to stay."

"Is that...?" a passer-by started to say to her companion as McGregor kicked Hazel in the shin and forced her back into the house.

"David," she pleaded.

"For fuck's sake, bitch, I'll stay."

"Mr McGregor, David McGregor!" the passer-by called out, her camera phone ready to take his picture if he turned. McGregor gritted his teeth and shoved the limping Hazel backwards, before slamming the door behind them.

"What the fuck!" he shouted in Hazel's face. "You are not a child. I will not be manipulated by you. What would your loving audience think of your attire?"

Hazel sank to the floor, her fight gone and tears streaming down her face.

"I didn't think," she whimpered.

"You never bloody think!" he screamed, his temper flaring. "If you ever fucking slap me again, you cunt, I'll, I'll…"

Hazel prostrated herself at the feet of her lover. "I'm sorry. I mean it, David. It will never happen again."

McGregor looked at her tear-stained face, the mascara running down her cheeks, and the red lipstick she had so carefully applied now smeared across her chin. Her chest heaved tantalisingly as her shoulders shook with her sobbing. The juxtaposition of her appearance as a dominatrix and her subjugation at his feet turned him on.

"Stand up," he ordered. "Now!"

Hazel looked up but didn't move. McGregor grabbed hold of her hair and pulled her up. With one hand, he grabbed her throat and squeezed until her breath came in ragged gasps. He kissed her swollen, red lips, feeling her laboured breaths in his mouth.

"On your knees, bitch," he spat, letting go of her so she fell hard onto the marble floor. He unzipped his trousers and pulled out his erect penis. "You better make me come, whore," he barked, not looking at her. Hazel whimpered slightly and leant forward, her warm lips encasing him in the wetness of her mouth. McGregor smiled to himself as she rocked, her tongue flickering over the tip of his cock, her lips locked around the shaft as she sucked. He felt the throbbing pulse inside, the tension needing to be released in a spray of semen straight down the bitch's throat. McGregor grabbed hold of Hazel's hair and thrust into her, she gagged slightly as he hit the back of her throat. Three more thrusts and he exploded, the sticky white fluid pouring into her mouth.

"Swallow," he ordered.

Hazel looked up, her face a mask of fear. She swallowed and then licked her lips provocatively, her expression changing to lustful dominance as she stood.

"Feel better?" she laughed, kissing him on the nose before skipping up the stairs, her seductive bottom bouncing free in the thin strip of leather.

"Fuck," McGregor muttered, realising he'd been played by a pro. Still, her arse did look good, and after a glass of Krug and a little morphine, he'd make sure she paid for her deception.

"Bring the Krug," she called from the top of the stairs. "You can drink it out of my pussy."

The Krug had been finished, along with a bottle of gin and the decanter of port Hazel kept for impressing TV executives. The mess they'd left in the bedroom would be cleaned up by Hazel's long-suffering assistant.

"Do you want to order in?" Hazel asked as McGregor's stomach rumbled loudly.

McGregor looked at her naked breasts and flat stomach as she smoked a joint of Triple H. He seriously considered reaching out and pulling on a red nipple, but his dick ached. Four hours of sex was enough to settle any man's appetite. Still? He reached out and pushed his fingers inside her, she squealed in delight as he massaged her clitoris and rubbed the taught skin between her vagina and bottom. Her thighs opened to give him better access. Abruptly, he pulled away.

"You've not been on the cover of a magazine in a while," he said spitefully. "Let's head to Beckwoods. You're sure to attract the attention of the photogs."

Hazel smiled. McGregor was a cruel bastard, but he was her cruel bastard. Her body ached from the sex, and the last thing she wanted was another hour of being fucked. Her faked delight had stopped him while if she'd shown pain, he'd have grabbed the big black vibrator on the cabinet and shoved it so far inside her she would have bled.

"Beckwoods," she said, trying to sound

disappointed. "Will you make a reservation while I get ready?"

McGregor took the implied compliment with a nod. He agreed with her. His name was more likely to secure a last minute reservation than a daytime presenter's. He dialled the restaurant.

"Beckwoods," the man answered.

"It's David McGregor," McGregor said. "Can I have a table in say, forty-five minutes?"

McGregor could hear paper being shuffled and a muted conversation in the background. "Will you be dining with Miss Woods?"

"Yes."

"We have a table for two in an hour."

"Fine," McGregor said. "Can I have a bottle of Krug at the table on arrival?"

"Of course, sir. Anything else?"

McGregor hung up the phone, a smug smile crossing his face. All the best restaurants were open to him these days, and it appeared maître d's now kept up with his social life.

Hazel stepped out of the shower and wrapped a large towel around her slim figure. She'd need to wear a long dress to hide the bruising. Laura, her assistant's, name flashed on her telephone screen.

"Yes," she said quietly into the receiver.

"I called Beckwoods and reserved your usual table at the front, and I've tipped off the press to expect you and Mr McGregor in an hour. I hope you don't mind, but I hinted at this being a special occasion."

"You wonderful girl," Hazel gushed. "Can you sort the mess here while I'm out? And help yourself to a bottle from the fridge."

"Of course, Miss Woods, or should I say Mrs McGregor?"

Hazel giggled and hung up. This assistant was a

treasure. She never complained, always seemed to understand the needs of her employer and yet was discreet enough to blend into the background.

"You've thirty minutes," McGregor called from the living room.

"Plenty of time," Hazel replied, rubbing the creamy lotion into her skin and dreaming about a wedding spread in Hello magazine.

The Town Car arrived just as Hazel was finishing her elaborate hairstyle. Her long hair had been twisted into curls and pinned loosely on top of her head in one of those carefree effortless styles that took skill, time and pain to achieve.

"Hazel!" McGregor shouted up the stairs. "I'll leave you here if you don't get your arse downstairs."

Hazel pushed her hands into her dress and lifted her breasts to create a round cleavage, took one last look in the mirror and smiled.

"Mrs McGregor," she whispered to herself. Maybe not tonight but soon. It was only a matter of time.

The pair stepped out of the Town Car to the flash of camera bulbs. Hazel clung to McGregor's arm and smiled at the paparazzi. Laura was a gem, Hazel thought as the photographers called out her name. Maybe she would be a little nicer to this one. After all, her fat dumpy body was of no interest to McGregor, and Hazel would need an assistant to plan a wedding.

The polite maître d' showed them to their table in front of the window and poured them a glass of champagne. Hazel reached over the table and took David's hand, gazed endearingly at his masculine frame, her face glowing with happiness.

"The photographers are looking, David," she hissed.

McGregor raised his eyebrows but didn't pull his hand away.

"Smile, darling, and look in love, you need the

column inches just as much as I do."

McGregor smiled, his hand locked with Hazel's as he leant over the table and kissed her. The flashing of bulbs exploded on the other side of the glass as the press tried desperately to capture the private moment. Hazel pulled back first and then with a shy smile pretended to just notice her audience. She blushed demurely, seemingly embarrassed at being caught in such an intimate way.

"They'll never believe it," McGregor hissed.

"Oh yes, they will," she smiled. "I'm every girl's best friend, and you, my darling pervert, are every housewife's wet dream. Together, nothing can stop us."

McGregor was about to comment, but the waiter came to take their order. "Is it a special evening?" he asked, refilling their glasses.

"Every evening is special with David."

"David McGregor? Is that you?" a sensual voice purred from across the room.

McGregor turned to look at the luscious figure of Clara Huntington walking towards him. The page three model's breasts practically burst out of the tight silver dress, but nothing could distract people from the angle of her eyebrows and swollen mess of her lips.

"My man tells me you want to do a story on me."

McGregor frowned. The last thing he needed was the Associated Press thinking he had anything to do with the botched Botox. He stood up, his body blocking her from the view of the journalists outside the window.

"Yes," he replied, placing a genteel kiss on her cheek. "I was so distraught about the incompetency of your surgeon I just had to offer my services to put it right."

"That's so kind of you. I was just saying to my dinner companion Lord Mowbray how I should have gone to you first. Your clinic treats his daughter, I believe."

McGregor nodded. "Why don't you come in next week, and we can talk about treatments. Maybe get you on

Morning Wake-up the week after."

"That would be marvellous."

"Well, I mustn't keep you from Lord Mowbray," McGregor said pointedly, "Hazel and I would ask you to join us, but this is something of a special occasion."

He moved slightly so Clara could see the collected paparazzi. Her face paled noticeably, although McGregor wasn't sure if it was the thought of being photographed with swollen lips or with the esteemed Lord Mowbray.

"Maybe you could nip out the back after dinner," McGregor suggested. "The maître d' is very skilled at sneaking celebrities away from the press."

Chapter 22 – I am afraid

Patrick woke in an empty bed in an empty house. Carole hadn't returned home. He'd seen her briefly at breakfast on Saturday as she rushed out of the house to some fitness appointment or another. Whichever fad diet or celebrity health kick she was on this time was actually working. As she'd bobbed out of the kitchen in her now baggy tracksuit bottoms and vest top, he'd felt attraction towards her for the first time in years. Her skin glowed and the new haircut made her red hair bounce as she walked.

"Shall I book a table for this evening? Beckwoods?"

Carole had looked back briefly as she stuffed something into an oversized handbag. Why women felt the need to carry so much crap about evaded Patrick.

"I'm sorry, dear," she'd muttered, putting on her shoes. "I made plans with Bethany for this evening. I expected you to be busy with those foreign friends of yours."

Patrick knew she meant the Bolivians, but like all career wives, Carole chose to ignore the illegal side of her husband's business in favour of Prada and Jimmy Choo.

"I thought it might be nice to spend some time together," he'd replied lamely.

Carole had stopped what she was doing and looked at her husband. She'd smiled and walked over to him, planting a friendly kiss on his forehead. "If you'd just said something earlier," she'd replied. "But I really can't cancel. I'm not one of those friends who cancels just because her husband is free for the evening." Carole's hazel eyes narrowed challenging him to disagree.

"I wouldn't want you to do that, dear."

"I know you wouldn't. It's why our marriage works. We understand each other."

The loaded sentence hit home. Carole had

forgiven numerous affairs and ignored his gambling addiction as long as it didn't affect her lifestyle. His last affair had nearly ended in divorce, and Patrick had needed to end the messy relationship with a significant payoff. He'd promised Carole it was the last time he'd be unfaithful, and he'd meant it. Patrick didn't class paying for sex as cheating. It was more making sure his carnal pleasures were satisfied without bothering his prim and proper wife.

"How's Robert getting on at Fitzroy's?" he'd asked, suddenly wanting to delay her departure.

"He says he's doing well, long hours and a lot of courting clients. In fact, he seems to be spending as much time wining and dining as in surgery."

Patrick had smirked. He knew exactly what sort of entertaining his young nephew was doing, and it had nothing to do with courting clients and everything to do with getting pissed and high. He'd considered warning Robert Sutherland about David McGregor but had decided the fallout would be far more fun to watch.

"As long as the boy is enjoying it," Patrick had replied. "He'll be getting a lot of experience with old Fitzroy."

"I think that celebrity surgeon David McGregor has taken him under his wing. He really seems to know his stuff. I just love listening to him on Monday mornings. You should do something similar. It would be wonderful to see you on TV."

Patrick had frowned. "I am afraid, Cupcake, I don't have the looks for television. Besides, discretion is important to my clients."

"I'm sure it is Patty Cake, but still," Carole had persisted. "I'd love to boast to the girls about my celebrity husband."

Patrick had frowned at his wife. Why could she not see that the cunt McGregor earned less from his celebrity clients than Patrick earned from his underground contacts? The man was all show and no substance. He was half the surgeon Patrick was and relied on looks rather than a scalpel. And who would want to be saddled with the drunken, oddball Fitzroy?

Carole had taken the not-so-subtle hint and closed her mouth. "I must be going. Can't keep Andrea waiting."

She had grabbed her bag, placed another kiss on Patrick's forehead and wafted out of the kitchen, leaving a trail of Joy perfume in her wake. Something was different about her, and Patrick wasn't entirely sure he liked it. He'd absently taken a gulp of hot black coffee. It burnt his mouth, and he'd spluttered the dark liquid all over his white shirt.

"Bastard!"

Mae had walked into the kitchen as he was removing his shirt. "Ah, Mr Sharp, what have you done? Quick, give it to me, the coffee will stain."

Patrick had smiled. "Whatever would I do without you?"

"Mr Sharp, you would fade from hunger and go to work in a wrinkled shirt."

Patrick had laughed. "Talking of food, do you by any chance have some of those magnificent pancakes?"

Mae had tutted. "You know I make them fresh. If you want a pancake, just ask."

The housekeeper left at two Saturday afternoon, and his wife hadn't returned home after lunch. He'd spent a lazy day watching sports and cursing his bad luck, especially when Chelsea lost, drinking excessively and pigging out on the casserole Mae had left for him. He woke on Sunday morning with a hangover and a feeling of dread. His mother had claimed to be a psychic and put these uneasy feelings down to a premonition of bad things to come. His shrink friend, Smith-Jones, called it free-floating anxiety and linked it to personal trauma. But Patrick blamed it on a lack of food and not enough whisky. Both of which he intended to rectify immediately.

Patrick was unnerved by the oppressive quiet as he gingerly made his way downstairs. Normally he could hear his wife talking on the telephone to one of her many girlfriends or bustling around the kitchen creating another huge flower display for the church. He would see Mae as she cleaned or smell the aromas of delicious food coming from the kitchen as she prepared another succulent meal. Instead, the house was cold and quiet. The bottles and dirty dishes he'd left by the sofa were still there on the floor. The sticky mess of tissues he'd used last night as he watched the babe station were stuck to the leather of the chair like a modern art sculpture. He'd considered booking Layla for the night, but unsure of Carole's movements, he had decided against it.

Layla had become a regular in his life. He'd seen her three times more since their first encounter, and the sex had been intense. The second time, her face had been covered with thick, cheap make-up. He'd insisted she remove it immediately. Underneath the thick foundation was terrible bruising. Layla's voice had remained dispassionate as she explained some punters liked to beat the whores before fucking them. Outraged, Patrick called Mr Costa to complain. Costa offered him another girl at half price for the inconvenience. When Patrick had tried to explain it wasn't about money but about Layla's health, Costa had laughed and told him to fuck off. It had been gentle Layla who revealed the truth of the matter. She had no rights. She belonged to Trae La Muerte. If they were paid so she could be beaten, then she was beaten.

"Can't you leave?"

Layla had laughed, "And go where?"

"I could put you in an apartment."

"Trae La Muerte would find me. I am worth too much to them. When I am forty, they will put me to work in a brothel for £25 fucks, and when I am fifty, they will put me on the streets."

"Why do you do it?"

In a quiet, unemotional voice, Layla had explained the circumstances surrounding her passage to England. Trae La Muerte recruited in the cities and villages of Bolivia, promising cleaning jobs in big houses or modelling opportunities for those stupid enough to believe them. For the girls who refused, abduction and rape at the hands of Trae La Muerte's men. Layla pretended she believed the lies and willingly gave her passport to Costa's men, but she knew enough to know she was being trafficked as a whore. It was the way of things in Bolivia. Her family were poor, and even the small allowance she would be permitted to send home would make the difference between life and death for her mother and sister. She could endure anything if Katricia didn't have to make the choices she had needed to. Patrick listened in stunned silence as she explained. Layla was so brave. He vowed sincerely to do something to help, and Layla had kissed him with a loving tenderness full of genuine emotion. In those moments of intimacy, he'd meant to do something, but he'd forgotten as soon as she left. The next time they met, she never mentioned the beating or his promise to help Katricia.

Patrick wandered from the lounge into the kitchen. He'd left the casserole out of the fridge, and the leftovers had congealed into a greasy mess. He opened the fridge to find it as empty as his house. Patrick's unease settled into a strange feeling of dread as if something horrible was about to happen. He shrugged the feeling off as senseless and decided breakfast at the Boot Room was the best solution to satisfy his need for food and human contact.

The streets of London were eerily quiet so early on a Sunday morning. Joggers bounced past in colour-coordinated Lycra with high-tech gadgetry to tell them how far they had run and how many cream cakes this entitled them to eat. Patrick had no time for joggers. He considered them a scourge on society. Upper middle-class twats with not enough to do and without the common sense to realise that surgery was a better option to shed the pounds. They probably ate granola bars and sipped fruit smoothies, counted calories and when no one was looking scoffed the entire box of chocolate and stuffed down a KFC value bucket for four. Patrick imagined running over the daft bitch in the shocking pink mini shorts and matching headband. The image of her brunette hair and soft pink limbs colliding with the windscreen made him smile. In the small square park near Belgravia, couples walked oversized dogs while fashionable ladies carried miniature poodles and shih-tzus in designer carry cases to protect them from the distress of getting their paws dirty. Patrick despaired of London and the arseholes who lived there. For a moment, he wanted nothing more than to earn enough to retire back to Ireland, buy a large rundown farming estate and spend his latter years pottering around as a man of the people. Patrick didn't even mow the lawn. How he intended to manage an estate, he had no idea. Pig muck and wellies really weren't his forte, but the idea of Carole milking the cows had a particular vindictive charm, he could employ people to run the rest.

This early in the morning, the Boot Room's valet service wasn't available, so Patrick pulled his black Merc into a parking space in front of Wellington's.

"Mr Sharp," Jones greeted him as he pulled open the large doors. "It's unusual to see you on a Sunday. Will you be wanting a table for breakfast, or are you joining someone?"

"No, just me, Jones."

"Right you are, sir. If you'll follow me. Chef has a delightful smoked salmon crepe this morning."

"Bacon and eggs and black coffee, please."

"As you wish," Jones said, leaving Patrick at a table with a newspaper.

Patrick smiled as he looked at the Mirror

newspaper, complete with the racing supplement. Jones was the ultimate gentleman's butler. He understood the needs of his members even before they did. Patrick had only just finished circling races at Doncaster and York when his breakfast arrived.

"Mr Danny and Sir James are in the sampling lounge if you desire any company," Jones said.

Patrick nodded and bit into the thick, freshly made bread. The bacon juices mixed with the melted butter to dribble down his chin. The salty bacon was cooked to perfection, the meat tender and the fat just off crispy. The yolk of the egg broke on his second bite, mixing with the bacon and butter in a deliciousness that lightened his mood. He took a sip of the delicious black coffee and sighed contentedly.

"See," he said to himself. "The only thing I needed was food. Bugger Smith-Jones and his free-floating anxiety."

"Pardon, sir?" Jones said from across the table.

"Nothing, I was just mulling something over. Sir James is here, you say?"

Patrick finished his breakfast and another pot of strong coffee served on a silver tray. He leisurely finished the paper and text in a few bets to Mr Green before deciding a bit of gentlemanly company and a cigar was just what the doctor ordered. He opened the oak door to the sampling room, the smell of Cuban cigars mixing with the cedar wood panelling in a welcoming mist. With the expensive extractor fans turned off, the room had a smoky haze of decadent disregard. A man dressed in a white shirt and black waistcoat stood behind the polished counter that held the keys to each member's exclusive collection of cigars. He bowed his head as Patrick entered and headed towards him.

"Good morning, sir," he said, handing Patrick his key.

"Good morning, Fredrick," Patrick replied.

"Could you have Christopher fetch me brandy?"

"Certainly, sir, the usual?"

Patrick thought for a moment. "Something a little fruitier, the Aberlour 12-year-old, I think."

"Excellent choice. It goes very well with the Havanas."

Patrick delayed the moment he opened his personal cigar locker. The anticipation was a tender moment of suspense. Like a boy looking through the window of a sweet shop with ten pence clasped in his fingers. Patrick turned the key slowly, listening for the sound of the click as the lock gave way to his eager hand. He gently pulled open the door and pushed his face into the locker, inhaling the heady aroma of his personally selected tobacco before the smells of the room invaded the space. He chose a small Partagas in its ebony tube and closed the door.

"Would you like me to prepare it for you, sir," Fredrick asked as Patrick returned the key.

Patrick nodded and handed over the metal tube. "I'll be over with Sir James."

"Ah, Patrick old boy," Sir James said, "I was meaning to call you."

Patrick walked over and sat on the gestured chair. "Well, no need now. Your wife's appointment went well, and her boobs have been booked in for next month," Patrick replied, assuming the tight bastard wanted to make sure he was getting the agreed-upon discount.

"Ah, that's good," Sir James muttered, turning a little puce. His expression of unease seemed out of place. "Last time we met, I was a little pissed. I may have been a little indiscreet." Sir James swallowed hard. "Danny boy tells me I might have let slip some information that I, well, to be frank, I shouldn't have."

Patrick stared at the red-faced older gentleman but didn't say anything. If the old goat was having second thoughts about insider trading and the legality of divulging information, it was too bad.

"It seems my information may have been a little premature." Sir James paused and looked at his feet. "I hope you didn't act on my indiscretion because the information is, well, to be frank, incorrect."

Patrick didn't say anything as a numbness started in his toes, crept through his abdomen, grabbed hold of his heart and progressed painfully to his head. Slowly, he closed his eyes, hoping when he opened them, he would be staring at his bedroom ceiling. This conversation would be a dream and Sir James' confession wouldn't mean he had provided corrupted information to the Bolivian cartel.

"Sir," Fredrick said politely. "Your cigar."

Patrick opened his eyes and looked at the silver tray in front of him. The cigar was expertly cut and displayed on a small cedar stand on top of a white cotton serviette with an extra-long match and a double brandy with three small cubes of ice floating on the amber liquid.

"You okay?" Sir James asked. "You seem to have gone a little pale, old boy."

Patrick stared at the small ice cubes bobbing on the sea of viscous alcohol. Sir James' words penetrated the numbness but didn't make sense. He slowly tore his eyes away from the silver tray and looked into the face of his demise. This stupid, self-important nobody, this drunken arsehole whose ego was larger than his fucking gut. How could Patrick have been ruined by this toff bastard?

"Sir?" Fredrick said again.

Life quickened as if someone had suddenly hit the fast forward button. Without saying a word, Patrick grabbed the brandy and downed the smooth liquid in one gulp. He stood, knocking the silver tray out of Fredrick's hand, and rushed out of the sampling room, his phone already in hand and dialling.

The bastard wouldn't answer at this time in the morning. He was probably in bed with some Trae La Muerte whore. The answer phone clicked on, and Patrick left a hasty message. He redialed and redialed and redialed. Each time the automated voice told him the user was unavailable, he hung up and redialed. By the time he reached his car, Patrick had called Mr Green eight times, his messages getting more and more panicky as he realised the mortal danger he was facing. Patrick choreographed his demise in painful and gruesome ways, each redraft becoming more violent and exotic as his mind raced. He needed to call Carole and get her to go stay with her mother for a few weeks. Andrew could take care of himself, but Gwen and Sasha would need to be warned to stay away from Costa and his crew. Patrick typed a text message to Mr Green and sent it three times to be sure. Then he phoned Carole. The relief at hearing her voice was short lived as he realised it was a recorded message.

"Carole, do not go home until you have heard from me. Call Mae and tell her to take the week off. Go to the bank on Monday, one far away from where you are staying, and draw out as much cash as you can, and for God sake, don't use your plastic. I'll be in touch when I can."

He hung up and dialled Mr Green again. Still no answer. Patrick had a momentary panic as he held his thumb over the electronic key to his car. Could the cartel have planted a bomb? Patrick pursed his lips and frowned. He was being stupid. A dead surgeon couldn't repay a debt. He was worth more to Costa alive, unless... Unless he would be used as an example to those who thought they were untouchable. Patrick stood, locked in an internal battle over common sense and self-preservation. His thumb paused a millimetre from the button on the key fob, his delicate surgeon's hand shaking as he tried to think. The phone in his other hand vibrated and then rang. The sharp sound made him jump, and his thumb to hit the unlock button. Instinctively, he threw himself to the ground, expecting an explosion on this quiet London street. He lay huddled until he realised the only sounds were his adrenaline-filled breathing and the shrill ringtone of his phone. Patrick looked at the screen and with a trembling hand swiped to answer the call.

"Hello," he said, his voice shaking with fear.

"Good morning, Mr Sharp. We need to talk."

Chapter 23 – Great idea

McGregor slapped the make-up artist on the bottom and she giggled. He looked in the mirror at his tanned face covered with a thick coat of stage make-up. He looked young for his age, and if the giggle of the twenty year old make-up girl was anything to go by, still attractive.

"Mr McGregor," the young girl squealed as he pulled her onto his knee, "you'll get me the sack, especially if Miss Woods sees."

"I guess we had better make sure she doesn't see then," he replied, his finger wandering up her skirt to rub tantalisingly against her.

"Why don't I lock the door?" she suggested but didn't move from his knee as his thumb started to stroke the delicate skin in between her vagina and bottom.

"Great idea," McGregor agreed, pushing his thumb into her anus and his finger inside her wet pussy. The girl gasped in surprised pleasure as his fingers moved inside her. McGregor had no intention of locking the door. Being caught fondling the help was part of the excitement, besides, he had nothing to lose if Hazel discovered their tryst. She was as likely to join in as she was to throw a hissy fit. One never knew with Hazel. McGregor dropped his head into the girl's cleavage and teased out one plump nipple with his teeth. He bit hard, tugging deliciously on her pert breast until she cried out in pleasure.

"Mr McGregor, your make-up," she gasped as he turned his attention to the other breast and covered her white blouse in tanned foundation.

This young brunette wasn't the first to have been branded an easy lay by the stains of his stage make-up, neither would she be the last, but her concern was tantalisingly naïve.

"You'll just have to reapply it," he laughed, "unless you'd like me to stop."

The girl bit her lip, torn between desire and fear. McGregor pushed his thumb deeper inside, massaging the soft skin he encountered. This new and erotic sensation broke any reservation she may have had. She pushed herself into him, her head thrown back to allow him easier access to her neck and breasts, her nails digging into his thighs as she bucked on his knee.

"Not yet, my little darling," he growled, grabbing her by the waist and lifting her off his knee so she stood facing the mirror. Using his foot, he pushed her legs wide and then bent her forward. He grabbed at the thin fabric of her blouse and ripped it open, exposing her large breasts. While one hand remained on her back, the other unzipped his trousers and guided his erect dick inside her. Her lava hot wetness encased him in a tightness that only came from inexperience. He pulled backwards slowly, enjoying the cold sensation of the air, and then thrust forward, impaling her on his erection. He looked at her in the mirror. The expression of passion in her dark eyes, the wonder and admiration, the full red lips open in desire, her breasts bouncing as he took possession of her voluptuous body. His focus changed, and it wasn't her he looked at as he came. In the moment of release, he looked at his steely reflection and enjoyed his domination. He held her still as the semen pumped out of him. Then, slapping her on the bottom, he withdrew.

"Pass me the box of tissues," he demanded.

The girl did as she was asked, then righted her clothing. Her blouse was ripped beyond repair, but McGregor didn't care, it wasn't his problem. He removed the condom, wiped himself clean and zipped his trousers, smiling at the musky scent of sex on his skin. He looked at himself in the mirror, ignoring the presence of the make-up girl. If she created a scene, he'd have her fired. The girl calmly took a pair of scissors from her make-up case and cut the sleeves and collar off her blouse. Then she wrapped it around her in such a way it not only hid the stains but gave her a fashionable plunging neckline. Without a word, she picked up the make-up brush and started to reapply McGregor's foundation.

"Will that be all, Mr McGregor?" she asked when she'd finished.

McGregor was impressed. She acted like nothing had happened. No wailing hysterics like his last workplace conquest, just calm professionalism.

"No." He paused. "Thank you," he added.

The runner tapped on his dressing room door.

"Mr McGregor, five minutes."

Hazel was already on set, her slim figure shown exceptionally in a rockabilly green dress. Her hair was piled high in a fifties style she thought gave her an air of glamour on morning TV.

"David," she gushed, leaning forward and kissing his cheek. Her nose wrinkled slightly as she detected the salty smell of sex, but gracefully she straightened her face before sitting back down. It wouldn't do for the crew to think there was disharmony in the McGregor-Woods partnership.

"Hazel," McGregor greeted a hint of mischief and challenge in his voice.

A technician walked up to the pair and started attaching their mics and earpieces, taping wires underneath their clothes and getting them to test the connections. Barry, the director, spoke in McGregor's ear, asking him if he could read from the teleprompter to check lighting and camera angles. The next half hour was taken over by technical support, reviewing rewritten scripts and checking facts for the onscreen titles. It wasn't until the two presenters sat down for the show's credits to run that Hazel leant over to whisper in McGregor's ear.

"So who was it? The new runner, the whore of a

receptionist or Olivia, the tasty make-up artist?"

McGregor didn't say anything.

"You do realise you've had my sloppy seconds." McGregor turned sharply to look at Hazel. "Didn't you realise how adventurous she was? I was between her legs before you," she bragged.

"You should have invited me to watch," he hissed torn between fury and frustration.

Hazel shrugged. "Maybe next time, we will," she said noncommittally.

McGregor was about to reply when Barry spoke in his ear, "Five, four, three, two, one, and you're live."

Hazel tilted her head slightly to give McGregor one last challenging look and then smiled professionally into camera one.

"Good morning," she said. "Welcome to another Monday morning with me, Hazel Woods, and my regular Monday guest, Doctor David McGregor. Today we'll be discussing how to bake the perfect cake and what to do when diets don't work. We'll also be looking at the latest celebrity fashion. Mark will be talking to Scott Holden about his heavyweight victory. James is out in Nottingham to bring the news from the search for little Fiona, who went missing on Friday, and we'll have music from Five Spokes. But first, Doctor McGregor is going help me welcome our studio audience and tell us all about the benefits of Botox and fillers as a preventive to aging."

Hazel turned to McGregor.

"As we all know," she smiled self-mockingly, "I've been known to have Botox on the odd occasion. In fact, the good doctor here is the one who holds all my secrets." She placed a friendly hand on McGregor's knee.

McGregor smiled into the camera. "And, of course, as your viewers also know, a doctor will not divulge the medical or treatment history of any patient. At the Fitzroy Clinic, like any good cosmetic surgery, we are bound by patient confidentiality. I guess what I'm saying,

Hazel, is your secrets are safe with me."

The audience laughed. One of the reasons Monday's studio tickets were so difficult to obtain was because of the undeniable chemistry between Hazel and her doctor. That and the chance to see Britain's very own Doctor McDreamy.

McGregor read the script he'd written last week from the teleprompter. He confidently explained how Botox had come into use and what the effects were. Expertly providing the audience in the studio and at home the knowledge to decide for themselves if Botox was for them.

"The most important thing to remember with Botox is that it is the practitioner who creates the results. It is crucial you research the clinic and talk to people who have used them before. Don't rely on publicity images on glossy marketing material. These might have been provided by the product companies or photoshopped to look better. Luckily, Botox errors are fixable and the effect temporary, but the last thing you want is to spend three to six months regretting a treatment."

"So David," Hazel said, "how can we tell a good clinic from a bad one?"

"Firstly, look at the people in the clinic. If the staff look like plastic imitation Barbie dolls and the people in the waiting room are over-treated, then walk out. Secondly, be aware of upselling. After all, you're not buying a pair of shoes, so buy one get one free isn't a good thing. It's a warning sign that maybe their treatments are not up to standard. Thirdly, look for the certificates on the wall. Medical qualifications and insurance documents should be well displayed."

"Helpful tips, David," Hazel said. "We have a few questions from the studio audience, and then I believe you're going to give us a demonstration."

"That's correct, we have a willing victim," McGregor laughed. "Unless you need a top up." He winked at the camera, leaving everyone with little doubt about Hazel's use of the anti-aging treatment.

"As you well know, David," Hazel said, wiping her hand across her smooth brow, "I had my treatment last week."

The camera zoomed in close on Hazel's face. She wiggled her eyebrows, causing absolutely no movement on her forehead. She giggled girlishly, and the audience laughed.

"Okay, our first question is from Mel of Hartlepool. Where are you, Mel?"

The camera swung round to Mel, who stood up and asked her question. McGregor had been notified of the questions and had answers already prepared. The segment in conversation with the audience passed quickly. Did it hurt? How long before you could see results? What happened if like some celebrities you ended up with a wonky eyebrow? How much did it cost?

McGregor answered with his usual charm and wit, making the audience laugh and yet giving them the information they needed to make informed choices. Segments like this made people think cosmetic surgery and procedures were commonplace, everyday things, like getting your hair cut or having your nails done. This was important, an attitude change cosmetic surgeons were working towards. Because as soon as a treatment became a beauty treatment, people stopped asking questions about survival rates and risks and started asking when and how often. McGregor was a hero to the entire profession. Even competitors like Patrick Sharp benefited from McGregor normalising cosmetic surgery to the average person. The danger was if you removed the elitism of the treatment, you removed the elitism of the practitioner. So instead of qualified surgeons raking in the money, you had upstart nurses thinking they could wield a syringe, then dentists and beauty therapists. As much as the industry needed plastic surgery to be for the masses, the godlike surgeons needed to retain control of the cash cow.

"We have time for one last question," Hazel said. "Janie from Kent, what's your question for David?"

Janie stood up and set her face in a stony glare. "Botox is a controlled substance. Why then are doctors prescribing Botox for patients they haven't seen?"

McGregor blinked. This wasn't one of the questions he'd been expecting. The government, with pressure from FOBPS, had deemed Botox a controlled substance to be prescribed by a doctor. While this was supposed to shut down non-practicing medical professionals carrying out Botox treatments, it had, in fact, just provided unscrupulous doctors with a means to quick cash. It was a known fact some doctors were charging twenty pounds to sign prescriptions for patients they had never met. McGregor knew of several doctors who had quit practicing medicine, instead staying at home to sign hundreds of scripts a day for Botox clinics all over the country.

"Well," McGregor said, collecting his thoughts, "I've heard rumours of this happening. Botox is a controlled substance, and it is important a patient is seen by a doctor before having a treatment. This helps to avoid side effects." McGregor mentally kicked himself for using the word patient. "In some rare cases, Botox is contraindicated. Only doctors can prescribe Botox, if you don't see a doctor before your treatment, the chances are that this Botox has been obtained unscrupulously. Either on a prescription for someone else or possibly as an illegal import. While I know of no doctor breaking FOBPS recommendations on this matter, it doesn't mean it doesn't happen. I can only reiterate my previous statement. Make sure you use a reputable clinic. If in doubt, find a different practitioner."

"Great advice," Hazel smiled into the camera. "You need to make sure you have trust in the person holding the needle."

Janie looked like she was going to challenge McGregor's assertion that prescription fraud was limited to a few rogue doctors, but the camera had moved, and she could do little more than sit down. Hazel filled the silence with a few inane comments before moving on to the next segment, a pre-filmed competition.

McGregor pulled the earpiece out and threw it on the floor. "What the fuck?" he demanded to the worried director. "The questions are supposed to be pre-screened. Can you imagine the phone calls I'm going to get this afternoon?"

"It's live television," Barry said with a shrug of his shoulders.

"You handled the question very well," Hazel added, putting her hand on McGregor's thigh

"Fuck off, bitch," McGregor spat, not yet having forgiven her for the taunt about the make-up girl.

"Mr McGregor," Barry warned. "The audience."

McGregor balled his fingers into a fist and considered punching the fucker in the face, but a glance over Barry's shoulder showed him the audience was watching every movement. With the mics turned off, they couldn't hear anything, but it was obvious to anyone with eyes that a confrontation was occurring.

"Let's set up for the make-over segment," Barry suggested. "We've two minutes before dead air."

McGregor snarled and stormed away. Hazel's interest was piqued. As a presenter, she had very little interest in investigative journalism, but a big story would help her break into the American market. They liked their presenters to be both brains and beauty. To be able to validate their skills on camera with their research off camera.

She walked over to her assistant Laura. "Find out all you can about our thorn, Janie. In fact, invite her for an after show meet and greet."

Chapter 24 – An audience

The alarm clock buzzed waking him from a pleasant dream about Lady Elizabeth, the droning noise getting louder and louder until Robert hit the snooze button. He rolled over thinking nine more minutes of sleep would be an incredible luxury, but as he turned, his whole body spasmed. Pain exploded in his legs, agonising throbbing cramps erupting in both calves simultaneously. Robert sat bolt upright or attempted to. His arms wouldn't work. He tried to remember what he'd taken last night but couldn't. He panicked, his heart beating faster as he tried to breathe. He laid still and waited for the fear to subside. When it did, he flexed his feet and reached down gingerly to massage the back of his legs. The pain eased, and he was able to sit up. On the floor next to his bed was a heap of sweaty gym clothing and a book on nutrition. He'd fallen asleep reading up on the best foods to eat to lose weight quickly. The pain was not from some concoction of Will's but from his own stupidity. He was a doctor. He understood the human body and what exercise would do to his flabby frame. Yet inspired by a pair of slim legs and a beautiful face, he'd ignored common sense and pushed his body beyond its limits.

Robert hobbled to the shower, each step burning agony. He needed Will's advice before he killed himself.

"What the fuck have you done?" Will asked as Robert gingerly limped into the clinic.

"Exercise."

Will's laughter brought Fitzroy out of his office and Kate from behind reception.

"Great, just what I need, an audience," Robert groaned as his three colleagues watched his slow shuffling progress across the reception.

Fitzroy shook his head and went to the

218

medication room, returning with a bottle of oxycodone. He threw the bottle of white capsules at Robert, turned and sauntered away. Kate more kindly fetched him a glass of water, and Robert swallowed two of the tablets.

"You need some help?" Will asked.

"Nah, I can manage," Robert replied, limping away.

"I meant with an exercise plan that will have you in shape rather than dead in the ground."

Robert halted his shambling progress and turned to look at Will. He nodded then grimaced, as even nodding caused pain in his shoulders.

"Lunch time," Will announced.

Robert groaned.

"Those pills will kick in soon," Kate sympathised. "Go sit in the staff room, and I'll fetch you a coffee. You don't have any appointments until ten."

Kate and Fitzroy were right. The pills took away every bit of pain, and Robert bounced through his morning consultations. He spoke a little too fast and enthused a little too much with his compliments on the client's clothing, choice of surgery or photographs of their children. But as the clients agreed to the exorbitant prices he quoted, and McGregor wasn't around to notice, no one commented on Robert's hyperactive frenzy. At one o'clock, Will threw a small black bag at Robert, inside were a pair of shorts and a vest top.

"Kate nipped out while you were in consultation and picked you up some trainers," Will informed him. "They're in a box behind reception. Go grab them, and we'll head to the gym for an hour."

"What about McGregor?"

"He has a consultation with a celebrity. He'll be at least another hour. We'll be back before he's finished."

"Best if you go out the back," Kate said from behind the reception desk. "The paps are camped outside already."

"How do they know who's here?" Robert asked, looking over the reception desk at the computer screen. The space in McGregor's column read Miss H.

"Her publicist," Kate said in a tone clearly expressing her disapproval, and maybe envy.

Robert shrugged and followed Will out of the back of the clinic. He could never understand a person's need for fame. Money yes, but fame came with inconvenience. McGregor was a fame whore. He craved the limelight and required attention to validate his achievements. Robert's uncle, Patrick Sharp, on the other hand, shunned the attention, preferring to operate in the shadows. Robert had once asked him why. His uncle's answer had confused and troubled him. He had answered with one word, control. Robert knew his uncle's family had some involvement with the troubles in Ireland and that Patrick's father had been killed in some insignificant IRA action. But Patrick Sharp was the poster child for English capitalism, a true Thatcherite. Robert couldn't understand why Uncle Patrick would ever feel controlled as he made thousands of pounds each day. The working class boy had attended university with the grants provided by the system he had been raised to despise, by a father who fought against everything his son now stood for. Robert's Aunt Carole had met Patrick in London, but the details were a little sketchy. Her marriage had ended any career aspirations she might have held, and Robert had been brought up hearing about his sly Aunt Carole, who had moved to London to snag a rich husband.

Robert's mother had remained in Leeds and married an electrician. Her life had been difficult. Coping with a lack of money and a son who never quite fit into his father's world of skilled labour. Robert's childhood hadn't been unhappy, but it hadn't been happy, either. Life had sort of happened while Robert stayed in his bedroom and escaped into the world of books. As Robert had grown older, his father became increasingly distant, choosing contracts that kept him away for weeks. A teenage Robert had blamed himself for his father's absence, but as an adult, he'd realised it was his mother's promiscuity that had broken the family apart. When he was eighteen, and just weeks before he moved into Leeds University dorms, his mother had died. A drunk driver had careened into the bus stop where she'd been waiting for the number 29 bus to Halifax. His father had attended the funeral and then run away to Spain with Mrs Evans from three doors down. University was supposed to be his fresh start, a chance to remake himself in the image of popularity. Instead, he retreated into himself. Fictional stories were replaced by textbooks, and his life continued in much the same seclusion as before.

"Robbie!" Will shouted.

"Uhhh?"

"Come on, mate, we've only an hour to get to the gym and back."

Robert roused himself from his contemplation of the past. It didn't matter how many nights he'd stayed at home listening to the rowdy noises of his peers as they drank, fucked and generally enjoyed themselves. What mattered was now. Now he was popular, now he had a chance to have a relationship with an heiress, and now for the first time in his life he fit in.

The ultra-shiny, hi-tech gym intimidated Robert, but having Will at his side boosted his confidence, and he strode purposefully towards the reception desk.

"Hey, Jemi," Will greeted the young black lad behind the counter. "How many in today?"

"Three and a half."

"A half?"

"Yeah, she could be good-looking if she tried. The other two are drop dead, just your sort."

Will flexed his muscles and smiled. "Robbie here can have the half. Don't think he could handle a bombshell he hadn't paid for."

Robert blushed, finally understanding their coded conversation.

Jemi came from behind the counter and wrapped his arm around Will's shoulder. "Come on, mate, I'll show you the half."

Jemi pointed to a curvy woman running on the treadmill. Her back was to the three men, but as she jogged, her bottom bounced temptingly. Her mousy brown hair tied back in a ponytail to keep it off her face as she exercised, swayed on her shoulders. Her waist wasn't as slim as it should have been, but even from this angle you could see the full curve of her breasts. The woman was familiar, but Robert couldn't put his finger on from where. Was she a client?

"Fuck," Will gasped.

Hearing his voice, the woman turned. "Will!" Claire exclaimed her eyes dropping to the floor as her neck flushed with embarrassment. Her skin glowed from the exercise, and with her hair tied back in a ponytail, Robert could see the attractive bone structure of her face. The dermal filler he'd injected into her lips had given her a gentle and seductive pout.

"Claire?" Will said, his voice questioning the evidence in front of his eyes.

"I was on my lunch break. I've only taken forty-five minutes, I promise."

Will couldn't speak. His mind couldn't get away from the seductive bounce of her bottom or the curve of her hips in the tight leggings. Had it been that long since he'd seen her naked? He tried to think back. A quickie in the supply cupboard, a blow job after surgery. Even the night she'd stayed at his place, he'd fucked her on the sofa, his hand wandering up her skirt without the seduction of undressing her.

"Claire," he repeated, not sure how he felt about the strange woman standing before him. Claire grabbed her water bottle and towel, hurriedly greeted Robert and fled.

"See what I mean, man?" Jemi said. "Arse to die for, but the face needs work."

Will turned and grabbed hold of Jemi's T-shirt. He pulled the younger man towards him, lifting him off his feet. "You fucking touch her, and I'll…I'll…You don't want to know what I'll do, but you wouldn't wake up."

Jemi put his hands up in surrender and tried to step back. "Hey, man, if she's your sister or something…"

Will frowned, the cold look in his eyes solidifying into hatred. "She's not," he hissed, pushing Jemi away from him. "Robert, weight room."

In the changing room, Claire burst into tears. She looked in the mirror at her red sweaty face. Who was she kidding? The look of revulsion in Will's eyes had told her everything she needed to know. She was a quick fuck, and that was all; a hole to push his dick into when nothing else was available. To him, she was no more than a convenience. The tears rushed down her face in a salty flood of desolation. She'd have to find another job, another life. But a life without Will seemed a cold, heartless place. She'd talk to Fitzroy about getting a reference, and until she found new employment, she'd just have to avoid Will. Claire looked at herself with new clarity. She'd worked so hard in the last three months, and finally her efforts were beginning to have an effect. Her stomach no longer had the overhanging muffin top, and while she'd never be slim, her figure had taken on a curvy shape rather than the usual potato bulge. She had cheekbones for the first time since her teens, and the filler Robert had injected into her lips made her feel almost attractive. But her daydream was over. There would be no happy ever after for her. Life wasn't fair, and the sooner she accepted that fact, the happier she'd be.

Robert's body ached worse than it had that morning. Will pushed him beyond his limits, his rage at seeing Claire taken out on Robert's flabby body.

"Ten more reps," Will growled as Robert sat up, gasping for air.

"I can't."

"If you want to look like me, you'll do ten more reps."

Robert looked at Will's toned body, the perspiration glistening on his skin while rivers of sweat pooled around Robert's crotch and underarms. Will's breathing was strained but even, while Robert gasped for air to cool his burning lungs.

"I can't."

Will looked at Robert with contempt. "No motivation," he spat, turning away from the exhausted surgeon and returning to his own pull-ups.

Will knew he wasn't angry with Robert but with himself. His reaction to Claire had been inexplicable. What was she, after all, but a quick fuck at lunch time? He'd pushed Robert until he collapsed when the real direction of his fury was his own body. His arms burned with exhaustion as he used the last reserves of his strength. Will's left arm gave way first, his fingers losing their ability to grab hold of the bar. He bent his knees and landed almost gracefully on the padded matting. What was it about Claire that had gotten him so wound up?

"Hit the shower," he said, barely looking at the collapsed Robert. "What we need is a night at Bankers."

Robert struggled to sit up. A hot shower sounded fantastic, but the last thing he needed was a night at the notorious sex club. What he needed was an early night and three more oxycodone.

"Maybe?" he said, but Will was too far ahead to hear.

"What have you two done to Claire?" Dylees

shouted as Robert and Will returned to the clinic. "I'm supposed to be liaising with the Five Spokes PR company to get the band into the clinic without the press finding out. Instead, I'm cleaning up your mess."

Will and Robert looked at their shoes.

"I will not ask you again. What have you done to Claire?"

Robert fidgeted. "Nothing. She was at the gym, that's all."

"And?"

"And Will might have reacted badly."

"Should I go and apologise?" Will asked, not able to meet Dylees' disappointed glare.

"No, she's with Kate. You can cover reception and leave the poor girl alone. Permanently," Dylees barked, turning on her heels and storming off.

Robert had an urge to laugh but resisted on account of Will's clenched fists and troubled expression.

"I think I'll go and check on my list," Robert mumbled lamely as he rushed away from the enraged anaesthetist.

Chapter 25 – Cut a few lumps off

"Mr Costa," Patrick said nervously, the words tumbling out of his mouth.

"Mr Sharp. A car pick you up in fifteen minutes."

"I'm not at home."

"We know, Mr Sharp. Jerry be with you shortly."

The phone went dead. Patrick briefly considered running, but where would he run to? He contemplated walking back up the steps of Wellington's and stabbing Sir James in the chest or hiding out in the lavatory. Instead, he slumped onto the kerb, his face in his hands, his knees up to his chest. There was nothing he could do other than accept the inevitable. Patrick Sharp had fucked up royally. The man who had made everything had lost everything in one bastard moment. There was nothing he could do other than wait and hope Costa was in a rush to finish him. Images of headless corpses floating in the Thames flashed through his mind. Smashed knee caps, broken fingers, toenails pulled from screaming victims. It was rumoured Costa had a private torture chamber complete with an ECT. Ten thousand volts of electricity flooding the human body until every muscle snapped and the heart stopped.

"Mr Sharp. If you wouldn't mind," Jerry said, holding the passenger door of the Town Car open. "Mr Costa is waiting for you at his St James' apartment."

Patrick tried to stand, but his legs wouldn't hold his weight. He crashed back onto the kerb, his heart beating so quickly in his chest he was sure Jerry could hear the hammering fear. In the end, Jerry lifted him to his feet and helped the shaken man into the car.

"Have a whisky," Jerry said sympathetically.

This wasn't the first time Jerry had driven some unlucky punter to Mr Costa's penthouse apartment. Occasionally, he was called to take them home or to the hospital for treatment, but more often than not, this car journey was the last time anyone saw them alive. Jerry breathed a sigh of relief. So far Costa had never called for him to dispose of a body. He wasn't high enough in the ranks of Trae La Muerte to be trusted with corpse removal, and he intended for it to stay that way. Jerry liked the fat surgeon. He was a proper gentleman. He'd been nice to Layla and even tipped Jerry on occasions when he'd been lucky at the boxing. It was a real shame he'd lost favour with Mr Costa. Jerry grimaced. How would he break the news to Layla? She had a very soft spot for Mr Sharp.

Patrick sat in the back of the car, his face dripping with sweat, his shirt stuck to the leather seat. He'd spilt half of the expensive whisky down his front. His whole body trembled with fear as he thought about the torture that awaited him in the luxury apartment. What would his IRA dad think about Paddy, the coward? The thought straightened his backbone a little. Whatever happened, he'd face it as a true Irish man. Patrick wiped away the tears and mucus with the back of his hand and poured himself another whisky. He tipped the glass to his lips and downed the alcohol. The shaking eased slightly, so he touched the bottle to his mouth and drank. The liquid ran down his throat and chin in equal measure, drenching the fabric of his shirt as he descended into the dizzying haze of inebriation. Whatever fate Patrick faced, facing it drunk would be easier.

"Mr Sharp," Costa said as the fat surgeon was hauled by two of Costa's bodyguards into the lounge of the exclusive apartment. "You seem to be little worse for wear."

The two men half-dragged, half-carried Patrick to the chair Costa indicated and unceremoniously let go. Patrick fell to his knees on the plastic sheeting laid out on the hardwood floor. He remained knelt as the implications of the sheet sunk into his drunken mind. Patrick tried to keep his eyes open and look at the man who held his life hostage, but the slackness of his muscles made focusing impossible.

"I called as soon as I knew," he slurred.

"And that was considerate of you," Costa said, his voice scarily even. "However, you appreciate intent has very little effect on losses. Help him to the chair."

"I tried," Patrick blurted while one of the thugs lifted him onto the orange plastic chair.

"Again, while very honourable, I still lose money." Costa smiled.

Patrick broke down. Tears poured from him uncontrollably, and he felt sure the wetness in his trousers wasn't sweat.

"Patrick... You don't mind me calling you Patrick, do you?"

Patrick shook his head dejectedly.

"Good, Patrick, then I set your mind at rest. I have way you can work off debt, including the money I lost on Faunaceutical."

Patrick looked up hopefully. He knew whatever Costa suggested would be illegal, probably involving supplying Trae La Muerte with drugs to cut and sell on the streets. But at this moment, he didn't care. He'd agree to anything to get him out of the room with all his body parts still functioning. "Anything."

"I was hoping you take this position." Costa's chilling smile made Patrick shudder. Whatever Costa wanted was far worse than knocking off the drugs cabinet.

"I've shipment coming in next week. Let's say, the livestock need neutering."

Patrick looked confused.

"My lady-boys want to be ladies. You make it happen."

"Gender reassignment?"

"Cut a few lumps off, stick a few lumps in. Not much to it really. Just make sure they beautiful and ready to work in a month."

"I'm not…" Patrick started to object.

"Well, that is shame," Costa growled. "It only way for you to pay your debts. I guess we have to use traditional methods of extraction. Thank you for time, Mr Sharp." Costa turned to the two thugs. "Please show Mr Sharp to car."

"I'm not able to have them ready to work in a month," Patrick blurted. "It takes at least six weeks for a vagina to heal."

Costa gestured for the thugs to step back. "Are they able to walk?"

Patrick nodded.

"They can give blow jobs and anal until they fixed," he shrugged. "I am so pleased we see eye to eye on this matter. Jerry will take you home, and I will be in touch as soon as shipment arrived. I suggest hot bath," Costa said, wrinkling his nose. "Fucking cunt," he added as the door closed behind Patrick. "I have no respect for worms. No backbone, these Irish bastards."

Danny Rossin, the sopla, had called the moment he'd heard the Faunaceutical deal had fallen through. Costa had been able to sell while the market was unaware of the termination of negotiations. Trae La Muerte had made a nonfatal killing, but he wasn't about to let Sharp know. The fearful surgeon would provide unlimited free plastic surgery for Costa's newest acquisitions.

Jerry asked Mr Green to repeat himself twice before he believed he was being asked to pick up Mr Sharp and not his corpse. Jerry had been sure Patrick Sharp's journey was one way and that the surgeon would be leaving Costa's apartment in a suitcase. Yet as he pulled up outside the Royal Chambers in Jermyn Street, there was Patrick, slumped against the lamp post. Jerry lifted the semi-conscious man into the car. He had instructions to take Mr Sharp back to the Wellington Club, but he knew the man was incapable of driving home.

Jerry pressed a few buttons on his mobile phone. "Layla," he said when she answered. "You fancy a bit of off the books work?"

"Depends," she said cautiously. "How much trouble am I to get into?"

"None, as long as we don't mention anything. Think of it as charitable volunteering."

Jerry quickly filled Layla in on what he knew and the state of the man in the back of his car.

"Pick me up," Layla replied and hung up the phone.

Patrick woke up naked and disoriented in a soft bed. Why was he not floating in the Thames? What had he agreed to? Slowly, the room stopped spinning. The white ceiling coalesced from fog into a solid, then the haze receded into walls and furniture. A large dresser and wardrobe seemed oddly familiar. Panic reasserted itself as he looked at the well-known clock on the recognisable bedside table. His hands bunching the expected high-count cotton sheets in crisp white.

"You're awake," said a voice that didn't belong in his home. "Jerry thought you not wake up at all. We nearly called for ambulance, but we didn't want you to have questions."

"Layla," Patrick croaked as he tried to force himself upright. She shouldn't be here, couldn't be here. His wife could be home at any minute, and here he was naked in a dishevelled bed with a prostitute. Divorce would be the easiest thing he'd suffer if Carole found Layla ensconced in their home.

"You have to go."

Layla looked hurt.

"My wife," he explained.

She smiled and relaxed. "Your wife not here. She left message on answerphone. Says she listened to your voicemail and had no idea what you ramble about. But she stays at Casandra's."

Patrick slumped back onto the damp bedding.

"It time you have bath," Layla said, holding her nose to emphasise her point. "You out of woods now. Time to not smell of shit."

She walked over to the bed with the confidence of someone who belonged in the spacious house and not the jealous interloper. As she manhandled him towards the bathroom, her strength surprised him. When he stumbled, she sat him on the toilet and undressed.

"We have shower together. I will wash you, but no funny business." She winked and Patrick felt his lip twitch into an involuntary smile. The last thing on his mind was funny business.

Layla ran her hands over a small bump on her usually flat stomach and hoped Patrick didn't notice the weight gain. She didn't understand it. All the vomiting and loss of appetite, and still she was putting on weight. She knew what happened to fat whores. They were pimped out on the streets, expected to get into the cars of punters and turn tricks for cash payments. She looked at herself in the full-length mirror of Patrick's bathroom and bit her lip in frustration. Her skin looked grey rather than rich tan. She must go to the gym more and eat healthily, get more sleep and try to take care of herself. The late nights and heavy drinking had taken their toll on her body, and the constant requirement to satisfy the needs of others had left her feeling weary and tarnished. She looked at the beautiful furniture and expensive ornaments, the posed picture of Patrick and his wife in the bedroom. The oversized bath and jet-powered shower must have cost more than she had been able to send to her sister in the last three years. How could one person have so much and another have so little? She resented the absentee Mrs Sharp, the poised woman who had everything and yet didn't appreciate any of it. She knew Patrick was no saint. He regularly drank too much, paid for whores and gambled, yet he also provided a home and a life free from worry. Maybe if Mrs Sharp were a better wife, Patrick wouldn't have strayed. Layla had never asked Patrick about his family, never wondered if he had children. But as she'd wandered around his luxurious house while he'd slept, she'd realised his house wasn't a home. The large framed pictures were contrived. Personal clutter had been replaced by stylish interior design to an issued brief. No sign of children's paintings on the kitchen fridge or desktop photographs of graduation. The building cried out for someone to love it, and Layla felt the same was true of Patrick Sharp. What the man in front of her really wanted and needed was for someone to take care of him, to support him and make him happy. Layla knew if given the chance, she would have grab hold and never let go. She looked in the large bathroom mirror at her abused body, resenting the woman she'd never met but whose life she envied. Fighting back the tears, she'd turned her back on the spent whore and faced the broken man she wished to fix.

Patrick looked at Layla through bloodshot eyes. She had never looked so radiant. Her body was fuller, and she glowed like an angel as she helped him into the shower. Gently, she massaged his body, washing away the sweat and fear with cleansing soap. Slowly, she brushed back his hair with soft fingers. And when he began to cry, she held him close, her damp skin pressed against his until the shaking subsided. When he was with her, things made sense. The worry of money and prestige, the trappings of London life didn't matter. He could see a simpler life as his mother had lived. A two-up, two-down terrace on an estate in Derry, living hand to mouth, week to week. Never able to save, but always a unit of solidarity, facing the hardship of life together as a family. Patrick had achieved so much more than his father, or had he? No children, no legacy other than NuYu and a wardrobe stocked with the designer shoes and clothes of his wife. What would the world remember about Patrick Sharp if

Costa killed him? Who would miss him if he disappeared? Carole? Patrick came to the stark realisation that the woman who had loved him over three decades ago had gone. The woman he was living with now had no time to share with her tainted husband. They shared a bed, but they didn't share a life. He thought earnestly about the last time they had socialised together, the last time they had shared a meaningful conversation, a kiss or even a meal. Layla gently kissed the top of his head, pressing his face into the warmth of her chest. This gesture of loving care came from a woman he'd bought and paid for. A woman who by all rights should hate him, and yet here she was showing compassion in his darkest hour. Patrick pulled away from her and swallowed his self-pity. Firmly, he held her by the shoulders and looked into her eyes. Her look conveyed trust and friendship.

"Layla," he said the word torn from his dry throat. "Layla, I am a useless man. I am selfish and arrogant." Layla started to disagree, but Patrick silenced her. "Let me finish," he pleaded. "I'm not sure what will happen to me. I've made bad choices, and for that I have to face the consequences. But I remember what you told me. You had no choices. I promised to help and I didn't." Patrick shook his head. "I have not been the man I should have been. You've shown more compassion and courage just by being here than I have in my entire life. I offered to help your sister, and I want to honour that promise."

Tears streamed down Layla's face as she looked at him. These weren't words of false hope, but a genuine pledge of help, that would make a difference.

"Have you an account you send money to?"

Layla nodded.

"Give it to me, and I will make sure £10,000 is transferred into it."

"That's…," Layla choked, the tears blocking her throat and preventing her from speaking. Instead, she leant forward and kissed him, not a deep sensual kiss of erotic passions, but a gentle, affectionate kiss of love. The tenderness shocked both of them, stirring emotions they had thought impossible. "The water is turned cold," Layla stammered, taking a step backwards.

"We better get dried," Patrick agreed. Both knew it was an excuse to put a little distance between them while they worked out the newness of these strange feelings.

Chapter 26 – Always a pleasure

"Would you like me to have your driver bring the car around the back?" McGregor asked the beautiful woman looking in the mirror.

"How kind, David," she replied, her New York drawl lengthening the short sentence. The slim woman brushed back the stray strand of strawberry blonde hair that had escaped the elaborate style. "But you know these vultures. They'll be waiting at the back door as well."

McGregor knew that wasn't true. Miss Hallie Robinson wanted her photograph taken and splashed across the front pages of the tabloids. Her movie premiered at the end of the week, and nothing brought out the photographers like a speculative plastic surgery story. Experts would be paid extortionate amounts of money to compare photographs from last week to those of her on the red carpet. McGregor enjoyed reading the gossip columnists guesswork. Does her nose look a little different? Are her boobs larger? Hallie Robinson pushed large, dark sunglasses onto her heart-shaped face and reapplied her pink lipstick.

"You look beautiful," McGregor said, kissing her on the cheek. "We'll schedule the lipo for next month, plenty of time to heal before filming starts."

At five foot eight and in high heels, her pale blue eyes were level with McGregor's as she looked at him over the oversized glasses. "Thank you, David," she lingered on his name before leaning in to air kiss his cheek and give him a full view of her round breasts and slim waist. The seductive effect was slightly reduced as he was the surgeon who had lifted and augmented her tits twelve months ago.

"Always a pleasure, Hallie."

He opened the door to the consultation suite and escorted her to reception. He glanced in the large mirror over the white table to check his hair and make-up before opening the front door. The flash of cameras was momentarily blinding. But Hallie, the consummate expert, twisted her hips to show off her sensual figure in a tight pink dress and feigned an expression of shocked annoyance at this gross invasion of privacy. McGregor stood behind her, his stiff back displaying protective masculinity.

"Miss Robinson would like to get to her car if you could please step back," McGregor said, holding his hand out in front of Hallie as if to block the cameras.

"Miss Robinson, what did you have done?" a voice shouted from the left.

"Hallie, over here," another photographer shouted.

"Hallie, are you in a relationship with your co-star Callum Edwards?"

Hallie looked over to the questioner and smiled. "I'm sure you understand my relationships are a private matter. Now I'll pose for a few photographs, but then really you must move on. Mr McGregor has a business to run, and I'm sure you are interfering with his other clients." Her voice oozed sensuality, and it was easy to see why she was such a success in Hollywood.

"So you're a client?"

David stepped in. "Miss Robinson and I have been friends for many years. I cannot comment any further." He raised his eyebrow slightly implying a not so platonic definition of their friendship to the gathered press. Flashbulbs exploded. To enhance the charade, McGregor kissed Hallie goodbye and waved her driver to take his place as bodyguard.

"Goodbye, David," Hallie breathed huskily, fluttering her long fake eyelashes. If the cheeky sod was going to get some free publicity from her, she'd augment the rumours with a little flirting. A love triangle with her in the centre would fill column inches and sell tickets to her new critically acclaimed film.

David turned back into the clinic, smiling to himself. He should have known better than to try and get one over on the savvy Hallie Robinson. Still, she'd played along, and the rumour would not only add to his reputation but provide free marketing for The Fitzroy Clinic and piss off Witch-Hazel. He'd teach the bitch to fuck without permission.

"Dylees," he called as he headed back to his office, "where's Will and Sutherland?"

Dylees stuck her head around his door. "Gym."

"Arseholes," McGregor snapped.

He'd decided to take a late lunch and had elected to give his underlings the benefit of his esteemed company. He briefly thought about taking the witch to lunch. She should be finished at the studio by now. But he dismissed the idea. She hadn't stewed enough just yet.

"Fitzroy?"

"Not arrived yet. He has Lady Elizabeth booked in this afternoon so should be rolling in soon."

"Call the fucker and send a car."

Dylees acknowledged his request.

"I'm off to Beckwoods for a steak. Do you want anything fetching back?"

"Can you bring me a dessert, please?" Dylees replied. "Whatever is on the specials board."

McGregor nodded. "Phone ahead and tell them I'm coming. Call me when my consultation arrives, but get Sutherland to start without me."

"Mr McGregor, your table is waiting," the maître d' said, showing McGregor to a table. "Miss Dylees asked us to open a bottle of 74 Domaines Barons de Rothschild for you."

"Did she ask you anything else?"

"She asked we remind you about dessert."

McGregor laughed as the maître d' poured him a glass of red. The viscous liquid coated the crystal glass as he swirled the blood-red wine. The vibrant smell of grapes roused his need for a rare fillet steak and a quick fuck. A waitress arrived to take his order, giggling appreciatively at his compliments making her tits wiggle deliciously. Maybe she'd be able to satisfy both his needs? She lingered at his table until the maître d' coughed discreetly.

McGregor smiled at her departing back. Her bottom jiggled pleasantly, and while she wasn't a stunning beauty, she had those homely looks that made a girl eager to please a more attractive suitor. A quick fuck in the back alley would be the perfect accompaniment to his steak. The thought filled him with warm feelings of expectation, and by the time the girl fetched the rare fillet, his dick was hard and ready for action. McGregor pushed his chair back slightly, and the girl noticed the bulge in his suit. He smiled as she blushed.

"I was thinking about you," McGregor said.

"Were you?" she giggled, not able to take her brown eyes away from his crotch.

"What do you recommend for dessert?"

"The crème brulee is very nice, sir."

"I was thinking of something a bit more salty and moist."

The redness spread from the girl's cheeks to her neck, colouring her breasts with a rosy glow.

"Do you think you have anything that could satisfy me?"

The girl nodded, biting her lip.

"Do you have a break coming?"

She nodded again. "In a quarter of an hour, sir."

"I better eat this quickly, and then I can eat you."

The girl practically quivered at the thought. The maître d' coughed again and started to walk over to the table. McGregor leant forward, covering his erection with the tablecloth, and picked up his knife and fork.

"Is everything to your satisfaction, sir?"

"Very much so. Your girl here was just explaining

the dessert options. Can I have five crème brulees to take away? My staff would strike if I forgot to take them a dessert."

"And for you, sir?"

"I don't have a sweet tooth. I prefer my desserts a little more savoury."

The steak tasted even better with the promise of a quick shag. The bloody juices soaked into the mashed sweet potato and slid down his throat with delicious, full-bodied flavour. He finished the bottle of wine, swirling the contents of his glass around to appreciate the last of the opulent, fruity aroma. The girl brought an elegant paper bag to the table with his bill.

"Your desserts, sir," she said, opening the bag so he could see five small boxed desserts and a pair of black silky knickers.

McGregor placed five fifty pound notes on the table and whispered, "Behind the restaurant?" He raised his voice, "Keep the change."

It took only moments for McGregor to be on his knees, the girl's skirt pushed up around her waist and his tongue deep inside her wet pussy. Unlike the witch, this girl had a thick bush of dark blonde curly hair. The sight turned him on, and his fingers reached up to tug on the damp pubes near her clitoris. The girl gasped in pleasure, her fingers clawing at his shoulders. McGregor had intended to force her to her knees and cum in her mouth, but her naive excitement was infectious. He pushed his fingers inside and found resistance. A thin layer of skin blocked his path. The girl tensed slightly but didn't push him away. McGregor stopped for a moment as realisation dawned.

"Don't stop," she begged, her legs shaking with desire. "I want this."

McGregor pushed a little harder but didn't break her hymen. This was a delicious pleasure he was going to

239

savour. Slowly, he removed his fingers and stood up. He placed his lips against hers and kissed her, his tongue pushing deep inside her mouth so she could taste her own wetness. She responded, clinging to him, her breath ragged with desire. McGregor unzipped his trousers, pulling out his firm penis. The girl reached down with hesitant, inexperienced hands, her fingers touching him with fumbling innocence. McGregor endured her grope for a moment before pinning her hands behind her back and pushing himself inside her. She tensed as his dick pushed against her hymen and bit her lip as he slowly, almost tenderly, pushed through to claim her virginity. McGregor growled as she relaxed against him. The tightness of her pussy was a pleasure worth savouring, but the flood of blood over the tip of his penis pushed him beyond sanity and into a raw animalistic need to rut. His hips tilted as he pushed deeper and deeper. His grip on her wrists tightened, his teeth biting into her neck as if she was a bitch in heat. He heard her scream, but it was a distant sound, only just penetrating his own ecstasy as he came. It was moments before he realised she was clinging to him, feathering gentle kisses on his neck. He pulled out and straightened his clothing before kissing her again.

"Thank you," she said, pulling down her skirt and straightening her blouse.

The simple statement surprised McGregor. Sex to him was about his pleasure, not another's, and yet this girl had thanked him for tearing away her virginity in a dirty back alley. He hadn't stopped to think about her needs or the morals of being her first. He had encountered the thin layer of skin and immediately wanted to discover the tightness of what lay beyond. The macho attitude of discovery, the animalistic pleasure of being alpha. McGregor felt something. Not shame or regret because he wasn't capable of those emotions, but something. Perhaps a twinge of remorse at not being a better person.

"Will I see you again?" the girl asked.

"No."

"I didn't think so," she replied, kissing him softly on the cheek.

She wasn't judging him for his lack of integrity but quietly accepting it. She turned and walked away, leaving McGregor stunned at her low expectations of his character. His phone rang, an operatic melody jolting him from the self-indulgent wallowing.

"McGregor?"

"Who else would be answering my phone," he barked.

"Don't get snotty with me, David," Dylees snapped.

"Sorry."

Dylees paused, taken aback by the simple apology. "Your client is here. She's filling in paperwork with Robert."

"Thank you," he replied, hanging up.

There was a hum of quiet chatter in the waiting room. Clients sat on the comfortable chairs flicked absently through magazines while speculating in hushed voices on what procedures Hallie Robinson had elected. The photographs of her and McGregor were already trending across the internet, and the gossip had started. McGregor strode into the waiting room, all conversations stopped. McGregor basked in the warm glow of admiration, forgetting all about the young virgin he'd seduced in a dirty alley. He strutted over to the reception desk and leant over to Kate, knowing the view of his backside in the tight black trousers was sure to make a lasting impression on the ladies.

"Can you get me a coffee?" he whispered.

Kate looked confused and then glanced over McGregor's shoulder, she shrugged at the absolute devotion on the faces of the waiting clients. If they knew what a man-whore McGregor was, would they still be lining up to have a piece of him? Probably. McGregor turned and smiled at his devotees and without a word headed for his office to leave them to gossip about his muscular frame and brooding eyes. Fitzroy barrelled out of the consultation suite, knocking into McGregor.

"Sorry, old boy, didn't see you there," Fitzroy apologised.

Fitzroy was pissed. His shirt was a crumbled mess with coffee streaks staining the white fabric. Congealed egg clung to the side of his mouth and his breath stank of stale alcohol. "Is Lady Liz here yet?" Fitzroy boomed. "I caught a few winks waiting for her."

"Dylees!" McGregor boomed.

Dylees popped her head around the corner, her arms ladened with towels and bedding. "What?" she yelled back.

"For fuck's sake, get this bastard cleaned up. And make sure Sutherland is with him when he examines Lady Elizabeth. The last thing we need is a judge wanting to screw us. So make sure the old sod doesn't try to screw his daughter."

"Why do I have to be the one?"

"Because you are excellent at bed baths, or so I hear."

"Watch yourself, McGregor," Dylees warned, her eyes narrowing. "I want hazard pay."

"Done, £40 do it?"

"Make it £50."

McGregor nodded. "Your dessert is in the staff room. Crème brulee.

Dylees shrieked like a little girl and ran over to kiss McGregor's cheek. "Thanks, boss," she laughed, emphasising the word boss disrespectfully. "Come on, commander," she said, linking arms with Fitzroy, "let's go give you a wash."

Fitzroy's eyes twinkled. "Only if I get to return the favour."

"In your dreams, old goat. You're so old you've forgotten what to do with it."

"I'll show you what I can do with it," he replied, slapping Dylees' bottom.

Dylees smiled affectionately at the commander in chief.

"Clara," McGregor greeted, opening the door to consultation suite two. "Has Mr Sutherland been looking after you?"

"Quite," Clara gushed, placing her hand on Robert's leg. "He's such a doll."

"Mr Fitzroy needs you in consultation suite three," McGregor ordered, dismissing the junior surgeon with a wave of his hand. "Now Miss Huntington, let's have a look at what we can do to rectify your face."

McGregor looked at the swollen lips and lopsided eyebrow. The eyebrow was easy to fix with a little Botox injected into the frontalis muscle. He gently touched Clara's lips with his gloved hand. The mass under his fingers was hard and plastic. Whatever had been injected into Clara's mouth had not been dermal filler. He consulted her notes.

"Did your surgeon try injecting hyaluronidase?"

Clara nodded. "It hurt and seemed to make the swelling worse."

The information Clara provided didn't add up. The texture of the lips was wrong. Far too much scar tissue. And when he ran his hand over the edge of her lips, he could feel a sharp edge, almost as if the surgeon had used permanent sutures.

"Did the practitioner inject the filler?"

"I don't know. I was under a general anaesthetic."

McGregor's fingers paused in his examination. "Miss Huntington, I think we have a significant problem. I'm almost positive you have not been injected with dermal filler. I have a suspicion you've been given Gore-

Tex implants. Was this procedure carried out in the UK?"

Clara's cheeks flushed with embarrassment.

"I didn't think so. When will you people learn?"

"I didn't want my picture in the tabloids," Clara cried. "I thought if I went away, when I came back to England, I'd just look better."

"Well, that didn't work, did it?" McGregor snapped heartlessly.

Clara burst into tears.

"Dylees," McGregor shouted. "We have a queen."

Dylees opened the door to the consultation suite and glared at McGregor. "What have you done?"

"The silly bitch has Gore-Tex implants in her lips and, I'm the villain."

Dylees put her arm around the sobbing Clara. "It's not as bad as it sounds, Miss Huntington. Mr McGregor here is one of the best surgeons in the country. He'll be able to remove the implant and then fill your lips once the swelling has gone down. The first thing to do is get you an x-ray so we can see what's happening. Isn't that right, Mr McGregor?" Dylees' angry stare bore into him.

"Yes, that's correct. Nothing is unfixable. Dylees will arrange an x-ray and put a little Botox in your eyebrow today to rectify that mistake," he said, already at the door. "I'll see you when the results come back and get you onto my list."

The door slammed shut, and Dylees was left with the tearful page three girl.

"Is it really that bad?"

"It isn't good, but McGregor is amazing. He'll have you smiling in no time," Dylees replied, handing Clara a tissue to dry her eyes.

"I just wanted to be beautiful."

"You are beautiful," Dylees replied, preparing for the Botox injections. In theory, she knew what she was supposed to do, an injection to weaken the muscle and lower the eyebrow.

"That's not what Lord Mowbray said. He told me the only thing that my lips were good for kissing was his dick."

"Maybe it was a compliment and you're just very good at blow jobs?"

Clara sniffed. "I am pretty good at giving head. Lord Mowbray says I'm the best cowgirl to have a ride."

Dylees raised an eyebrow.

"He likes me to wear cowboy boots and a Stetson. I have to pretend he's a stallion and wave my two Smith and Wesson pistols in the air." Clara giggled. "He certainly neighs like a horse when he comes."

"Every time?"

"Yes. He has a bridle in his desk, and he trots around the room while I use a whip to tame the mustang. It's fun most of the time."

"Sounds it," Dylees replied, not sure what else to say.

"He's a very well-endowed man, and when he bends me over his desk and pushes inside me, I just melt. It really is like being mounted by a stallion."

Lady Elizabeth was next door with Fitzroy. Did the judge's daughter know about her father's mistress or his Wild West fetish? What would happen if the two ladies met in the corridor? Dylees' asked Clara to lie back on the paper-covered couch.

"After this, we can get you booked in for an x-ray. If it is Gore-Tex, then we'll need to make an incision and pull out the strips. Hopefully, Mr McGregor will be able to carry out the procedure intra-orally so you won't have a scar. When your lips are healed, we can then inject a little dermal filler to fill out the lips and avoid excessive tissue. Can I ask you a personal question?" Dylees asked as she lifted the eyebrow and injected a little Botox. Clara nodded. "Why stay with Lord Mowbray when you know there isn't any future in it?"

"I love him," she replied quietly. "Before the big

cartel trial, he was kind and wonderful. Even the Wild West thing was fun. All gingham shirts and daisy dukes. I'd put my hair in pigtails, and he'd wear chaps. But the things he has to listen to in court," she paused, not sure what to say. "It's changed him into a darker, angry man," she finished lamely.

Dylees made notes in Clara Huntington's file about the sex games and verbal abuse

McGregor was on the internet when Dylees knocked quietly on his door.

"Has Cuntington left?"

"Yes. I'm concerned, McGregor."

McGregor looked up from his monitor. "So am I."

"I think she might be in over her head with the Judge."

McGregor stared blankly at her. "And?"

"And I'm concerned."

"None of our business what people get up to in their sex life."

Dylees frowned. "So what are you concerned with?"

"This fucking Gore-Tex. I've already persuaded Wake-up to cover the story and Hello to do a before and after spread. If I can't get the implants out, it's going to screw the PR story."

Dylees turned and stormed away.

"What's her problem?" McGregor said to himself and returned to his research on Gore-Tex facial implants.

Chapter 27 – Faulty implants

Patrick Sharp looked at the clock in his empty kitchen. Costa had called Layla with a client booking, and she'd had to leave. Patrick had felt a surge of jealousy as she took the call and then something deeper, a sense of protectiveness that made him want to hold onto her and never let her go. It was stupid. Layla was a whore, she fucked people for money. Yet the feelings she'd awakened wouldn't be suppressed.

"I'll talk to Mr Green," Patrick announced as she was leaving, "I could pay him to let you go back to Bolivia."

"Don't," Layla pleaded her voice just above a whisper. "If he knows I here, he kill me, or worse use me make you do things. He tell Costa and Costa like to beat whores. Please don't draw me attention."

Patrick looked at the kitchen clock again. The hands seemed to have jumped forward, robbing him of the time to censor his thoughts and emotions before facing the clinic. Gwen had telephoned just after Layla had left, her voice a welcome distraction from the anxiety he felt for his life and Layla's. Patrick's strained tone worried Gwen. Patrick might slink off for long boozy lunches or spend too much time gambling, but he was always first in the clinic in the mornings. He liked the quiet peacefulness of walking through the empty hallways, looking into the neat yet welcoming consultation rooms, smelling the cleanness of the surgical suites. Gwen had known his absence was more than him taking a morning off as he claimed. The reluctance in his voice scared her. Something bad was about to happen, and nothing she could do would change the outcome of whatever sequence of events Patrick had started.

"You've clients from one, Patrick," she'd told him, her voice professional and calm even though her pulse was racing. "And Mrs De-Costa's husband has booked a consultation for a business acquaintance at six. I tried to explain we don't take appointments outside of clinic hours, but he said you had cleared it."

"It's fine, Gwen," Patrick had replied, his heart sinking. "I'll be in by twelve thirty."

The grandfather clock in the hallway chimed midday. Patrick closed his eyes and counted slowly to ten. Simultaneously, he opened his eyes and stood up. Without giving himself time to think, he grabbed his keys and left.

Andrew was stood behind the reception desk when Patrick opened the doors.

"Where's Sasha?"

"Having her nails done," Andrew replied, smiling. "Heavy night?"

"Heavy weekend!"

"Gwen's covering your Botox clinic, so I'm the stand-in Sasha." Andrew fluttered his eyelashes and pretended to file his nails. "Do you know how many coffees Gwen's made me make her?"

Patrick smiled despite himself. Andrew's humour was infectious.

"Shall I make you a cup, boss? Looks like you could use one."

Patrick shook his head. "Who's in at one?"

Andrew looked at the paper diary. "Holy shit, Sasha's handwriting is appalling! She should be a doctor." Andrew squinted and turned the page sideways. "Mrs Roberta De-Vargas, she's in for the afternoon. I'll go and grab her file because I can't make out anything else."

Patrick laughed. Sasha's handwriting was shockingly bad, and she regularly made up her own shorthand. A practice Patrick had encouraged. Patient notes were confidential, but appointment books weren't.

Andrew returned with a thin, brown folder containing Roberta Juan De-Vargas' medical records. This

248

was her first treatment at NuYu, although she wasn't new to cosmetic surgery. Patrick flicked through her notes. Tummy tuck, rhinoplasty and breast augmentation in Bolivia. This visit to NuYu was to correct faulty implants. Patrick looked at the photographs he had taken during her consultation. One implant had definitely burst, leaving the left breast lumpy and deformed. The scarring of the right breast was still angry and red twelve months after surgery. Patrick intended to remove both implants, debride the breast tissue from the left and then play it by ear. He had two options, remove tissue from the unaffected breast or use two different sized implants. The first option was the more surgically recommended, but the second would be quicker. It all depended upon the level of silicone seepage.

"Andrew," Patrick said, looking up from the notes. "This isn't straightforward. We'll probably need to keep her under for longer, and there's going to be an extensive amount of cutting."

Andrew thought for a moment. "I'll increase the epinephrine dose and keep a close watch on her stats."

"Can you make sure we've plenty of saline and Gwen is aware of the possible contamination? We'll need to report to FOBPS on this one. The implants will need to be kept for analysis."

"Right you are, boss," Andrew replied. "Sasha should be back in ten."

Patrick focused on the task ahead, clearing all thoughts of Costa, Layla, his wife and the late night appointment. This surgery promised to be challenging. It was always difficult cleaning up another surgeon's mistakes, and unfortunately, it wasn't the first time he had seen faulty implants from abroad. Patrick walked into the surgical suite. He checked the trays of tools, precise cold steel skeletons waiting to be wielded by his skilled hands. He checked the machines that bleeped and buzzed in a language only a proficient anaesthetist could interpret.

"Are you okay?" Gwen asked quietly from the

hallway.

"I am now," Patrick replied, his fingers itching to touch the scalpel. "This room always makes me feel anything is possible." Patrick paused. "Is Mrs De-Vargas here?"

"Yes. Sasha's filling out the consent forms with her, and Andrew is making friends with her security team."

"Team?"

"Three of them. Nasty-looking bunch. Scared Mrs Fox into paying without complaining." Gwen smiled.

"Maybe we should see if we can keep one," Patrick laughed. Mrs Fox never paid without complaining.

"I'd rather have one of the attractive ones Mrs De Costa has. That Luis maybe?"

Patrick felt a cold shiver run down his spine at the mention of Costa's name.

"I was only joking, Patrick," Gwen said as the colour drained from his face.

"I know, Gwen. Long night." Patrick took a steadying breath and looked at the steel instruments again. "Besides, who'd do any work if you and Sasha were mooning over hunky security?"

Patrick briefly greeted Roberta De-Vargas and explained the procedure and the risks before handing her over to the capable Andrew. He scrubbed in, enjoying a moment of peace in the ritual of washing.

"We're ready for you," Andrew said poking his head around the door.

"Right behind you."

Andrew wheeled Roberta De-Vargas into the surgical suite. In her prone position, the imbalance in her breast tissue was acute. The right breast stood like a small hill with the rosy nipple erect in the centre. The left breast flopped underneath her armpit, the bumpy tissue mass creeping down her ribcage.

"Hell!" Andrew exclaimed as Patrick pulled back

the green surgical sheet to reveal the uneven boobs.

Gwen rubbed gauze, saturated with the blue sterilising solution, over the breasts.

"It's worse than I thought. The silicone has seeped lower and under here," Patrick said, running his fingers over the side of her chest.

"Lymph nodes?" Gwen asked.

"I can't tell, but I'm hoping not. The best thing we can do is cut her open and have a look."

Patrick picked up a scalpel and touched it to the underside of the right breast, running his blade along the existing scar before removing the implant. He passed the jellylike sack to Gwen and turned his attention to the left breast while Gwen inspected the implant for damage.

"Patrick," she exclaimed as she moved the implant in her hands, "there's no serial number."

Patrick stopped his incision. "What?"

"There isn't a serial number or maker's mark."

"Is it intact?"

Gwen ran her fingers around the smooth implant, applying pressure to check for damage.

"It doesn't look right, but there is no leakage."

"That's something. Bag and tag it for investigation."

Patrick returned his attention to the left breast. He cut along the underneath of her breast, lengthening the existing incision. Carefully, he removed the half-empty implant and passed it to Gwen.

"I'm going to have to open her up. I can see fuck-all."

Patrick ran his scalpel up to the nipple and around the areola then peeled back the skin to expose the tissue underneath.

"Shit." Andrew gagged as the smell of septic pus filled the room.

"It's fucking industrial silicone," Patrick growled.

"What? How?" Gwen gasped as she looked at the

yellow pus surrounding the globules of cream-coloured industrial silicone.

"We're going to have to debride most if not all, of her breast tissue, pack the area and keep her sedated overnight."

"We aren't registered for in-patients."

"What do you suggest? An NHS Ambulance outside isn't good for business or our health!"

Gwen looked as if she was about to argue. Her mouth opened and closed. In front of her lay the sedated wife of a Bolivian gangster, her chest cut open, and three not very nice bodyguards waited for news of their ward in the staff room. She sighed and reached for the cannula.

"If this goes badly, Patrick Sharp, and I end up answering questions at an inquest or worse, in a Bolivian basement, just remember I objected to this course of action."

"It will not go badly," Patrick answered, taking the cannula and starting to suction the infected areas.

Gwen passed Patrick the scalpel and mopped the sweat from his forehead.

"Light," he said, pointing at the lower part of Mrs De-Vargas' breast. Gwen altered the light, giving an unnerving brightness to the semi-transparent goo that seemed to ooze over the red tissue.

"Suction," Patrick said. "I want this removed as soon as I cut."

Gwen held the suction ready, her arm shaking slightly as she waited for the moment Patrick pulled back his scalpel. Patrick took a deep breath and cut into the healthy tissue surrounding the industrial silicone. Slowly, methodically, he removed all traces of the non-medical grade, illegal substance.

"It's not caught the lymph nodes but it appears some has seeped onto her ribcage."

Gwen winced involuntarily as Patrick scraped his scalpel over the bone. The semi-transparent, silicone stuck to the blade like commercial adhesive. He growled and threw the scalpel in the dish on the table.

"Bastard third world surgeons," he grunted, picking up another scalpel. "They might as well have pumped Unibond sealant into her tits."

Patrick picked up another scalpel and continued scraping at bone and tissue until his back ached and his eyes stung. Taking a last look, Patrick stepped back.

"Have a look," he said, nodding at Gwen.

Gwen carefully inspected the tissue. Four hours had elapsed since they'd started the surgery. By now, they should be suturing the incisions and wheeling the unconscious patient to the recovery room.

"Clear," she confirmed.

"Good," Patrick replied. "Scalpel."

"It's the last one," Gwen warned.

Patrick used the blade to scratch at the remaining muscle tissue until bright red blood flowed, then rinsed the area with saline. With Gwen's assistance, he packed and taped the wounds on both breasts, inserting a drain under each arm.

"Stats?" Patrick asked.

"All good, boss. I can keep her under for another hour or bring her round but keep her groggy," Andrew replied.

"Groggy is fine. We need to keep her calm. She'll need to go under in the morning so we can reconstruct."

Gwen placed a kiss on Patrick's cheek as he left the room. The surgery had been difficult and time-consuming, a less skilled surgeon would have panicked, and his patient would have ended up with a mastectomy and a two-month wait for reconstruction.

Patrick wearily made his way to the staff room.

"Can you please call Mr Vargas and ask him to contact me. Tell him his wife is doing well, but a complication means an overnight stay here rather than Re Vive. I'll explain in person or over the phone, whichever is his preference."

One of the men nodded.

"You're welcome to stay as well, but I'm afraid we are not set up to provide accommodation."

"Here is fine," the man answered, gesturing at the couch in the staff room. "You show me Mrs De-Vargas." He turned to his colleagues and spoke quickly in Quechan.

"Sasha can provide you with bedding and order food for you," Patrick explained, pointing in the direction of the lounge.

The man nodded at Patrick and then with a slight tilt of his head sent one of the men to the front of the building while the other pulled out a phone and dialled.

"Mrs De-Vargas?" the man in front of Patrick demanded.

"She's heavily sedated," Patrick explained as they walked towards the recovery room, now a makeshift ward.

Andrew had efficiently set up the monitors and drips. As they entered he stood over the prone patient, double-checking her vitals. The bodyguard looked over at Mrs De Vargas and Andrew before turning to walk out of the room.

"Chair," he demanded.

"There's one in the room," Patrick replied.

"Chair here," the man said, standing still as a statue in the hallway.

"Are you sure?"

"Sure."

Patrick shrugged his shoulders and fetched a small chair from his office. The man took the chair and sat, looking straight in front of him and ignoring Patrick. Effectively dismissed by the bodyguard, Patrick shrugged again and left with the distinct impression the bodyguard was not so much a protection detail but a prison guard.

"Mr Vargas will speak you."

Patrick jumped. The large man had approached without a sound and now stood with a mobile phone thrust into Patrick's face.

"Thank you," Patrick stammered, his heart pounding in his chest. "Mr Vargas, Patrick Sharp here."

"Mr Sharp," Vargas hissed menacingly.

Something about Vargas' quiet calmness frightened Patrick. The man didn't ask after his wife but instead let the silence draw out between them as an inaudible threat.

"Roberta, I mean Mrs De-Vargas, is doing well. I have just checked on her, and while the complication has made things difficult, I assure you the outcome is positive." Patrick paused, waiting for a response, and when one didn't come continued. "The implants your wife had were substandard. Dangerous is a better description. The implants were not made of medical grade silicone, but industrial grade, similar to what you can buy at a DIY store. When the left implant ruptured, the industrial silicone spread across your wife's ribcage and into the surrounding tissue. We have successfully removed the implant and the infection, but this has meant removing much of her breast." Vargas' sharp intake of breath caused Patrick to falter in his explanation. "I assure you," he stammered, "we can reconstruct the breasts. However, we needed to leave the area packed and open overnight to ensure the antibiotics are working and we have indeed removed all the infected tissue. Your wife's health would suffer if we weren't so cautious."

"The implant?"

"We have sent the implants to FOBPS for investigation. I'm afraid we are obliged to in these circumstances. Any information you can provide about the surgeon would be helpful. He needs to be prosecuted for his misconduct."

"The surgeon of no concern. He will be dealt with."

A cold shiver ran down Patrick's spine as he thought about the ramifications for the Bolivian surgeon and his own possible future if he failed to return Vargas' wife in perfect condition.

"Will you be coming to see Mrs De-Vargas this evening?"

"No."

"Alright, we shall see you in the morning, Mr Vargas."

"No. My men will return her to me when surgery is complete. Have Esteban inform me of progress."

Vargas hung up without saying goodbye, and Patrick handed Esteban the phone.

"Mr Vargas says you are to keep him informed."

The man grunted that he already knew his orders, muttering about piqui, kutana and wanushka under his breath. Patrick shrugged, he didn't understand any of Esteban's comments but got the distinct impression they were probably insulting. He looked at his watch. It was six o'clock. All he really wanted was a bottle of whisky and a couple of pills to take the edge off. Instead, he had the unknown client of Costa's and the imminent possibility of death via two generals of Trae La Muerte to look forward to.

"Patrick," Sasha murmured, "your six o'clock appointment is here. Can I get off home now?"

"Of course, Sasha. Thank you for staying and helping out in these difficult circumstances."

Sasha smiled shyly. "We're a team, Patrick. Besides, I expect a gift card from Serenity."

Patrick laughed, "Mud treatment and caviar facial it is. Take Gwen with you."

Sasha placed a reassuring hand on Patrick's shoulder. "You'll sort it," she said.

Patrick pursed his lips. If only he had Sasha's confidence in his abilities but her loyalty and assertion he could cope helped straighten his shoulders. Patrick pulled on the cuffs of his shirt sleeves and walked towards the lounge area.

Chapter 28 – Never been so outraged

Robert's arms ached. Will had roused, threatened and pushed him passed the point of exhaustion while hardly breaking a sweat.

"Think about the ladies running their fingers over your ripped abs," Will had encouraged when Robert collapsed after twenty C-sit crunches. Robert had tried to think of anything but the pain in his legs and the wobble in his stomach muscles as he worked to follow Will's instructions.

The shower had helped a little, but even after turning the water to almost scalding, the aches still persisted. Now he sat in a consultation suite chair that McGregor must have modified to rub at his delicate back, torturing his arms and legs by forcing him to sit awkwardly straight. The ostentatious man in a tailored grey suit sat in front of him had been talking for the last ten minutes. Robert knew nodding and smiling were only going to move the consultation along so far. He looked at his notes and tried to block out the niggling discomfort.

"Can I take your GP's name?"

"You've already asked me that," the gentleman snapped his pale blue eyes flashing angrily. "When is McGregor going to appear?"

"He should be here any moment, sir," Robert replied. "It's standard procedure for me to get the paperwork out of the way before Mr McGregor carries out your consultation."

"Well, I don't like it," the man said pushing his lips into a pout and smoothing his flawless dark hair. "This is a delicate matter, and I will not discuss it with some underling."

Dylees watched from the linen cupboard as McGregor skulked outside the consultation suite. He was quite a comical figure, bent over with his ear pressed against the door, listening to Robert and the client. He was so engrossed in the conversation he didn't hear Dylees until she was stood next to him.

"What you doing, David?" she whispered, patting him on the shoulder and causing him to jump.

"Waiting for the perfect moment," he replied, yanking open the door and storming into the consultation suite. "Mr Sutherland is not an underling. He will be assisting me in surgery, you cunt."

"You little fucker, I've never been so outraged! I will report you, you overstuffed celebrity whore!" the man yelled, jumping up to face the infuriated McGregor.

"Report me then, you shrivelled twat. Just remember I know where the skeletons are buried."

"Of course, you fucking do. You buried them with me."

The two men stood nose to nose, each puffing out their chests in a ridiculous display of virility. They stared at each other, their eyes narrowed and mouths set. Robert sat open-mouthed, unable to force himself to intervene as he watched the strange confrontation.

Unexpectedly, McGregor's lips twitched into a smile, and the other man's followed suit. The two combatants threw their arms around each other, laughing and slapping each other on the back.

"Collins, how are you? It's been what, five years?"

"That it has, McGregor. The last time I saw you I was married to the redhead."

"So you were. I did her boob job and tummy tuck for you."

"Shouldn't have bothered. The bitch used those tits to land herself a footballer."

McGregor laughed again. "Maybe we should repossess them. You paid for them, after all."

"I'll draw up the papers, and you can be my expert witness. Not really worth the effort. The bitch put me off women for life. I prefer men now." Collins gave McGregor an appraising look.

"I always had a suspicion you were bent."

"Sexually or legally?"

"Both! What you doing here?"

"Getting fucking nowhere with your boy, here."

McGregor frowned at Robert. "What's a bastard like you here for anyway? Didn't think a crook like you put much stock in your looks. Your arse need tweaking?"

"Ah, as subtle as always. You've heard about the Trae La Muerte trial."

McGregor nodded.

"Well, I'm representing Mr Costa himself. I'm going to be a TV celebrity just like you."

"And you're worried your wrinkles will show on camera."

"I need to be ready for my close up, Mr Director." Collins giggled, pouting at McGregor with a suggestive glint in his eyes.

McGregor laughed and grabbed hold of Collins' mouth, pulling him forward and locking lips in a passionate kiss.

Collins pulled away, wiping the back of his hand across his mouth. "You've been practicing," he said, tilting his head as he considered McGregor's bi-willingness.

McGregor sat down, deeming it time to acknowledge Robert's presence.

"Collins, meet Sutherland. He's a promising new surgeon with a few too many morals. Sutherland, meet Collins, an old friend and the best, bent barrister in England."

Robert stood up and shook the man's hand. It seemed the right thing to do, even though, the formalities of introduction had happened half an hour earlier.

"Right. Brass tacks, what can you do to make me look good?"

"Paper bag?" McGregor suggested.

"What for? The cash you're going to give me to bribe the judge at your next indecent exposure hearing?"

"Bag? For the money you charge to mount a defence I'd need to give you a suitcase," McGregor retorted.

The banter continued until it seemed even McGregor had run out of ingenious ways to insult his old friend.

McGregor looked at his watch. "Can you go assist Fitzroy with his examination of Lady Elizabeth?"

Collins raised his perfectly plucked eyebrows at the name while Robert felt his insides turn to jelly at the thought of examining the lovely Lady Elizabeth. Would she remember him from the coffee shop, or would she have forgotten the incident altogether? He had the small bag she'd left behind stashed in his locker, waiting for the moment he could present it to her and win her heart. Well, maybe not, but in his fantasies she would be grateful for the return of her purchase and agree to dinner.

"You know he's the judge in the Bolivian trafficking case," Collins said.

"Who?"

"Lady Lizzy's dad."

"I think I'd heard something about it. Hazel mentioned wanting to cover the proceedings on Wake-up."

Collins looked thoughtful. "You're still fucking Witch-Hazel then?"

"When it suits. She's a dirty whore at heart, and I must say she keeps things entertaining."

"Can you introduce me?"

"You thinking of changing teams again?"

"No, but then the witch has a bigger dick than most men. I believe we could be useful to each other. A few interviews, maybe a bit of leaked information to give my clients an advantageous urban image..." Collins left the sentence hanging. Even Hazel Woods couldn't spin a

Bolivian drug cartel a positive media light. "Cameras aren't allowed in court, but they are allowed on the steps of the courthouse. Certain statements could be put out exclusively now the trial is at the point where they're starting to question Franco Costa."

"It's your head-fuck," McGregor said. "I'll tell her to expect your call. Actually, you've done me a favour. This will get me off the hook for fucking her make-up artist."

"David McGregor!" Collins exclaimed in mock horror.

"James Collins, you wannabe media whore, what can we do to enhance your appearance."

By the end of the consultation, McGregor and Collins had made plans to suck a little of the fat from Collins' middle so he could comfortably wear slim-fit tailored suits during media interviews. They decided against any procedures on the face, barring a few ThreadLifts next week and a touch of Botox which McGregor promptly called Dylees to carry out. "I've had a few at lunch," McGregor explained. "Dylees is amazing with injectables. She'll have you looking ten years younger."

In truth, Dylees needed the practice and McGregor was itching to Google the trial Collins led defence for. If he gave Hazel exclusive insider information, she'd owe him. He'd be able to get more air time and possibly break into the lucrative make-over shows. To date, Hazel had blocked his efforts to move to evening entertainment. The contract he'd signed two years ago prevented him from appearing on rival shows, and Hazel deemed any show she wasn't involved in as rival.

"Hazel," McGregor purred into the telephone. "I'm so sorry we fought this morning."

"So am I," Hazel gushed. "And over a silly little make-up girl. It's not as if she meant anything."

"Maybe we could invite her for dinner?"

McGregor replied.

"Oooh!" Hazel giggled, understanding McGregor's train of thought. "She could be dinner. Shall we invite her to Bankers?"

"Precisely."

"David McGregor, you are incorrigible."

"And you, Hazel Woods, are scandalous. I have another surprise for you." McGregor waited as she begged for the surprise, her voice lowering as she described the devious sexual acts she was planning to reward him with for his gift.

"As delightful as that sounds," he laughed. "This surprise is more professional than personal."

He could almost hear her profuse sulking on the other end of the telephone as he started to explain his encounter with an old friend. However, by the end of the conversation, she was practically wet with excitement.

"He's with Dylees at the moment. I said you'd call when you were free."

"Keep him there. I'll be over as soon as I've finished with the research team. Whatever you do, David McGregor," she shrieked, "don't let him leave until I get there!"

"Relax, I'll bring him to Bankers tonight."

Robert heard Hazel's shriek as he rushed passed McGregor's office on the way to the staff room. Lady Elizabeth's check up hadn't played out the way Robert had hoped. She'd ignored the junior surgeon, lavishing her attention on the red-faced Fitzroy. She'd answered questions in as few words as possible while Robert was examining the sutures and cringed as he'd touched the still tender skin with gentle pressure.

"When will the bruising go?" she had asked Fitzroy.

"It will be a few weeks, my dear. The body needs time to heal."

"But I'm in Haut Monde's charity catwalk show next week, and you know what the press is like. My photograph will be splashed across the front pages, especially with Daddy's drug trial."

"You will have to endure, my dear. Cover up a little."

Lady Elizabeth had laid a gentle hand on Fitzroy's arm. "That would be worse than showing the bruising. Could you imagine the rumours? Pregnant? Drug addict? Beaten by a boyfriend?" She'd paused, "When can I have my nose done?"

"Whenever you like, my dear."

"I'm not sure it is a good idea to have any more surgery until you are fully healed," Robert had interjected.

Lady Elizabeth's head had instantly snapped to the side to look at the northern upstart. "And who do you think you are to challenge a skilled surgeon like Mr Fitzroy?" Her eyes gleaming with anger and distrust.

"I'm not challenging Mr Fitzroy's knowledge or skill," Robert had said tactfully, when he'd wanted to shout, 'I'm challenging his greed, you stupid woman.' "All I meant to say was with your father's current media attention maybe having such drastic surgery is unwise. Won't you be photographed constantly?"

The girl needed counselling or maybe to hear the word no occasionally. Robert strongly suspected body dysmorphia but knew better than to voice his suspicions in front of her. He'd talk to Fitzroy after she'd left and try and reason with the man before Lady Elizabeth ended up deformed.

The check up appointment ended abruptly, and Robert ran down the corridor to get the little Tiffany's bag Elizabeth had left in the coffee shop. He needed to make it back to reception before she'd managed to disentangle herself from Fitzroy's embrace. He grabbed the bag and barrelled past McGregor's office, stopping momentarily to straighten his tie. He took three deep breaths and pushed open the door to reception.

Lady Elizabeth didn't even turn as he walked towards them.

"I'll get Daddy to give you a call," she said, kissing the air next to Fitzroy's port-stained cheek. "I'm sure he'd love lunch at Wellington's."

"Lady Elizabeth," Robert said politely.

She turned and looked at him over the rim of her dark glasses. "What?"

"You left this in the coffee shop."

Lady Elizabeth looked at the small bag Robert held as if it were a bag of medical waste. "I'm sorry," she replied. "I have no idea what you are talking about, Mr Sutherland." She turned back to Fitzroy and kissed the air beside his other cheek, entirely ignoring the junior surgeon.

Robert stood, his arm outstretched, the small Tiffany's bag dangling from his hand like an unwanted gift from an undesirable suitor. His face turned red as the rest of the waiting clients stared at him. Robert let his arm drop to his side. He backed away from the dismissive heiress until he could feel the door handle against his back. Then he turned and fled.

Robert pushed the gift bag back into his locker. The contents were worth a month of his salary, yet her ladyship had discarded the gift and him as worthless. Robert scowled. Fuck her and her upper-class snobbery. What did she have that he needed anyway? Sure she was beautiful and sophisticated, and her eyes crinkled mischievously as she smiled. Her desirable lips were impossible to take your eyes off, and her laugh made his insides melt. But how much of Lady Elizabeth was real, and how much had been injected or sucked out at the Fitzroy Clinic? He ground his teeth together in frustration. He hated the stuck-up bitch, yet his nights were filled with dreams of her beautiful legs. He woke every morning with a stiff dick and images of her on top of him. Her pert breasts bouncing in front of his face as she lowered herself onto him, riding him until he came. Well, the bitch was on her own. Body dysmorphia or not, she'd have to deal with the situation herself. He was through mooning over the entitled whore.

"What are you doing in there?" Dylees asked.

Robert pushed the door of his locker closed with a guilty start.

"Nothing."

"Doesn't look like nothing. If you're taking drugs for recreational use, you need to make sure Will knows so he can reorder."

"I'm not," Robert stammered, horrified and intrigued by the idea. "But if I was?" he left the question hanging.

"If you were, you'd be as idiotic as the rest of your kind. However, Will keeps a stash in the locked cupboard in the pharmacy. Just ask him for the key, and for god's sake, stop taking the meds meant for patients."

Robert had been steadily increasing his tolerance to ketamine and morphine and a dozen other drugs. McGregor or Will were always on hand with a drink, pill or smoke that sent his head foggy. He knew he should abstain, but the need to be one of the team outweighed his common sense. Each time, he swore it would be the last, his determination lasting until McGregor held out his hand with the next fix. It had never occurred to him to ask where Will procured the drugs McGregor supplied.

"McGregor wants you to take over his appointments at Re Vive. Nothing much, just examinations of last week's surgeries."

"I'll head over to the spa in five minutes."

Robert's mind was whirling. A ready supply of drugs and a fucked-up an heiress might make for an interesting evening. If she didn't want to socialise with him for him, her medical files suggested she might for a quick fix. Once he had her in his apartment, Robert was sure something in Will's staff supply would loosen the bitch up enough that she would give him a chance.

"Will?" Robert said, walking into the staff room. "Dylees tells me you have a key."

Chapter 29 – Professional ethics

The effeminate man sat on the plush chair in the lounge sipping a latte, his little finger pointing out while flicking absently through a Marie Clare. His crossed long legs were encased in slim-fitting leather, leaving nothing to the imagination. The man looked up at Patrick through heavy false eyelashes and smiled.

"Ah, Senior Sharp," he said in a heavily accented voice. "It is good to meet you."

Patrick held out his hand. "Patrick Sharp."

The man took his hand, twisting his fingers slightly, so instead of shaking the man's hand, Patrick was left holding long, delicate fingers with red painted nails. "Eloise," the man introduced himself. "Mr Costa tells me you are answer to prayers."

"Did he?"

Eloise dropped his hand to his side and stood. He was at least four inches taller than Patrick. His slim form was clearly displayed in the tight-fitting clothing, and as Patrick studied his figure, Eloise's dark eyes sparkled mischievously. "Ever been with a transsexual?" he smiled, taking hold of Patrick's arm. "I tell you, Layla has nothing on me."

Patrick coughed and stepped away, his face flushed.

"We whores talk," Eloise giggled. "If nothing else, it passes time between being fucked. Mr Costa thinks I could earn him more with tits and a pussy." He took hold of Patrick's arm again. "What do you think?"

"I think Mr Costa knows what he's doing. If he says you need gender reassignment, and it's something you want, then that is what shall happen."

"What if I didn't want?"

"I am bound by professional ethics. If you don't want the surgery, then I will not perform it. Everyone has the right to choose."

Patrick tried not to think about the ramifications of not performing the sex change op. If Eloise told him he didn't want surgery, what would he do? Did he really have the courage to refuse?

"How naïve," Eloise giggled. "I will have surgery. I will fuck men until I am old, and then if I lucky, I will be put to use in brothels keeping young ones in line. If not, I will end up dead in the gutter. But I will be pretty corpse after you finished with me. Shall we?"

Patrick led the way into the consultation room, unnerved by Eloise's calm acceptance of life.

"Are they mine?" Eloise asked as they passed the staff room with the Bolivian bodyguards asleep on the couches.

"No, we have another patient in the clinic."

Eloise raised his perfectly shaped eyebrows but didn't comment.

"Mr Costa tells me you are best," Eloise said as he seductively undressed. Patrick was impressed by the skill with which he slipped off the skin-tight trousers. He was sure any other person would have been stumbling, pulling and grunting in their efforts to remove the fitted leather. Eloise noticed the attention and smiled alluringly, "Seen something you like?"

"You are a tease, Eloise."

"I know."

"I'll need to take a detailed medical history and then some measurements. But first, what is it you are wanting?"

"You!"

"Incorrigible."

"Maybe if I knew that word, I would have it? Instead, I have list." Eloise removed a paper from his small Mulberry clutch bag. "The obvious tits and pussy, of course, but also Adam's apple removed and make chin smaller, please."

Patrick leaned forward and touched Eloise's face. He ran his hands expertly from the ears to meet in the middle of the chin. The man had a beautiful face. Large dark eyes and high cheekbones, a small feminine nose and large full lips. The jaw line was strong in comparison, making Eloise an attractive man, but not a beautiful woman.

"This we can do. We can reshape your jaw without affecting your range of movement."

"This is good, range of movement is important," Eloise teased, licking his lips suggestively.

Patrick ignored the comment, running his fingers down Eloise's neck and feeling his Adam's apple. "This could prove more challenging. The scar might not be worth the results."

"It must be done," Eloise said, his voice firm and solemn.

"Very well," Patrick agreed, "but the scar will be visible."

Patrick reached for his notebook and started to take a medical history.

"All we need to do now is take some measurements, a few samples of blood and urine and then we are done."

"Or we talk about payment!"

"Mr Costa has sorted payment," Patrick replied.

"I think of something more personal in way of payment," Eloise whispered, his hands reaching down and caressing Patrick's thigh. When he found no resistance, he moved his hand upwards and brushed his long fingers over Patrick's penis. Patrick felt himself harden involuntarily. The idea of being with a man had never crossed his mind, and yet here he was letting this girly-man touch him.

"You see," Eloise smiled, licking his lips, "we plenty to talk about."

Patrick jumped as someone knocked on the door. Eloise laughed and stepped backwards, allowing Patrick to readjust himself before opening the door.

"Gwen."

"Who else would it be?"

Patrick rubbed his hand over his head. Today he wouldn't be surprised if Father Christmas himself walked into the clinic with a bag of coke and a desire to have a bit of lipo.

"What is it?" he sighed.

"Mrs De-Vargas is awake. She wants to know how the surgery went."

"Well, tell her."

"That's your job," Gwen said pointedly and stormed away.

Patrick turned back to Eloise. "Please excuse me for a while. I need to see to my other patient."

Eloise assented, intrigued by Patrick's mystery client. Vargas? When did the general get married, and to whom? Eloise had been one of Vargas' imports until Costa took over the UK prostitution ring. Vargas had been good to Eloise, and the lady-boy held a fondness for the ruthless leader that many wouldn't have. Being a prostitute in the UK was difficult but being transgender in Bolivia was a death sentence. Unwittingly Vargas had saved Eloise's life by trafficking him to Britain. The internal politics of Trae La Muerte were not common knowledge among the lower ranks, but Eloise was smart enough to know Vargas had been shafted by Costa in one way or another. Maybe this unknown wife could give him more information. Suddenly, getting one over on Costa's annoying favourite whore by seducing the hopeless surgeon wasn't so important.

Patrick caught up with Gwen and apologised.

"I should think so," she huffed, refusing to be placated until he told her Sasha was booking the two of them into Serenity.

"You just remember, Patrick Sharp, where your

bread is buttered, and who is doing the buttering."

Patrick nodded. He'd been forgiven, and being told off occasionally was just the price you paid for Gwen's caretaking. "Can you take bloods and samples from the client in consultation room one."

Roberta De Vargas was sat up in bed, her face had lost its healthy glow, and the glazed look in her eyes told Patrick she was still under the influence of the sedative.

"What happened?" she mumbled.

"There was a complication. We had to remove most of your left breast."

Roberta grabbed at the sheets with numb fingers, trying to rip off the bandaging in her panic to see.

Patrick calmly laid his hands on top of hers. "Don't, you'll pull out the sutures. It's not as bad as it sounds. Tomorrow, after you've had a good night's rest, we'll take you back into theatre and reconstruct your breasts. You might have to avoid bikinis for a few months, but that's all."

Roberta's hands stopped clawing at the sheets, and she relaxed back into the cushioned bed. "My husband?"

"He sends his love and will see you tomorrow."

A small cynical smile twitched on her lips, but she didn't challenge Patrick's assertions. "Can I have glass of water?"

"Yes a little, but no food, I'm afraid. Surgery will be tomorrow, so you are nil by mouth."

She looked confused.

"We need your stomach empty so the anaesthetic works."

"Ah," she replied.

Patrick helped her to drink a little water and then stayed with her until she drifted to sleep. He checked the drains and monitors before leaving. The reddish fluid in the drain was worrying, but he could do nothing until the antibiotic drip took effect.

Patrick could hear two chatty voices followed by high pitched laughter as he walked towards the consultation room.

"He didn't!" Gwen giggled.

"He fucking did!" Eloise laughed. "Right up to the point where he realised I'd padded my bra with more than chicken fillets. But with his dick up my arse already, he had to let me go."

"Well, that's one way to smuggle drugs."

"To beat system, you have to corrupt it. And most corruptible part is dick."

"Eloise, you are terrible."

Patrick breathed a sigh of relief. For one horrific moment, he had thought they were talking about his earlier indiscretion. Instead, Gwen was getting an intimate knowledge of drug smuggling. Patrick knocked on the door and entered without waiting for permission. They were in enough shit without being accomplices after the fact in some drug mule ring.

"Gwen, Eloise. Have you taken the samples?"

"Yes," Gwen replied, nodding at the dish with four vials of blood and a urine sample.

"Will you test to see if I pregnant?" Eloise giggled.

"If you think it is a possibility?"

Eloise tossed back his head and laughed. "Why these tests?"

Patrick's face took on a serious expression. "We need to test for blood type, infections, any sexually transmitted diseases. Also, we need to know what drugs you have taken in the past, and if you're taking any now. Mr Costa warned you about drug usage preventing the surgery."

"He did," Eloise replied earnestly. "I have abstained since last month."

With Gwen's help, Patrick measured Eloise,

examined the skin over his chest and carried out an internal examination. Patrick then sat down and explained the procedures in detail, the recovery time and the need for rest after treatment.

"We'll need to arrange an x-ray at the hospital and wait for the blood work. But I'm happy to go ahead with the surgery. We'll perform the gender reassignment first, including the breast augmentation, and then the more cosmetic stuff as you heal. Do you have any questions?"

"How big?" Eloise asked, holding his hands out in front of his chest.

"Probably a C cup, maybe a little bigger, but the tissue needs time to stretch. We will use a saline implant and make them as big as we can. We can carry out another procedure at a later date to increase the size if you want."

"Have you lived as a woman?" Gwen asked.

"Part-time," Eloise answered. "I am not man, I am not woman. I am exotic. Men like fact they do not know."

"It might be a good idea to dress as a woman between now and your surgery," Gwen suggested. "You'll need to get used to people looking at you differently."

"My darling Gwen. They already do."

Gwen laughed and linked arms with the likable whore.

"Who's in the room?" Eloise asked as they left the consultation room.

"What room?"

"The guarded one. Is it wonderful Mrs De-Vargas?"

"You know Roberta Juan-De-Vargas?"

Eloise covered his shock by stumbling in his high heels. "Of course, I know Roberta. We grew up together. Do say hello to her from me."

"She's sedated at the moment. Otherwise, I would take you in to see her."

"What's she had done, the sneaky bitch."

"Patient confidentiality, I'm afraid. I can't say."

Patrick collapsed into the comfortable chair in his office. The trauma of surgery and Eloise's calm acceptance of life had caught up with him in an overwhelming bone-weary tiredness. His head felt like it was stuffed with cotton wool, his mouth as dry as the Sahara. He felt cold, yet sweat poured from him, dampening his shirt. Thoughts whirled around his head, shocking images of death and destruction. For the first time, he felt the weight of his misdeeds. He could no longer blame his dead father for his addiction to gambling. He could no longer blame his wife for his affairs, or his upbringing for his need to own more and more. He had made the choices that had brought him to this point in his life. He was the author of his destruction. Images of his home in Ireland formed out of nowhere. The green pastures behind the cottage they'd moved to after his father's death, the crumbling walls and peeling paper now adding character rather than poverty to the small two-bedroom house. Two children skipped into the daydream, laughing hand in hand as they twirled faster and faster under the tree. The children had dark hair and tanned skin. They looked at him with dark brown eyes, their smiles growing wider as they ran to him. Patrick held his head in his hands and wept for his past and a future that would never exist. He screwed up his eyes, trying to close out the painful image, and the idyllic scene was replaced by a bright, red light flickering into a horrifying lake of blood. His nightmares came to life. Layla gagged and bound, her stomach cut open, her face twisted with fear and horror. The decapitated corpses of Andrew and Gwen, arms and legs tangled in the heap they had fallen in. Carole strung up, her legs dangling in the air while she screamed his name over and over again.

"Patrick!" Carole screamed. "Patrick!"

Patrick opened his eyes. Carole was leaning over him. He tried to focus, but her face was so close that all he could see was the distorted vision of her from his dream.

"Carole," he gasped, grabbing hold of her arms in a painfully tight grip. "Are you okay?"

She winced as Patrick's nails dug deeply into her bare arms. "You're hurting me," she cried.

Patrick let go and stood up. He enveloped her in a bear hug, lifting her off her feet and then holding her at arm's length to check for injuries or harm.

"Patrick, what's wrong with you?" she gasped after enduring his inspection.

"Nothing, everything's fine," he muttered.

"Patty Cake, if there's anything wrong, you must tell me. Maybe I can help."

"Cupcake, it's nothing. Well, nothing I can't handle."

"Patrick," Carole warned. "I know far more than you think. You might believe all I do is host charity events and shop. But I had a life before moving to London with you. Leeds is one of those places you learn quickly or you get dead."

Patrick shook his head. He'd met Carole over twenty years ago. A young, attractive croupier who had caught his eye at an underground card game. He'd bet big to impress the slim, beautiful woman and had won. Carole's refusal to go home with him to celebrate that night, or any other, had meant he'd ended up marrying her just to see if what was secreted beneath the smart black and white uniform matched her flame red hair.

"It's gambling debts, isn't it?" Carole said, interrupting his thoughts. "Who do you owe money to, Patrick? Please tell me it's not the Irish."

Patrick laughed. "No."

"Who?"

"Some South Americans."

"Who?"

"A Bolivian gang. They operate the boxing, bookies and a few other illegal enterprises."

"Such as?"

"Cupcake, you don't want to know."

"Yes, I do."

"Drugs, girls, the usual."

Carole sat down. "Tell me everything."

"Well, you'll just have to carry out the surgery," Carole said when Patrick had finished explaining. "It's us or them after all."

"But what about my oath? What about the fact I don't specialise in gender reassignment or the laws I'll be breaking?"

"What about your oath to me? Stop being a baby Patrick, and read a fucking manual. You gambled away your prerogative to be squeamish. Mr Costa and Mr Green are not men to be messed with. You'll do whatever they say, and you'll do it with a smile and a deference to the men who hold your life in their hands."

Patrick couldn't remember mentioning Mr Green by name, but he must have. Carole was right. If he wanted to keep those close to him safe, he had to smile and do as he was told.

"I'm sorry, Carole," Patrick said, and for the first time in his miserable life, he meant it. "I'm sorry I'm not a better husband. I'm sorry I'm a selfish prick and dragged you into this. I'm sorry…"

Carole placed a gentle hand on his cheek. "It's alright, Patty Cake. Just do as you're told, and we'll be okay."

Patrick's shoulders shook as the tears flooded down his cheeks.

Chapter 30 – Beasts in the vault

McGregor arrived at Bankers at ten, Collins in tow. Hazel had agreed to be there at eight with the slutty make-up artist, but she was always late, and besides, she deserved to be kept waiting. The smartly dressed waitress passed McGregor two large Black Pearl cognacs.

"Almost makes me want to go straight," Collins laughed, unable to take his eyes off the diaphanous bank uniforms. "Doesn't leave much to the imagination," he said as the curvaceous waitress bent down to grab a bottle of port from the lower shelf.

"It does change one's opinion on making a deposit."

Collins laughed. "But where are the boys?"

"They tend to be consigned to the vault."

"Then what are we waiting for?"

"We need to be called into the club through that door." McGregor gestured to the staff entrance to the back offices of the old bank. "It takes a little time when you bring a guest."

Collins raised an eyebrow.

"They need to do a quick search on your background. Make sure you're not a criminal or a copper."

Collins laughed. "I'm a barrister. Isn't that worse?"

"Undoubtedly, but I think they'll make an exception if you promise to be bad."

McGregor had just finished his brandy when the black hostess walked up to them. "Mr McGregor and guest," she said, consulting her clipboard. "If you'll follow me."

"Gladly," McGregor said, gazing at her upturned nipples through the thin fabric of her shirt. She smiled at McGregor's inspection, her full lips revealing perfect white teeth.

"See something you like, Mr McGregor?"

"I do, but I wouldn't dream of breaking the rules."

"Shame, I heard you enjoyed breaking rules," she replied, her hand brushing his dick as she turned to show them into the heart of Bankers.

Collins coughed at McGregor's shock. "So old boy, occasionally something does catch you off guard."

"The staff are off limits. We're not allowed to touch, but I guess the rule only goes one way. I just never thought about it."

The hostess turned and flashed a wicked smile at them, her illicit intentions towards McGregor reflected in her dark brown eyes. McGregor imagined running his hand over the velvety brown skin, his fingers tangling with hers as her long legs wrapped around him, pulling him deeper.

"Sold," McGregor said, his voice full of devious plans for the beautiful black hostess.

"Mr McGregor, you can't afford me." She turned to enter the code on the keypad on the wall, pushed open the door and stepped aside for the men to enter.

"Enjoy your evening, gentlemen," she said, bowing slightly and handing them a Banker's parcel each. "There's an orgy in the boardroom and a performance by the Beasts in the vault."

The door swung shut, leaving McGregor with his thoughts firmly on the filthy things he would like to do to the hostess.

"Beasts?" Collins asked.

"This way."

The performance was already in full swing when they entered. The members of Bankers stood around the walls of the vault, their hands wandering over each other and their eyes firmly fixed on the male duo on the small stage. Both men were stripped to the waist, their muscled chests oiled and gleaming in the dim candlelight. The first man prowled the stage, a fur loincloth wrapped around his waist, the top half of his face covered by a hideous, hybrid mask. Feathers surrounded a feline face in a strange perversion of a mane, and a vicious beak protruded instead of the regal nose of a big cat. His animalistic dancing undulated from side to side, his bare feet stamping and hands clawing at the air to the tribal drumbeat. The audience swayed with the rhythm, captivated by the heady, ritualistic atmosphere. The second man was chained to a cross, his arms and legs bound by heavy steel chains. His face was covered in tight leather, preventing him from seeing the man who stalked his vulnerable body.

The drumbeat grew louder and more frenzied, and the audience involuntarily held their breaths as the part man, part beast crept closer to his chained captive. Then without warning the beast launched himself at his prey, his nails digging into the man's chest, drawing bloody scratches across the torso. The captive screamed in pain and fear. The beast howled and circled, clawing at the man's bottom and thighs until the thin fabric covering his lower half was rags. The beast used its teeth to tear the tattered material from the man, leaving him naked and afraid. The audience didn't move, so engrossed in the performance that even the casual fondling stopped. The beast growled and sat at the feet of his captive. Then very slowly he stood, its face pressed against the skin of the man. It licked the bloody gashes and nibbled on the inside of his thighs before enveloping a nipple in its mouth. The man's cry was fear and pleasure as the beast's teeth sunk deeper into his flesh. The beast dropped to his knees, its claws digging into the man's naked bottom, forcing his hips forward and his manhood into its waiting maw. It lapped at the man's dick until it hardened. The man groaned again, this time with pleasure as the heat encased him. The beast moved, its nails digging deeper into flesh as the man writhed in pleasure. The man's arms strained against the chains as his body tensed, and he exploded in orgasmic pleasure. The beast turned to the audience, white cum dribbling from its mouth before returning its attention to the victim. Its tongue slid up the man's toned abdomen and rippling chest until it claimed his mouth with its own in a long passionate kiss. The man fought, pulling with all his strength at the shackles holding him captive. He managed to get one arm free, his finger scraping at the wooden cross behind his head. The sound of splintering wood echoed around the vault as he ripped a large pointed shard from the cross. Gripping the shard until blood ran from his palm, he plunged the stake into the beast's back. The beast convulsed and fell. The man slumped forward a scream torn from his throat.

The audience remained frozen as the drumbeat ended. No one spoke as they watched the life drain from beast and man. Then the crowd broke into rapturous cheers, stamping their feet and clapping until the sound filled the vault with a crescendo of noise. The men on stage didn't move until the sound died away. Then both men removed their masks in a flourish and bowed to the audience. The beautiful man, who had been the beast, untied his partner from the cross and, hand in hand, they greeted their fans.

"Fucking hell!" Collins exclaimed. "Why haven't you brought me here before?"

McGregor's answer was cut off by a pair of manicured hands that encircled his waist and grabbed hold of his erection.

"I thought Damon's performance would do it for you," Hazel whispered into his ear.

McGregor turned and grabbed Hazel around the waist with one arm, his other hand pushing under her flowing skirt. He encountered stockings and suspenders before finding the wetness of her pussy. His fingers pushed deep inside her. "His effects seem to be mutual.

You appear to have forgotten your knickers, my dear."

"Olivia has them," she laughed.

McGregor raised an eyebrow.

"The make-up girl. When you weren't here, we started without you," Hazel smirked.

"How incredibly rude," McGregor growled, slapping Hazel across the face with his damp hand.

Hazel grinned, took hold of his hand and sucked on his fingers. "I taste good." She smiled, a red welt forming on her cheek. "As good as Olivia, but you already know that, don't you?"

McGregor laughed and pulled her towards him, his mouth claiming hers in a passionate battle for supremacy. Collins wolf whistled, and the pair pulled apart. Hazel's lips were full and bruised, McGregor's bleeding.

"Now I have a reference sample," McGregor growled, licking his lips. "May I introduce you to my friend, Collins?"

Hazel and Collins wandered over to the Beasts, the slender barrister quivering in anticipation. McGregor considered finding Olivia to fuck her senseless while Hazel was otherwise engaged, but a poor defenceless girl alone somewhere in the depth of Bankers turned him on. The fear she would experience in this alien environment would make her all the more pliable when they took her back to his hotel suite. He licked his lips in anticipation of the pleasure to come. Out of nowhere, powerful hands pinned his arms against his side. He tried to struggle, but the more he fought, the tighter the grip became.

"Did you see the fight?" Scott Holden whispered in his ear.

McGregor relaxed and then lashed his head backwards, connecting with the boxer. He heard the satisfying crunch of bone, but the grip on his arms didn't lessen.

"If you have damaged my good looks, you'll be

fixing them for free," Scott growled. "You owe me."

McGregor could feel Scott's warm breath on his neck and hear the rasping pant of desire. He curled his hand back to caress the muscled thigh of the man holding him captive.

"You want to replicate the show?" he asked, his hand moving up the boxer's leg to touch his hard erection.

"The chairman's office is free?"

McGregor glanced over at Hazel and Collins, still engaged in conversation with the Beasts. "Lead the way," he said, blood pounding through his body.

The muscled boxer smiled coyly as he took McGregor's delicate surgeon's hand in his massive fist.

The chairman's office was a private room where members lived out fantasies of punishment and domination. An array of props were kept in a steel filing cabinet, from glasses and dictation notepads to whips and handcuffs. The participants could role play numerous scenarios using the antique oak desk or the leather Victorian sofa. Many a lady had ended up on her knees on the plush carpet or pressed against the flocked wallpapered walls. McGregor remembered his last time in this room. How he'd dictated his dirtiest thoughts to Witch-Hazel as she sat in the secretary's chair, the glasses on the end of her nose her only item of clothing. Now he stood in the room with a large green-eyed boxer. The man's head was shaven, giving him a thuggish look. The blood from the split lip McGregor had inflicted earlier had dried, and it cracked as he smiled. Scott's eyes flashed dangerously as he closed the door and unbuttoned his shirt. McGregor was toned, but Holden's torso was hard-ripped muscle. His pectorals bulged beneath a fine down of ginger hair.

"Do you want to undress me?" Scott asked, strutting over to McGregor. "Or should I blow you?"

"Both," McGregor whispered, the thought of the masculine dominant boxer on his knees pleasuring him making his dick throb.

Carefully savouring the moment. McGregor pushed the white shirt from Scott's shoulders and then unzipped the man's trousers, pushing them to the floor along with the underwear to reveal Scott's hard, straight erection protruding from auburn pubes. Scott sank to his knees and McGregor moaned as his dick was encased in the heat of Holden's mouth.

"Stop," McGregor growled as he felt the pulsing throb of orgasm. "Stand."

Scott did as he was told, allowing McGregor to turn his large frame and bend him over the desk. McGregor inserted his fingers into Holden's tight anus, massaging until the muscled thighs were quivering with delight. Slowly, almost gently, he pushed inside, his cock surrounded by the hot tightness. Scott's fingers clenched around the edge of the desk as McGregor's hand snaked around his torso to stroke his dick. McGregor thrust forward, claiming his domination over the man. The groans of pleasure from both men echoed around the room as they sated their lust. Together, they came in one epic heartbeat, leaving them spent and gasping for breath.

"Next time, I win," Holden gasped, each word forced out between ragged breaths. "I will take you."

He gently kissed McGregor's lips then picked up his clothes and walked naked into the depths of Bankers. McGregor tilted his head, considering Holden's firm arse and the implications of the promise. Absently, he straightened his clothing and went looking for Hazel and Olivia.

"Where have you been?" Hazel demanded.

"The bar," he replied, not wanting to share his passionate moment with her.

"Did you find Olivia?" she asked, her eyes narrowing suspiciously.

"No darling, I thought I'd wait for that pleasure with you."

Hazel leant forward and kissed him, her tongue

forcing its way into his mouth. He didn't taste of the sweet girl. Maybe McGregor had learnt his lesson. She smiled slyly. David McGregor loved her, and this act of restraint proved it.

Chapter 31 – Make me beautiful

The night had been the longest Patrick Sharp could remember. He'd checked in on Mrs De-Vargas at half hourly intervals for the first four hours, and then hourly after that. The naps he'd stolen in between had been haunted by nightmares of gender reassignment surgeries. Patients bleeding out on his table while he stood helplessly, holding their genitalia in his hands. Clients waking up after the surgery and demanding why he'd removed their cocks, pleading with him to reattach the members they thrust into his face. At five in the morning, Patrick gave up on sleep and turned on his computer. If he was to get any peace from his overactive imagination, he needed to research the correct techniques for dick to pussy surgery.

"Patrick," Gwen whispered her hand on his shoulder.

Patrick opened his eyes and looked blurrily at her.

"You dozed off. Stop worrying about the gender reassignment surgery. You're going to pull in outside assistance?"

"Of course," Patrick lied. "How's our patient?"

"As well as can be expected. She's woken up, still groggy. You need to explain what happened now the sedation has worn off."

Patrick pushed his hands through his hair and stood up. His lower back hurt from sleeping hunched over his desk. He gulped back the cold coffee sat next to his keyboard and smiled at his nurse.

"What would I do without you?" he asked as they walked to the recovery room.

Patrick carefully explained the procedure to Mrs De-Vargas, detailing again what had been done and why. He held her hand gently as she cried. "Don't worry, Mrs

De-Vargas, I've removed all the damaged tissue, and we'll take you into surgery as soon as the anaesthetist arrives. The next time you wake up, you will be smiling. I promise."

Mrs De-Vargas held Patrick's hand tightly. "Make me beautiful again," she pleaded.

Patrick squeezed her hand reassuringly. "I just need a few details of your surgeon," he said, handing her a notepad. "Name, address, those sorts of things, as much as you can remember."

Patrick headed to the surgical suite to give Gwen the details he had on Doctor Guillen for the FOBPS investigation. He paused outside the surgical room as he heard Gwen laugh.

"Patrick will be here any minute." Gwen giggled.

"And?" Andrew laughed, making strange murmuring sounds.

"And I haven't found the time to tell him about us yet. He has so much on his plate at the moment."

"Well, this would be the perfect way to let him know I'm in love with you."

Gwen squealed with delight as Andrew kissed her. Patrick stood still. He felt he was intruding on a private moment of happiness, yet just by listening to the genuine love in their voices, he felt almost part of it.

"Not here," Gwen sighed.

"Tonight? We can take the kids for dinner and then put them to bed early with a DVD."

"Sounds good to me."

"And when they're sound asleep," Andrew whispered, "I'll put you to bed and…"

Patrick backed silently away. It was one thing to listen to his beloved Gwen when she was declaring her love for the worthy Andrew, but another thing to eavesdrop on their sexual fantasies. He was genuinely pleased for the two of them. Andrew had never been in a serious relationship. He'd played around a bit but had never found someone who could keep him interested. Gwen had three children to an abusive husband who had knocked her around until she divorced him. Both of them deserved happiness. Patrick smiled. The quick-mouthed Gwen would keep Andrew on his toes, and Andrew would make an excellent father, he was half-child himself. The incident made Patrick think about his marriage. The feelings he'd felt for Carole when he'd seen her at the underground casino. Her resistance to his sexual advances until they were engaged, and the joy he'd taken in her naïve body. He tried to think when her inexperience had turned into prudishness and realised she had never really enjoyed sex. Marriage to him had been about securing her future, not love. Patrick pictured Andrew playing with Gwen's children in the park, throwing a ball or just chasing each other round in circles until they all collapsed in a laughing heap. Carole had never wanted children. She worried pregnancy would change her lifestyle. When they'd found out she was infertile after the miscarriage, it had been a relief for Carole while Patrick had stored away the hurt and loss. He dreamt of having little ones clinging to his feet, begging for another story or piggyback. Was it this that had caused him to seek comfort elsewhere? Did Carole shoulder some of the blame for his infidelity?

"Ah, there you are Patrick," Gwen said, interrupting Patrick's train of thoughts. "Andrew is in."

A smirk spread across Patrick's face. "Is he now?"

"And what is that supposed to mean, Patrick Sharp?"

Detecting the edge in her voice, Patrick didn't pursue the line of thought. "Well, he should be checking on Roberta De-Vargas, not making coffee. She's awake and ready for him. I have the details of her previous surgeon if you could pass them on to FOBPS while I scrub in."

Gwen looked as if she was going to say

something. Her eyes narrowed, and she studied her boss
for a long time before taking the notes from his hand and
walking away. Patrick smiled. 'Good on you, Gwen,' he
thought but didn't have the balls to say.

Andrew wheeled Mrs De-Vargas into the surgical
suite. Her eyes were taped shut, and the tight bandaging
around her chest had been cut away. Patrick looked at the
clear fluid in her drains. He removed the surgical tape and
opened the flaps of skin on the left breast. The tissue
underneath was a healthy pink, the muscle fibre dark red
and firm. He removed the packing and double-checked his
removal of the silicone.

"She's one lucky lady," Andrew said, pointing at
Mrs De-Vargas.

"I know another one," Patrick teased, keeping his
face lowered so they couldn't see his smirk.

"Scalpel?" Gwen asked.

"No. I think the pocket underneath the muscle is
perfect. There's still a definite separation between both
breasts, and I can't see any silicone masses. Saline, please."

Gwen jetted saline solution over the tissue and
used the suction to extract the liquid and any particulates.

"Pass me the 300cc implant."

Gwen removed the sterile implant from the
packaging and handed it to Patrick. Patrick weighed the
implant in his hand, testing the texture and consistency
under experienced fingers. Satisfied, he pushed the implant
into the pocket underneath the muscle to reform Mrs De-
Vargas' breast from a saggy mess into a perfectly shaped
tit.

"Agreed?"

"Agreed," Gwen replied, looking at the size and
shape.

Patrick sutured the incisions and massaged the
breast to make sure the nipple was in the right place before
performing the procedure on the other side. When he was
finished, Gwen pressed the small green button that lifted

the patient into a sitting position. Roberta's breasts now had a natural fullness to them. Patrick removed the camera from the cupboard and took a photograph.

"Send it to Mr Vargas when we are out of here. At least it will get one general off our backs."

Gwen wasn't stupid. She knew the Bolivian clientele were less than upstanding, but she'd never heard them referred to in such military terms before.

"Is there anything we should know, Patrick?" she asked. "I have the kids to think about."

"Everything is fine, Gwen. It doesn't concern you. Let's just get Roberta De-Vargas safely back to her loving husband."

The noise Gwen made was anything but ladylike. Andrew placed a restraining hand on her arm. An intimate gesture Patrick would have missed had he not overheard their earlier conversation.

"I'll be in my office. Let me know when she is awake."

A hot coffee and the morning's post were on his desk when he walked into his office. Sasha was already at her place in the waiting lounge, her gentle, happy humming as she sorted the patient files drifting through the clinic. Patrick smiled. In about ten minutes, she'd poke her head around his door and offer to fetch everyone breakfast from Feast. The mail was nothing exciting, a couple of bills that needed paying, a query from a solicitor to see if he was interested in testifying as an expert witness and a hospitality invite from a drugs company. The image on the front of the hospitality invite caught his attention, and he picked it up again.

'Mr Patrick Sharp is cordially invited to attend Faunaceutical launch of Hemafen.'

Patrick shook his head. They'd kept that bit of information out of the press. No wonder they'd decided not to sell at any price to Beijing Biochemistry Laboratories. The shareholders would have been insane to sell with a profitable drug hitting the market. Hemafen was a pain relieving topical medication based on the chemical constituents of hemp. The cream was being marketed as a breakthrough for targeted pain relief after surgery. If it hadn't been blasted Faunaceutical, Patrick would have gone and revelled in the debauchery, drugs, alcohol and women. Launch events had a habit of turning into orgies right after the sales pitch ended. What better way to get surgeons to part with their ill-gotten gains than to get them drunk and fucked by a sexy call girl or boy. Many of his colleagues had awakened the next morning to find they'd purchased a five years' supply of drugs while licking temazepam of some whore's breast. Shit, Patrick himself had signed up to trial PRP therapy while plastered, but the girl had been hot as hell. He screwed up the invitation and threw it into the bin with the other junk mail. He had enough problems without adding another financial burden to his already overstretched budget.

"Bacon and eggs?" Sasha asked, poking her head round the door.

"Please."

Sasha walked down the hallway to catch Gwen before she examined Mrs De-Vargas.

"Breakfast?"

"Can you get me a bowl of muesli and an apple?"

"Gwen, you are so bloody good. Don't you fancy a sausage sandwich occasionally?"

"No. Have you asked Andrew and the bodyguards if they want anything?"

"They're rather scary," Sasha gulped.

"They'd be scarier hungry."

Sasha twitched. "If you say so."

Gwen smiled as Sasha went in search of Andrew. She'd put a tenner on the fact Sasha would get Andrew to ask the Bolivian thugs if they wanted anything to eat.

"Mrs De-Vargas," Gwen said, knocking on the door to the recovery room.

Roberta opened her eyes at the sound of someone entering the room. She swallowed and tried to wet her lips a little.

"Would you like a drink?"

Roberta nodded, not able to speak through the dryness in her throat. She drank gratefully from the glass of cold water touched to her lips.

"Tits?"

Gwen smiled. "Yes, you have beautiful breasts. The surgery was a complete success. You'll need to keep taking the antibiotics and stay at Re Vive for the rest of the week, but everything went according to plan."

"Thank you."

"It's Mr Sharp you need to thank. Are you up for a visitor?"

"Husband?"

Gwen shook her head sadly. She'd emailed the photograph of Roberta's new boobs to Mr Vargas and gotten a curt message in return. When she informed him that he would be able to visit his wife in two hours, the reply had been one word, 'busy'.

"No, I'm afraid your husband is tied up, but he is looking forward to you going home. We had an old friend of yours in yesterday. He says he'd like to visit and catch up if you are feeling up to it."

Roberta looked confused. "I have no friends in England."

"Eloise. He was in here yesterday. He said you grew up in the same village as you."

Confusion changed to fear. "He knows I here?"

"Yes. He wanted to know if he could visit."

"No," the word was uttered with such venomous hatred that Gwen took a step back. "He bad man. You tell Mr Sharp. No trust him." Roberta's accent became stronger as she spoke. "Ama chaski quillqa qon. Qon runa sipiy."

"I don't understand?"

"Eloise come England before me." Roberta's voice trembled, and her body shook. "You keep him away me. Blame me for street life. He kill me."

Gwen wrapped her arms around Roberta. "You don't have to see him if you don't want to. I will phone him and explain you are already back home with Mr Vargas."

Roberta looked relieved. "Tell him Vargas very happy with wife, not need chinaku."

Gwen comforted the distraught Mrs De-Vargas until she fell asleep. How could the small effeminate man put such fear into anyone? He seemed more likely to call you names and condemn your fashion choices than physically harm you. Could Roberta have a real reason to fear the lady-boy?

Chapter 32 – Party on the weekend

Robert had waited in the coffee shop until it closed every day since his failed attempt to return Lady Elizabeth's bag. His infatuation with the wild aristocrat had grown into a destructive obsession. The stolen moments with Elizabeth over coffee had been the happiest in his life. He knew they had made a real connection and only his tactless remarks had soured their relationship. If she'd just give him the chance to apologise, he was sure they could recapture the magic of new love. He'd rehearsed what he was going to say as he sat hour after hour, drinking cup after cup of overpriced coffee waiting for her to turn up ladened with bags from a shopping trip. His days at the clinic blended together a meaningless cut, stuff and stitch as the numerous bodies of Fitzroy's and McGregor's clients were wheeled into the surgical suite. Robert's stash of drugs from Will's cupboard helped with the pain of Elizabeth's absence. A little armodafinil or Ritalin in the mornings to get him out of bed, a little morphine to take the edge off in the evenings. He'd not meant to use the stash of drugs he'd appropriated, but the loneliness crowded in on him, an oppressive weight that the morphine lifted. McGregor and Will had suggested a Friday night in the West End, but Robert had been afraid to miss his chance to talk to Lady Elizabeth he'd refused their offer. He wasn't sure what it was about her that fuelled his desires. He never stopped to question which came first, the fixation or the drugs. He just knew that with her life would be better.

"Another latte?" the waitress asked.

Robert looked at the cold cup of milky coffee he was nursing. "Yes, please," he said, placing a fiver on the table and staring out of the window again.

Robert didn't see the pitying look she gave him as she set the latte in front of him and took the crumpled five pound note. He didn't notice the man he barrelled into as he rushed from the coffee shop after the leggy blonde strutting across the busy road. His eyes were fixed on her back as she weaved confidently through the traffic and into the elite beauty spa across the street. Robert's stride halted abruptly at the pavement, as he gazed through the large, dressed window of the Serenity Spa. He could see a cream waiting room with oversized sofas and an ornate reception desk. He watched Lady Elizabeth talk to the uniformed girl behind the desk before being ushered through a door and out of sight. Robert stood on the street, his mouth open wide, an expression of total adoration plastered across his vacant face. She was an angel in human form, the most beautiful woman he had ever seen. One way or another, he had to have her. Robert stood until his feet hurt and his back cramped. He could have been waiting for one hour or five. He had no recollection. Just a need to not let the beautiful, ethereal creature escape. In his mind, Lady Elizabeth had become more than a woman. She had become a symbol of his worthiness, the thing he needed to complete himself. Without her, life was not worth living.

Robert closed his eyes and opened them, blinking slowly. The object of his affection, his fantasy and reason to live, was stood inches away, her face a mask of horror and repulsion.

"You bastard!" she exclaimed, slapping him across the face. "What gives you the right?"

"I, I, I…" he stammered, still not sure the creature in front of him was real.

"You what?" she demanded, poking him painfully in the ribs. "You think standing outside while I have my nails done makes you anything but a total frigging freak?"

"I, I have a gift for you?" Robert mumbled, trying to find the planned speech in his jumbled mind.

"What could you possibly have that I would want?" Lady Elizabeth screamed, her face so close to

Robert's he found it difficult to focus.

"Morphine, ketamine, lidocaine."

She stepped back slightly, her expression changing from one of anger to interest.

"I have access to medical grade drugs, anything you want, really," Robert continued. "McGregor keeps a supply for staff. I can get them for you if you like," he finished lamely.

"When?"

"Now. I have some back in my apartment."

Lady Elizabeth looked unsure.

"What better way to party on the weekend?"

She took her phone out of her bag and tapped on the screen. She waited a few moments and then tapped again.

"Do you have any mazzie?" she asked.

Robert nodded. He should have known, temazepam was an ideal party drug. It gave you a sense of invincibility, eradicated your inhibitions and allowed you to explore the hidden depths of your soul. Taking mazzie recreationally usually resulted in public sex and occasionally the user being pulled down from the ledge of tall buildings because they thought they could fly.

"Well," she said impatiently when he didn't move, "lead the way."

Robert couldn't believe it. After days of imagining, planning and hoping, here he was, walking towards his apartment with Lady Elizabeth. He had a bottle of champagne in the fridge for just this occasion. He was positive that once they were away from prying eyes, she'd open up to him. They'd have a real conversation about the important things in life, and she'd realise they were meant for each other.

"Not bad," she said as he opened the door to his apartment. "I expected something more northern." Elizabeth cringed as she spat the word, as if being from Yorkshire was a character flaw.

Robert smiled. "My Uncle Patrick owns the NuYu clinic. While my family isn't part of the establishment like yours, you can see I'm from a wealthy family."

While far from the truth, Robert felt a little embellishment wouldn't hurt his wooing of the young, troubled heiress. "Have a seat. Would you like some champagne?"

"Whatever for?"

"I thought you might be thirsty?

This wasn't going according to plan. In his imagination, they'd be sat in front of the fire, sipping champagne and revealing their most intimate secrets to each other.

"I'm in a little bit of a rush. J-Collie is expecting me with the Mazzie."

"Sit," Robert said. "Please, I'll get you a drink, and then I'll get you the temazepam."

Lady Elizabeth sighed but took a seat on the leather sofa. Robert rushed off to the kitchen and grabbed the bottle of Cristal. He filled two flutes, dropping a crushed flunitrazepam into the champagne and giving it a quick stir. Lady Elizabeth didn't know what was good for her. James Collroy was a first-class arsehole, pictured in the tabloids with a different woman each week. Robert knew he needed to protect Elizabeth from the advances of such a worthless suitor, and maybe if she relaxed a little, she'd stay. He walked back into the living room and passed Elizabeth the spiked glass.

"The pills?"

"Drink first and tell me how much you want. You want the drugs only for personal use, right? I can't be caught supplying."

Elizabeth looked deep into Robert's eyes and smiled. Raising the glass to her lips, she sipped the sparkling drink before running her tongue around the rim of the glass suggestively. She looked into Robert's eyes and smiled.

"Robert... I may call you Robert?"

Robert nodded.

"I just need a little for me and my friends. I promise not to tell them my source, okay?"

Robert choked slightly on the dry sparkling liquid. "As long as you promise."

Elizabeth leaned forward, resting her hand on his leg. "I promise."

Robert felt a tingle of excitement run up his thigh. "Maybe we could get something to eat one evening?" he ventured.

Elizabeth removed her hand and picked up her glass. "I'm not sure it would be appropriate, Robert."

Robert felt as if his heart would break. With seven words, Elizabeth had crushed his hopes of children and a picket fence. Of coming home from a day's surgery at his own clinic paid for by Elizabeth's trust fund to a happy wife with dinner on the table. In his daydream, dinner would be followed by an evening of passionate lovemaking while the nanny saw to their beautiful children.

"Ohh," he managed to say.

Elizabeth looked at her watch. "J-Collie will be waiting for me if you could?"

Robert frowned as he stormed out of the room. He grabbed a handful of pills from the stash in the bottom drawer of his dresser and stuffed them into a clear plastic bag. It wasn't temazepam, but she wouldn't know. The oxycodone would mix poorly with the flunitrazepam he'd already given her, but the bitch deserved to puke her guts out. He returned to the living room, his mood darkening with each step. How dare the stuck-up bitch refuse to have dinner with him? The plastic media whore would be lucky to have someone as genuine as him. He knew all her dark secrets from studying her medical records and still wanted her. The failed suicides, the excessive surgery, the numerous times McGregor had pumped her stomach on the QT when she'd overdosed on party drugs. She might not sleep with him for love, but she'd sure as hell do it to prevent him revealing the truth about daddy's little princess.

"I don't feel…" Lady Elizabeth began to say as the glass slipped from her fingers and shattered on the floor. She looked at the shards of broken glass in amused amazement, her hand reaching out to touch the delicate fragments. She picked up a sliver of glass and held it tightly in her palm. It cut deep into her flesh, but she didn't cry out in pain. Instead, she let go of the shard and brought her hand to her mouth. Robert stared as Lady Elizabeth teetered on the edge of the sofa and then fell forward.

"Elizabeth!" he cried out, rushing to her and lifting her off the floor. A bruise was already forming on her cheek, and the red blood from her hand had smeared across her dress.

"You're bleeding," he said.

"Bleeding," she repeated.

Robert grabbed her by the shoulders and looked into her eyes. Her pupils were dilated, her gaze glassy as she looked at him without comprehension. Her lips slackened and fell into a strange lopsided grin. Robert waved his hand in front of her face, and she reached out for his fingers.

"Do you want water?"

"Water," she repeated.

Robert sat her on the sofa and fetched a glass of water. She looked at the glass in her hand as if it was a peculiar, wonderful and yet unknown object.

"Would you like to go to bed with me?" Robert asked, forcing the words past the lump of uncertainty in his throat.

"Bed," she repeated.

A thin, evil smile spread across Robert's face as he took hold of Elizabeth's arm and lifted her from the sofa. With a deliberate knowledge of where his actions would take him, he led the semi-conscious woman into his bedroom. He stood her in front of the mirror and slowly undressed her. Peeling her outer clothing from her to reveal the black lacy underwear. He unclasped her bra, letting her pert breasts bounce playfully in his hands.

"Is that nice?"

"Nice," she repeated.

"Should I go on?"

"Go on."

Robert knew what he was doing was wrong, but the hardness of his dick and the residue of drugs still in his system suppressed his conscience. He ran his fingers between her breasts and down her stomach to her small thong. Hooking his fingers underneath the fabric, he pulled downwards. Robert gasped at the beauty of her pussy. The smoothness of the skin and the lack of any hair made his dick ache with need. He sank to his knees in front of her and devoured her with his mouth, sucking and licking until he felt her wetness and excitement meet his own.

"Look at me," he ordered as he looked up at her from his knelt position. "Look at me while I make you cum."

Elizabeth did as she was told, looking down at the man at her feet. She felt something wrong and struggled inside herself to grasp hold of what it was. The more she tried to find the answer, the further she seemed to slip into herself until the only thing she could feel was the pressure of something inside her.

Robert pulled his mouth away and replaced his tongue with his fingers. He pushed deep inside her vagina with his fingers. He stood up and kissed her, his lips pressed hard against hers. Her mouth opened to accept his tongue as she submitted to him. Robert quickly shed his clothing before turning her to face the large mirror in his bedroom. He stood behind her and guided his erection into her. He knew he should be gentle, but his excitement was too profound. Weeks of imagining, dreaming and fantasising came together at that moment. He pushed deep inside of her, his hands clasped over her breasts to stop her from moving away. Robert felt the tightness of her surrounding him, the sheer joy of his dick inside her, the softness of her breasts in his hands. He thrust ten times and came. The explosion of pleasure left him panting for breath. Gently, he kissed her back and nibbled on her neck as he came down from the orgasmic high.

He redressed himself, and then Elizabeth, straightened her hair and pushed the pills into her handbag. He called a taxi using her phone and sent a text message to James Collroy confirming she had the drugs. The message gave the impression she'd be able to score from the commoner anytime they needed as long as she was nice to him. Robert hoped J-Collie would push Elizabeth into more late night liaisons for the promise of free drugs. He kissed her one more time before leading her from his apartment to the waiting taxi.

Elizabeth didn't know where she was. Her head felt as if it was stuffed full of cotton wool, and her clothes seemed wrong somehow, almost as if they weren't her clothes. She peered into the darkness, trying to make out her surroundings.

"That's fifteen fifty," a man said from the driver's seat.

Elizabeth turned her face the noise and tried to focus on the person in front of her.

"That's fifteen fifty, miss," the man said again.

Elizabeth's stomach heaved. She reached for the handle to the door and pushed it open. Falling forward, she managed to get her head out of the vehicle before she emptied the contents of her stomach onto the pavement.

"Stuck-up bitch," the cabbie yelled, yanking open his door and rushing around to the side where Elizabeth half-hung. "If you've hurled in my cab, you'll have to pay an extra fifty clean-up charge."

Elizabeth looked at him, trying to focus on the arm reaching to pull her out of the black cab. The man grabbed her purse and rifled through it to find a fifty pound note.

"Thanks for the tip," he growled, pushing her purse back into her hand and leaving her wobbling on the street.

Elizabeth managed to take three faltering steps away from the kerb, her high heels tottering unsteadily beneath her. The lights of the cars' headlamps hurt her eyes, and the constant buzz of noise, maybe music, droned in her ears, making concentrating impossible.

"Where have you been?" a familiar voice asked, although she couldn't place him.

"I, I, I," she stammered, her legs giving way as she fell forward into the strong arms of James Collroy. "I don't know."

Chapter 33 – A hatchet job

Hazel woke first. Her body ached in the delicious way that announced her body had been abused by McGregor. She smiled and stretched. Sunday mornings were always a pleasure. A full day to do nothing but relax and fuck. McGregor's gentle snoring beside her made her smile. She turned and looked at his smooth, muscled body, his warm tan from a fortnight in the Maldives fading slightly. Hazel ran her fingers over his taught stomach. Her red nails tracing a path through the trail of blonde hair running down from his navel, her private highway to pleasure. McGregor stirred at her gentle attention but didn't wake. This is the man I will marry, Hazel thought, her mind drifting to a celebrity-studded wedding with Hello or OK vying for the rights to the photographs. An elegant 1940s Hollywood cream gown designed by Alexander McQueen, a honeymoon in the states to discuss their move across the Atlantic as the newest British power couple. McGregor's career as a surgeon to the stars would guarantee her access to the Hollywood elite and, more importantly, the men who made the big screen decisions. Hazel had been dropping hints for the past few months, discreetly slipping information to the press on their impending engagement, tipping them off when she was at McGregor's apartment. For all his rough exterior, Hazel knew in her heart McGregor loved her. It was only a matter of time, a waiting game until the inevitable proposal.

McGregor moved his hips so her hand slid lower. Hazel smiled as the sleepy McGregor unknowingly pushed his dick into her waiting hand. Hazel wanted to do something special for McGregor, something to keep his thoughts from lingering on the nubile make-up girl they had shared their bed with for the last two nights. Olivia had been a marvellous addition to their lovemaking, her eagerness to please coupled with her lack of boundaries had made her the perfect girl to share with McGregor. She'd willingly gone along with all their games and revelled in being tied up and whipped into submission. Hazel was sure Olivia would be a regular player in their sexual encounters. Thinking about her made Hazel wet with pleasure, but also cautious. McGregor needed to know where his loyalties lay, and that was with her. This morning's wake-up call would be the ideal way to remind him of the perfection of their relationship. Hazel leant over and encircled McGregor's penis with her lips, gently nibbling and licking until he was firm. She pushed the full length of him into her until he touched the back of her throat. McGregor stirred but didn't fully wake as her fingers massaged his balls. Hazel felt his thighs tense and knew he was ready to come. With expertise that came from knowing every inch and pleasure point of his body, Hazel inserted her thumb into his anus and sucked. McGregor opened his eyes and lifted his shoulders from the bed. His hands reached for her head, his fingers tangling in her hair and pushing her deeper. His body tensed, and he orgasmed.

"Are you awake, my lover," Hazel asked innocently.

"I am now," McGregor replied.

Hazel snaked her mouth up his body and locked her lips with his. McGregor responded, his tongue diving in and out of her mouth, sending tingling fire through her body. As suddenly as he responded, he stopped.

"Coffee and paper?"

Hazel knew he wasn't asking if she wanted to read the morning newspaper with a milky latte in bed, he was placing an order. Hazel got out of bed, her hips swaying seductively as she walked naked from the bedroom into the kitchen. The erotic display was lost on McGregor, who had already closed his eyes and drifted back to sleep.

McGregor opened his eyes and sat up in bed. The bed was cold. Hazel should have been back by now with his black coffee and, if she was lucky, a repeat of the morning's entertainment. He threw back the sheets and stormed into the kitchen. Hazel sat at the breakfast counter, her back to him, the newspapers spread out in front of her, two coffees discarded on the side to go cold.

"Where the fuck is my coffee?" McGregor barked.

Hazel turned to face him. Her skin was as pale as morning snow, yet a blotchy redness had crept up from her chest, corrupting the smooth whiteness. Her lips were set in a thin line, and anger emanated from her bloodshot eyes. Hazel grabbed the newspaper and threw it at him.

"Did you know?" she accused.

"Know what?" he asked, bending to pick up the crumpled paper at his feet.

"The whore!" Hazel screeched, throwing herself across the breakfast bar and shoving the rest of the newspapers onto the floor.

McGregor ignored her histrionics and looked at the front page of the Mail on Sunday. Emblazoned across the cover was a full page picture of Olivia Chatsworth in a lacy red teddy he'd bought for Hazel. It showed off her slim waist and long legs in a way it had never clung to Hazel's body. The big black headline read, 'My Weekend Threesome with Hazel Woods and David McGregor.'

"The bitch," McGregor spat, turning to page five.

Across a double-page spread were two more photos. The first, Olivia tied in bondage gear with the caption, 'She Tied Me Up While He Whipped Me'. The second of, the make-up artist in a schoolgirl outfit above the words, 'I Was Dressed Up as a Schoolgirl While Hazel Went Down on Me, McGregor Took Photos.' Hazel's shrieks made it impossible for McGregor to concentrate on the words. Calmly he walked over to her, grabbed her by the shoulders and slapped her hard across the face. A red welt appeared immediately, her left eye swelling slightly from the forceful blow.

"Fucking shut up. I need to think," McGregor growled.

Hazel dangled from McGregor's grasp, yelping pitifully like a puppy separated from its mother as she desperately tried to hold in the screams. McGregor let go, shook his head dismissively and returned to the newspaper. The article was a hatchet job, leaving the reader with no doubts about the depravity of McGregor or his lover Hazel Woods. It detailed Olivia's first encounters with the two, the sexual advances and trysts in their dressing rooms, the off camera spats. The article divulged details about Bankers, although thankfully not by name, instead calling it a well-known sex club in London. Chronicled Hazel's invitation to spend the weekend at the Carmine Hotel and in graphic, horrifying detail Olivia related the perverted sexual games they had played in the luxury suite. McGregor skim read the rest. He'd have been turned on by the article if he didn't know the impact it was going to have on his career. Hazel would no longer be seen as a girlfriend to confide in over coffee. And he'd not be able to sell himself as the housewives' favourite or lambast about corruption in the world of plastic surgery now he had been outed as a heavy-drinking, sexual deviant.

"The fucking whore," he snarled as Olivia described in intimate detail his enjoyment as he watched the women playing children's games in the nude.

Olivia was repeatedly quoted, her inflammatory comments highlighted in bold black text. 'He recited nursery rhymes as we skipped about naked,' and 'McGregor had his hand on his cock while we played hopscotch and asked if we wanted to lick his lollipop.' Olivia revealed Hazel's eruptive personality, her hysterics on set and her need to control those around her. 'Hazel, also known not affectionately as Witch-Hazel by her colleagues, is a control freak. Yet in the bedroom she submits to the needs of her lover David McGregor. He controls her every move and delights in punishing her for unseen transgressions.'

"What do we do?" Hazel whimpered as the telephone rang. McGregor picked up the phone.

"Fuck off," he yelled, slamming down the receiver. "Fucking press." McGregor stormed over to the window and looked out. "The cunts are camped outside."

Hazel trembled. It was bad enough having her intimate life exposed, but to have to face the press and explain was all too much. "David, do something."

In reply, McGregor walked over to her and slapped her so hard he knocked her to the floor, standing over her menacingly while she cowered in the corner.

"I told you to fucking shut up. I can't think while you're shrieking at me."

McGregor picked up the phone and stomped into the bedroom, slamming the door shut behind him. Hazel waited for a moment and then cautiously crawled over to the bedroom door. She pushed her ear against the door and listened.

"Press is outside," McGregor said, his voice muffled through the door.

"Yes, it's true… Hazel's here… I'm not sure about that…" A long pause while McGregor listened to the person on the other end of the telephone conversation. Eventually, he responded. "Well, if you think it's for the best, I guess it can be temporary." Another pause. "I'm following your lead on this one if you think it will work."

Hazel could hear McGregor's footsteps moving towards the door and she scuttled backwards to the kitchen breakfast bar where he'd left her.

"Gabriel is sending a car," McGregor said.

Hazel stood up, narrowly missing the edge of the table, and threw herself at McGregor. "Please, please don't send me out there to face them on my own."

McGregor pulled her away from him and looked at the shaking woman in his arms. Hazel flinched, expecting a backhanded blow, but instead he pulled her back to him and embraced her in his strong arms. Hazel melted into the embrace, her face pressed against his chest as he soothingly stroked her hair.

"It's going to be just fine," McGregor soothed. "Gabriel is sending a car with some of your things, a make-up artist and hairdresser and a ring. Gabriel is one of the best PR men in the business. It's all sorted."

Hazel burst into tears. Her shoulders shook as the trauma and hurt of the day flooded out of her. McGregor was her protector. He had a plan, and all she had to do was go along with it.

"We need to get out in front of the story," McGregor explained. "Show a united front and divorce ourselves from Olivia and her exposé. If we deny anything, the article will grow legs. So instead Gabriel's plan is to confirm she spent the weekend with us and then give them something bigger to talk about."

The bell rang, and McGregor sat Hazel on the breakfast stool before going to answer the door. Hazel stared unseeingly at the table in front of her, the newspaper pages a blur of words and images that made no sense. She closed her eyes and tried to take deep steadying breaths. A gentle hand touched her shoulder, and Hazel turned to look at the pretty woman stood in front of her.

"Miss Woods," the woman said, "I'm Saffy. I'm your make-up girl. Jenny, the hairdresser, is just fetching up the clothes and stuff, but I just couldn't wait to get up here and congratulate you. Thank you so much Miss Woods for letting me be a part of this big day."

Hazel didn't understand a word she'd said. Big day? Congratulations? Her world was crashing down around her, and this ridiculous girl wanted to be part of it?

"What's the ring like? Which designer have you chosen for your gown? Have you set a date yet?" Saffy asked as she applied foundation to cover the nasty bruise forming on Hazel's face. "No of course you haven't set a date yet. I'm being silly. You only just got engaged."

Hazel grabbed Saffy's hand. How dare this stupid girl make fun of her? But the girl wasn't making fun of Hazel's sad situation. Her face showed a genuine joy. "Oh, I'm sorry, Miss Woods, did I catch that nasty bruise?"

"It's a little sore," Hazel mumbled trying to comprehend Safi's words.

"Good, we wouldn't want you looking in pain as you announce your engagement to the world." The doorbell rang again. "That'll be Jenny. She's such a sweetheart. You'll love her and the dresses they've sent over. Wow, if I could ever wear a dress like that, I'd be in heaven." Saffy babbled on while applying eye shadows and blushers. Hazel tuned out. Engagement, ring, giving the press a bigger story. The truth began to sink into the fog of Hazel's mind. Gabriel had suggested an engagement as a means of giving their relationship legitimacy, and McGregor had agreed. Hazel's heart stopped beating for a moment as she held her breath until stars floated in front of her eyes and the world started to spin. David McGregor loved her and meant to marry her.

"David!" she screamed, letting the air out of her lungs and her heart lurch back into rhythm.

"Yes, my love," McGregor said, poking his head around the door. He was wet from the shower, his face clean shaven and a towel wrapped around his waist.

"We're going to get married?"

"That's why I proposed, darling."

Hazel rushed to McGregor and threw her arms around his neck, pressing her lips to his and kissing him. McGregor blushed slightly and smiled at the two girls stood with their mouths open wide.

"This morning's newspapers have given Hazel a fright. Our sex life is a little unconventional, but I think that should be our business and no one else's."

"I agree entirely," Saffy said. "The bitch is only after money."

"Just wants to be famous for five minutes," Jenny added. "Not like you, Miss Woods. You have real class, but Olivia Chatsworth is a tart."

"Thank you," McGregor said untangling himself from Hazel's grasping arms. "We hope everyone will be as understanding as you." He turned Hazel to face Jenny and with a gentle pat on her bottom sent her stumbling towards them. "Let the ladies finish your hair, love. I need to go put some clothes on." He smiled self-effacingly, knowing full well the devastating effect his tanned abdomen was having on the assembled gaggle of women.

Hazel dutifully sat on a stool and let Jenny mess with her hair. She half-listened as they talked about that horrible Olivia. But that conversation was soon replaced by speculation about J-Collies and his on-again, off-again girlfriend. Hazel heard something about embarrassing photographs of a drunken Lady Elizabeth puking outside a London nightclub. A new song released by Five Spokes and the start of a gang trial that promised to be as exciting as any TV show. Hazel sighed contentedly. She was engaged to McGregor, something she had wished for. Maybe McGregor expected a long engagement, but Hazel had other ideas. She knew where his skeletons were buried, and now she had a ring, she wasn't about to give it back without a fight.

"You look beautiful, Miss Woods," Saffy exclaimed as she emerged from the bedroom in a tight-fitting red suit. "If I can just touch up your lipstick?"

"Call me Hazel." Hazel beamed. Saffy had worked wonders. Her face glowed radiantly, and even the purple bruise couldn't be seen underneath the make-up. Hazel made a mental note to get Saffy on staff at Morning Wake-up. It would be a good idea to have a few allies in the studio. Olivia had been well-liked, and Hazel knew she'd burnt many bridges with the studio crew. Maybe Jenny needed employment as well?

McGregor walked into the living room and took a

step back. "My, my, who is this beautiful creature standing before me?" he gushed, rushing to kneel in front of her. "You look radiant, my darling. But there is one thing missing." McGregor reached into his back pocket and pulled out a large diamond ring, the five carat princess cut stone stood proudly in its platinum setting. "You left this in the bathroom, dear."

As McGregor pushed the ring onto her left hand, Hazel felt butterflies fluttering in her stomach. Saffy and Jenny cooed in the corner, honoured to be present at this pure moment of loving intimacy. McGregor ignored them, looking deep into the face of his beloved. This was what needed to be remembered and reported by the media, these spontaneous displays of affection between him and his fiancée. McGregor looked up at the two girls, smiled warmly and winked. The girls giggled.

"Now if the press asks you any questions, just tell the truth," he said. "We have nothing to hide, so please, if you can make a little money on the side, go ahead. You can buy me a drink with your ill-gotten gains."

Jenny giggled while Saffy replied, "Mr McGregor, we wouldn't share anything with the press."

"Call me David," McGregor said, taking hold of Saffy's hand. "I'm very impressed by your integrity. However, in this instance I give you permission to tell the press what you have seen here. Right down to the horrid bruise Miss Woods received at the hands of Olivia Chatsworth."

Saffy gave McGregor a big hug and then rushed over to hug Hazel. "I'm so happy for the both of you," she gushed.

"Thank you, dear," Hazel replied. "And I agree with David. I wouldn't have any problems with you talking to the press. I know you'd not make anything up. Just tell them how happy we are together."

Hazel kissed Saffy and Jenny on their cheeks before taking McGregor's arm and leaving the apartment.

Behind her, she could hear their faint conversation.

"They are so in love," Jenny said.

"Hazel's so amazing," Saffy added. "Not at all like the paper made her out to be."

"Maybe we can do the make-up and hair for the wedding."

"Fingers crossed, Jenny."

Hazel smiled as she stepped into the elevator. If those two were anything to go by, then this cover-up would work and, better still, give her everything she wanted. "Olivia Chatsworth, thank you so much. I hope you were paid very handsomely because I am going to destroy you," Hazel whispered under her breath.

"What was that dear?" McGregor asked.

"Nothing darling, just thinking out loud. A summer wedding, don't you think?"

Chapter 34 – A little chat

Patrick's weekend had dragged. Carole had been out all Saturday with her girlfriends. Spending exorbitant amounts of money in Harrods, lunching at the Ritz and having her nails done at the overpriced Serenity Spa. She called at seven o'clock and left a message on the answerphone for him to get himself something to eat as she was going to be late. He was asleep before she arrived home.

Sunday morning, she was quiet over breakfast. Surprisingly, he missed her usual nagging banter and inane gossip about this friend or that relative.

"You're quiet, dear," he said, pouring himself another cup of black coffee. "Is something wrong?"

"No, no," she replied. "I was just thinking I haven't seen Maxine for a while."

"Weren't you with Maxine yesterday?"

"Yes, of course," she snapped. "I meant I haven't seen her on her own for a while. You know, without the other girls. I worry about her, and we just didn't have a chance to chat."

Patrick smiled. Carole would be able to chat underwater.

"What's so amusing?" she asked.

"Nothing, Cupcake," he replied, using her pet name in an attempt to soothe her ruffled feathers. "It's just you amaze me with your concern for your friends."

"I am always concerned for my friends," she snapped.

"I know that's what I meant. You're a good friend and a good wife. In fact," he said, standing up and kissing her on the cheek, "you are just an incredible woman."

Carole almost cringed at his touch but reminded herself to relax. "I have to pop out later. You'll be okay here, won't you? Or you could go to the club?"

Patrick felt disappointed. Carole looked magnificent, the new hair style and clothes suited her, bringing out the blue in her eyes and hugging her figure beautifully. "Have you lost weight?" he asked, noticing her regained slim waist.

Carole twirled in front of him. "A little, but it's the clothes really," she lied.

"Do you have to go? Couldn't we nip back upstairs?" he asked, grabbing her around the waist and pulling her to him.

Carole pushed him away. "Patrick," she laughed. "In the middle of the morning? What would Mae say?"

"Who cares?"

"I do. I will not be gossiped about when she meets with her other housekeeping friends, and besides, I've just done my hair."

When she left, Patrick thought about going to the Boot Room, but he couldn't face the smoke, noise and inane masculine banter that dominated the conversation. My dick is bigger than yours, is a conversation you can only have when you are not in a reflective and depressed mood. Besides, his dick didn't feel very big after being rejected by Carole in favour of the book club.

He considered going into the office, tidying up the paperwork relating to Mrs De-Vargas' botched boobs. He'd submitted the report to FOBPS and been interviewed over the telephone by an officious surgeon who didn't seem to know his arse from his elbow or his medical silicone from his sealant. Patrick had been informed the police would be making enquiries and to ensure he was available. The ramifications of performing the surgery without a licence had been hammered home repeatedly during the conversation. Patrick had been as contrite as possible, explaining the emergency nature of the procedure and the judgement call he'd made. At no point did he mention the metaphorical knife to his throat or the part this had played in his decision to go ahead with the reconstruction. The office was not the place he needed to be at the moment. He couldn't go to the boxing, and looking at the papers to see the race odds was just masochistic as Mr Green refused to take his calls. He'd not seen Layla since she'd brought him home, and he doubted he ever would again. If he wasn't allowed to gamble, he wouldn't be allowed to hire a whore. Patrick had never felt so alone or out of his depth. He closed his eyes and slowed his breathing. Self-pity never got you anywhere. If only he could see Layla, he'd feel better, but he didn't have her telephone number. Patrick held his head in his hands, trying to think of a way to get in contact with her. He jumped up, bashing his knee on the table as he remembered she'd called Jerry from his phone. Maybe he could persuade Jerry to pass on a message to Layla? It was a long shot, and he didn't know if she'd take his call or risk the consequences of meeting him without Costa's approval, but he had to try. His whole body ached with the need to see her. He hobbled to the telephone and dialled Jerry's number like a teenage boy, his fingers shaking, his palms sweaty.

"Jerry, can you get a message to Layla? I'll make it worth your while."

"Hang on," Jerry replied, passing the phone to his passenger.

"Hello," Layla breathed, ensnaring Patrick in the richness of her voice.

"Hello," he stammered.

"Patrick," she whispered, "are you okay?"

"Yes, no, not really," he mumbled. "I need to see you. Can you get away?"

"I am on way to client. I get Jerry to bring me after," she hung up without saying goodbye.

"I love you," Patrick whispered into the dead line.

Patrick rushed around the house. "Mae, Mae,

clean the bathrooms and kitchen and then have the afternoon off. With Carole out for the day, I can take care of myself." He felt as giddy as a young boy waiting for Christmas, certain in the knowledge dreams can come true if you close your eyes and just wait for your presents to arrive. He jumped into the bath, scrubbing himself clean of his self-indulgent pity.

"I'm going, Mr Sharp," Mae shouted from the bottom of the stairs.

"Right you are," Patrick yelled back from the bathroom.

Patrick was towelling himself dry as the doorbell rang. He ran downstairs, the towel clasped loosely around his waist and pulled open the door expectantly.

"Mr Sharp."

"Rebecca," Patrick replied. "Are you still using that name?"

"Rebecca is fine, Mr Sharp. Perhaps I could come in, and you could put some clothes on?"

"Rebecca, as I assured you last time, we have nothing to talk about. I am expecting a guest, so if you'd excuse me." Patrick started to close the door, but Rebecca placed a surprisingly strong hand against the wood.

Patrick puffed out his chest in annoyance and grabbed her arm. Instantly, he heard the sound of car doors opening, and two men emerged from the unmarked Town Car. Patrick paused as he took in the muscular, armed figures.

"I see we understand each other, Mr Sharp," Rebecca whispered. "Now if you let me in for a little chat, I can be gone before Layla Arze arrives."

Rebecca was terrifyingly well-informed. Had they tapped his phone, or Layla's phone, or the Trae La Muerte's vehicles? What did she know about his agreement with Costa? Patrick felt a prickle of fear run down his back, and the heat of panic made him sweat even in just a towel.

"Should I put the kettle on while you get dressed, Mr Sharp?" Rebecca said, closing the door behind her and walking into the kitchen.

Patrick nodded, unable to disagree. This conversation was going to take place regardless of his attire.

When he returned to the kitchen, he could smell the rich, roasting coffee. Rebecca was sat at the breakfast table, photographs spread out on the pale wood. She pointed at a chair. "Sit," she ordered. Patrick did as she commanded and took the offered coffee. "We have a lot to talk about," she said. "Firstly, your connections to Trae La Muerte are without doubt."

Patrick opened his mouth to refute her claims.

"Now, Mr Sharp," Rebecca warned, "this will go a lot quicker if you don't try to deny things that are already in evidence." She threw a set of photographs at Patrick. "As you can see, we know about your preference for Layla Arze, a trafficked prostitute from Bolivia. We know about your gambling debt, and we have interceded on your behalf with the Federation of British Plastic Surgeons with regard to the De-Vargas case."

Patrick looked at the photographs. The first few were of him and Layla at various hotels. He was stunned by her beauty, the darkness of her eyes, the prominence of her cheekbones, the naturalness of her imperfect loveliness no surgeon had ever touched. The second set was of Patrick at various boxing events or greeting the wives of high-ranking Trae La Muerte generals at NuYu.

"What the fuck," Patrick exploded as he turned to the last three images.

"You didn't know?" Rebecca said patronisingly.

The photographs had been taken using a telephoto lens through the window of a penthouse hotel suite. The subject of the surveillance, Mr Green, was naked and knelt at his feet in a leather basque was Carole Sharp.

"We chose the less explicit images to print," Rebecca said, clearly enjoying herself. "In other frames, the material is quite pornographic."

"Carole," Patrick said, his mind crushed by self-absorbed misery. He conveniently forgot his affairs and constant use of prostitutes. Carole's infidelity seemed more profound than anything he had ever done. Her inability to experiment sexually with him had always been a conflict in their marriage. Yet here in these photographs, Patrick saw a woman who knew her body, acted out her fantasies and enjoyed it. In full colour, Patrick saw a woman in love with herself and the man she had chosen to experiment with. He pushed the photographs away.

"What do you want?"

"I want to tell you a story, Mr Sharp. Some of the story you already know, but I think the ending will come as a bit of a shock. Once upon a time," she started, "there was a plastic surgeon who got into bed with the wrong wolf. Now some people may think that anyone who plays with a wolf gets what they deserve, and maybe they're right. This little plastic surgeon performed numerous surgical operations and received lots of money for his work, none of which he declared to the authorities. Then one day, the wolf asked the plastic surgeon to carry out a boob job on Mrs Wolf. The greedy plastic surgeon agreed, but he made a mistake. The implants were cheap, and they ruptured, and Mrs Wolf's boobs sagged. The wolf was angry and went to the plastic surgeon, demanding answers and money and then, just to be sure, he bit off the plastic surgeon's head." Rebecca threw another pile of photographs at Patrick. "Our friends in Bolivia provided these."

Patrick gagged and rushed over to the kitchen sink. His stomach heaved, and Mae's famous pancakes were regurgitated into the basin.

"As you can see, Mr Sharp," Rebecca said, laying

out the photographs of the decapitated surgeon, "Trae La Muerte does not take kindly to mistakes. Your colleague here, Doctor Guillen, wasn't given the chance to explain his medical negligence to the authorities. His body was found three hours after you gave the Federation of British Plastic Surgeons his name. It took longer to find his head."

Doctor Guillen's blood-soaked body had been disposed of in a back alley next to a rusting skip. Thrown inside the skip and photographed separately, his head. The ragged tissue of his neck was a clear sign the decapitation had not been quick.

"We think, from the photos, they used a hacksaw," Rebecca mused. "We are not sure how long he was conscious."

Patrick puked again.

"I have nothing to say," he said, wiping his hand across his mouth. "If you'll please leave."

Rebecca stood up and straightened the piles of photographs. "I'll leave these here with you. Should you change your mind, you can reach me at Scotland Yard."

Patrick still had the photographs spread out on the kitchen table when Layla arrived. She took one look at the contents of the images and ran to him, wrapping her arm around his shoulders and rocking him like a baby until his shaking stopped.

"Layla," he croaked his voice dry and gravelly. "What should I do?"

So consumed was he by his own fear, Patrick didn't notice Layla's ashen face or see the terror in her eyes. She'd come here to tell him something, to give him news that both terrified and delighted her. Yet somehow she couldn't bring herself to say the words after the atrocities in those pictures.

"It be okay, my love. We find solution," she said into his hair. The words sounded hollow and false. A lie to appease a child, a fiction to make you feel better for a while until the horror of the truth invaded every part of your being. Patrick was a dead man, and if she didn't report his dealings with the police to Costa, so was she. "Let go for walk," Layla suggested, moving the photographs away.

"What if we are seen?"

"It not matter anymore."

Patrick misinterpreted her lack of concern for one of confidence in Costa's indifference. "I'll go get my coat."

They walked along the leafy streets near Patrick's home and crossed the small bridge to the square communal gardens. Layla breathed in the fresh air, the sweet smell of the trees and listened to the sound of birds perched on the branches. This is what she missed most about back home, the green open spaces where people and animals lived together in small corrugated shacks. Families had nothing apart from the most important thing, each other. The London she knew was dirty and smelly and painful. It was darkened clubs and hotel suites. It was sex and drugs and being forced to do things she didn't want to with men she didn't know. London was servitude, punishment and the threat that if you didn't do as you were told, the people you loved would suffer. She had resigned herself to the fact that her life was worthless in the hope her sister could have a bright future. But now things had changed. Her affection for Patrick and that first night of unprotected passion had left her wanting and needing more. Her priorities had changed, and with the money Patrick had sent Katricia, life could possibly be better.

"Tell me of this Rebecca?"

Patrick recounted his meetings with Rebecca, and the information she had provided.

"Layla, she knows everything. If I don't cooperate, I'm imprisoned, but if I do, I'm dead."

"Can she protect if you testify?"

"You know as well as I that she can't."

"Patrick," Layla said, taking his hands in hers, "I'm pregnant."

Patrick stared in blank disbelief. "Is it Costa's?"

Layla slapped Patrick hard across the face, her small frame delivering enough power to knock his head sideways. "It yours," she hissed. "The first night in hotel. I sleep only you with no condom. Then and always."

"Mine?" he said, the reality of a tiny life growing inside Layla starting to take root in his brain. A little foetus, so small it wouldn't yet show up on a scan, yet so precious. A billion genetic instructions that would grow into a person, half Layla, half him. His face broke into a silly grin. His shoulders shook with laughter as he hugged Layla to his chest.

"A baby. My baby, Layla," he stammered, unable to put his words into any coherent form. "I don't know what to say."

"Say you love me, and it be all okay."

"I do love you," Patrick declared.

"Kayak," Layla responded.

Chapter 35 – Mr Witch

Doctor Smith-Jones looked up from the doodle on his notepad and considered the gentleman laid on the blush consultation sofa. The self-important man's legs were crossed over the arm of the couch, his expensive shoes wet from the rain staining the yellow fabric.

"And now I am fucking engaged to the bitch," McGregor fumed, sitting up to check the doctor was listening.

"How does that make you feel?" Smith-Jones asked, buying time until he could work out what the arrogant twat was talking about.

"Trapped, frustrated. I want to make the bitch, Olivia Chatsworth pay for her betrayal. Make her beg for mercy while I squeeze my fingers around her neck. I want to slap the smug smile from Hazel's face and beat her into submission. I want to ..." Spittle flew from McGregor's mouth as the impotent fury spewed forth.

Smith-Jones looked at McGregor over the metal rim of his glasses. "Mr McGregor while I can sympathetic to your plight and bound by patient confidentiality, I must remind you that I am duty bound to report and threatening behaviour to the authorities."

McGregor swung his legs to the floor and sat up. "What the fuck do I pay you for then," he growled.

Smith-Jones scribbled 'narcissistic aggressor with an overwhelming need to control those around him,' on the notepad. "We need to find the cause of your anger Mr McGregor. Your self-destructive behaviour with women must stem from your childhood. Tell me about your relationship with your mother."

McGregor's mouth set in a thin frown and his eyes narrowed. "I don't have a problem with my mother. I hardly saw the bitch. I have a problem being engaged to a twisted conniving whore who wants to get married and make babies."

"The why did you get engaged if you don't want to get married?"

"Olivia fucking Chatsworth. Haven't you been listening?"

At Hazel's insistence, Saffy and Jenny were drafted as the replacement Morning Wake-up make-up girls. The associated press had been more cynical than the two young, star-struck girls, but the chance to sell papers had been too much of an incentive to not run the story. The Sun, in particular, ran a full page spread. Giving front page coverage to the announcement of the McGregor-Woods engagement, mainly out of rage that the Mail had beat them to a scoop. The Daily Mail stuck doggedly to the story of Hazel's and McGregor's exploits with Olivia. Revealing more salacious details about McGregor's fondness for dishing out pain and Hazel's submissive responses. Hazel spread the array of newspapers on the dressing table. Her beautiful, composed face stared back from the pages. She picked up The Daily Express, absorbing their report. Bless Andrew Percy. He'd even quoted Saffy describing the horrific bruising Miss Chatsworth had inflicted in a fit of jealousy. Hazel laughed. The article made Olivia out to be love-struck as well as greedy.

The show's producers hadn't been pleased by the recent scandal, but the hordes of people camped outside for a chance to congratulate the happy couple seemed to have dulled their anger. In fact, to make the show an extra special one, they'd insisted David McGregor host the full show as co-presenter, rather than just participating in his usual cosmetic surgery slot.

McGregor walked into Hazel's dressing room, holding a large bouquet of flowers.

"Are those for me?" Hazel sighed. "David, you are so wonderful."

"They aren't from me," McGregor snapped, plonking the flowers on her dressing table. "There's about forty more downstairs."

Hazel plucked the card from within the arrangement of pink roses. "To Hazel and David," she read aloud. "Many happy returns on your engagement. Love your biggest fans, the canteen ladies in Leeds. Oh, David, are they all for us?"

McGregor bowed his head. "We've played it right. Gabriel is worth every pound the bastard charges us."

Hazel placed a chaste kiss on McGregor's cheek. She'd decided she needed to be more demure around the studio now she was an engaged woman.

A runner poked his head around the dressing room door. "Sorry to interrupt, Miss Woods, Mr McGregor, but this is your five-minute call."

"Thank you, Jim," Hazel replied politely.

McGregor raised his eyebrow. Since when did Witch-Hazel know people's names, let alone say thank you? Jim was as surprised as McGregor. He turned to leave and tripped up over his feet, muttering, "That's alright, Miss Woods."

Hazel and McGregor sat hand in hand on the red sofa, waiting for the director to finish his countdown.

"In five, four, three, two, one. We are live," Barry said over the earpieces pushed into McGregor's and Hazel's ears. "Camera one, pull in tight to Hazel so McGregor can't be seen. Hazel, autocue is rolling."

The music faded, and on screen all the viewers saw was Hazel's face. She smiled shyly and started reading from the autocue. "Good morning to you all. I'm Hazel Woods, and this is Morning Wake-up." She paused and smiled as if considering something for a moment. "I'm sure you're all aware of the recent press coverage of my personal life. It is not something I wish to dwell on. What has been said has been said, and I'm afraid that bell cannot be un-rung. Olivia Chatsworth was a good friend and the complete betrayal of my trust has left me reeling. Olivia, as a friend, I reach out to you and hope you seek some help. This need for attention is something that will pull you down into places you don't want to go."

The director was screaming in her ear to return to the script, but Hazel ignored the yelled instructions. She was going to have her say, her way. This was live TV. What were they going to do, but keep the cameras rolling and hope for the best?

"Olivia knew I was announcing my engagement on Sunday morning and felt the need to overshadow my marvellous news with this sensational story. What happens in my bedroom is my business, and I will not seek to justify myself when all I am guilty of is exploring my sexuality within a committed relationship." The director's panicked shrieking grew louder and McGregor's grasp on her hand tighter. Hazel took a deep breath. "All that aside, I have the great pleasure of introducing a new co-host to Morning Wake-up." Hazel took a breath and waited dramatically.

McGregor narrowed his eyes. This co-hosting was supposed to be for one day only. How the fuck was he supposed to run a successful clinic if the majority of his day was spent being Mr Witch?

The camera closed tightly onto Hazel's beaming face, her radiance dispelling any misgivings the audience might have about her co-host actually being her replacement. "I give you my fiancée and co-host, Mr David McGregor."

The camera pulled back to include David sat gracefully on the sofa, hand in hand with Hazel. Quickly, he altered his expression from annoyance to happiness. "Thank you, Hazel," McGregor read the autocue, adhering to the words he'd been provided while hastily working out how contractually bound he was by Hazel's announcement. "I'm almost as excited about co-hosting as

I am about our engagement. I said almost," he winked at the camera as Hazel playfully tapped him on the arm. "Now before we move on to our first segment, I want you to show the viewers at home. Those who haven't bought a newspaper yet, what all the fuss is about."

Hazel's smile could have lit up the heavens. "Of course, David," she said, holding out her left hand as the camera zoomed in on the perfect diamond ring. The studio lights glinted off the faceted stone, making it appear as if a rainbow exploded from its centre. "David has such good taste, don't you think?" Hazel asked. "Later in our phone-in, we'll be talking about proposals. Was yours romantic? Unusual? Or just plain weird? Did the type of proposal reflect your marriage, or was he a total letdown after popping the big question? We want to know your stories, fun, sad or romantic. This is your chance to share."

"Now, with our engagement being announced yesterday," David read, "this show is dedicated to love and marriage. We're going to look at what you need to do to get ready for your big day, from cosmetic procedures you might want to consider to the perfect wedding breakfast. But first, we are going to catch up the news and weather."

"Mark, it's over to you," Hazel added.

"Thank you, Hazel, and may I add my congratulations to the both of you."

"Thank you, Mark," David replied.

"And in three, two, one, out," the director said over the earpieces. "Well done, David, a perfect performance. What the fuck, Hazel? You nearly gave me a heart attack bleating on about Olivia Chatsworth."

"The audience loved it. Don't be such a fucking baby, Barry."

"Welcome back, Hazel," McGregor laughed.

Hazel shot him a look that spoke volumes. "Get ready for your segment on cosmetic treatments for the big day while they file the audience in."

"How the hell did they put this all together so

quickly?" McGregor asked.

"The show's outline is always a little fluid, but my team is just really good. With our engagement, this was a show too magnificent not to make."

McGregor watched as the audience filed in to hushed oohs and aahs as they saw McGregor and Hazel stood together. Hazel flashed her ring at the people getting seated and walked over to talk to them.

"So sorry we had to keep you waiting outside. We didn't want to spoil the surprise, and with tweeting and Facebook, it was bound to get out."

Chapter 36 – My record is

The weekend blurred into a horrifying fuzziness. Robert drank until he couldn't think because each time he sobered he was either racked by guilt at his actions or halfway out the door to shag the bitch again. Sleep gave him no peace. She came to him in his dreams. Her naked body laid across his bed, her legs an open invitation for him to touch her pale, delicate skin. He didn't eat, he didn't wash. He sat in stinking sheets, looking into the mirror where her image haunted him.

An insistent noise penetrated his fog, an annoying buzzing as if a bee had flown into his ear and made its way into his brain. The notion annexed thought. Taking over his mind, filling him with the incessant fear the invading bee wouldn't be able to find its way back out. Robert leant his head to one side and then the other trying to shake the bee from its lodging in his auditory canal. Eventually, he stuck a finger into his ear to dig the bloody creature from his head. The banging started just as the buzzing stopped, and Robert realised something was hammering on his door. He lifted his aching body from the bed and stumbled towards the door. He collapsed against the wall and only after several failed attempts managed to turn the key. The door opened, and a figure loomed in front of him.

"For fuck's sake!" Will exploded, seeing Robert slumped against the wall. "Of all the days to turn into Fitzroy."

Will grabbed Robert by the neck and half-dragged, half-carried him into the bathroom. Dumping him in the shower, Will turned on the cold tap, drenching the drunk in freezing water. Robert spluttered and coughed, the water spilling over his face to run down his back in rivulets of ice.

Will poured the body wash he'd found underneath the pile of dirty towels over Robert's head. "Clean yourself up, man. You're a fucking disgrace."

The body wash stung Robert's eyes, the excruciating pain bringing him back to his senses. He pushed his face into the cleansing water and undressed, rubbing his body with the foaming wash until his skin was red from scrubbing and he felt sanitary again.

He emerged from the bathroom to the smell of cooking bacon. "What're you doing here on a Sunday?"

"It's fucking Monday," Will replied, pushing a bacon sandwich in front of Robert. "McGregor is in the studio all day, and you need to cover his surgery."

Robert blinked in confusion. Why was McGregor in the studio? Why wasn't it still the weekend? "I'm not sure I can," he said, holding his hands out to show Will the tremors vibrating along his fingers.

"What you taken?"

"I don't know. Something, everything, a lot of alcohol."

"Sutherland, you are a dick. Eat that, and we'll rehydrate you at the clinic."

It took two hours and an I.V. drip before Will was satisfied Robert could safely see clients. It took longer for Robert's addled brain to understand McGregor had gotten engaged.

"McGregor's getting married?" he kept repeating as if somehow continually asking would change the answer.

Will thrust the Mail on Sunday into Robert's hand. "Damage limitation, dick," he said and marched away to check on the list of operations due for the afternoon.

The press camped outside the clinic had expected to catch McGregor in hiding. Instead, they had to make do with Carl Fitzroy. "I'm to be the best man at the wedding," he chortled while posing for the camera. "Yes, of course, I knew. The lad's my protégé, taught him everything he knows."

"Even how to bang two women at once?" a reporter shouted.

"My record is four," Fitzroy laughed, "but don't tell the Mrs... Damn good publicity, this," he chuckled, bumping into Robert as he sauntered towards his office. "We'll have to get you engaged, too. Double the exposure."

"I'd rather concentrate on my career," Robert replied.

"Good idea, my boy, Cut 'em or fuck 'em, but never tie yourself to one. What do we have booked in for today while McGregor is on the lam?"

The day's appointment list was manageable. Several clients had cancelled their procedures last minute, claiming press invasion. Kate stated her opinion that the ladies had been more concerned about the morals of the tarnished McGregor than appearing in the tabloids. Claire nodded her agreement with Kate's statement, but secretly thought the cancelling patients were more annoyed that they hadn't been David McGregor's chosen playmate. With a light list, Fitzroy sober for the first time in years and Robert competent enough to assist, the capable Kate soon had the clinic running smoothly.

"Kate, you are a dear," an abstinent Fitzroy beamed, kissing her on the cheek.

"What's with the commander?" Claire asked Kate as she walked past with a pile of gowns.

"Relief from his McGregor allergy!"

Claire laughed, and Kate looked carefully at her. "Seems to me Fitzroy isn't the only one recovering from an oppressive mental illness."

"I don't know what you mean," Claire replied, blushing with embarrassment.

Kate smiled as Claire fled. She hadn't meant to embarrass her. In fact, she'd meant her comments as a discreet compliment. In the last few days, Claire had avoided all contact with the womanising anaesthetist. The exercise at the gym was paying off, and Robert's light touch with the dermal filler and Botox was noticeable but not over the top. Kate smiled and picked up the phone to Serenity Spa.

"Have you any appointments for tonight? Two cut and blow dries and two caviar facials… You have? Brilliant. Can you bill the Fitzroy Clinic? Actually, make it for three." Dylees deserved a treat as well. Fitzroy and McGregor owed them after all the shit they'd put up with in the last month.

Fitzroy skipped along the hallway towards the surgical suite. "Come on, my boy," he said, slapping Will on the shoulder as he danced past. "Lady Time waits for no man, especially those like us who crusade against her."

"What's he snorted, and can I have some?" Robert said, coming up behind Will.

"Nothing. He's sober, and don't you think you've fucking had enough?"

Robert held his hands up in surrender. "Look, Will, I'm sorry about this morning, but don't you think you're over reacting? It was the weekend, and I just had a good time. Like you taught me!"

Will scowled. "I don't care what you do as long as it doesn't affect me. Just stay out of my way," he growled, staring at Claire's slim legs and curvaceous bottom as she bent down to pick up one of the gowns she'd dropped.

"What's got into you? Or is it more what you haven't got into?" Robert asked, suddenly understanding the direction of Will's anger. "Maybe if you were nicer to her?"

"I said stay out of my fucking business!" Will yelled, grabbing Robert by the shirt and pulling him forward so the two men were nose to nose. "Keep your opinions to your fucking self."

Will stormed off, leaving Robert standing in the middle of the corridor. Claire turned and looked at him.

He shrugged. "I don't know what's up with him, but I'd stay clear if you don't want your head bitten off."

"Robert, dear boy, if you would join us," Fitzroy shouted impatiently from the end of the corridor.

Dylees wheeled the patient into the surgical suite as Robert scrubbed in.

"Classic Roman nose," Fitzroy commented, looking at the patient. "Did you know, Robert, that nose jobs were carried out at the height of the Roman Empire? Anlus Corneruis Celsus published the De Medicina which detailed the procedure. It amazes me how far we've come and yet how little we have changed."

Robert mumbled he hadn't known and steeled himself to be ridiculed.

"Well, I have a copy if you're interested, young Robert," Fitzroy said. "A little music, don't you think? What would you like, Dylees?"

"Abba?"

"Abba, it is. Let's get this dancing queen a straight nose." The music blasted out of the expensive sound system as Carl Fitzroy picked up the retractor. "Well, girls and boys, it's show time." Fitzroy pushed the retractor into the patient's nostril and then indicated that Robert should hold the instrument in place while he picked up a second retractor and inserted it into the second nostril. "Can you see the cartilage?" he asked Robert. "If we cut here and here," he pointed with the surgical scissors, "we will be able to remove the hump with minimal bruising."

Robert nodded. Fitzroy reached for a scalpel and cut into the skin of the nasal septum, following the red line he'd drawn earlier.

"Scissors," Fitzroy said, and Dylees handed him the sharp surgical scissors. "Osteotome." Dylees passed Fitzroy the small chisel along with the surgical hammer. "This is why I love you," Fitzroy laughed, taking the hammer. "You don't even need to be asked."

The sound of breaking bone always turned Robert's stomach, the hollow tap, tap, tap followed by the identifiable click as bone gave way to the surgeon's steel. Fitzroy massaged the bone between his thumb and forefinger. "What do you think?" he asked, taking hold of the retractor so Robert could feel the work. Robert ran his fingers up the nasal bone. The lump was gone to be replaced by an even continuous line.

"Okay, my boy, grab the rasp and let's smooth the bone a bit."

"Me?"

"I don't mean Will! He's only good with sharp, pointy things." Fitzroy looked pointedly at Will's crotch.

"We each have our own skill set," Will laughed.

Robert's hands shook as he took the rasp. He looked at the file for a moment before swallowing his trepidation and inserting it up the patient's nose. The resistance of the bone to the rasp surprised him.

"Steady. It's not like filing your nails. No calcification has occurred in a patient of this age, so the bone is almost flexible. You need to move slowly and with a little more pressure." Fitzroy indicated Dylees should take over holding the retractor and then placed his hand on top of Robert's to guide his movements. "Perfect," he said after a minute. "Now use the fine rasp to smooth and polish the bone. Then we can move on to the cartilage. Dylees, if you can direct the saline."

Robert did as instructed until Fitzroy was pleased with the results.

"Sutures, please." Fitzroy sutured the cartilage into place and then pulled the skin back over the nose. "A suture here, please," he said to Robert, passing him the needle and indicating he should stitch the nasal septum.

Dylees handed Fitzroy a nasal splint and tape. Fitzroy fixed the splint in place as the shades of bruising began to form. The master surgeon stepped back. The procedure had taken just under two hours. The skill with which Fitzroy's hands seemed to flow without thought left Robert astounded and he was forced to reassess the older surgeon. He'd learnt more in a day with Fitzroy than in three weeks of working alongside McGregor.

"Phone call for you," Claire said as Robert emerged from surgery.

"For me?" Robert replied, his heart skipping a beat as for one precious second he thought Elizabeth might have called.

"Yes, he says he's your uncle."

"Uncle Patrick!"

"How should I know? Go find out."

Robert walked slowly to reception. What could Patrick want? It must be important for him to call The Fitzroy Clinic.

"Robert, my boy," Patrick said warmly when Robert muttered hello. "I'm been meaning to pop in and see how you've settled in."

Robert smirked at the blatant lie. Patrick had no more intention of stepping a foot through the doors of the Fitzroy Clinic than McGregor would willingly enter the lounge of NuYu. Robert had the distinct impression that if either surgeon entered the sacred doors of the other's lair, they would instantly burst into flames and hell would open beneath their feet.

"I'm fine, Uncle Patrick, just a little pushed for time. I've two buttock augmentations before I'm finished. Was there something I could help you with?"

"Glad they're keeping you busy over there. I was hoping you'd be able to assist me in some off the books work."

Robert hesitated. Off the books meant not strictly legitimate, but it also meant cash. If he was to impress Lady Elizabeth on their second date, he needed money. Patrick Sharp's illicit work might be an ideal source of income.

"What sort of surgery?"

"Standard stuff mainly. Breast implants, nose jobs, that kind of thing. It's cash in your pocket."

"If we can keep it between the two of us. When?"

"Seven."

"Tonight?"

"The client is pressed for time. If it's inconvenient, I can get someone else." Patrick paused, hoping Robert wouldn't call his bluff.

"No, it's fine, Uncle Patrick. I'll walk over as soon as I'm finished here. You can brief me on what needs to be done when I get there."

In stunned contemplation, Robert put down the phone. It was the first time Patrick Sharp had ever shown any interest in helping him. Aunt Carole had practically blackmailed his uncle into letting the apartment to Robert. Even then Patrick had insisted on a complicated lease and a nominal rent so he could, in his words, 'Kick the scrawny-arsed wimp on to the street if he made even a coffee stain on the pure wool carpet.' The insults Patrick Sharp had thrown at Robert over the years still offended, but money was money, and it was better in his pocket than some other surgeon's.

"You sorted?" Dylees asked, walking past.

"Nearly," Robert replied. "I just have a quick phone call to make."

"Your Botox and fillers are here, and your B.I.G. will be prepped in thirty minutes."

Robert muttered acknowledgment, his mind far away on the luscious legs and firm breasts of Lady Elizabeth. He picked up the phone again. "Could you deliver three dozen, no make it five dozen red roses to The Penthouse, Royal Chambers, Jermyn Street, St James." He'd memorised her address from her medical notes. "The card?" He paused. "Just put Yours Always Robert and a couple of kisses." The four-hundred-pound price tag made him gag slightly, but he gave over his credit card details and with a self-satisfied smile hung up.

"What's with him?" Will asked as Robert walked past whistling. "This morning I had to practically give him CPR, and this afternoon he's bouncing about as if he's about to burst into song."

"How should I know? But as long as it keeps him moving until McGregor makes an appearance, I don't care," Dylees replied.

Chapter 37 - Most eligible bachelor

McGregor ripped the mic from his shirt and stood up. Morning Wake-up had just finished.

"If we can just get a couple of publicity shots with Hazel for the website?" a young lad with a camera asked.

McGregor glanced at the Morning Wake-up ID around his neck and nodded.

"Hazel darling, can I tear you away from your fans for a moment?"

Hazel looked over her shoulder and flashed an adoring smile at her fiancé. "Not a chance, dear. But the two of you can come over here and take some photographs. Would you like to be on our homepage?" she asked the two pensioners sat in the front row.

The grey-haired lady's hands went immediately to her hair while her friend grabbed her beige handbag and ferreted for her coral lipstick. As he posed with the old dears, McGregor noticed Gabriel, mobile pressed to one ear, scribbling frantic notes on the back of a cigarette packet. He raised his thumb indicating another successful negotiation. Throughout the morning, Gabriel had been fielding interview requests, photo-shoot offers and calls for quotes from every national magazine, newspaper and show. At present count, McGregor was expected to play the loving fiancé eleven times.

"The After Ten Show," Gabriel mouthed. Gabriel hung up the phone and walked over. "Four grand each," he whispered to McGregor before turning to the huddled fans. "I'm afraid I'm going to have to steal Miss Woods and Mr McGregor away from you. Haut Monde has just arrived to interview them."

McGregor smirked. The PR man was talented. The journalist Haut Monde had sent to interview them was evidently chosen to get a reaction from the fragile Hazel. The twenty-year-old had the same blonde curls, blue eyes and voluptuous figure of Olivia Chatsworth.

"Miss Woods," the journalist gushed. "It's such an honour to meet you."

"I'm sure it is," Hazel replied acidly before McGregor kicked her ankle under the table. "It must be quite a big story for you to cover," she added more diplomatically.

"It is Miss Woods. You have won the heart of Britain's most eligible bachelor. We at Haut Monde are such romantics, and we want to know, how do you do it?" Her eyes sparkled mischievously.

McGregor reassessed the journalist. She wasn't just a physical replica of Olivia. She had Olivia's hunger for fame as well. He'd have to watch what he said or be the victim of more press attention.

"Okay, from the start, can we get the questions about Olivia Chatsworth out of the way? Then we can quickly move on to the exciting wedding plans?"

McGregor raised his foot, ready to kick Hazel again.

"Of course, my dear," Hazel purred. "You wouldn't be doing your job if you didn't ask. David and I have nothing to hide."

The journalist looked disappointed at Hazel's calm response. She'd obviously wanted to report on a Witch-Hazel hissy fit rather than the size of the diamond in the engagement ring.

"I'm afraid I need to stop it there," Gabriel said after fifteen minutes. "David and Hazel have three more interviews before filming a celebrity make-over. I do hope you got everything you needed?" He didn't wait for the young journalist to answer and ushered her out of the green room that had hurriedly been repurposed as a press area.

"I need to be out of here by two," McGregor said, looking at his watch. "The camera crew are with Clara Cuntington till one and then setting up at the Fitzroy

Clinic. I need to make sure none of the fuckers says anything they shouldn't."

"Three more slots. Cosmo, Marie Claire and Woman's Own. Fifteen minutes a piece, and you'll be finished," Gabriel said.

McGregor posed for the Woman's Own photographer, his arm casually around Hazel's shoulder while she leant lovingly into him. The engaged couple smiled tenderly at each other as the camera flashed.

"I'm afraid that time is up," McGregor said, affectionately kissing Hazel's cheek. "I'll meet you on the Ann Thomas Chats set."

"Make sure you eat something, darling," Hazel called to his departing back.

McGregor strode purposefully towards the car park, his mind already on the complex lip reconstruction he was about to perform on camera. Lesser surgeons would be intimidated by the procedure. Pulling Gore-Tex from the lips resulted in unsightly scarring, and only a very few practitioners had the nerve to attempt the treatment. He would need to remove the strips intraorally by cutting into the inner lip tissue, known as the wet vermilion. It was a technically simple procedure but held a high risk of something going terribly wrong.

Dylees had everything under control at the Fitzroy Clinic. The camera crew were busy setting up in treatment suite one. Clara Huntington was happily chatting with a surprisingly glowing Claire. Fitzroy and Sutherland seemed to be coping with their lengthy surgical lists. In fact, Fitzroy appeared to be adapting a little too well to his re-found leadership role. McGregor would need to act before the old drunk reasserted himself and it became even more difficult to get the bastard to retire.

"Clara, my dear, is Claire looking after you?"

"Perfectly, David," Clara beamed. "We have such a lot in common. She has become a firm friend."

McGregor nearly choked on the espresso Claire handed him. He couldn't imagine two women with less in common.

"Good, good," he spluttered. "We'll just wait for Dylees to get out of surgery and then get you sorted."

Even with the door open, treatment suite one felt oppressively small. The camera equipment, lighting and sound boom were squeezed in between the medical equipment. The studio's technicians stood shoulder to shoulder against the walls, trying not to get in the way as surgeon and nurse prepped the patient for her procedure. Clara Huntington laid on the white couch, her eyes closed as McGregor injected lidocaine into her gum lines.

McGregor turned to the camera and spoke directly to his audience. "While the lidocaine takes effect, I will outline the procedure we are about to perform. Miss Huntington's Gore-Tex implants have been inserted subcutaneously, this means under the skin, to give her a permanently fuller lip. While popular in the nineties, their use in the UK has ceased due to the unnatural appearance of the lips after the procedure." He paused for a close-up shot of Clara's swollen lips. "Dermal filler provides more natural results, and while you still need to be careful which practitioner you choose, mistakes can be easily fixed." McGregor turned to Clara and touched her lips with his gloved hands. "Are you numb?" he asked.

Clara nodded, and McGregor lifted her top lip to show the camera the inside of her mouth. "I am going to make an incision here, just below the gum line, and gently pull out the Gore-Tex strips." McGregor touched his index finger to Clara's fraenum. "By using this method, we can minimise the visible scarring and be able to inject the filler once the lips have healed." Letting go of her lip, McGregor placed a reassuring hand on Clara's shoulder. "Okay, Clara, you will feel a slight pressure, but nothing more."

He nodded to Dylees, who used both gloved hands to roll back Clara's top lip. McGregor wiped the moisture from the skin, placed the scalpel against the inner lip and cut a half millimetre incision. He picked up the surgical tweezers and grabbed hold of the white strip that protruded from the blood bubbling on the surface. Taking a steadying breath, he slowly pulled. The strip caught as if it was made of Velcro instead of Gore-Tex. He pulled harder and felt the rip of tissue as the strip jerked free. McGregor placed the piece of Gore-Tex in the steel dish and showed it to the camera.

"As you can see, this strip has been attacked by the body's immune system. The yellow and white substance you see is the antibodies trying to break down a foreign object. This is often the reason the lips seem to get bigger over time. The benefit of dermal filler is that it doesn't work against the immune system. It is designed to allow the body to break it down over time and is removed by your lymphatic system, the body's own waste disposal."

McGregor returned his attention to Clara and removed the other strip of Gore-Tex in her upper lip. He put a small dissolvable suture in each incision before moving on to treat the bottom lip in the same fashion. The procedure took no more than thirty minutes, but it felt like hours. McGregor sat back and stretched, almost knocking over the sound engineer.

"Cut," he growled as the off balance technician's boom landed on Dylees shoulder.

"Make-up," the site director yelled down the corridor. "We'll get a few close ups of Clara and then break until the local anaesthetic has worn off."

"Claire," McGregor shouted. "Get me a coffee and a fag."

McGregor pushed his way out of the crowded room and sought sanctuary in his office.

With her make-up reapplied, Clara posed for a few after shots before exclaiming she really must use the loo and dashing from the treatment suite. What she really needed to do was confirm her dinner arrangements with Lord Mowbray, but she couldn't do that in front of a television crew. Her lips still felt numb from the lidocaine.

"Darling," she mumbled into her phone. "Of course it's me," she added when the judge demand she prove her identity.

Clara was crying when she hung up the phone. Lord Mowbray's verbal abuse was getting worse, and while she promised herself she wouldn't let his mood swings hurt, being constantly victimised by the man who claimed to love her was soul-destroying. The receptionist, Claire, had the right idea. She'd taken control of her life and ditched the dick who was using her. It gave Clara hope that maybe she would be able to do that one day. She dried her eyes and looked at herself in the mirror. A slight bruising was beginning to form, but the ugly lumpiness had gone. McGregor had warned her that when the swelling reduced, she'd need a bit of dermal filler, but for now her lips looked fantastic. She pouted in the mirror and smiled.

"Would you like a girly coffee and lunch one day next week?" Clara asked Claire as she waited for the film crew to finish setting up.

Chapter 38 – Rain check

The afternoon flew by. Botox, fillers, lifting threads and two quick buttock implants with the newly sober Fitzroy. All the time he was injecting, cutting and suturing, Robert was thinking about the radiant face of Lady Elizabeth Mowbray as she opened the door to receive his gift. Would she call him immediately and thank him for the delightful present? Or be more coy and casually bump into him in the coffee shop, he thought of as their special place? Maybe she would be bold and turn up at his apartment dressed in black lace knickers under a fur coat, begging him to shag her over and over again?

"Where are you off to, my boy?" Fitzroy asked as Robert almost ran out of the door. "Thought I'd take you for a quick drink at the Boot Room to celebrate a successful day without the Rabbit." Robert looked confused. "My pet name for the vain David McGregor. He fucks like one, so I call it as I see it."

Robert laughed. "I can't tonight, sir. I have an errand to run for my uncle."

Fitzroy's eyes narrowed slightly. "That would be Patrick Sharp?"

"Yes."

"The man's a shark. Just be careful what you get mixed up in, my boy," Fitzroy said, placing his hand on Robert's shoulder in a fatherly manner.

"I will, sir," Robert replied. For a brief moment, Robert wondered what his life would be like if Fitzroy had been his mentor instead of McGregor. Would the commander in chief have stopped drinking long enough to guide his student to excellence? Without McGregor's ridicule, would Fitzroy have risen to the challenge of being a better person? And would he have flourished under Fitzroy's tutelage? "Could we take a rain check?"

"Of course, lad," Fitzroy spluttered. "It's not like

you're going anywhere." He liked the strange northerner with his odd dress sense. When he had interviewed Robert, he'd thought the working class accent and hardworking attitude might be a welcome relief from the southern dandiness and muscle flexing he suffered from McGregor and Will. Silently, he wished he'd insisted on mentoring the boy, but McGregor had ruthlessly pointed out that Fitzroy was a drunk and a dinosaur. It was true. Carl Fitzroy hadn't been the same since his wife died. The clinic was all he had left, and instead of valuing the thing he loved most in the world, he'd let it become tarnished and abused by the likes of McGregor. "Things are going to change," he muttered as he watched the young man run down the steps. "Just you wait and see."

Robert ran from the top of Blow Row to the bottom, arriving at NuYu out of breath and panting. The doors to the clinic were locked and all the lights were out. Robert began to get the uneasy feeling, his Uncle Patrick hadn't been entirely honest about the patient they were about to treat. He knocked on the door softly, almost hoping no one answered. Instead, the front door was jerked open, and Patrick Sharp's large hand reached out and pulled Robert in.

"You're late," he hissed.

"McGregor was only in the clinic for an hour then rushed back to the TV studio. I've had to cover two lists."

Patrick snorted. "Fucking media whore. The arse wallows in shit and comes out smelling of roses as your Aunt Carole would say. How he managed to pull two birds in the first place amazes me. The prick must have a big dick."

Patrick looked at Robert, waiting for him to defend his boss. When he didn't, Patrick shrugged his shoulders "Been a slight change in the surgical plan," he said, heading towards the surgical suite. "It's a boob job and gender reassignment. We will be here to the early

343

hours of the morning."

"What?" Robert gasped. "But I've never…"

"Easy as any other surgery," Patrick lied. "Just nip, tuck and push. I'll be lead, so just do as you're told."

Robert gulped and tried not to think about the numerous things that could go wrong. "Who else is in with us?"

"Just you and me. I'll administer the anaesthetic, and you can monitor the vitals."

"But this type of surgery needs four people."

"For fuck's sake, where are your balls, boy? You don't get big off the books money if you aren't prepared to improvise occasionally." Patrick threw the notes at Robert. A loud bang at the front door stopped his tirade. "That's the patient. Now act professionally, or I'll string your useless corpse up outside that cunt McGregor's clinic."

Robert was taken aback by the venom in Patrick's voice. He was aware of his uncle's disdain for David McGregor, but even so, his level of hostility seemed excessive. The tickle of apprehension on Robert's neck turned into a sharp stab in his brain. What the hell had he gotten mixed up in?

"Good evening," Patrick said as he opened the door. Two men pushed past Patrick, dragging a third. "Where's Eloise?"

"Change of plan," Robert recognised the South American man from the doorstep of NuYu. "Mr Costa says you do this one." He deposited the slim, bruised man on the chair by the greetings desk.

The slight man's tanned and exotic features were hidden by extensive bruising. His delicate, handsome face was ruined by a deep gash on his cheek that had swelled until his left eye had closed. Finger-shaped bruising was starting to develop on his neck, and dried blood caked his white shirt. He leant uncomfortably to one side as if trying to ease the pain in his back as he stared blankly at his feet.

"I can't perform surgery on someone I've never

seen," Patrick blustered. "I need to run tests, blood analysis, check for infections."

"Run whatever tests you want, but surgery tonight."

"I need to talk to the patient first."

"He speaks no English."

"I must talk to Mr Costa. This is not what we agreed," Patrick said trying to keep the hysteria from his voice. "Robert, can you please clean up our patient and take him to the consultation room."

"I stay with him," the man said, lifting the would-be patient from the chair in his vice-like grip. The man winced in pain and cringed away from the muscle-bound man.

"That's okay," Robert interrupted. "I'll help him into the consultation room. You can follow." Robert hooked his arm around the slim waist and pushed his shoulder under the man's armpit. The man weighed nothing, and Robert lifted him easily as if he were a child. "Sorry," Robert said when the man grunted in pain. The man turned to look at Robert, his dark eyes reflecting nothing but fear. "I'm Robert," Robert said helplessly. "I'm going to get you cleaned up and give you something for the pain."

"It doesn't speak English," the man said as if Robert were slow.

"Then translate," Robert snapped, finding a store of courage he hadn't realised he possessed.

Patrick walked into his office and slammed the door shut. Fuck Costa. There was no way he was carrying out surgery on an unknown. He needed to run tests before any procedure. The last thing he needed was to contract AIDS or hepatitis from some South American rent boy. Patrick grabbed the telephone and stabbed at the buttons, his moral outrage bristling right until Costa's voice boomed on the other end of the line.

"Mr Costa, this is most irregular. I agreed to this

arrangement only on the strictest of guidelines. This goes against everything I stand for as a surgeon."

Costa listened patiently while Patrick detailed the dangers of surgery to a patient with bruising and lacerations. "Mr Sharp," he said calmly. "This matter not for discussion. Fabio will have surgery, and you will perform surgery. Jose there to translate."

"He could be carrying infection or disease. You can't expect me to put myself at risk."

"Is your problem. Fabio is there, and Eloise is not. You carry out surgery, or Jose will make you wish you did. Need I remind you, you have much money you owe me?"

Patrick's blood ran cold. Costa didn't need to go into gory details with his threat. The presence of the two armed thugs was enough of an incentive. They weren't there to prevent the misfortunate man from escaping but to leave Patrick in no doubt about what lay in his future if he refused.

"Is lovely Gwen assisting this evening? My wife talk about her affectionately."

Patrick stifled the scream building in his throat. "Gwen is not here," he replied, his voice sounding hollow.

"Ah, is shame. She is good nurse, I think. Let's hope whoever is helping is as good. A body would not be easy to go away."

Mine or Fabio's Patrick thought? "This is the first and the last, Mr Costa. I need to assess the patients before surgery in the future. I need to know if they are mentally prepared for the changes they are about to go through."

Costa laughed. "Not your concern. Leave Fabio with his dick. Give him large breasts and big bottom. Make him look pretty. Some men like their lady-boys with both options. They get bigger price."

Costa hung up without waiting for an answer. Patrick grabbed the whisky bottle on his table and poured himself a large glass of Midleton's. Thoughts of the dead Doctor Guillen flashed into his mind as he gulped back the alcohol. Trae La Muerte was not known for its understanding, and Patrick Sharp had no intention of turning up with his throat slit in some dark alley. The fiery liquid eased Patrick's conscience. After all, it wasn't as if he was cutting off the man's dick. In theory, if Fabio wanted, he could have the breast and buttock augmentations removed and go back to life as a man. Patrick unashamedly refused to think about the likelihood of Fabio ever escaping life as a whore for the Bolivian cartel.

Patrick walked with false purpose into the consultation room. Robert had cleaned Fabio's facial wounds and glued the nasty gash. Fabio had removed his shirt, and Patrick could now see the purple and green bruising along his rib cage and torso. Jose stood quiet and threatening in the corner of the room, a constant reminder of the consequences of noncompliance.

"Mr Sharp," Robert said. "This man is in no fit state to undergo surgery."

"I am the senior consultant," Patrick barked. "I will decide who is fit and who is not fit. Draw bloods and go get the cross match."

Robert opened his mouth to object, but Patrick's ominous expression told him not to voice his concerns in front of the thug who now guarded the door. "Very well, Mr Sharp. I shall bow to your better judgement."

Patrick walked over to the man. "Translate please," he said to Jose. "In a little while, we will be getting you ready for surgery."

Jose translated and Fabio nodded.

"Are you allergic to anything?"

Jose translated, and Fabio shook his head.

"Do you have any diseases I should know about? AIDS, Hepatitis, TB, blood clotting?"

Patrick waited while the question was translated, and Fabio answered. He pointed to his heart while talking.

"Nothing is wrong," Jose replied.

"Does he have a heart condition?"

Jose looked concerned.

"It will not prevent surgery, but it will make things more difficult if we do not know. He might die!"

Jose and Fabio spoke rapidly in Quechan. "Fabio has heart murmur. He takes bisoprolol and heparin."

Patrick grimaced. It meant they needed to work quickly and monitor Fabio more carefully. It was irregular, and imprudent, to carry out a procedure without more information. But nothing about this surgery was regular. One more complication wouldn't make a difference to the likely outcome. Patrick explained the two procedures he was about to do, and Jose translated. Fabio looked confused and then resigned to his fate. Nothing in his demeanour suggested excitement or even relief at finally starting the change from male to female. He shrugged his shoulders when Patrick asked if he had any questions and stood when told so Patrick could make the guiding marks on his body.

"After the surgery, we will put a little Botox and filler into your face to give you a more feminine appearance," Patrick explained. "This will last between six and twelve months, and then you will need it done again. If you ever need anything," Patrick stressed the word anything, "reversing, then we can do that for you."

Hope flashed in Fabio's eyes for a moment and then extinguished as he looked at the menacing face of Jose. What hope did a rent boy have of escaping the Trae La Muerte cartel, especially after the investment of cosmetic surgery? Fabio and those who followed would be fiercely guarded and well-used until they no longer became profitable. Then they would be murdered or worse, left on the streets to be deported back to South America.

"Please put this on," Patrick said, holding out a gown. "I will be back shortly to take you to anaesthetics." Patrick turned to Jose. "You can accompany Fabio to anaesthetics and then join your friend in the lounge. Help yourselves to coffee, and I will come and get you when the surgery is completed. Follow me."

Jose grunted.

Patrick left Fabio and Jose to scrub in and check Robert had prepared. He found Robert at the sink, manically scrubbing his hands and arms with the hard brush and surgical foam.

"Uncle Patrick, this is wrong."

"Keep your mouth shut and do as you're told," Patrick replied. "These people are not the sort to accept no as an answer."

"The man is clearly under duress. We should call the police."

Patrick turned to face Robert, his eyes narrowed, his mouth set. "I will say this only once. You will not live to see the morning if you even mention the police outside of this room. These men are Trae La Muerte. They are not fucking around. The last surgeon who made a mistake was found dead with his fingers broken, throat slit from ear to ear and, just in case he still lived, a bullet to the back of his head."

The colour drained from Robert's face until his skin resembled the white walls of the clinical scrub room.

"I'm glad you understand," Patrick hissed.

Robert had never performed breast augmentation on a man. The tissue over the ribcage was tougher, the soft connective tissue replaced with fibrous muscle. Patrick worked quickly and efficiently, cutting a deep gash in the skin to form the underside of the breast and then carefully separating the adipose tissue from the underlying muscle to form a pocket for the implant.

"Pack the area," Patrick instructed. "Let's see if we get some give in the skin."

Robert did as he was told, using his gloved hands and packing to lift the skin.

"At a push, we should be able to get a D cup inserted into the pocket. It'll be uncomfortable for a while,

but better Fabio's discomfort than ours," Patrick said.
Patrick looked back down at his patient and continued his
work. When he was satisfied with both pockets, he lifted
the cannula. "You insert the implants and suture while I
start the lipo. We can use the adipose tissue in the buttock
area. It'll be quicker than implants."

Cheaper, too, Robert thought but didn't voice as
he picked up the silicone implants. Patrick wiped over
Fabio's stomach area with the blue antiseptic, made a small
incision and then pushed the cannula into the cut. While
Robert worked to make sure the breast provided a
feminine cleavage, Patrick pulled and pushed the 4mm
cannula, sucking out the yellow fatty tissue and giving
Fabio a more womanly waistline. Patrick paused for a
moment, considering the contents of the suction canister.
He'd needed a little more adipose for an effective buttock
augmentation, but if he took any more from the waist the
bruising would be terrible. Patrick looked at the man's
face, relaxed in sleep but still showing the signs of his
beating. What was a bit more bruising? He pushed the
cannula back into the soft tissue and reduced Fabio's waist
by a few more inches. A flat stomach would be a positive
in Fabio's line of work, Patrick thought, justifying his
actions.

"Finished," Robert said. "Do you want to check
my work?"

Patrick gave the breasts a cursory glance. They
looked even, and with his new slim waistline, Fabio's torso
had a definite seductive appeal.

"Right, let's get him turned. We'll have to do this
quickly," Patrick said, pulling out the cannula.

Robert helped turn Fabio onto his side, padding
the underside of his new breasts with a surgically wrapped
pillow.

"I'll push the fat cells, and you make sure it's
even," Patrick instructed, pulling the adipose tissue into
ten large syringes. Robert watched in strange fascination as

the transformation from manly flatness to womanly curves occurred in front of his eyes. "Turn her," Patrick said.

The two men manoeuvred Fabio onto his other side, and Patrick repeated the procedure, pumping the last of the fat cells under the skin. Patrick took one last look at his work and stood up.

Placing his hands on his lower back, he groaned. "I'm getting too old for this," he mumbled to himself.

"Pardon?"

"Nothing lad, you did well. Let's get Fabio here into recovery. Pad under his…or is it her now," Patrick tilted his head and raised an eyebrow at his inability to specify Fabio's gender, "thighs and lower back. Make sure there is no pressure on the buttock area. I'll been there in a moment to check the drains."

Robert wheeled Fabio out of the surgical suite, leaving Patrick alone with his thoughts. What he had just done had been morally and surgically wrong. He had broken every oath he had sworn to uphold, and yet surprisingly, he felt very little other than the weariness of long surgery. He thought about Fabio's future and shrugged. Each person made their own way in life, and if it ended badly, they had no one to blame but themselves. Patrick removed the three sets of surgical gloves he'd been wearing. It was by no means a guarantee of protection against the viruses and diseases a male prostitute might be carrying, but it had been better than nothing. He pulled on the thick yellow rubber gloves used for cleaning and for the first time in his career set about sterilizing the tools and table.

Robert wheeled Fabio into the recovery room, the man or woman or some strange hybrid of the two was still unconscious. His delicate features looked peaceful, almost attractive, underneath the bruising. Robert checked Fabio's vitals and examined the sutures before settling him with towels and cushions on either side of the very swollen and curvaceous bottom. Unintentionally, he ran his hands from Fabio's slim waist up to his newly acquired breasts. Robert shuddered as waves of painful spasms started in his stomach. His whole body heaved, and he thought he was going to be sick all over the patient in front of him. The ramifications of the surgery they had performed seeped into his conscious mind. His legs began to shake, his heart beating so fast he thought he was having a heart attack. Why? Why? Why? The question echoed in his head endlessly. He tried to justify his actions. He had needed to save Uncle Patrick from the Bolivian gang. He needed to stay alive. Fabio would be better off after the surgery, lady-boys were paid more. He needed the money to impress Elizabeth Mowbray. He wanted to astonish his Uncle with his skills as a surgeon. But Robert knew these excuses didn't have any foundations in a court of law or with his conscience. What they had done to this man was wrong. It didn't matter that they had been threatened. Patrick and Robert had taken a healthy young man and turned him into a freak show. It would have been different if the patient had been through the proper consultation and counselling. If Fabio had chosen to make these changes to his body of his own free will. Then they would be helping him become the person he wanted to be. But instead of freeing Fabio from a body he felt was not his own, they had trapped him in a body that would be used for the pleasure of others. Robert pulled at his clothes. His whole body felt as if it were on fire. His thoughts tumbled from one place to another, trying to run away from the horror of his own part in this grievous assault. He couldn't breathe, his vision turned fuzzy, his head spun.

"What the fuck?" Patrick screamed from the doorway.

Robert opened his eyes and looked at his enraged uncle.

"What do you think you're doing?"

Robert dragged his gaze from Patrick's face and

looked down at the hands that seemed to belong to someone else. Clutched in the unfamiliar fingers was a syringe filled with morphine, the point of the needle firmly embedded in Fabio's neck.

"Step away from the bed," Patrick ordered.

Robert let go of the syringe and stepped backwards. "I," he muttered, trying to remember when he had picked up the needle. "I," he muttered again, sitting down on the floor, his face in his hands while the tears streamed down his face.

"You bastard!" Patrick screamed. "You pussy face cunt! You have no place in surgery. Get the fuck out."

The words released Robert from his paralysis, and he ran from the recovery room, away from the demons of his actions and out of the door of NuYu. He didn't stop running until his legs burnt and his chest constricted. No longer able to hold himself upright, he sank onto the pavement. After a few moments, he looked around. He knew where he was and where he had been going. Their special place, the coffee shop that symbolised his and Elizabeth's relationship. He had been making his way to the place they shared. Robert wept with joy at the thought of her. Somehow he knew she'd be waiting for him. She'd be sat in the window, hoping he'd walk around the corner. She'd take one look at his strained face and wrap her arms around him. She'd take all the pain and fear away. They'd sit talking until their drinks were cold, and then they would return to his apartment and make love over and over until the monsters had been chased from his mind. Robert stood and ran around the corner. His head lifted expectantly to smile at her beautiful, warm face. Instead, he found the coffee shop closed, the dark windows mocking him in their empty, hateful way. The closed sign ridiculed his foolish hope. He limped home, opened a bottle of whisky and drank himself to sleep.

Chapter 39 – Sexual liberation

David McGregor sat on yet another sofa while another make-up girl brushed powder over his face and checked his hair. Another inane presenter sat smiling at him, and Hazel clutched his hand as if her life depended upon it. This was the eighth interview of the day. He'd been asked everything from where he bought the ring to what celebrity friend might play at his wedding. So far, all the presenters had avoided questioning the couple's sexual exploits. The media savvy Gabriel had seen to it the presenters knew the boundaries, but this was the After Ten Show. The presenter, a one-time hack, was known for in-depth interrogation and an invasive style of interviewing.

"You need to talk about Olivia Chatsworth tonight. Otherwise, the press will think you have something to hide," Gabriel had advised. "Jeremy King is a friend of mine. Offer him some free Botox, and he'll make sure you come across as the injured party."

McGregor smiled at Jeremy King and tried to remember he wasn't supposed to reach across the small space between them and tear his head from his shoulders.

"The more you give me, the more I have to work with," Jeremy instructed. "You tell all, and I'll keep it funny. I'll have you coming across as sexual liberators rather than twisted freaks."

"Thank you," Hazel smiled, placing a hand on Jeremy's thigh, her long fingers just a little too high for polite society. "It's wonderful to find such an open mind. I find people are so judgmental sometimes when all we were doing was exploring our inner sexual animals."

Jeremy gulped as Hazel's finger brushed the delicate skin just beneath his cock. "I understand. How could one resist the charms of the lovely Olivia Chatsworth?"

Hazel's eyes flashed with anger, and she pulled her

hand away from the presenter. "I hope you understand that I am the victim here. Olivia Chatsworth is a media whore. She misrepresented herself from the moment we met and manipulated the situation to make money."

McGregor groaned. This light-hearted interview was going to be painfully long. Not only did he have to chat with the self-proclaimed comic, but he also had to sit on camera and pretend to be interested while two other celebs were interviewed.

"We've just had confirmation," Jeremy beamed. "Hallie Robinson is going to be our fourth guest."

"Now this should be interesting," McGregor muttered quietly. "Hazel and Hallie in the same room, the gravity of two stars in one small space, surely the world will explode."

"Oh, I do love Hallie. She's a dear friend of David's. Isn't she darling?"

McGregor nodded.

"Maybe you'll have a threesome in the green room?" Jeremy joked.

"Mr King, that is not funny," Hazel fumed. "Unless you intend to join us," she added with a sly smile, and the presenter flushed.

"I think we're about to go live," he stuttered. "Can you inform Laura Philips in the green room she'll be on in half an hour?"

The interview went well. Jeremy resisted the urge to make more than three jokes about Hazel not wearing white at her wedding, and Hallie showed enough sympathy for it to appear real. The only tricky moment had been when Jeremy had raised the rumours about McGregor's and Hallie's love affair. Hazel turned red, and her lips pursed together in an unflattering expression. Luckily, the cameras were focused on Hallie as she laughed and placed a hand on McGregor's arm.

"David and I are old friends," she sighed huskily. "I can't say there isn't chemistry between the two of us, but Hazel got there first."

Hazel managed to get her expression under control as the camera swung in for a closeup. "I'm hoping Hallie will become a close friend," Hazel gushed. "It's so difficult for women in the media. We are either slags or bitches. It's time people realised we're human. We all have our flaws, although Miss Robinson's are obviously few and far between." She paused for the audience to laugh. "But at the end of the day, we're just people doing a job."

Hallie clapped, and the audience followed suit.

"Will you be inviting Hallie to the wedding?" Jeremy asked.

"Of course," Hazel replied. "But after today, I'm sure there will be an invitation for you, Jeremy, and Laura too."

As promised, Olivia Chatsworth came across as a money-grabbing opportunist and Hazel a poster child for women's sexual liberation. McGregor realised his role in the threesome had all but been forgotten. It was the ladies the public were interested in.

"Wonderful to see you, David," Hallie said, kissing him on the cheek as the credits finished and the runners came to detach them from their microphones.

"I watched you on the red carpet. You looked sensational," he replied. "Your visit to the clinic worked. You were on every cover."

"And you took more bookings," she laughed.

"Obviously. Who wouldn't want to be treated by the surgeon Hallie Robinson trusts?"

"Horrible business with that Chatsworth girl." Hallie screwed up her face in disgust. "You should choose your bed companions better." She shot Hazel a scornful look.

"It was perfectly pleasurable," McGregor smirked. "And the aftershock has been handled."

"But you're engaged to the witch!"

McGregor leant towards Hallie and whispered into her ear, "A temporary condition, darling."

Hallie's eyes sparkled. "Well, when you need a shoulder to cry on about the breakup, call me."

"And you'll have your PR call the press."

"But of course, what better story than an old friend comforting the heartbroken McGregor."

Hazel had finished talking to Jeremy and turned her dazzling smile on Hallie.

"I hope my fiancé isn't monopolising your time, Hallie. I know you're incredibly busy and probably have a hundred things you'd rather be doing."

"I was to fly to the states this evening, but with this impromptu interview, I've missed my flight. I was going to ask you and David to join me for dinner."

Hazel didn't like the way Hallie lingered over David's name as if their history was much more intimate than a client-surgeon relationship. "That would have been delightful, Hallie, but we agreed to dine with Jeremy," Hazel replied, waving at the presenter as he kissed Laura Philips goodbye.

"Perfect, we shall make a foursome."

Hazel pursed her lips in futile frustration. She didn't want to go to dinner with anyone. What she wanted to do was take McGregor to bed and prove being engaged was valuable in more ways than just good PR.

At Hallie's insistence, the two ladies were escorted to the studio's wardrobe room, where they picked out sexy and complimentary evening gowns. Their make-up was reapplied with the emphasis being camera lenses and natural light rather than film footage and studio lighting.

"What an excellent trap," Hallie giggled conspiratorially to Hazel as the hairdressers embarked on glamorising the duo's hairdos. "One would almost think you planned the whole thing to get McGregor down the aisle."

"David loves me very much. He proposed before

that Chatsworth whore talked to the newspapers."

"Come now, Hazel, we all know David McGregor isn't the marrying type. This engagement reeks of Gabriel. He's so brilliant at cover-ups."

"I will not tolerate this abuse!" Hazel shrieked "David and I are in love. We've already set a date for the wedding. We will be married in the spring."

"That soon?"

"What's the point of waiting when you know what you want?" Hazel regretted the words as soon as they left her mouth. Hallie clearly didn't think Hazel was a worthy dinner companion let alone the hand of David McGregor. The bitch lorded her international success over Hazel as if somehow she was better because her face was recognised on both sides of the Atlantic. "The fact is we want to get married quickly so we can move to the states. David will open his own clinic, and I have offers from daytime television."

"What marvellous news," Hallie gushed. Hazel was lying, and Hallie knew it. McGregor would never leave London. His identity and self-worth revolved around the city. Take McGregor out of this cosmopolitan world, and he'd fade like a flower severed from its roots. "But you must be more discreet, my darling. The walls have ears." She looked knowingly at the two hairdressers, who in their raptured eavesdropping had stopped styling and stood, hair brushes in hand and mouths open.

The four celebrities left the studio after signing autographs and posing for photographs. McGregor instructed the driver of a large black Town Car to head over to Beckwoods then reached into his jacket for his phone and passed it to Hallie. Hazel frowned.

"Hallie's going to tip off the press," McGregor smirked. "She can hardly do that from her phone, can she?"

Hallie dialled the number she'd memorised after her first starring role. Putting on a believable British accent, she informed the journalist she had it on good authority the scandalous David McGregor and lovely Hallie Robinson, would be at Beckwoods in twenty minutes.

"No, I have no idea if Miss Woods will be with them," she added.

"Am I not enough of a media name?" Hazel fumed.

Hallie laughed. "My dear, they will come because of the speculation. Will she, won't she be there? If I'd told the truth, where is the story?"

Hazel gritted her teeth and swallowed the malicious comment welling in her throat. Jeremy King tried to fill the awkward silence by chatting, but when neither responded, he sat back in defeated discomfort. McGregor smirked. Hazel needed her ego knocked, and Hallie was just the Hollywood star to carry out the demolition.

The car pulled up at Beckwoods, and the four emerged into the flashing bulbs of the paparazzi. Shouts of 'Miss Robinson, this way,' mingled with 'Miss Woods, let's see the ring.' Jeremy was effectively pushed out of the way as McGregor and the ladies posed for pictures and answered a stream of repetitive questions.

Eventually, McGregor stepped forward. "Thank you, but we really must get inside. The maître d' will give our table away if we aren't in soon."

The reporters and photographers laughed and moved to the side so the four could make their way to the door.

"Mr McGregor," the maître d' greeted. "Can I show you and your guests to your table? I've opened a bottle of Remoissenet, Gustave Gros, Richebourg '59 for your enjoyment, with our compliments."

"Thank you," McGregor replied, following him to a table near the window so the press could get clear photographs of the four celebrities as they dined.

"Your waitress," the maître d' said, waving his arm to a young girl stood shyly in the shadow.

"Good evening," she said, smiling at the ladies, "Good evening, sirs," she added, looking at Jeremy King but refusing to look at McGregor.

McGregor gritted his teeth. Of all the fucking bad luck. He'd forgotten his quick shag with the innocent waitress in the alley until she stood in front of him, a menu held protectively across her stomach. The memory of her tight, untouched body came back to him, and he felt aroused. His fingers inched across the table towards her firm thigh before remembering the waiting press and his companions. He pulled his hand back and thrust it into his pocket, finding a hard dick instead of solace. Hallie and Jeremy were looking at the menus, but Hazel's eyes locked on McGregor and his reaction to the pretty girl. She placed her hand on his erect cock and pressed painfully.

"Don't even think about it," she whispered into his ear. "That girl will run to the press as quick as drop her knickers."

The thought hadn't occurred to McGregor. Would the waitress, whose name he still didn't know, run to the journalists outside with a kiss and tell story? All thoughts of repeating the lunchtime's entertainment disappeared, and his eyes narrowed as he looked at her slim form. The four placed their orders, and the waitress returned to the kitchen.

"I need a piss," McGregor said, standing up.

Hazel grabbed his arm, digging her fingernails into his flesh. "Don't be long, darling, the entree will be here soon."

McGregor headed in the direction of the toilet and, when out of Hazel's sight, veered towards the kitchen. He caught the young waitress as she backed out of the kitchen door, her arms full of plated food.

"Mr McGregor," she squeaked, nearly dropping the plates. "You scared me."

"I'll do more than scare you if you think about talking to the press."

The girl's face turned red with embarrassment. "Why would I do that?" she asked, looking at her shoes.

"Money, fame, revenge for our liaison ending."

The girl looked at him. "Why would I want it to continue?"

The question was so genuine and unaffected. McGregor took a step back and looked into her face.

"You didn't feel used or rejected?"

The girl laughed. "Quite the opposite. I enjoyed being with you, and it rid me of a problem."

"And you don't want to do it again?"

"In a dirty alley with, and please don't take this the wrong way, a serial fucker. No thanks."

McGregor laughed uncomfortably.

"Mr McGregor, I think you should return to your table."

McGregor looked again at the young girl standing before him, strength of character shining from her eyes. "Can I call you?"

"No," she replied, walking away to serve four businessmen in sharp suits.

McGregor had been dismissed. It was a strange feeling, a sort of hollowness in the pit of his stomach. He looked in the mirror behind the bar and saw himself through her eyes, an older man in make-up trying to be young. The late nights and booze had aged him, dark circles ringed his eyes and his skin seemed sallow underneath the tan. Mulling over this newfound modesty, he returned to his table.

Clara Huntington was stood chatting with his dinner companions.

"David," she sighed kissing both his cheeks. "I was just saying to Miss Robinson how marvellously you have corrected my lips."

McGregor gently ran his fingers across her mouth,

feeling the texture underneath. "In a few days we'll be able to put in a little filler to give you back your famous pout."

Clara smiled and managed to thrust her chest out at the same time to give the paparazzi a magnificent shot of her cleavage.

"Would you like to join us?" Jeremy asked, unable to take his eyes from her breasts.

"I'd love to, but Lord Mowbray is a little camera shy. We are pushed right at the back of the restaurant in case his wife finds out about the affair," she giggled.

"More romantic that way, don't you think?" Hallie asked.

"It definitely makes it easier for him to eat his dessert," she laughed, pointing at the chocolate stain on her dress. "Now I must dash. There's a Clint Eastwood marathon on this evening, and I need time to get the judge into his bridle."

"Dylees tells me Lord Mowbray has a pony play fetish," McGregor explained as the page three girl bounced away. "Clara Cuntington is happy to oblige by dressing as a cowgirl and firing his guns while he fires his load. Two guns and a ten gallon hat?" McGregor shook his head. "As a fetish, it's definitely one that takes commitment."

"What do you say, Hazel? Fancy dressing up for McGregor's pleasure?"

"Hallie, if you want to join us this evening, you only need to ask," Hazel retorted. "I have a spare schoolgirl outfit."

Chapter 40 – His next fix

The nightmares became more horrific as the week progressed. Robert couldn't sleep unless he swallowed three diazepam with a bottle of whisky, and even then the bruised face of Fabio haunted him. In his nightmares, Fabio would be laid on the surgical table, bleeding from the aggressive liposuction, his blood gushing onto the tiled floor. Robert would lift his red hands to his face as he gave up trying to stem the bleed. His feet would slip on the slick floor, and he'd land in the pool of sticky blood. In another desperate dream, Fabio danced naked in front of Robert before being forced into vile sexual acts with crazed men. His full breasts and erect penis a testimony to Robert's skills as a surgeon. Fabio would look up from his torture to ask Robert why. But the worst hallucination, the one that left him shaking and drenched in sweat, was when Elizabeth slipped into his bed only to metamorphose into the Bolivian lady-boy. He couldn't function at work without Ritalin. Even getting out of bed was a herculean task, first one leg and then the other, sit up and push. McGregor was so caught up in his own world, the dilemma of being famous and successful, he didn't notice or care about the state in which Robert rolled into work. Uncle Patrick had left messages on his answerphone both at home and on his mobile. The voicemails were becoming increasingly more aggressive and agitated.

Days blurred into one long, monotonous grey. He felt very little and thought even less. Robert barely did more than put one foot in front of the other. His brain working on automated pilot as he cut and sutured, suctioned and stuffed. The string of bodies pushed in front of him didn't register as people, more as tasks he had to perform before he could get his next fix.

Elizabeth was constantly on his mind. He stalked her on the internet, following the trending media stories about her and watching her Facebook and Twitter accounts for any morsel of information. He sent her dozens of messages and when she didn't reply, he posted messages to her Facebook friends until his account was suspended. He sent gifts to her apartment, using up the money his uncle had paid him and maxing out his credit card. He waited in desperation for her to respond. When she didn't, his drug-befuddled mind blamed her friends. J-Collie and his gang disapproved of his relationship with Elizabeth. They didn't think his Leeds pedigree good enough for their precious Lady Liz. He convinced himself the only reason he and Elizabeth were apart was the poison spouted by her upper-class social circle. If only he could find a way to get to her.

"You fancy a night out?" Will asked as he walked past the staff room. "You look like you need a good meal and a good fuck."

Robert looked up from the press photograph of Elizabeth on his phone.

"I've something I have to do," he muttered, pulling his coat from the hook and walking out of the clinic with a purpose he hadn't felt in a week.

Will shrugged his shoulders. "Claire," he yelled down the empty corridor, "you fancy a quick bite then back to mine?"

Claire shook her head. "I don't think so, Will."

Will studied Claire as she turned away from him. Her newly acquired confidence shone in every movement. Kate and Dylees had persuaded her to have her hair cut in a short pixie style that emphasised her cheekbones and gave her face a heart-shaped beauty. He'd not been able to stop thinking about her curvy figure since seeing her on the treadmill at the gym.

"How about we just go for something to eat, and we can talk?"

Claire tilted her head to the side and studied Will. Something had changed in the way he regarded her. "I think... that would be nice." She smiled shyly.

Outside, Robert pulled his coat firmly around his shoulders. Even with his jumper underneath the thick winter coat, the cool air bit into his flesh with sharp needle-like teeth. He looked in his wallet. He had a few coins, but not enough for the tube let alone a taxi. His credit cards were maxed out and his bank account overdrawn. He lifted his collar around his neck, resigned to walking the long distance to St James. As he walked, he played the impending scene in his mind. He'd push his way past the doorman and rush for the lift. He'd barge the door of Elizabeth's apartment, his shoulder locked to force it open. The wood would splinter and give way to his manly strength. James Collroy would challenge him, barring his way to Elizabeth. Robert would clench his fists and, in a gentlemanly manner, ask Mr Collroy to step out of the way. He'd obviously refuse, and Robert would be forced to punch him in the nose. Elizabeth would run to him, her arms outstretched to hold him close. Robert held out his arms and stumbled forward, his legs giving way, and he crashed into the pavement. He felt the cold flagstones, and a numb sensation ran through his legs and into his chest and head before he passed out. Robert couldn't open his eyes, and his whole body shook uncontrollably. He felt wetness on his face and a warm sensation around his crotch. He tried to make his arms move, but the pain in his chest prevented his brain from sending the simple instruction.

"Can you tell me your name, mate?" a voice asked.

Robert concentrated and managed to open one eye, his vision blurred by a pink haze of blood.

"Elizabeth," he said.

"I need your name, sir," the man knelt beside him said, "and I don't think it's Elizabeth."

Robert looked at the large man in a fluorescent jacket. He had a kind face, one of those people who looked like they knew how to take care of others without making judgements. He smiled and closed his eyes.

"He must be high," the man shouted over his shoulder. "Geoff, can you bring the oxygen and trolley."

"Right you are, Dave," the other paramedic shouted from the back of the ambulance.

"Tells me his name is Elizabeth," Dave laughed as he ran his hands over Robert's legs and arms. "Doesn't seem to be anything broken. A nasty cut on his face though." Dave paused. "Here have a look in this," he said, pulling Robert's wallet from his coat pocket.

"Robert Sutherland," Geoff said, looking in Robert's wallet. "And this must be Elizabeth," he added, showing Dave the picture in the wallet. "Quite the looker for a drug addict. What's he taken?"

"Not sure, but this might explain," Dave answered, his fingers closing around the empty medicine bottle in Robert's coat pocket. "It's morphine and not prescribed to him."

"Bloke's a surgeon," Geoff said, pulling out Robert's ID card from the Fitzroy Clinic. "At one of those fancy cosmetic surgery clinics off Harley Street."

"Explains a lot." Dave turned his attention back to Robert. "Now Robert, we need to get you on the trolley. We are going to lift you in one, two, three."

The two men lifted Robert onto the trolley and wheeled him into the ambulance. Dave climbed into the back while Geoff went around the side and sat behind the driver's wheel.

"Better stick on the blues and twos," Dave ordered as Robert started fitting again. "His withdrawal would be better in A&E."

"Right you are." Geoff pressed the small button inside the cab. The blue flashing lights and sirens started as he pulled the ambulance out into the waiting traffic.

"Robert, can you hear me?"

"Elizabeth," Robert croaked.

"Would you like me to call Elizabeth?"

"Yes, phone," Robert tried to gesture to his pocket before the shaking started again and he faded back into the grey fog.

Robert felt as if his head had exploded. His face was on fire, and he couldn't feel his legs. The lead weight across his chest made breathing impossible. He reached out for the bottle of morphine he kept on his nightstand to relieve his pain and get him moving. His hand collided with a laminated cabinet. The cabinet wobbled, and a plastic jug crashed to the floor. Robert opened his eyes. Beyond the white laminated cabinet that very definitely hadn't been there when he went to sleep was a blue and white striped curtain and a tiled floor. He could hear people moving about and talking. Their voices loud enough to hurt his ears but not to make out their conversation. Robert swallowed, trying to ease the dryness in his throat, then pushed himself into a half-sitting slump.

"Ah, Mr Sutherland, you're awake. You gave us quite a fright," a nurse said, pulling back the curtain and checking his vitals. "Drink this."

She lifted him into a sitting position and held a glass of lukewarm water to his lips. He drank slowly, the water dribbling from his numb lips.

"Elizabeth?" he croaked.

"I'm afraid there wasn't any answer." The nurse looked sympathetically at Robert. "Can I call anyone else?"

"No."

"Your mum?"

"Dead!"

"Alright, but you'll need someone with you when you are discharged. We had to pump your stomach and give you naloxone, so you'll feel every ache and niggle."

Robert scowled. The naloxone had not only removed the emotionally dulling effects of the morphine, but its pain relieving properties as well. His face throbbed in time to his laboured breathing and even staying still hurt.

"Will Harrington," he managed to say through gritted teeth. "Call Will."

The dreams were worse without the dulling effects of the benzodiazepines. The images were more vivid and somehow more real. Elizabeth stood over his broken body, playing with Fabio's breasts while Fabio cut off Robert's dick and then made love to Elizabeth with his limp phallus as a dildo. McGregor, his face pressed close to Robert's, demanded to know why he'd used all the drugs. The scene metamorphosed into Uncle Patrick's battered body slumped in the corner, with the Bolivian cartel's thugs laughing at his corpse. Robert woke screaming into his pillow, his hospital gown and sheets wet with sweat. The calm, kind nurse cleaned him up and tucked him back in bed while he begged her to give him just a little something to take the edge off the pain. He grabbed at her as she refused, crumpling her neat uniform with his dirty hands.

"Enough of that, Mr Sutherland," she barked, breaking his ineffectual grip with one movement.

Light was filtering through the striped curtain when Robert opened his eyes again. He remembered waking in the near darkness, the sterile flicker of light from the overhead strip lighting making it possible to see the shadows of ghosts walking up and down the empty corridor. But this new light was the gentle warmth of morning sunshine flooding into his enclosed cubical. He could hear voices on the other side of his curtain and knew he was the topic of discussion.

"He's had a difficult night," the nurse explained. "I'm afraid it will be a long road back from his addiction."

"How'd he end up in here?" Will asked.

The nurse consulted her file. "He was found passed out at the north end of Harley Street. His notes say he wasn't competent enough to give any details."

"And what was in his system?"

"Morphine, benzodiazepines, ketamine and a few others. A right concoction. Do you work with Mr Sutherland?"

"No, we're just friends."

"Ah, I was going to report this to the police. It looks like Mr Sutherland has been helping himself to the medical supplies from his work."

"Oh," Will replied innocently. "Do you know where he works?"

"His ID says the Fitzroy Clinic. Isn't that the one at the top of Blow Row, where the dishy Dr McGregor from the TV works?"

Will flashed the nurse his charming let-me-take-you-out smile and placed his arm around her shoulder. "Can I deal with this? David McGregor's a close friend. He's only just gotten engaged, and this news would ruin his happy moment." He let his finger run up her arm in a suggestive way. "Maybe I could take you for a drink, and you could fill me in on Robert's condition so I could best help him recover."

Inside, Will was fuming. Of all the fucking things to do, overdosing on clinic drugs was the worst. Will and McGregor had been happily supplying themselves and their friends for years without drawing attention. Now he was going to have flatter and charm nurse plain Jane just to keep her quiet. It wouldn't have bothered him generally, a quick fuck and a promise to call. But he and Claire had talked all last night. They had sat cuddled on the sofa, actually getting to know each other over a bottle of wine. For the first time in his life, he had told someone he loved them and meant it. He didn't want to risk destroying something what could develop into more by flirting with a nurse.

"Well, I wouldn't want to spoil Hazel's big moment," the nurse agreed. "I'm a bit of a fan."

"I could ask her to pop in and say hello," Will suggested, relieved that there was an alternative to keep the nurse quiet. He knew full well Hazel was a fame-hungry whore, and this would make a great story on Wake-up.

"You think?"

"Here's my number. Call me, and I'll arrange something with Hazel. Now, shall we go check on Robbie?"

The curtain was tugged back, rattling the metal rings on the pole. Robert jumped at the unexpected noise and groaned in pain.

"Robbie," Will gushed, rushing over to Robert's bed, "are you okay? What happened? Why didn't you tell me you were in trouble?"

Will laid a hand on Robert's shoulder and smiled. "Don't worry, man, I'll get you home, and we'll fight this addiction together."

The nurse smiled in admiration. Robert Sutherland was lucky to have such a good and attractive friend. Will waited until the nurse was far enough away she couldn't hear his threatening whisper.

"What the hell? Of all the fucking stupid things to do. You fucking arse, do you realise what you've done?" Will pressed heavily on Robert's shoulder, causing a yelp of pain to erupt from Robert's throat. "If this comes back on me, you dick, I'll... I'll..." Will's anger overflowed in a torrent of rage, his face turned red and spit flew from his mouth. "I'm going to talk to your consultant. The quicker you're discharged, the fewer tests they can run, and the fewer questions are asked." Will stormed out of the room, leaving Robert to dwell on the injustice of life.

Will returned to the ward with the lost property clothing the nurse had found. He threw it onto the bed and stood with his arms crossed. The only way Robert could leave the hospital was if Will agreed to stay with him while he detoxed. The next forty-eight hours were critical. If Robert could stay sober and clean, they would admit him to a rehab clinic on Monday.

"Thank you," Robert croaked.

"Don't fucking thank me. What McGregor will do with your sorry ass is anyone's guess. Of all the stupid bastard things to do. That supply wasn't just for your personal use. Show some self-restraint, man."

Robert apologised as Will pushed him in the hospital wheelchair to the car and shoved him into the passenger seat.

"This thing won't go away," Will chastised. "I thought we were mates, man. But you're just a screwed up cunt. Why'd you take all that shit in the first place?"

Will's rant continued to Robert's door, his anger overflowing in a torrent of abuse. Partially, Will felt guilty he hadn't noticed Robert's addiction, and to some extent, he felt scared it could have been him laid in a hospital bed. Maybe it was time he took a long, hard look at his own life. Will took the keys from Robert's shaking hand and opened the apartment door. He deposited the shaky Robert on the sofa and marched towards the exit.

"Get yourself cleaned up. You look like a tramp," Will spat.

"You said you'd stay with me?" Robert pleaded, trying to force his legs to move.

"Yeah, I'm your mother now. Claire's snuggled asleep on my sofa. She's a prettier breakfast companion. See you Monday, clean and sober."

The door slammed shut, leaving Robert alone and desperate.

Chapter 41 – Declaration

Patrick was on a high. Gambling with his life had dulled the need to gamble with his money. His wife was having an affair with a senior member of a drug cartel. His favourite prostitute was pregnant with his child. His business had turned into an illegal gender reassignment clinic, which paid handsomely. Or it would when he'd paid off his debt to the cartel. And the lovely Rebecca was waiting in reception with some officious looking man. They were no doubt going to try and persuade him to testify against the cartel. Patrick smiled to himself. What would the prim and proper Rebecca say if she knew that only this morning Mrs De-Vargas and Mrs De-Costa had been in the clinic for their check-ups? Or that tomorrow while the clinic was closed, he had a lop and stuff procedure booked. Now if only his bastard nephew would return his calls. Life on the edge was exhilarating, and Patrick found he had a spring in his step.

"There's a bitch in reception," Sasha said, poking her head around the door. "Says her name is Rebecca but won't give me a last name."

"No worries, Sasha," Patrick beamed. "Show her into my office, will you? And fetch us some coffee."

"The little man with her?"

"Yes, him too."

Sasha showed Rebecca and her companion into Patrick's office and left to get the coffees. Patrick regarded the two people in front of him. Rebecca was as she had been in their two previous meetings, elegantly dressed in tailored clothing that couldn't disguise her feminine curves. Her long hair was tied up in a conservative knot, and her minimal make-up enhanced her natural beauty. The man with her was quite a contrast. His ill-fitting suit looked like it had been bought a decade ago although his shoes were polished and well cared for. His thinning grey hair had neither style nor purpose, and his slight frame showed the stoop of someone used to sitting at a computer screen for long hours.

"How may I help you, Rebecca?" Patrick said warmly, directing her to one of the four chairs surrounding the antique coffee table. "Sasha will be back soon with coffee."

"Thank you, Mr Sharp," Rebecca replied primly. "Can I introduce you to my colleague, Mr Francis?"

"Mr Francis," Patrick said, holding out his hand to shake the bony fingers of the man.

"Mr Francis is from the Inland Revenue," Rebecca continued.

Patrick's smile faded from his face as the colour drained from his skin. "What can I do for the Inland Revenue, Mr Francis?"

"Rebecca drew our attentions to you a few weeks back," Mr Francis said.

Patrick looked at Rebecca, and she smiled slyly.

"Since then, we have been outside your establishment. We have monitored the number of clients and estimated the amount of money you have taken. Would it be fair to say you have increased your turnover of late?"

Patrick frowned. "A little."

"Ah, that's what we thought. We estimated a 100% increase in business revenue from last year's declaration. Could we see your electronic diary and any other records?"

"I'm afraid, Mr Francis, we're not as technologically advanced as our competitors. We still rely on pen and paper."

"That's a shame."

The door opened, and Sasha rushed in, followed by Gwen. "There are men in suits taking the appointment books and card receipts!" Sasha exclaimed.

"They're in the supply cupboard as well," Gwen

added.

"As you can see, Mr Sharp, Her Majesty's Inland Revenue is quite efficient. For every unaccounted pound from the last two weeks, Mr Francis here will assume the same has been miss declared for the last five years."

Mr Francis nodded. "We have calculations for these things. Now if I can just take your computer and the details of your accountant, I will be out of your hair in no time."

Without waiting for Patrick's answer, the little man started unplugging Patrick's computer and emptying the drawers of his desk into the briefcase he was carrying.

"You bitch," Patrick spat at Rebecca.

"Manners, Mr Sharp, cost nothing. Not cooperating with the authorities, now that's expensive. Mr Francis estimates your tax bill at somewhere between £450,000 and a million. Payment won't be a problem, will it?"

"You know as well as I do I don't have that sort of money."

"Well, we could always come to some agreement."

Patrick held his head in his hands, he had believed himself untouchable. Prided himself on remaining under the radar, never flashing his cash in the wrong circles. Maintaining paper records so there wasn't an electronic trail of money changing hands. Client records were confidential, and they would never be able to subpoena those. He'd not counted on the bastards sitting outside his place of business.

"You can't do this," he blustered.

"I am afraid tax evasion is a serious crime, Mr Sharp," Rebecca explained. "With the economy as it stands, Her Majesty's government can't afford not to claim every penny owed. We can do this and will do this. The men confiscating your drug supply will be collating purchases against prescriptions. Anything out of place will be logged and investigated."

"You'll destroy me."

"Well, Patrick, you know this can all go away if you would just testify to your involvement with Trae La Muerte."

"I can't!"

"That's a shame. I do believe you have a phone call."

Patrick looked confused. "Phone call?"

Rebecca held her hand up for Patrick to be quiet.

"Mr Sharp?" Sasha whispered from the doorway. "Mr Lowry is on the telephone. He says he's from the Federation of British Plastic Surgeons and wants to talk about the unlicensed operation you carried out on Mrs De-Vargas."

Rebecca tilted her head and placed a small business card on his desk. "The walls are closing in, Mr Sharp, and only I can open a window for you to escape."

"I'm a dead man. Do you understand, you bitch?"

"We'll leave you to your phone call, Patrick," she said, her honey-smooth voice a deadly trap with him the fly caught in its sticky sweetness. "Good day, Mr Sharp. We will be in touch at the end of our investigation. Unless you want to visit with me at Scotland Yard."

Mr Francis and the other Inland Revenue staff filed out of NuYu, their arms loaded with heavy cardboard boxes containing the papers which made up Patrick's business. The boxes were piled into the black van parked across the road, and the men stepped into the black Jeep parked next to it. Patrick watched in detached fascination as his life's work travelled away in the back of the two government vehicles.

"Patrick what just happened?" Gwen exclaimed.

Patrick turned away from the departing vehicles and looked into the face of his nurse and friend. "The end, Gwen, just the end of everything."

He took a look around the decadent reception. The furniture he and Carole had so lovingly chosen to compliment the original features of the Victorian building. The ornate reception desk he had fallen in love with, and the threadbare rug he wouldn't throw out because it just fit the ethos of his clinic. He picked up an expensive vase full of delicate red roses and threw it at the wall. The satisfying splintering of porcelain echoed around the room, breaking the debilitating sludge in Patrick's brain.

"Fucking bitch," he screamed at the top of his voice. "Get Sir James on the phone. I'll have the whore's throat slit before I take this shit."

Sasha looked at Gwen. Gwen nodded, and Sasha rushed away.

"Patrick, we'll have clients in soon. You go into your office, and Sasha and I will clear up this mess. Have a cigar, have a drink, have anything, just calm down."

Patrick stormed into his office and poured himself a large glass of Midleton's. He emptied the amber whisky down his throat and then threw the glass at the wall. Patrick grabbed a chair and swung in at the desk and then pulled his certificates off the wall and smashed them onto the floor. If the fucking governmental whore expected him to bend over and take it, she was very much mistaken. He'd destroy everything in this building before he let the bitch get anything out of him.

"Sir James is on line one," Sasha said, poking her head around the door and then backing away when she saw the destruction Patrick's rage had inflicted on the orderly room.

Patrick snatched up the phone, his fingers pressing so hard on the keypad his knuckles turned white.

"Sir James," he yelled, "I need you to make some calls and get a bitch off my back."

Patrick explained the situation as Sir James made sympathetic noises over the phone.

"Which government department is she with?"

"Fuck if I know, the bitch won't even give me her real name."

"That doesn't sound promising. Seems almost clandestine."

"She's based at Scotland Yard."

"Okay, leave it with me, but Lord Mowbray is sitting the Trae La Muerte trial, and he's not my biggest fan."

"You owe me, James!" Patrick screamed. "Just get it fucking sorted or get me in touch with someone who can." He slammed down the phone and slumped back into his chair. Sir James had been his last desperate chance of making something out of this mess. If he couldn't get the bitch called off, Patrick was as good as dead.

Gwen and Andrew walked into Patrick's office.

"Fuck off!" he screamed at the pair.

"We will if you don't behave. Now tell us what mess you've gotten us all into."

"Nothing. I'm sorry. I just need to go home. Can you handle things here?"

Andrew put his hand on Patrick's shoulder. "Of course we can, but you don't need to handle this on your own. Is there anything we can do?"

"Yes. For the sake of my sanity, propose to Gwen," he placed his hand affectionately on Gwen's face, "and when he does, say yes."

Gwen looked like she was about to deny their love affair, but Andrew put a restraining hand on her arm. "Consider it done, boss."

Patrick wasn't sure how he arrived home. He drove on autopilot, his mind struggling to comprehend the consequences of the day. If his assets were frozen, he'd be unable to perform surgery and, therefore, unable to pay back Costa and he'd be a dead man. If he agreed to testify, his business would survive, but Trae La Muerte would kill him before he went to court, and he'd be a dead man. If he admitted his downfall to Carole and they ran away together, she'd hate the lower standard of her life, and he might as well be a dead man. Thoughts of Carole brought other emotions, hatred, distrust, revulsion. He couldn't decide what he was going to do about the bitch who had betrayed him. Confiding in Carole wasn't an option. Her affair with Mr Green had transferred her loyalties from her husband to the cartel. What a fucking mess he'd made of his life. He gritted his teeth in frustration as he sat in his car in the drive. Carole would have heard the iron gates opening, and if he waited in the car any longer, she would be suspicious something was wrong. Steeling himself to play the doting husband, he pushed his key into the lock on the front door. Patrick stood in the quiet, dark house and for one blissful moment thought his scheming wife might be out, probably fucking the little Bolivian worm.

"Is that you Patty Cake?" her sickly voice called from the lounge.

"Who else would it be?"

"I'm in the den. I have a fire lit and a bottle of red open. I thought you might need it after today."

"What's that supposed to mean?"

"Nothing," Carole stammered. "I meant after the transvestite's surgery, we haven't talked. I thought it might have been difficult keeping it from Gwen and Andrew."

"Oh," Patrick replied, throwing his jacket onto the old leather chair and taking the glass of red wine she offered. "I thought you meant something else. Today has been fine. No questions at all."

Carole looked suspiciously at her husband. He was hiding something, his red face and inability to look her in the eyes confirmed her misgivings. What had the prick done this time? "You don't seem too sure."

"I have a lot on my mind," Patrick said, stalling for time. "Sir James' eighth wife wants everything doing, your nephew is dodging my calls and Gwen and Andrew seem to be an item."

"About bloody time," Carole laughed. "The pair of them have been dancing around each other from the day you opened the clinic."

"Really?"

"Oh yes, I've always said Gwen needed to make a move on your attractive anaesthetist before some would-be wag sank her claws in. They make such a perfect couple. A bit like you and me, Patty Cake." She leant over and kissed him on the cheek. Part of Patrick wanted to pull away in revulsion, while the curious part wanted to know how far this new and sensually empowered Carole would go to keep him in line. He pulled her onto his lap and kissed her, his tongue pushing into her mouth. She resisted like she had done all throughout their marriage, then forced herself to relax and opened herself to him.

"Don't you have bridge tonight?" he asked, wanting nothing more than to push the whore off his knee.

"I cancelled so I could spend the night with you," she breathed huskily. "We don't spend enough time together these days."

"I'm famished, Cupcake," Patrick replied. "Has Mae left us any food? We can be bad and eat it here in front of the TV."

"I'll go and see. You find something to watch," Carole replied, jumping off Patrick's knee as if his skin had suddenly become painfully hot.

"Bitch," Patrick whispered.

Carole returned with two bowls of pasta and meatballs covered in a greasy orange sauce. "So tell me all about Gwen and Andrew," she said, plonking herself on the rug next to the fire and stuffing one of the meatballs into her mouth.

Patrick looked at the woman he'd fruitlessly lusted after for over twenty years. Her slim figure and confident swagger had returned, and she looked every inch the sexy croupier he'd fallen in love with. He dragged his eyes upwards to her face, and the heartless expression in her eyes made his blood freeze and his dick limp.

"They're keeping it very hushed, so I have no idea how long it's been going on, but I get the impression it's serious. Gwen's children like him."

"Do I need to buy a hat?"

"At some point maybe, but don't be ordering a Philip Treacy just yet. My bank balance couldn't take the hit."

"Well, a few more surgeries for your Bolivian friends, and that should be behind us."

"Carole, you do realise that this will never be over, don't you?"

"Mr Costa is a man of his word. Once you've worked off your debt, I'm sure Ricardo Green will have everything back to normal."

Patrick tried not to scowl at Carole's disclosure. Ricardo? In the years Patrick had been placing bets, Mr Green had never divulged his first name, but then again, Patrick had never had Ricardo's dick in his mouth.

"Let's hope so," Patrick agreed. "Then you can buy all the Philip Treacy hats you want."

"Do you think he'll propose? Let's hope they're as happy as we are."

Chapter 42 – Mr Collins

McGregor found balancing media interviews with his regular schedule of work almost impossible. He needed to rely heavily on Sutherland, but the boy just didn't seem to have his mind in the game. Fitzroy was reasserting himself, Hazel was pushing for a date for the wedding and Gabriel appeared to have forgotten this little sham engagement was temporary. Instead of getting Hazel to back off, the bastard kept lining up interviews and taking meetings with creatives who wanted to pay for the privilege of being involved in the biggest celebrity wedding this side of the Atlantic. The clinic was busy with ladies wishing to sneak a peek at the most eligible bachelor in London before he tied the knot. In fact, McGregor was swimming in offers of clandestine liaisons he couldn't accept because the fucking press followed him everywhere. And Witch-Hazel was up to something. He felt unsettled and out of control.

"Mr Collins is here for his appointment," Kate buzzed over the intercom.

"Show him through," McGregor snapped, thinking that maybe he could persuade the gay goat to go for some lunch with him after his ThreadLift treatment. At least he'd be able to have a drink and a moan in peace.

Collins strode purposefully into McGregor's office, his slim frame displayed to perfection in the tailored pinstriped suit.

"What the fuck happened?" Collins laughed. "Witch-Hazel finally shackled you in her dungeon until you agreed?"

"Piss off, homo! I'd sooner let you put a ball gag in my mouth and your dick up my arse than walk up the aisle."

"I knew it was a media stunt. Gabriel?"

"The one and only. Bloke's a genius and a greedy

bastard. You should see what shit he's lined up," McGregor said, slapping Collins on the back. "Have a drink before we go through to the treatment suite. I'm in no rush, you?"

Collins shook his head. "Lord Mowbray is reviewing some evidence in the Trae La Muerte trial. Until he rules, I'm at a loose end."

"Lunch?"

"I didn't bring the ball gag!"

McGregor stuck two fingers up at the barrister then picked up the phone. "Kate, book a table at anywhere but Beckwoods in an hour." Collins raised his eyebrows. "I'll tell you about it over lunch. You're buying. You can write it off as client hospitality."

The photographers snapped photographs of the two men as they left the clinic an hour later. Collins posed happily for the cameras with his new ThreadLifted and Botoxed face.

"Will Mr Collins be representing you against the Mail?" a journalist shouted.

"Mr Collins is an old friend. He's here for social reasons only. Besides, I can't afford him."

The collected press laughed and snapped a few more shots.

"How do you feel about your upcoming trial, Mr Collins? It must be nerve-racking defending the Trae La Muerte cartel?" a man at the very back of the press crowd shouted.

Collins turned to stare at the man. He didn't look like the usual tabloid paparazzi. His grey suit was a little too well-cut, his smile a little too false even for a journalist. He was the sort of man you quickly forgot.

"I cannot comment on an active case. However, if you contact my office, we will happily provide you with the press releases and inform you of any public statements." Collins paused and looked as if he wanted to say something else. Instead, he closed his mouth and turned to McGregor. "Move," he whispered as the small man triggered a memory.

"What was all that about?" McGregor asked.

"That man wasn't press. I think he's government. I've seen him before at the courthouse. He was with a tall stuck-up bitch, calling herself Rebecca."

McGregor lost interest. Collins was always knee-deep in shit. It came with the territory of defending murderers and cartels. If somebody weren't following the barrister, McGregor would be more surprised.

"Tell me about why we couldn't go to Beckwoods."

McGregor laughed and launched into the story of the sordid affair.

"What do you mean, he's at lunch?" screamed Hazel as she stood at reception at the Fitzroy Clinic. "We have a meeting with the wedding planner at one."

"I'm sorry, Miss Woods," a nervous Claire stammered. "He never mentioned anything."

"Where the fuck is he?"

"I can find out Miss Woods. He's with Mr Collins."

"The gay barrister?"

"I don't know."

Hazel's eyes narrowed as she stared at the terrified receptionist. She was very plain. Why McGregor employed her, Hazel had no idea. Maybe she made the clientele feel more beautiful after their surgery? Collins was the little fucker who had accompanied David to Bankers. He'd spent the evening with the Beasts after their explicit performance and, by all accounts, the homo barrister had put on his own show worthy of an audience. The bastard had promised her exclusive access to the cartel trial but as yet had provided nothing worth using. Hazel paused to think. At least David wasn't off shagging some waitress or actress. But what else could he be up to? Hazel's mind began to twist. Prenups, wills or a way to get out of marrying her?

"Find out where they are, and I'll join them," she said, her mind already plotting against McGregor. It would cost her the contract she'd lined up with Central Broadcast America, but it would be worth it to secure McGregor's hand in marriage.

"Hazel McGregor," she whispered to herself as Claire rushed off to find Kate. It had a stylish sound to it.

"Don't look now," Collins laughed as he saw the figure strutting towards their table, her high heels clicking on the floor. "But I think your affianced isn't pleased with you."

McGregor scowled and ran his finger across his throat, sticking his tongue out as he mimed his death.

"David," Hazel's high pitched voice grated like nails running down a chalkboard. "We have a meeting in five minutes with Julian."

"I forgot, darling," McGregor purred, standing to kiss her cheek.

Hazel glared over McGregor's shoulder at Collins as if it was his fault her fiancé had gone AWOL. When she was positive she had imparted her displeasure to the egotistical barrister, she pulled McGregor's lips to hers, kissing him in a way that made even Collins uncomfortable. Satisfied she'd made her point, Hazel pulled out a chair and sat as a waitress came to take her order.

"I'll have a glass of iced water, please," she smiled. "We'll not be staying."

McGregor tried not to laugh at Collins pulling a childish face while Hazel's head was turned.

"We have so little time to arrange this wedding, David," Hazel whined pointedly, ignoring Collins.

"Well, don't let me keep you from your appointment," Collins smirked. "I can make my own way back to your clinic, grab my stuff, and head out. In fact, Hazel can have my dessert, and you can pick up the bill."

"How kind," Hazel gushed. "I wish all of David's friends were so gentlemanly. Can I call you later to set up an interview?"

"Of course Hazel." Collins had never been referred to as gentlemanly before. He stood and kissed McGregor and Hazel, ignoring the evil look McGregor was shooting his way. Things couldn't have worked out better for him. Collins whistled a tune as he practically skipped out of the restaurant.

"We need to talk," Hazel said her tone serious. "I've put up with a lot of shit from you over the years, David McGregor, and it's going to stop."

McGregor narrowed his eyes and waited for her to continue. His lip lifted into a snarl as he considered the number of sentences he would allow before he knocked the stupid expression from her smug face.

"I know this engagement was all Gabriel's idea," she didn't pause for him to deny it but continued, "but I will not be embarrassed by you calling it off. The Chatsworth scandal was enough. I will not tolerate being ditched." Her voice levelled into a calm whisper. "Remember that segment on Botox on Wake-up? A woman in the audience asked a question about prescriptions being written without the patients being present. Well, after the show I did a little digging. It seems not only is it unethical, it's illegal and surprisingly widespread. In fact, if you know where to look, the evidence is very easy to collate. Records are kept of the number of prescriptions a surgeon writes. Can you believe some doctors are writing two hundred scripts a day?"

McGregor felt his collar was suddenly too tight. He loosened his tie and pulled uncomfortably at his neck.

"My sources tell me doctors are getting paid as much as £25 a script. My math isn't brilliant, but conservatively, this could earn them up to twenty-five grand a month. That's over a quarter of a million a year."

McGregor's palms started to sweat, and his mouth felt dry.

"Now most of the doctors involved in this scam have been advised by their accountants to declare their illegal earnings to avoid tax fraud. While this means they are unlikely to be investigated by Inland Revenue, it does make it easy to track the additional payments."

"What do you want?" McGregor hissed between gritted teeth.

"Nothing, my darling," Hazel beamed. "I have no intention of embarrassing my husband by exposing his dirty little secret."

McGregor heard the sound of wedding bells clanging like iron bars on a prison cell. He'd admired Hazel for her willingness to step beyond the usual sexual boundaries. He'd appreciated her beauty and enjoyed her depraved appetites. But McGregor had never considered her an intellectual. She was a pretty face on TV, the dumb blonde who made people feel comfortable. She was not an investigative journalist who chased leads and broke stories. Hazel remained silent while the gravity of the information sank into the recesses of McGregor's brain.

"Shall we have a spring wedding at the Clarmile?" she whispered.

McGregor closed his eyes, he couldn't breathe. A pain erupted in his left arm, spiking up into his chest in agonizing spasms. There was no escape, and he knew it. Taking a deep breath and letting the air rush out of his mouth, he opened his eyes.

"Sounds perfect, darling. When are we meeting Julian?" he asked, suppressing his anger and despair.

Hazel smirked happily as the waitress put the pannacotta in front of her. "In quarter of an hour. I told him to meet us here."

Collins admired Hazel. The witch had baited a trap, and McGregor had willingly stepped into the cage. All that remained was for Witch-Hazel to fit a collar and hobble her prey. Regardless of her intentions towards his old pal McGregor, she had provided Collins with just the opportunity he needed to get into McGregor's empty office. Collins had briefly considered bribing his friend, but he was too tight to spend the cash Costa had given him. The bundles of used fifty pound notes were stuffed in an ice cream box in his fridge and would stay there until he was able to get them out of the UK and safely into his Swiss bank account. No, theft was a far cheaper solution.

"You," he barked at the receptionist as he walked into the Fitzroy Clinic. "McGregor is with Witch-Hazel, and I didn't want to be roped into page boy duties. I'm just going to pop back and get my briefcase."

"Mr McGregor doesn't like people in his office when he's not there," Claire replied.

"You could call him and check, but by now Julian will be busy discussing flower displays and colour themes. But by all means, interrupt Hazel in her moment of victory."

The colour drained from Claire's face. Even her new coral lipstick seemed to lose some of its shine as she considered Collins' words. "That's okay, Mr Collins. If Mr McGregor said it was okay, who am I to disagree?"

"Nobody," his voice oozed venomous bitchiness. "I'll show myself through."

Claire looked over Collins' shoulder at the three women waiting to see Fitzroy. The ladies smiled sympathetically, but Claire suspected their compassion lay with Mr Collins having to deal with a stupid receptionist, rather than with Claire being verbally abused by the arrogant barrister.

Collins turned and walked through the doors and into the domain of his friend. He refused to look back, sure at any moment, a giant hand would clamp onto his shoulder and pull him back to demand he leave. The building was unnervingly quiet, the doors on either side of the corridor closed with blue engaged notices pulled. Collins picked up his pace as he saw the white door to McGregor's inner sanctum. His arm refused to move, sweat prickled on the back of his neck. Behind him, he could hear the sound of muffled talking. Someone was walking towards the door from a consultation suite. Collins reached out and pushed the handle down. Quietly, he slipped into McGregor's office and shut the door as he heard the voice of the little prick Sutherland escorting a high-pitched woman to reception.

"Well, if you're sure fat injections are the way to go," she screeched as she walked away.

Collins felt his heart trying to explode in his ribcage. He closed his eyes and took three steadying breaths. The room stopped spinning, and his heart slowed. Move! He opened his eyes and looked around the room. Next to McGregor's desk was his briefcase. He looked past the battered leather case and at the steel filing cabinet. Please let it be unlocked, Collins willed. The last thing he needed was to have to rifle through McGregor's desk drawers looking for the key. Slowly, as if he was walking towards a dangerous animal, Collins crept over to the filing cabinet. His hand reached out to touch the cold metal surface. He pulled on the top drawer and held his breath. The drawer moved, the quiet scraping of metal on metal seeming as loud as a fire alarm. Collins waited for the inevitable sound of running feet, the shouts of thief as he was dragged away kicking and screaming. No one came. Collins let out the breath he had been holding and sneered. His quick fingers moved through the drawer, his eyes taking in the names on the top of the name tags. Lady Celeste Brown, Laura Philips, Scott Holden, Sarah Wilson and then the one he wanted, Lady Elizabeth Mowbray. His eyes scanned the rest of the files to make sure he hadn't missed anything. He was tempted to take Hazel Woods' notes or sneak a peek at Hallie Robinson's, but he resisted. His fingers flicked absently across the manila tags until

Clara Huntington's name screamed out in bold black letters, Lord Mowbray's mistress. Collins pushed the two thick files of medical notes into his briefcase. The intimate and personal details from mistress and only daughter, a perfect blackmail tool for a corrupt judge.

"Did you find it?" Claire asked when Collins reappeared in reception.

"Find what?" Collins asked a guilty flush spreading across the back of his neck.

"Your briefcase, Mr Collins."

Collins held up his briefcase and smirked. "Blind as well as thick. McGregor sure knows how to hire staff." His acidic comments hid his relief.

With Lady Elizabeth's notes, he had leverage, and with leverage, he could get the case overturned. If that didn't work, he could always leak the details in Clara Huntington's file to the press, forcing Lord Mowbray to be replaced with a more pliable member of the judiciary. Dylees had made some excellent notes about bridles, sploshing parties and verbal abuse in the margins. He rubbed his hands together in anticipation of the nice fat bonus he'd need to hide in an offshore account.

Chapter 43 – No suicide

Robert sat on the sofa until the sunshine from the window became painful to his sensitive eyes. He squinted, rolling out of the light, and his stomach rumbled hungrily. He willed himself off the soft cushions and, like a man three times his age, stumbled to the kitchen. Robert had to stop halfway across the open-plan apartment to catch his breath and wipe the sweat from his eyes. He pulled open the fridge with a shaking hand. Inside was a few bottles of overpriced beer, a bottle of curdled milk and half a moulding loaf. The cupboards offered the same uninspiring options. Robert pulled out a box of porridge oats and mixed in half a cup of water. He shoved the bowl into the microwave and smelt the out-of-date yoghurt pushed to the very back of the fridge. It smelled tangy, but his stomach cried out for food, and in his lightheaded state, anything seemed better than nothing. The microwave pinged. He pulled out the lumpy gruel and poured the soured yoghurt over the top. The thick gloop stuck to the back of his throat, but he managed to force it down. Surprisingly, he felt better, less shaky. He managed to make it back to the sofa and flopped onto the soft cushions. He turned on the TV and spooned the porridge into his mouth. A vibrant, beautiful head shot of a laughing and carefree Elizabeth flashed on the screen of his television. The wind had caught her hair as the photo had been taken, pulling the long blonde mane off her face to expose her aristocratic features. Robert dropped his bowl, the sticky gruel creeping across the floor like some prehistoric protostome. He grabbed for the remote to turn up the volume.

"Lady Elizabeth Mowbray's body was found earlier today at her penthouse apartment in London. Her body had remained undiscovered for nearly a week as she was thought to be abroad avoiding the nightclub scandal.

Her family are said to be devastated by the news and believe foul play may be involved," the monotone voice of the presenter announced.

The screen changed from the picture of Elizabeth, beautiful and alive, to paparazzi shots of her stumbling towards James Collroy.

"Lady Elizabeth was photographed recently outside a well-known London nightclub. At the time, it was widely reported Lady Elizabeth had been intoxicated. Friends and family have always denied this claim, believing she had been the victim of crime and possibly drugged."

The screen flashed to outside Elizabeth's apartment, where the now live feed showed forensic experts carrying things in small plain bags and cardboard boxes to the waiting police van.

"Evidence is being collected to try and make sense of this tragedy. Police have informed us that no suicide note has been left, and at this time, they are not able to rule anything out of their enquiries."

Robert sat in stunned silence. Had James Collroy killed her in a fit of jealous rage? He picked up the phone and started to dial the police. His fingers froze over the final digit. For the first time in days, possibly weeks, Robert was clean and sober. His mind analysed his actions. Racing through the moments he'd spent with Elizabeth, the messages he'd sent, the drugs he'd supplied in a clear plastic bag, the pleasurable, incredible sex she hadn't consented to. He rushed to the kitchen and vomited porridge and bile into the stainless steel sink. What had he done? How could he explain? He grabbed for his phone and deleted the text messages he'd sent before stuffing the phone in a plastic bin bag. He snatched his laptop from the kitchen work surface. Removing all the comments he'd posted on her Twitter and Facebook page, suspending his account and erasing his history. The laptop went into the black plastic bag. He rushed to his bedroom, fear giving him the strength and determination to ignore the pain tearing through his body. He pushed the empty bottles of drugs, the discarded bottles of alcohol, the bra he'd kept as a memento of his love into the bin bag. Like a madman, he cleared away evidence Elizabeth had been in the apartment. He got down on his hands and knees and scrubbed the carpet where she'd stood, then showered, rubbing his skin until it was raw, hoping to scour away all evidence and his guilt. Robert knew what he had done. Blaming Elizabeth or McGregor or his uncle or anyone else was a waste of time. Trying to get rid of the evidence in his apartment, when the proof of his infatuation was documented in intense psychotic postings on the internet and her phone, was futile. Robert collapsed in a heap on the floor and waited for the police to come and arrest him.

The waiting drained Robert of his resolve to be brave. His body tensed at every sound in the corridor, his brain on high alert for the sound of sirens. But no one came. No police kicked in his door to drag him off for an interview. No enraged relative threatened his life for driving Elizabeth to suicide. No press knocked on his door asking for comment. He wished the police would hurry up and get here so he could face his punishment.

Robert crawled from the bedroom into the lounge. The television was still on, the news replaying the same scenes over and over again. Flashing photographs of Elizabeth, the taped-off crime scene and now interviews with her friends and family over crackly telephone lines. Robert wanted to turn the screen off. To be done with the torture of seeing her face, but his arms refused to obey him, and he sat, his eyes glued to the flashing images. A red bar appeared at the bottom of the television screen. A critical update had been released. Robert crawled nearer to the screen until he could reach out and touch the gentle face of his infatuation and downfall. The picture disappeared to be replaced by the smart-suited newsreader. Robert screamed, tormented by the loss of his last connection to the woman he loved.

The newsreader shuffled some paper and looked solemnly into the camera. "New evidence has come to light in the Elizabeth Mowbray investigation. We have just been informed by the MET that her tox screen has shown high levels of flunitrazepam and oxycodone.
Flunitrazepam is more commonly known as Rohypnol, the date rape drug. When combined with opiates such as oxycodone, it can cause respiratory depression and lead to death. The police are no longer looking at this matter as a suicide and will be updating the public as and when they know more. As always, our thoughts are with the family in these tragic times."

Robert tore at his face, clawing terrible red lacerations down his cheeks as he processed the implication of this new information. He wasn't just a rapist, he was a murderer. He'd given Elizabeth the oxycodone knowing it would react with the flunitrazepam he'd spiked her drink with. He hadn't meant her to die, just get a little sick. Robert couldn't face the truth sober. He grabbed the last bottle of spirit in his apartment, a nasty clear vodka he'd been bought as a home warming present. He drank straight from the bottle, the burning liquid spilling in rivers of fire down his lacerated skin. The effect was instantaneous on his empty stomach, warming his body and making his head swim in a pleasing stupor of intoxication. He smiled to himself as he thought about joining Elizabeth. He stumbled over to the kitchen. Careening off the coffee table, knocking over the standard lamp and colliding with the breakfast bar. His hand groped along the marble surface until he found the handle of the drawer. Robert pulled it open, falling backwards into the fridge, his fingers clasping the large kitchen knife. He sank to the floor, his legs sprawled open at odd angles, his head slumped forward. He looked at the blade in his hand with blank, drunk eyes, trying to focus on the stainless steel and lift it to his wrist. He growled in desperation, the noise sounding animalistic to his ears. The knife moved, and he felt a sharp pain as he cut into his wrist. He tried to press harder, to cut deeper, but his hand refused to obey. In frustration, he threw the knife across the kitchen, watching in fascination as it slid across the floor and under the cooker.

"No!" he screamed, scrambling on his hands and knees to rescue his only hope of escape. His hands clawed at the edge of the blade and pushed it further into the dark murk. Robert rocked backwards, tears pouring down his face as he curled up into a foetal position and waited for his life to end.

As he sobered, the numbness dissolved into a painful throbbing. Light exploded in front of his eyes, and he craved the blissful peace of oblivion. The words flunitrazepam and oxycodone resounded in his head until they no longer made sense. He'd killed Elizabeth! He couldn't face the truth sober. He needed a fix, and he didn't care what pill he pushed down his throat as long as it made the pain go away. Robert crawled to his bedroom and emptied the contents of the bedside drawer onto the floor. Mindlessly, he opened each of the empty bottles and ripped into the used silver blister strips.

"No," he wheezed between dry lips until a single thought invaded his throbbing mind, "Will."

Will would have drugs! Robert couldn't find his phone, but Will would be at the clinic. In fact, drugs would be at the clinic.

To the world outside, Robert looked like another addict looking for a fix. His glazed expression and scratched face made people turn away from him as he stumbled drunkenly across London. The rank smell of blood and the vomit down his mismatched and borrowed clothes gave him the appearance of a man used to living on the streets. People crossed the road to avoid him, and one man gave him a couple of quid for a hot meal. Robert grinned inanely at the man, saliva dribbling from his mouth. Time meant nothing to him as he placed one foot in front of the other, his body unconsciously taking him towards his goal. A horn sounded as Robert stepped off the pavement. The driver of the car wound his window down and threw the remnants of a cold coffee at the tramp.

"Oi, dick head, look where you're going!" the man shouted as he sped off.

Robert stumbled up the steps of the Fitzroy Clinic and turned the handle of the door. It refused to move. He tried again, his body rocking violently to the side as he lurched forward. His fingers grasped the cold metal handle a second time and he pushed again. Robert tilted his head to one side and squinted. Was he at the right door? He looked again at the silver plate on the side and sounded out the words. Fitzroy Clinic. He stepped back, a stupefied scowl forming, tried to force the door again. The handle moved, but the door refused to open. Robert knocked loudly and, when that didn't work, kicked the door until his feet hurt.

A cleaning woman stuck her head out of the window opposite. "It's closed, dumb ass!" she yelled. "Besides, I don't think they would let you in anyway. Piss off before I call the police."

Robert tried to look in the direction of the voice, but he couldn't make his body move. He heard the window slam shut as he twisted and tripped down the steps. Robert didn't know he walked, just that each time he forced his eyes open, the scenery was different. The streets changed from the old three-story Victorian buildings to modern glass and concrete constructions and then terraced housing, rundown and boarded up. Robert's shoulder collided with something. It was darker here, the sun didn't shine and the cold damp ate through his clothing. The bricks of the arched railway tunnel were broken, and his feet slid on the moss-covered floor.

"Watch it," a man spat from his cardboard home. Sluggishly, Robert looked at the man. His clothing mirrored Robert's, a mismatch of dirty trousers and a ripped jacket covering filthy skin. The man grinned at Robert, showing blackened and broken teeth. "You got anything to eat?"

Robert shook his head.

"Pah," the man spat and turned his attention back to picking the scab on the back of his hand.

"Ketamine?" Robert rasped.

"Ed might, but it'll cost ya," The man pointed deeper into the darkness of the railway bridge.

Ed was as emaciated as a person could be without being dead. His yellow flesh clung tightly to his bones, showing sinew but no muscle. His back stooped as if his spine could no longer hold him straight. His tattooed face seemed to belong to some Hollywood horror movie rather than the everyday streets of London. He turned when Robert croaked his name and professionally appraised the man.

"Look like you need a fix," Ed cackled, his gravelly voice harsh in the silent tunnel. "Can you pay?"

Robert thrust his arm forward, showing Ed the expensive watch on his wrist.

"Is it real?"

"Gift," Robert croaked.

Ed looked at the man's clothing. It was old and stained, but his shoes seemed new and expensive. The man's skin was sallow, and he showed all the signs of an addict. Yet his hair was cut in a fashionable style and the watch on his wrist was a Tag. Ed weighed all the information quickly, his mind calculating the odds of Robert being a long-term client or a one-off punter. The watch was worth maybe a grand at a pawn shop, but from the looks of Robert, he'd either end up in rehab or be dead in a week.

"Look, mate. I have some meth if you want it."

Robert nodded, grabbing at the offered drug with

numb fingers.

"Slow down," Ed instructed, pulling his hand out of Robert's reach. "Ya watch first."

Robert fumbled with the clasp, eventually removing the watch from his wrist, and held it out for Ed.

"You need a needle?" Ed asked, inspecting the watch for serial numbers and trademarks.

"Please."

"Nice, the addict has manners," Ed cackled, handing Robert the crystal meth and a needle.

Robert fumbled, pulling the meth into the syringe and then pushing the needle into the vein on his left arm. He pushed the plunger, injecting the stinging liquid directly into his bloodstream. Calmness settled over Robert as his mind floated outside his body. The physical and emotional pain vanished on a gentle breeze as the meth took over. Robert didn't intend to stay under the bridge. He stumbled towards the light past the homeless man underneath the cardboard. When his legs refused to carry him any further, he slumped, his back pressed against the cold brick, his legs twisted underneath him and his vacant eyes looking towards a future he would never have.

"Elizabeth," he whispered, his hands reaching out to touch the breathtaking face of the woman he loved. Euphoria washed over him and he smiled at the hallucination that danced in front of him. He tried to stand to follow the spirit twirling and dancing just out of reach. "Elizabeth?" he shouted as she moved away from him.

His skin itched as if a million insects crawled over him. He felt cold and then too hot. He pushed himself to his feet and stripped off his clothing before following the apparition. He stumbled blindly along the dirt track and onto the street, following the mirage of a happy, skipping woman. Robert's heart beat with happiness, his breathing quickened, and he stepped out from the darkness and into the light. His fingers touched the silky fabric of Elizabeth's dress. She turned and smiled. The driver of the car didn't have a chance to swerve. The naked man stepped out from the darkness of the railway bridge and just stood in the middle of the road. A strange smile spreading across his face as the bonnet of the red Corsa crashed into his legs. The screech of brakes brought people running as Robert's body was thrown into the air and tossed over the roof of the car. The woman in the vehicle screamed in response to the wet thud of his body hitting the tarmac.

Chapter 44 – To be free

"Phone me back, you bastard," Patrick screamed into the receiver.

He'd left twenty messages for his nephew over the last four days and on Saturday morning had resorted to visiting his apartment. Patrick's temper hadn't been improved by the state of the apartment he'd so kindly provided for his cheating wife's only surviving relative. The smell that had greeted him as he opened the door was stomach-churning. Moulding food, body odour and the smell of decay and neglect mixed to form a depressing picture of his nephew's life.

"I'm going to kick the bastard out," Patrick had yelled as he'd scribbled a note and left it on the coffee table. If he hadn't needed the twat's skilled hands, he'd have changed the locks there and then. As it was, he needed Robert's assistance to perform a gender reassignment on Eloise.

The banging at the door of NuYu ended his rant into the telephone. He had a choice. Either call Andrew or try to perform the surgery himself. Patrick didn't want to bring the anaesthetist into the difficult situation, but he had little alternative. He dialled Andrew's home as he opened the door to let Jose, Riky and Eloise into reception.

"What?" Andrew asked sleepily as Patrick explained.

"Boss, why?"

"I'll explain later. How quick can you be here?"

"Half an hour. I need to get rid of Gwen first. I don't want her to be involved."

"Me, neither."

Patrick hung up, feeling a little more confident.

Andrew was a solid, good, loyal man. He turned back to the three men.

"My anaesthetist will be here in a while. Let's get you into pre-op."

Eloise smiled. "I look forward to being free."

Patrick stared at the lady-boy, trying to find the hidden meaning in the statement as he escorted Eloise down the empty hallway of NuYu. He shrugged as he showed his client into the consultation room, putting the unnerving sensation down to worry at having to involve Andrew in this unpleasant business.

"What the fuck is she doing here?" Patrick shouted as he saw Andrew and Gwen walk into the surgical suite. "I told you to leave her out of his mess."

"Patrick, you need a nurse if you aren't going to kill the guy. I don't have that sort of experience," Andrew explained. "Besides she wouldn't let me come alone."

"As if I was going to let the two men I love dig themselves deeper into this shit."

They were right, but being right wasn't enough. Patrick hated putting Gwen in danger, and knowing they stood a better chance of survival by working together didn't help ease his conscience.

"Well, you're here now. You may as well scrub in."

Gwen curtsied and then stuck two fingers up at Patrick. "A thank you wouldn't go amiss."

"Thank you," Patrick said meaningfully.

Gwen quickly and professionally summed up the situation. She rearranged the surgical tools and examined the medical notes as Andrew wheeled the unconscious Eloise into the surgical suite.

"Medical history?" Gwen asked.

"That is as much as we have. It's what you collected."

"Patrick, you're messed up. I thought you were

going to get a specialist to lead?"

Patrick shrugged. "It's sort of off the books. I couldn't risk them going to the police."

"Has he been on HRT?" Andrew asked.

"Must have been, look at his face," Patrick replied, waving a scalpel at Eloise's smooth, hair-free chin.

"Might have been illegally supplied birth control?" Gwen speculated.

"And you've given him 40mg of propofol?" asked Andrew.

Patrick nodded.

"Have you done this before?" Gwen asked, looking at Eloise's genitals.

Patrick shook his head. "In theory, it should be simple. I guess once we get started, we'll find out if I'm right. We will remove the testicles first, create a vagina and when happy with the results, carry out a quick breast augmentation. If we encounter any difficulties, we can always do the tits tomorrow." Patrick touched the scalpel to Eloise's testicles and made the first incision.

The surgery progressed surprisingly smoothly. Eloise's testicles were now comfortably cushioned on cotton wool in the steel kidney dish. The nerve bundle had been located and isolated, ready to form the clitoris, and the primary incision had been made dissecting the penis ready to create a vagina. Gwen wiped Patrick's head with a damp cloth, and he smiled at her. The gentle, bleeping rhythm of the machines Andrew monitored soothed his nerves, and he began to relax. He moved on to dissect the urethra from the shaft of the penis and cut away at the excess tissue to create a smooth, even appearance. Eloise's penis effectively joined his testicles in the kidney dish Gwen held.

"Halfway," Patrick sighed, blowing out the air in his chest and mentally preparing himself for the next part of the surgery.

Patrick took the offered needle and started to

stitch until he had created a cavity of skin inside the patient. He then positioned the urethra above the new vagina and sutured. Raising her eyebrows at NuYu's newest piece of medical equipment, Gwen passed him what looked like an oversized dildo covered in latex. Patrick inserted the vaginal form, ensuring it was placed correctly, and strapped it into place. He stepped back and looked at his work. The stitching was still red and raw, but he was pleased with the appearance of his first vagina. The skin was still a little tight, but it was possible to see clearly defined labia and clitoris. The urethral opening and vaginal opening were anatomically correct, and when the hair grew back, it would hide the telltale scarring.

Andrew patted Patrick on the back. "I didn't think you could do it. Congratulations on your first dick to pussy op."

Patrick smiled. "Let's get on with the tits before my back cramps so badly I can't stand."

Gwen shook her head at the exchange. She was as relieved as both of them that the surgery had proceeded well, but wished they realised their congratulations were premature.

"Breasts," she said, pointedly looking at the flat-chested Eloise.

"Scalpel," Patrick said, sticking his tongue out at Gwen behind her back.

"I saw that."

Patrick made an incision and prepared to carry out the routine procedure. Eloise moved. It wasn't a large movement, more a twitch.

"Andrew?"

Andrew looked at the monitors and the patient, his mind doing a few quick calculations. Eloise twitched again, and his eyes flickered under the surgical tape.

"Andrew?" Patrick repeated, more urgently.

"You said he hadn't taken anything."

"He told me he hadn't."

"And you believed him?"

The patient lying on the table started to convulse, his whole body shaking as his heartbeat increased.

"Do something!" Gwen screamed, holding down the semi-conscious man.

Andrew injected 10mg of propofol into the line. "He must be on something." The anaesthetic took hold and Eloise body went limp.

"Cocaine," Gwen exploded. "Your Bolivian friends are drug cartel. Why did I agree to be involved? The guy's stoned out of his brains on coke, and you bring him into surgery."

Andrew placed a restraining hand on Gwen's arm. "This isn't the time."

Gwen gritted her teeth. "Patrick Sharp, of all the stupid things to agree to. After this surgery, you and I are through. I'm leaving, and if you don't join me, Andrew Vergette, I'm leaving you, too." She grabbed a scalpel and waved it at Patrick's face. "Give this man his tits, and let's finish this. I want to be away from you as quickly as possible."

Patrick closed his eyes and took a deep breath. She was right to leave, and he wouldn't stop her. Patrick opened his eyes and worked as quickly as he had ever done. "Implant?"

Gwen passed the implant without looking at him. She couldn't let herself think too closely about what they were doing or what it meant for the future. Patrick was unethical and dangerous. She was right to leave, but the very thought of life without NuYu scared her. She desperately wanted to back down but knew if she did, she'd follow Patrick into hell. For the sake of her children, she couldn't do that.

"It's done," Patrick said, walking into the reception area where Jose and Riky waited. "It was a little tricky, but the surgery went well."

The two men shrugged. Eloise pulling through meant that they had a semiconscious body not a dead body to drag to the 4x4.

"You should be able to take him home in the morning."

"He goes now."

"He can't go anywhere until the sedation wears off, and even then he needs to remain still for twenty-four hours."

"Mr Costa tells us to take him to apartment, we take him to apartment."

"Get Mr Costa on the phone," Patrick sighed. The last thing he needed was to draw further attention from Trae La Muerte, but Eloise could not be moved.

"We'll leave at the end of the week," Andrew said to Gwen as he reset and sterilised the surgical machines.

"We leave today. I am not setting foot in this building again," she hissed.

Gwen's expression told him she didn't want to talk. He kissed her on the forehead and left to check on Eloise's vitals, leaving her in the surgical suite cleaning up the operating table.

Something was wrong. Even accounting for a little residual cocaine in his system, Eloise shouldn't be reacting the way he was. Andrew looked at the heart rate monitor. Eloise's heartbeat had increased to a dangerous high, and his skin felt clammy to the touch. Andrew pushed fluids into the I.V. and checked the bandages around Eloise's breasts and groin. Both were soaked in red blood. Andrew pressed the emergency call button on the wall and held a towel to the wounds to stem the bleeding.

Gwen rushed in to see Andrew's hands covered in blood, just as Eloise's body started to convulse. "Myocardial infarction?"

"Looks that way but…" Andrew left the sentence unfinished.

Patrick stood at the door frozen by indecision as Gwen attempted to get a tube down the lady-boy's throat to prevent him from suffocating. The monitors bleeped wildly, their disharmonious din adding to the melee.

"The coke must have been cut with aspirin!" Andrew shouted. "Get the charcoal."

"It's too late for that," Gwen screamed. "Patrick, call 999."

Patrick didn't move.

"Patrick!" Gwen yelled.

Patrick took one last look at the fitting body of Eloise, then turned and fled. Behind him, he could hear the panicked shouts of his staff and then the inevitable sound of one long bleep as Eloise's heart stopped beating, and he died. Patrick walked past the two body guards and out into the street. He knew he had no choice. To stay was to die. Keeping his face locked forward, he strode purposefully to his car and drove away.

Subconsciously, he knew where he was going, but it wasn't until he arrived at Scotland Yard that his conscious mind caught up. He abandoned his car on the double yellows, leaving the keys in the ignition and half-ran, half-stumbled into the building.

"Sir?" the security guard asked, noting Patrick's blood-stained clothing. "Can I help you?" he asked weighing up Patrick's threat level. The man's fingers twitched near his Taser.

"I need to see Rebecca."

"Rebecca who, sir?" the guard asked, deciding the man in front of him was a lunatic with blood from his victims on his clothes.

"Rebecca who is dealing with the Trae La Muerte case. I don't know her fucking last name," Patrick said, thrusting Rebecca's card at the guard.

The guard's expression changed. He spoke quietly into the radio on his shoulder. "Miss West will be with you shortly. If you will take a seat, sir?"

The last thing Patrick was able to do was take a seat. He paced back and forth in the sterile lobby, his mind racing. Carole could go fuck herself. She'd betrayed him with Trae La Muerte, and her future was of her own making. Gwen and Andrew were different, as were Sasha and Layla. If he agreed to testify, he needed them safe first. That was the condition of his cooperation. For the first time in a decade, Patrick would put the needs of his loved ones above his own.

"I need a fucking drink!" he muttered to himself.

"I have a lovely cognac in my office," Rebecca said, appearing from nowhere. "Shall we have a glass or two while we discuss your testimony?"

"I've conditions."

"People always do. Should we start with the extraction of Layla Arze?"

Patrick sank onto one of the plastic chairs, placed in neat rows for the desperate populace forced into Scotland Yard. Victims and perpetrators alike were forced to wait in panicked discomfort while the powers of bureaucracy decided their fate. Patrick had been outmanoeuvred, outwitted and out of his depth.

He nodded, unable to utter more than one word, "Baby."

Rebecca's face softened momentarily, and then her eyes focused. She reached for her mobile.

"Extraction of subject A is a go. Added complication, the subject is with child. If soft extraction is not possible, resort to a direct assault."

"Gwen and Andrew?" Patrick pleaded. "Gwen has children. I can't let anything happened to them. And Sasha, my receptionist. She wasn't there, but they might…"

"There are consequences to our actions, Mr Sharp," Rebecca said, disapproval sharpening her tone. "You should not have involved your friends. Where are they?"

Patrick recounted the morning's events, his fear rushing forwards uncontrollably as his whole body shook. Tears flowed freely down his face as he talked about Eloise and the failed gender reassignment operation.

"He must have taken something. Andrew thinks it was cocaine. I think he wanted to die. He must have known the surgery would go badly if he were high."

Rebecca looked disdainfully at the man in front of her. His green surgical scrubs were covered in blood, evidently belonging to the rent boy he'd effectively murdered. The consequences for Mr Sharp had suddenly become far more than losing his wealth and power. She could protect his staff from the fallout, but someone had to pay for the death of the male prostitute who had bled to death at Patrick's hands. She pushed the matter to one side. For now, she needed Patrick's cooperation. She focused on ensuring the safety of Sasha Haia, Andrew Vergette, Gwen Charles and her children.

"You left them at the clinic with Trae La Muerte enforcers?"

Her disgust at his actions shattered the last remaining thread of Patrick's composure. He nodded, collapsing onto the floor. Hysteria ripped at his mind as pain exploded in his chest.

"Shit!" Rebecca screamed. "Get the paramedics! The bastard's having a heart attack."

While the paramedics worked on the unconscious body of Patrick Sharp, Rebecca consulted with her superiors. She managed to convince them that the only way to secure Patrick's cooperation was to ensure the safety of his staff. She failed to mention their involvement in the death of a male prostitute or Patrick's critical condition. Her entire attention on saving the people who had unwittingly been pulled into this dangerous situation by a selfish man.

"I'll head up the team," she informed her superior.

"I know what we're looking for. If we hit NuYu now, we can extract Gwen Charles and Andrew Vergette, preserve evidence and potentially arrest two of Costa's enforcers."

Rebecca hung up and made a few additional calls. In ten minutes, a strike team was waiting outside for her command, and Luke had appeared to take over supervision of Patrick Sharp. "Call if there's a change in his condition," she ordered.

"Yes, ma'am," Luke replied, taking up a position a few metres from his charge as the paramedics worked to save his life.

Rebecca greeted the commander of the response team as he passed her a stab vest and escorted her into the waiting van. "We need to go in silent and hard," she explained. "We have two hostiles, two witnesses and a body I need preserved."

"Armed?"

"Most likely."

The commander spoke quickly to his team as the vehicle pulled out into London traffic. Rebecca closed her eyes and tried to think of all the angles to this operation. She listed in her head what she needed to preserve in evidence and what information she could give to the forensic team who would follow.

On a quiet Sunday afternoon, the unmarked van pulled onto Harley Street. The busy clinics and offices were closed for the weekend. The few cars parked along the street had probably been abandoned in favour of Friday night revelries. The van made a sharp left onto Blow Row. Silence fell over the people in the vehicle, a readiness for what was about to come.

"Johnson, you're primary. Oatway, take the second. Green and Parker, your responsibility is the hostages. Franklin, you're with me. Miss West, hang back until we've secured the building. If we can take the Bolivians alive, great, but don't put yourselves at risk."

The unmarked van pulled up, and the back doors

opened. With quick, professional movements, the six men jumped from the back of the vehicle, a battering ram in Johnson's grasp. Rebecca heard the loud crash of the ram against the door and shouts of warning as the armed response team entered. She heard four shots fired and a woman scream, and then silence.

"Captain says you can enter, ma'am," Franklin said, poking his head around the door of the van. "Bastards were armed. We managed to take one alive, but the big one took two to the chest."

"The hostages?"

"Both scared but very much alive. They barricaded themselves in the medical cupboard. The woman has a few choice words for that man at Scotland Yard."

Rebecca walked into the clinic. At first glance, it was disturbingly similar to her previous visits. The first change she noticed was a potted plant knocked over next to the leather Chesterfield sofa. Rebecca's eyes followed the trail of soil the armed response unit had trodden into the green carpet in their rush to get across the room. Two bullet holes marred the landscape painting on the wall. Rebecca followed the trajectory of the bullets to the dead body in the doorway, the two red stains on his chest growing larger before her eyes.

"The second Bolivian?"

"Handcuffed and in custody. Oatway's with him."

Rebecca acknowledged the information, diverting her eyes as she stepped over the dead body and walked further into the clinic. It wasn't until she reached the recovery room that the full horror unfolded. Eloise lay naked but for the blood-soaked towels, his lifeless eyes staring back at Rebecca.

"Make sure no one enters. We'll need a full forensic rundown. I want to know why that man died."

"Ma'am."

Rebecca could hear the muffled crying of Gwen,

her sobs muted by the chest of Andrew, who held her close and stroked her hair in an intimate comforting manner. Feeling she was intruding on their personal grief, Rebecca coughed.

Gwen pushed Andrew away and rushed at Rebecca. "My kids?"

"Tell me where they are, and we'll dispatch a car to get them."

Gwen quickly gave their location, and Rebecca spoke rapidly into the radio.

"And Sasha?" Gwen added.

"Our receptionist," Andrew explained.

"Is she involved?"

"Not really, but some of the bodyguards know her."

"I'm having her moved into protective custody."

"What's going to happen to us?" Andrew asked.

"You'll make a statement about what happened here today, and then we will relocate you and your children. You'll have to change your names, but think of it as a fresh start. You might be called to testify eventually, but don't worry about that now."

Gwen burst into tears, relief and fear robbing her of the ability to function. Andrew nodded his understanding. "Gwen, as long as we're together, it doesn't matter where we are." He turned to Rebecca. "I think you'll want this," he said, passing her a blood-stained letter. "I haven't read it, but it's addressed to Mr Vargas. I found it in Eloise's clothing when I was looking for what he'd taken."

Chapter 45 – Finished

The new make-up girl looked at him and giggled. It wasn't the flirtatious giggle of a girl trying to get his attention, but a humorous laugh at his expense. McGregor frowned and stood up, his dark expression fixed on the soon-to-be-unemployed girl. They'd finished filming Morning Wake-up, and he sat in his dressing room waiting for Hazel to finish signing autographs. They were having lunch with Gabriel before he rushed back to the clinic.

"Have you seen this?" Hazel screamed, throwing a newspaper at his head. "As if we didn't have enough shit to deal with, you go and get yourself on the front cover of the Mail again. Are you trying to fucking ruin us?"

McGregor wasn't in the mood. Will had just phoned. Robert hadn't turned up for work, and a large contract for the Crown Prosecution Witness Programme had fallen through.

"Fuck off," he growled, picking up the newspaper. While Hazel's blackmail meant that he had to go ahead with the marriage, he had no fucking intention of being civil to her.

"Read," she spat, turning her back and walking away.

McGregor picked up a newspaper to see a photograph of Candice Connelly on the front with the headline, 'Would You Have Plastic Surgery If You Looked Like This?' McGregor smirked. He'd not thought about the sexy blonde since his failed attempt to shag her after her consultation. He'd left a few messages, but with everything that had happened in the last few weeks, he'd sort of forgotten. He'd assumed she was a fame-hungry wannabe, and guessed this article was her first step on the route to stardom. He turned to the next page, expecting to learn about her new found career as a glamour model. If the pictures were good, he'd give her another chance.

"Fuck!" he screamed as he read the article, his fingers gripping the chipboard make-up table. 'Charley Street Reaches Ethical Low.'

Candice Connelly wasn't a fame-hungry whore. She was an undercover investigative journalist. The story described her dealings with ten well-renowned surgeons.

'My journey started with an appearance on morning television,' Candice wrote. 'I was lucky enough to be invited to volunteer for a consultation with the celebrity surgeon, David McGregor. While his on-screen persona is that of a caring doctor, his off-screen life is far from benevolent. After initially declaring me perfect, Mr McGregor invited me to dinner with the clear understanding I would be provided with cosmetic procedures in return for sexual favours. At my Fitzroy Clinic consultation, Mr McGregor explained the improvements he could make to my appearance.'

On the page was a small photograph of Candice in white utilitarian bra and pants. Red arrows pointed to her stomach, her bottom, thighs, her nose, lips and forehead with details of the surgery he had recommended and the associated costs. 'Mr McGregor suggested the surgery and injections could all be performed in one day and was willing to schedule surgery with no medical history from my doctor or counselling. In fact, David McGregor seemed more interested in my sexual past and satisfying his voyeuristic tendency than providing a worthwhile consultation. In my opinion, the Fitzroy Clinic stands as an excellent example of what is wrong with plastic surgeries.'

McGregor scanned the remaining pages. NuYu didn't come off any better. Neither did Giles from the Medispa or James Galway of PSI. Candice Connelly had written a hatchet piece on all the major players in the cosmetic surgery industry.

"I'll fucking kill the bitch!" McGregor yelled, storming out of his dressing room. "Hazel!"

Hazel was seething. Gabriel had just confirmed Vogue had pulled out from sponsoring her wedding and Hello had cancelled her photo shoot. McGregor was a dick led only by his greed and his raging hard-on. Why she wanted to marry the prick was anyone's guess.

"You incompetent arsehole," she screamed as he stormed through the door. "Don't you check out your fucking clients?"

"She was your fuck up. You were the one who invited her onto the show. How the fuck was I supposed to know she was a reporter?"

"Isn't that what you have Kate for?"

"Piss off." McGregor slapped Hazel so hard she flew across the room, her body crumpling against the dressing room wall.

"You bastard!" she screamed, flying at him, her claws aimed at his face.

McGregor grabbed hold of her shoulders and pulled her backwards into the hallway. The studio staff scattered in all directions, to avoid being involved in a violent argument between the two stars.

"If you would just keep your dick in your pants, maybe your brain would occasionally work."

"And maybe if you weren't such a twisted bitch, I wouldn't have to find innocent pussy to fuck."

"You think I'm going to stand for this shit?"

"You think I give a fuck?"

Their voices grew louder and more heated as they rained blows on each other until security stepped in to physically drag the two apart. Hazel kicked and screamed, her body spasming in her desperation to inflict pain on her fiancé. McGregor sneered, shook himself free of the restraining arms and marched away. How dare the bitch talk to him like that, how dare the cunt Connelly expose him like that, how dare the world look at him with such undisguised loathing? He was above all of them, every single one of them.

He dialled Candice's number and spat a vile message onto the answerphone. He called Gabriel and, when the bastard didn't answer, sacked him over voicemail. He got into his Jag and slammed the door on his fucked-up morning.

The clinic called. "I'm on my fucking way!" he screamed at Kate.

"Mr McGregor, the police are here."

"What?"

"The police are here. They need to talk to you."

"Did that bitch Connelly phone them? Tell them I was fucking about."

"It's about Robert Sutherland, Mr McGregor. Can you please get here as quickly as possible? They say it's urgent."

"An hour," McGregor growled. "I'm on my way."

McGregor arrived at the Fitzroy Clinic an hour and ten minutes after he'd hung up on Kate. The building was disconcertingly silent. Clients must have been cancelling in droves as the Daily Mail story spread. Claire stood next to a tearful Kate, the two girls holding hands, their sad expressions mirrors of each other. Will and Fitzroy spoke quietly to a police officer in the corner of reception, and Dylees rushed about serving coffee, her nervous energy the clearest warning that something was majorly wrong.

"I'm here. What the fuck is this all about?"

The police officer stood. "If you and Mr Fitzroy would accompany me into your office, I can explain, sir."

The three men sat in the comfortable chairs in McGregor's minimalistic office.

"Coffee?"

"No, sir, but thank you," the officer said, taking a deep breath before blurting out, "I regret to inform you of the death of Mr Robert Sutherland."

"That's not funny. Is this some sort of sick joke?" McGregor barked.

"Sir, I'm afraid Mr Sutherland's body was found on Sunday afternoon. We were unable to identify him until this afternoon. He had no wallet or personal items."

"He was mugged?"

"No, sir, he was hit by a car while under the influence of crystal meth."

"Crystal meth?" McGregor couldn't hardly speak around the lump of panic in his throat.

"Among other drugs, sir. Did he have a history of drug abuse?" We have forensics going over your drug room at the moment. However, it appears Mr Sutherland may have been helping himself to your supply of controlled medications. We believe when he couldn't gain access to the building, he purchased some uncut meth on the street."

"Why are we only just being told?" McGregor asked.

"Mr Sutherland had no identification. It appears he discarded all his clothes before walking out in front of the car."

McGregor looked at the officer and tried not to laugh

"Eventually we found his clothing and belongings with a homeless man," the officer continued consulting his notes. "We have a few questions."

"Oh," was all McGregor said as he tried to calculate his culpability. Medication had been ordered for personal use, but could the police prove it? The little fuckwit had screwed him royally if he hadn't been dead McGregor would have strung the bastard up.

"I know this is a difficult time for you and your staff, Mr McGregor, Mr Fitzroy, but a pressing line of enquiry has emerged. I'm afraid I have to ask you some questions about Mr Sutherland's involvement with Lady Elizabeth Mowbray."

"He assisted in her surgery," Fitzroy explained. "Helped with her follow-up appointments here and at Re Vive."

"And this was the extent of his involvement with Lady Elizabeth?"

"As far as I am aware," McGregor replied.

The officer asked questions about Robert's final movements and told the two men he'd keep them informed as the inquiry proceeded.

"His family?" McGregor asked, realising he hadn't a clue about Sutherland's family members.

The officer consulted his notes. "An aunt and uncle."

"Patrick Sharp."

"You know him, sir?"

"By reputation. He owns the clinic at the end of Blow Row." McGregor waved in the direction of NuYu. "Now I must get back to my clients."

"The Fitzroy Clinic will have to remain closed today while we investigate Robert Sutherland's death."

"Fucking perfect!" McGregor yelled.

McGregor's reputation as a man of the people had been shattered. Candice Connelly's article had painted him as a money greedy, dirty old man. Then, of all the selfish things to go and do, Sutherland runs bollocks naked into a car, so high on drugs the police felt the need to investigate his clinic. The intercom buzzed.

"Mr McGregor," Claire whimpered into the telephone, "I think you need to come to reception."

"Where's Kate?"

"Dylees has sedated her. She was hysterical."

McGregor slammed down the receiver. "What the fuck now?"

McGregor emerged into a reception full of cameras and flashing light bulbs.

"Can you comment on Robert Sutherland's

death?"

"Was he romantically involved with Elizabeth Mowbray?"

"Did you give him the drugs?"

"Who the fuck let these vultures in?" McGregor screamed at Claire.

Will stepped in front of Claire and held his arms out protectively. "Leave her the fuck alone. This is your pissing mess, not ours."

McGregor turned to the collective press. "Fuck off!" he yelled, waving his hands ineffectually at the crowd of photographers and journalists. "Just fuck off!"

The paparazzi didn't move. Instead, McGregor's outburst seemed to ignite their frenzy, and bulbs flashed as more questions were shouted.

"Did you and Miss Woods have a threesome with Robert Sutherland?"

"Was Candice Connelly involved with his death?"

"Do you have any comments on the article in the Mail?"

McGregor launched himself at the press, arms swinging, his face enraged. He caught one journalist across the face with a left hook and grabbed the camera from a photographer. He bludgeoned a third with the camera until his face was a bloody pulp. Those closest to the vicious attack couldn't escape as the rest of the throng pushed forward to get a better photo of the incensed surgeon. It was Will and Fitzroy who interceded to calm the situation. The two men stepped in front of the homicidal McGregor, placing a human shield between him and his targets. Dylees stepped behind him and discreetly injected him with enough sedative to drop a horse. She called to Claire, and they hauled his semi-conscious body from the reception. Fitzroy moved towards the gathered paparazzi.

"I'm sure you understand this is a difficult time for all of us. Robert Sutherland was like a son to David. That we didn't see this tragedy unfolding will haunt us all for years. A young man has lost his life. We must not forget this fact by sensationalising the story. We ask you all to give us time to grieve and come to terms with our personal loss. We will release a statement when we have spoken to his friends and family. Now if I could ask you to leave, as you are interfering with the police investigation. If you don't, I am sure the officer here will kindly ask the same."

Will Harrington looked carefully at his commander in chief. Will had written the older man off as a drunk has-been, yet here he stood, his shoulders straight and his head lifted high as he dealt with the Associated Press. The absence of McGregor over the last week had revitalized the man. His eyes, typically red and glazed, were clear and sharp. He might have lost weight, or it could just have been that he no longer stooped in drunken disarray. No longer overshadowed by the magnetic personality of his fame-hungry partner, Fitzroy had been given back command of his ship. McGregor might recover publicly from the media scandal, but his position as premier at the Fitzroy Clinic would never be regained.

Will ran his hand over his shaved head. Was he responsible? He'd removed all the drugs from Robert's apartment thinking that the young surgeon just needed to lay off the pills for a few days to get over his dependence. Instead, he'd forced Robert on to the streets looking for a fix. He looked at Clare her eyes red and swollen from crying. If only he'd been a better person Robert might still be alive. He walked over to the woman who he loved and wrapped his arms around her.

"It wasn't your fault," she said.

"I should have done something." He paused accepting his role in Robert Sutherland's death. "I will change, no more drugs, no more Bankers. Just you and me and the future."

Carl Fitzroy spoke a few quiet words to each of the journalists as they left. A quick 'Robert will be missed,' a subtle 'David made a mistake in his assessment of Ms Connelly's requests,' a gentle 'Yes, you can quote me on that' and a handshake. Appeased by Fitzroy's attentiveness, and with a story they could print, the newsmen left.

Fitzroy put his arm around Will. "Thank you for your help, William. Let's get the ladies and take them for lunch. I think we could all do with a glass of red in memory of Robert. Have you ever been to Wellington's? I'll have to take you."

McGregor read the note pinned to his chest. He screwed the paper up and threw it in the bin. He could hear the noise of police officers in the next room as they removed records and bagged up Sutherland's things. McGregor thought about his outburst, and his anger returned. Why had Claire allowed him to be ambushed? Why had Dylees sedated him when he was dealing with the parasites? Who had informed the journalists Sutherland had died? He absolved himself of any wrongdoing. Forgetting that the reason the press were at the Fitzroy Clinic in the first place had nothing to do with Robert's death and everything to do with Candice Connelly and his medical misconduct. The scribbled Post-It told him Fitzroy had taken the staff to Beckwoods and when he woke, he should join them.

"Fuck that," he snarled, grabbing his car keys.

He drove like a madman, weaving in and out of traffic, tailgating the cars in front until they moved, cutting in front of taxis and buses. He mounted the kerb as the traffic lights turned amber and nearly knocked over a man walking along the pavement. McGregor shook his fist at the bemused man and sped off down a side street. It wasn't until he pulled his car in front of Hazel's house he realised where he was going.

The reporters had already been on the phone. Hazel had refused to comment as she heard the details of

McGregor's meltdown. First Candice, and now a dead employee. McGregor was finished in the UK. Hazel had already been on the telephone to Gabriel confirming he'd lined up several chat show interviews in the states. If she managed to impress, she'd be a shoe-in for those insipid daytime panel shows, and then her own chat show. Americans loved scandal, especially when it involved the British and sex. Olivia Chatsworth had done her a massive favour if you looked at it from that perspective. Hazel Woods had been unknown across the Atlantic until now.

"David," she gushed, rushing into his arms as he yanked open her front door. "It's horrible! How are you?"

McGregor held her at arms-length, his fingers digging painfully into her arms. "Fuck off, witch," he growled, throwing her to the floor. "I'm only here because the press is camped out at my apartment and the clinic.

Hazel scrambled backwards, her feet sliding on the polished floor. His look of hatred and unrestrained anger made her heart pound in terror. For the first time in her relationship with McGregor, she felt fear. McGregor was normally so in control of his emotions. He'd manipulate, hurt, and degrade, but always in the tight confines of what he deemed acceptable.

"Gabriel will be popping around at six," she said, her voice shaking. "He's lined up a few jobs for me in the states and thinks he has an opportunity for you, too."

"I fired the fucker," McGregor spat.

"He decided to ignore your voicemail."

"Why?"

"I asked him to."

"Why?" McGregor's voice grew more acidic.

"There's nothing for us here," Hazel said, standing up and cautiously moving towards McGregor. "With Robert's death and the Mail's campaign against you, your career in London is over. You could move to Leeds or Manchester, but here in London no one will take your calls. Gabriel has it all sorted."

"He does, does he?"

"Yes, David, he does. We catch a flight this evening, look at the three houses he's chosen for us in Hollywood and do a few interviews on late night TV. We can have the contracts drawn up by midweek, and I should be offered a regular spot on Daily Chat. And Gabriel is working on a few things for you." Hazel raised her eyes and looked at McGregor. "It seems our sexual adventurousness has made us a bit of a hit. They would like you to guest on Sexperts."

"I'm a fucking surgeon."

"Gabriel is working on that, too. You'll need to sit some papers, but you can practice in the states. You can start with one of the big five and eventually have your own clinic."

"I have my own clinic," McGregor hissed, grabbing Hazel by the throat.

"But you don't anymore. The Fitzroy Clinic is finished. No one will want to be treated there. A sexual pervert, a drunk and a dead addict. Your clinic is as dead as Robert Sutherland."

McGregor dropped his arms to his sides. Hazel was right. Nothing he could do here in the UK would matter. If it had been one incident then maybe, but three major new stories? His medical and television career were over.

"David?"

"Thinking."

Hazel backed away. The cogs of David McGregor's mind were turning. Either he'd realise she spoke the truth or she'd be getting on a plane without him. Morning Wake-up had already pulled his contract and suggested she take a leave of absence to get over the death of Robert Sutherland. Hazel had tried to explain she didn't know the prick, but the executive producers had been adamant. Sources inside the MET had leaked information linking Robert's overdose to the suspicious death of Lady

Elizabeth Mowbray, and the studio wanted no more scandal.

Chapter 46 – Has this been confirmed?

Rebecca read the Daily Mail article with interest. Candice Connelly had certainly done her homework, and very few surgeons would be enjoying their Monday morning. She recognised a few of the names from her work with Patrick Sharp. David McGregor had that fancy place on the corner of Harley Street and Blow Row, while Fredrick Gavin had a garish orange sign above his door. She skim read about James Galloway and the little French doctor, Michelle Delvaux. The only clinician Candice had any praise for was an unknown northern practitioner who had refused to treat her on the grounds she didn't actually need anything doing. Rebecca sipped her tea and read the paragraphs about Patrick Sharp again.

'Mr Sharp has the appearance of a charming Irish gentleman until you notice the clientele in the waiting area and the racing pages spread unashamedly on his desk. In debt to many gambling houses, Patrick Sharp is more interested in your money than your emotional wellbeing. Insisting on calling me Candy for the entirety of our dealings, even though I had given him my name on several occasions, Mr Sharp recommended over £20,000 worth of treatment, including a labia augmentation. As a respected investigative journalist, I was a little shocked. Not only had I not mentioned this procedure at any point, Mr Sharp had in no way inspected that particular area.'

The diagram of Candice's body was covered with arrows. Breast augmentation, buttock lift, labia reconstruction, liposuction on her thighs, dermal filler in her lips. Rebecca considered showing the article to Patrick but decided against it. He had suffered a mild stroke, and the MET's doctors were fearful further stress could have long-term effects without adding public humiliation to the head-fuck.

"Miss West," a young officer said respectfully

from the doorway. "This has just come to our attention."

Rebecca looked up at the young officer and the brown file she held in her hands.

"What is it?"

"I think you should examine it," she replied, not wanting to commit.

Rebecca took the file and skim read the report before glancing at the photographs of a naked dead body.

"Has this been confirmed?"

"Yes, ma'am."

"Shit." The young officer stepped back as her superior cursed venomously. "Does anyone else know?"

"Not as yet. The body is in the morgue after autopsy, and there seems to be evidence linking this matter to the Elizabeth Mowbray death."

"Bastard," Rebecca swore. "Get me everything and make sure the coroner doesn't release any details without consulting me."

The female police officer saluted and left.

"Shit," Rebecca spat, standing up to go find Patrick Sharp in the medical suite at Scotland Yard.

The look on Rebecca's face drained the colour from Patrick. "Layla?" he gasped.

Rebecca shook her head. "Mr Sharp, Layla is fine, as are Andrew, Gwen and the children. Your receptionist Sasha is staying with her mother for now. Once you've been debriefed, you will be able to see Layla. But this is another matter, I am afraid."

"Carole?" Patrick asked, wondering if she'd turned up dead in a back alley or was in a hospital, beaten. Whatever happened, she deserved it?

"No word on her yet. We're still looking. I am afraid…" Rebecca sat next to him on the bed and placed a reassuring hand on his shoulder. "I am afraid, Patrick, your nephew has died of an overdose."

Patrick looked stunned. "Was it the cartel?"

"We don't think so. Mr Sutherland's involvement

with your current problems seems to be peripheral. His autopsy shows large quantities of drugs. Morphine, ketamine, oxycodone and methamphetamines. It appears he stripped naked and ran into the road. He was killed by a car sometime on Saturday. We were unable to identify him until now."

"I thought you said overdose?"

"He was high, Mr Sharp. He ran out into the road, but if he hadn't, he would have died in a matter of hours."

Patrick didn't know whether to laugh or cry. He'd never been close to his nephew, seeing him as a costly extension to his marriage, but the kid hadn't deserved to die. Patrick sat staring at the plain walls of the medical room they'd moved him to after his stroke and wondered why he felt nothing at the news of his nephew's death.

"There's more."

Patrick looked at Rebecca. Behind the concern, he could see hints of annoyance. "What is it?"

"Mr Sutherland has been implicated in the death of Lady Elizabeth Mowbray." Rebecca continued when Patrick didn't challenge her claim. "His DNA was taken when his body came into the morgue. While it didn't provide us with an ID, his DNA was in our system. It appears Robert raped Lady Mowbray shortly before her death and was somehow involved in supplying the fatal dose of drugs that killed her."

"I thought it was suicide?"

"The lead detective's working theory is that Robert spiked Elizabeth Mowbray's drink with flunitrazepam and then supplied the overdose that killed her. Evidence has been collected from his apartment, leading the task force to believe he was obsessed with the Lady."

"I own that apartment. I was there looking for Robert. Am I being charged as an accessory?"

Rebecca shook her head. "The investigation shows he tried to remove the evidence from his apartment.

Documents were destroyed, his laptop smashed. However, forensics found her DNA in the bedroom, and the tech team has uncovered text messages and emails from him to her and her acquaintances. His fingerprints have been compared to those on the bag of oxycodone, and they're a match."

"How did she die?"

"A fatal mixture of flunitrazepam and oxycodone. She left Robert's apartment with the flunitrazepam in her system and then took the oxycodone provided by Mr Sutherland while at the nightclub. Hours later, she died in her penthouse. Her body wasn't discovered for several days."

"So there's no doubt?"

"Very little. They have yet to compare his credit card purchases to the gifts and flowers she received after her death, but the chances of Elizabeth Mowbray's death not being connected to Robert Sutherland are remote at best."

"Bastard."

"My thought exactly."

"How will this affect my testimony?"

Rebecca tilted her head and reassessed the man lying on the bed in front of her. Patrick had asked the very question she had been anxiously considering since she received the report.

"A disgraced surgeon, blackmailed by a drug cartel, is an unsympathetic witness as it is. Add in a rapist nephew killed by a drug overdose stark naked, and I stand a good chance of being considered unreliable."

"Patrick, I understand your concern. It's one I share. Is your only connection to Robert Sutherland the apartment?"

"My wife gave him cash every now and again, and I paid his university fees."

"So denying your relationship would be easy to disprove?"

"The arseholes at Fitzroy's are aware of our relationship," Patrick said. His fingers gripped the starched linen sheets as he considered the implications of Robert's death for himself and those currently protected by Rebecca West.

Rebecca thought for a moment. Her only option was a cover-up. Robert Sutherland was dead and could not be punished for his crimes. Lady Elizabeth's death could be ruled a suicide if she leant on the right people and the body in the morgue could go back to being a John Doe. She'd need a cover story for his colleagues at the Fitzroy Clinic, but that wasn't an impossible task.

"What are you going to do?"

"That's not your concern, Mr Sharp," Rebecca snapped. "My colleague will be in shortly to take your statement, and then you can see Layla." If anyone had a reason to keep the gory details of Elizabeth's death in-house, it was her father. Not only would it be an embarrassment for the public to know his family's dirty secrets, it would also kill his career if the cartel managed to discredit the star witness in this media show trial. Rebecca had her phone out of her bag before the door closed behind her. "Rebecca West to speak to Lord Mowbray, please."

Patrick stared at the grey, unappetizing food the police officer had placed on the table pushed over his bed. Rebecca had not returned, but her second in command Luke Turner had questioned him for hours. Places, people, events, everything Patrick knew about the illegal operations of Trae La Muerte. A picture was emerging of the vast network of gambling, prostitution and drugs the cartel controlled in London and as far north as Manchester. Evidence had been collected from NuYu, medical notes of prostitutes, wives and girlfriends of the high-ranking cartel officers. Patrick was expected to fill in the blanks. Did Maria Lopaz-de-Costa live with Costa at the address listed in her notes? Was there conflict between Vargas and Costa? Was Roberta Juan De-Vargas afraid of her husband, and would she cooperate if offered immunity from prosecution? The questions came one after another until Patrick couldn't remember if he'd been asked the same question before. His eyes hurt from the flickering overhead lights, and his head swam as he tried to concentrate.

"I think you need something to eat," Luke had said as Patrick almost fainted.

Patrick looked at the grey slop. He wasn't sure he'd class the overcooked lump of meat and partially boiled carrots as something to eat. He picked at the offending food and sniffed at it. It smelt of nothing. He took a bite and chewed the tasteless, dry fare, swallowing it with difficulty.

"You call this food?" Patrick asked as Luke tucked into his fast food burger.

"I call it what you get after a stroke."

Arguing with the man was almost as pointless as begging for a bite of his juicy burger. "What's happening with Layla and the others? When can I see them?"

"Layla is with Rebecca. She's answering some questions."

"She's pregnant," Patrick interrupted.

"We know. She's been seen by a doctor, and everything is just fine. Gwen and Andrew are looking at mug shots to see if they can identify any unknown players."

Patrick pushed himself up in bed and leant towards the officer. "I want to see Rebecca now. I will not say another word until I know my friends are safe. I will not have them risking their lives testifying against the cartel."

"That is not your choice."

Patrick narrowed his eyes and looked at the man sat on a plastic chair in front of him. Luke stared back, playing a tactical waiting game to see who broke the uncomfortable silence first. Luke calmly finished his burger. Sharp was tough. He knew without him, the case against Trae La Muerte was weak. Luke tapped on the door. The officer outside opened it and stood to attention.

"Sir?"

"Can you ask Miss West to join us?"

"Sir."

"I want assurances Gwen and Andrew will be relocated, together with her children, and not prosecuted. I want Sasha looked after. I want Layla to be given a new identity and my bank accounts transferred to her name," Patrick said, looking up from his bed at the smartly dressed Rebecca.

"Anything else?"

"I want to see Layla."

Rebecca raised her eyebrow. She'd expected him to ask for immunity, yet he'd not mentioned it during questioning.

"Layla may be called to testify to your involvement."

"She will not testify, do you understand? I will sign anything you want and take a deal, but not if you force the people I care about to risk their lives."

"The paperwork will be drawn up. The best I can offer you is ten years for manslaughter. The Federation of British Plastic Surgeons will strike you off as a doctor but have agreed it is in everyone's best interest if the matter in regard to Mrs De-Vargas is hushed up." Patrick smirked. It wouldn't do for another scandal involving prominent surgeons to hit the newspaper stands. Luke had given him a copy of Candice Connelly's story. If he hadn't had other matters on his mind, he'd have laughed out loud. The sneaky bitch had stitched up half the surgeons in London. "Deal."

Rebecca wasn't expecting his reply. Patrick could

have bargained for five years in a minimum security prison. With good behaviour, he would have been out in three, joining Layla and their child. "I'll draw up the papers."

"But I need to see Layla now."

Rebecca motioned for Luke to go and fetch the pregnant prostitute. Patrick's heart leapt into this throat as he saw the woman he now knew he loved. She was shaken but alive. The extraction team had pulled her out moments before Costa's men arrived at the house in which she'd been held. Four other girls had been found, along with an older woman who claimed to be a victim but was clearly the Madame. Three other girls were out on jobs, but officers had been left to arrest them as they returned.

"Patrick," she exclaimed, running over and throwing her arms around the withered surgeon. "I thought I never see you again." She avoided looking at the heart rate monitor or the tubes coming out of his arms, concentrating on his face instead. "You okay?"

"It's all going to be fine, Layla. A little faint, that's all," Patrick soothed, brushing her hair from her face and kissing her. "Miss West is going to make sure you are safe. How would you like to move to Ireland?"

"With you?"

"I'll join you after I've served my sentence," Patrick reassured, hoping she didn't hear the tremble in his voice. Patrick knew testifying against Trae La Muerte was dangerous, but that didn't matter as long as his child and Layla were safe. It was the reason he hadn't pushed for a lighter sentence. Three years or twenty years, dead was dead.

"Oh Patrick, our baby…"

"Will grow up in a beautiful country, with a beautiful mother and a beautiful life."

Layla rested her head against Patrick's shoulder. Katricia had received the money Patrick had promised and moved with their mother out of town and out of the reach of Trae La Muerte. Now Patrick was offering her a way out of prostitution, a new start and, more than that, a family.

"Kuyayki," Patrick whispered into Layla's hair.

"I love you, too."

Rebecca coughed from the doorway. "I'm afraid we need to continue questioning Miss Arze."

Patrick started to object.

"The information she can provide will save many other girls in Layla's situation. She will not have to testify."

"I have to. Friends need help, too."

Patrick nodded, but he couldn't make his arms let go of her frail body.

"Five more minutes," he pleaded.

Rebecca knew it was against protocol, but what harm could it do. With Layla's information, she was already coordinating five separate raids on houses suspected to hold trafficked women, and two with new arrivals who faced the same fate as Eloise. Patrick had provided information on gambling dens and a St James' apartment the MET and other interested agencies had no previous intelligence of. Andrew and Gwen were being cooperative but knew very little about the cartel that threatened their lives. Mr Francis of the Inland Revenue was still carrying out his investigation. He was the most thorough and pedantic investigator the Revenue employed, and if Trae La Muerte had laundered any money through NuYu, he'd find it. Right now, her most pressing problem was the death of Robert Sutherland which called into question the character of her star witness. Luckily, Lord Mowbray was cooperating. He didn't want his daughter's personal life dragged through the courtroom. With his approval, she was going to take over the investigation and gently bury it as an unfortunate accident. Elizabeth Mowbray's public reputation would remain intact, and Robert's Sutherland's death would become just another junkie overdose. It was far from clean, but it was at least a neater.

"I'll have the MET's doctor check on Patrick Sharp in an hour. Call when they arrive, and I'll escort Layla Arse back to interrogation. I've made arrangements for her to fly from Gatwick to Dublin with a security detail this evening. Her new identity will be provided at the airport. Gwen and Andrew need to decide if they're getting married or never seeing each other again. I'll let you break the news to them."

Luke grimaced. "Thanks, ma'am. You give me all the best jobs."

"And after that, you can have a crack at the enforcer we arrested. Goes by the name of Riky."

"Ma'am." Luke smiled.

Chapter 47 – Do as I say

Hazel was right. He was finished in the UK. But having Hazel tell him he was finished was the suture that broke the surgeon's back. Fuck Robert Sutherland, fuck Fitzroy, fuck the TV execs and fuck Hazel. Actually, fucking Hazel would make him feel better, especially if he could hear the bitch scream. He turned to look at her, self-hatred oozing out of every pore in his body. Hazel took a step backwards and then another. She'd always known McGregor was a sick bastard, but he had always shown restraint. Pain wasn't what turned him on, it was dominance over others. Hazel realised she'd miscalculated. McGregor wasn't in control anymore. Everything he'd held in high regard had been eradicated, and all that was left to dominate was her frail body. The back of her heel hit the first step on the stairs. She looked back, trying to judge her footing. Her eyes left McGregor for only a moment, but it was enough to snap him out of his inaction. She turned back seconds before McGregor's hands encircled her throat, wringing the air from her lungs.

"Going somewhere?" he asked.

"No," Hazel croaked. "David, you're hurting me."

"But you like it rough. Isn't that what the papers say?"

Hazel clawed at his hands, her nails digging into them in a desperate attempt to loosen his grip.

"You know I like it when you fight."

McGregor spat in her face as he forced her backwards up the stairs. Hazel had two choices, and neither appealed to her terrified mind. Either she submitted and hoped her surrender cooled his fury or she fought. Her vision blurred, and she found it more and more difficult to think. She let go of David's hands and stumbled backwards up the stairs.

"Should we take this into the bedroom, darling?

You can tie me up if you like," she gasped.

McGregor slapped her across the face, the force of the blow knocking her head into the banister. But at least he'd let go of her throat.

"We could use the bondage swing. It's been months since you tied me up."

McGregor's hand came down across her cheek, splitting open her lip. She tasted blood. Licking her lips suggestively, she pivoted to ascend the stairs. McGregor grabbed her leg and pulled. She fell forward, her head crashing against the step, a fresh cut dripping blood into her eyes.

"Come and get me," she giggled provocatively, crawling up the stairs, her bottom swaying seductively inches from McGregor's face.

McGregor felt himself stiffen, the smell of blood and Hazel's uninhibited display both enraging and exciting him. How dare this slag flaunt herself so blatantly when she should be cowering in fear? He let her get halfway up the stairs before advancing. He wrapped his hands in her hair and pulled her head backwards, his teeth biting into her neck as a wolf's might when mounting its bitch. Her tore at her underwear, ripping the thin red fabric from her dry vagina. Hazel's screams of pain echoed through the empty house until McGregor forced her red lace knickers inside her mouth, his hand clamped over her face. His other arm circled her neck to prevent escape. McGregor thrust and thrust, his excitement blocking out any other thought, his need to dominate and control overwhelming him. Hazel submitted. He felt her body relax, the tension in her muscles gone. He'd won, and in the moment of victory, he came.

"See, slag, I own you," he growled into her ear, letting go of her neck.

Hazel fell forward.

"Get up, bitch."

Hazel didn't move. Her prone form slumped

across the stairs like a discarded rag doll.

"I'm not playing with you, cunt. I said move."

McGregor grabbed her hair and lifted her head off the step. Lifeless eyes stared back at him, red lace poking out from her mouth like the apple of Sleeping Beauty. McGregor let go. Her head smashed against the staircase, the noise reverberating in the silent house. McGregor turned Hazel's body over and felt for a pulse. He put his ear to her mouth and listened to the nonexistent sound of breathing. He shook her, shouting her name over and over again. McGregor knew she was dead. He grabbed for his mobile, ready to call the emergency services but instead scrolled to Gabriel's number. Instinctive, self-preservation took over, a calm calculation of the facts. Hazel was dead. Nothing he did could bring her back, even if he wanted to. But why should her death ruin the rest of his life? She had asked for it. Her manipulation and twisted sexual fantasies had brought them to this point. He looked at her lifeless corpse, a blue tinge already tinting her pouting lips. She looked almost peaceful.

"McGregor," Gabriel answered the phone.

"Hazel's dead."

"Dead tired from all the excitement of the last few days. Perfectly understandable, David. I'll be right over."

The phone disconnected, and David McGregor was left alone with the strangely beautiful body of his deceased fiancée. His fingers reached out to brush a strand of hair from her still warm face, her pale skin soft under his fingertips. He thought about removing the red lace knickers from her mouth, but couldn't bring himself to touch the instrument of her death. Instead, he sat next to her on the stairs, watching her sleep like he had done many times in the past.

"What the fuck!" Gabriel exploded. "You call me on the phone and tell me Hazel's dead. I'm assuming it wasn't natural causes?" He waved aggressively at the corpse, her shirt torn and her skirt gathered around her waist, exposing her naked bottom. "Did you call anyone else?"

McGregor shook his head. "I didn't mean to."

"Didn't mean to! You stuffed her pants in her mouth and choked her. What did you expect to happen?"

"I wasn't... I didn't... I... She made me so angry."

"Perfect. I get the pair of you out of shit and instead of thanking me and moving to America to live the celebrity lifestyle, you kill the bitch who made it all possible."

McGregor shook, his whole body trembling with sorrow and despair and anger.

"The bitch deserved it," he spat. "She thought she'd won. Well, I showed her, didn't I?"

Gabriel put a hand on McGregor's shoulder. "David, this is serious. You could be charged with murder. We can't deny your sexual contact. Your DNA will be all over her body. What we need to do is have you somewhere else when she died. Get the air con to full and fetch me a bottle of rum."

For the first time in McGregor's life, he did exactly as he was told without any questions. He walked to the drinks cabinet and fetched Gabriel a bottle of Havana Club.

"No, you drink it. You have to be drunk for this to work."

McGregor tipped the bottle to his lips and drank the smooth golden rum. Gabriel pulled a pair of latex gloves out of his pocket and a bottle of surgical spirits from the case he'd carried into the house. It wasn't the first time he'd touched a dead body, but his stomach never got used to the work his head accepted as part of the job. He cringed as he felt the cooling skin of Hazel's neck. He wiped the area with the surgical spirits, removing most of McGregor's DNA. He pulled the underwear from her mouth and placed them in a sealed plastic bag. Sex was impossible to deny, but McGregor needed to be able to claim he'd left Hazel alive.

"Did you move the body?"

"Yes."

"How was she when she died?"

"Turned away from me, a few steps up," McGregor gestured.

Gabriel repositioned Hazel's body on her stomach halfway up the stairs as if she had been fleeing her attacker. Her torn clothing would be seen as part of a vicious attack by a crazed fan. Walking back down the stairs, Gabriel knocked over the planter and dislodged the oil portrait of Hazel. He walked into the kitchen and grabbed an apple out of the fruit bowl and a heavy golden award from the display cabinet in the lounge. Gabriel took a deep breath and hit Hazel on the back of the head with the golden statue. He heard a sickening crunch as bone crushed beneath the blow. He stuffed the apple in her mouth and stood back to admire his gruesome work. McGregor was halfway through the bottle of rum by the time Gabriel had finished staging the crime.

"Loosen your tie," Gabriel ordered.

"What?"

"Do as I say. And remember, just after you called me, concerned about Hazel's exhaustion, the two of you had a fight. You were drunk, and she was manic, emotionally unstable. She attacked you, accusing you of continuing your affair with Olivia Chatsworth. When I arrived, we decided it was best if you cooled off at the bar before meeting at the airport. We'll go for a drink, and then I'll take you to Heathrow. It's essential you make a scene about Hazel's absence and break down when you think she's broken off the engagement. Do you understand?"

McGregor nodded.

"Good, now go turn off the air con. It will warm up over the next few hours and make the time of death difficult to discern. We'll leave making as much noise as we can."

The airport was crowded and noisy. McGregor's head hurt from the vast quantities of alcohol Gabriel had poured down him while they play-acted the roles of rejected lover and best friend. Gabriel's assistant had been to McGregor's apartment and had packed a suitcase of essentials. David now sat in the first-class lounge, his head in his hands, trying to block out the sounds of happy holiday makers.

"Mr McGregor, your flight is about to board."

McGregor looked up and tried to focus on the attractive air stewardess. Usually, he'd be thinking about ways of getting a quick fuck in the galley. Instead, he was concentrating on not puking his guts all over her shoes.

"Has Hazel arrived?"

"I'm afraid not, sir," she replied sympathetically, placing her hand on his shoulder. "Maybe she's been delayed and will catch a later flight."

McGregor gulped down the vomit in his throat. The air stewardess felt tears welling in her eyes. The poor man was so obviously distraught about that deplorable woman. Hazel Woods didn't deserve the devotion of such an incredible man if she could leave him waiting in an airport lounge.

"Is there anything I can do?"

"No, we had a fight... I think she's left me..." McGregor stammered. "The article made her so angry and I... I had to leave. I was afraid what she'd do if I didn't. I shouldn't have left." A solitary tear welled in the corner of his eye.

The stewardess moved her hand, gently touching his cheek and wiping away the tear as it trickled down his face.

"She doesn't deserve you," she smiled.

McGregor looked up and tried not to grin.

Collins sat in the Boot Room drinking a glass of port and waited. Lord Mowbray had initially refused to meet with him, explaining in detail judicial misconduct pertaining to case discussions out of court.

"If you have anything to say to me, Mr Collins, you can say it in my chambers with the prosecution present," he'd snapped.

"I'm quite happy to meet you in chambers Lord Mowbray. Maybe you could show me your two guns and hat."

Lord Mowbray had spluttered before agreeing that a more private meeting at Wellington's might be best.

Collins sipped the delicious red wine and considered which of the two files he should use to blackmail the judge. On one hand, the details of Elizabeth's addiction to plastic surgery, her regular use of prescription drugs for recreational purposes and her various injuries at the hands of unpleasant boyfriends provided ideal blackmail material. Yet the salacious details on the kinky Lord that Clara Huntington had divulged to McGregor's staff was something the man definitely wouldn't want in the public arena or a divorce solicitor's hands. Collins placed both brown files on the table in front of him. Maybe he'd let the judge decide which file to look at.

"Mr Collins," Fredrick said. "Lord Mowbray asks you join him in the cigar room."

So much for having the upper hand, Collins thought as he grabbed the two files from the table and followed Fredrick. The smart waiter opened the doors to the cigar room and stepped back to allow Collins to enter. The barrister was assailed by the opulent smell of tobacco and fragrant wood. The ornate cedar walls provided a touch of old world class that would have seemed out of place anywhere other than The Wellington Club. Lord Mowbray sat on a green leather Chesterfield chair, a brandy in one hand, a lit cigar in the other.

"Well, out with it man," he growled.

Collins felt off balance. He'd expected a cosy chat with the veiled threat of ruin. Instead, he was stood before the headmaster explaining why his homework wasn't in on time.

"Lord Mowbray, if I may sit."

"I'd rather you didn't. Say what you have to say and then be gone."

Collins scowled. "If that's the way you want it," he snapped, throwing the brown files on the table. "These are copies, obviously."

Lord Mowbray lifted the files from the table, looking first at the file with his daughter's name neatly penned on the front. He flicked through the white sheets of paper, emotions crossing his face as he read the medical notes. Without saying anything, he picked up the second file. "What do you want?"

"What any good barrister wants, my client to be free from willful prosecution."

"I said what do you want?" Lord Mowbray hissed.

"I want you to have a good look at the evidence and how that evidence has been collected. I'm sure you will find technical procedures have been ignored, witnesses coached to embellish their testimony against my clients and a general overreaching of the prosecution in the charges laid."

"You want me to rule in your favour."

"I want you to listen to the evidence and then decide on its merits based on new information."

"Collins, you're a slug, and one day someone will tread on you."

"Maybe, Lord Mowbray, but it will not be you." Collins smiled. "I'll leave you to your cigar and reading."

Lord Mowbray sat in silence for a long time, staring at the offending files. The bastard McGregor had made an enemy, and when the press had finished chewing him up, Lord Mowbray would bury him for leaking private files to scum. Collins wasn't the only one with friends in low places. For now, he concentrated on damage limitation. Rebecca West had already been on the telephone to cover up some prick's nephew's involvement in his daughter's death. She could bloody well make sure this new information stayed quiet as well.

His daughter had been a problem from the moment she could talk, demanding and obstinate. She thought the world owed her just because of her aristocratic birth. He'd wanted a son, but his prudish wife had gone off sex after having Elizabeth. In public, he'd played the doting father, but in truth, all he'd wanted to do was send the asinine bitch to boarding school and forget she'd been born. Clara Huntington, on the other hand, was a pleasure to be around, especially when she schooled him in the ring, her whip cracking on his haunch. But even she hadn't been able to keep her mouth shut. Waffling, gossipy bitches. Why were all the women in his life a liability? Maybe he should switch sides like Collins. Maybe having a dick up your arse prevented you from being fucked. He knew he had no choice but to accede to Collins demands. The government would force him to resign his judicial appointment if either scandal broke. How could he pass sentence if his judgement and moral fibre were called into question? There was nothing he was able to do but lean his rulings in the case towards the Trae La Muerte cartel.

Chapter 48 – Last week

"Doctor says you're well enough to be moved to protective custody," Luke informed Patrick.

"Layla?"

"Layla has been relocated to Ireland and given a new name. She's settled well into her new life. She'll be able to communicate with you through Miss West."

"Gwen and Andrew?"

"Mr Vergette and Mrs Charles have been relocated within the UK. You'll be pleased to know they married last week with Miss West and myself as witnesses. The children were very happy. It was a very emotional service."

"Sasha?"

"With her mother for the time being. We'll reassess the situation if a threat comes to light."

"Carole?"

"Still no word, but a possible sighting in North London."

"I guess that's it then?" Patrick said, pulling back the white sheets and swinging his legs out of bed. "Solitary confinement until the trial. Do I get breakfast before I go?"

"I'll have some arranged," Luke replied. He'd come to like the older man in the week he'd been interrogating him. Somewhere in his past, the man had made a wrong choice. His greed had cost him everything, but he wasn't bitter about it. Instead, he seemed to have embraced his change in circumstances, looking forward to the future as his chance to make amends. A week without alcohol or the stress of gambling and surgery had improved his health. The doctors were confident Patrick Sharp's heart condition was manageable with medication.

"Can I have a pen and paper, please?" Patrick asked.

Patrick quickly ate the contraband fried breakfast Luke had smuggled into the medical wing and wiped his greasy fingers on the bed linen. He knew he didn't have much time before he was transported to the Category A prison in Belmarsh. He picked up the pen and started to write.

'My wonderful child,

I never knew you, but I loved you with all my heart.'

Patrick wrote the words spilling from his heart and soul in a jumble of thoughts desperate to get onto the page. He told his unborn child all the things he'd wished his parents had told him and hoped his expression of infinite love would give her something to hold onto when darkness surrounded her. He explained how he'd loved her mother and had given his life to make sure they were safe. He imparted advice and guidance and his deepest wishes until his fingers cramped and he could write no more. He finished the letter with the words he never expected to be able to claim.

'Kuyayki, Your father.'

He sealed the letter in the envelope and placed it on the swing table next to his bed. Patrick closed his eyes for a moment and tried to imagine what his child would look like. In his mind, he saw a little girl twirling under an old oak tree, her dark hair flying wildly around her shoulders while she danced among the falling leaves of autumn. He would never see his child walk or talk or graduate university. He would never experience the joy of being a father and grandfather. He would never sit in front of an open fire with a little one on his knee while they listened to the rain on the window and told each other stories about witches and fairies and dragons. Patrick smile did not quite reach his eyes as he resolved to give his child and her mother the only gift he would ever be able to give them. The chance at a better life. A polite knock on the door told him his time was over. He pulled the old coat they had given him over the prison tracksuit and pushed his feet into the grey plimsolls.

"The guards are here," Luke said.

"Can you make sure Rebecca passes that on to Layla, please?" Patrick asked, waving at the plain white envelope.

"Of course, sir."

As he was escorted to the armoured vehicle for his journey, Patrick looked back once more at Scotland Yard.

At Belmarsh, the guards handcuffed him as they opened the doors of the van. Three prison guards stood to escort him into the grey building surrounded by steel wire and high fences. They searched his clothing and quietly explained what was expected of him. Patrick wondered if they knew his solitary confinement was to protect him from the cartel he'd agreed to testify against, or did they believe he was some kind of deviant sexual offender? His fingerprints were entered into the system, and his photograph taken. Then he was escorted to the small cell he would call home for the rest of his life. Patrick sat on the lumpy mattress on a metal bed, underneath a small window.

"Lights out in one hour," the guard said before closing the cell door and leaving Patrick alone.

"Gabriel's on the phone," Hallie shouted from inside the luxury villa.

"Tell him I'm on my way," McGregor replied, pushing himself up and out of a large heated swimming pool in the garden.

McGregor wrapped a towel around his waist and walked into the spacious white lounge, his wet feet slapping on the tiled floor.

"David, you're dripping on the sofa," Hallie chastised, passing him the phone.

McGregor reached for the phone, simultaneously pulling her against his tanned, wet torso.

"Gabriel," he greeted as Hallie squirmed her way out of his embrace. "What's the latest news on my contracts?"

"You've been booked again as an expert for Stitched. But that isn't why I'm calling." Gabriel paused.

"Spit it out, man."

"Hazel's body has been found."

David McGregor sat down on the cream sofa, leaving a wet stain on the expensive fabric.

"When?"

"Last night. Her assistant Laura was sent to fetch some paperwork for Morning Wake up and found the body."

"And?"

"And they think she was killed sometime after you left for America. They'll want to question you, but with no property missing and those fanatical fan letters you were always warning her about, the police think it was an obsessed fan."

Gabriel was being careful what he said in case the phone was tapped.

"But they have leads?"

"Yes, I gave them the letters. We all thought she was on a beach somewhere, drinking mojitos and corrupting some poor local boy."

"Will I be asked to return to the UK?"

"Not at the moment. The police tell me they have requested HPD send an officer to question you."

"This is sad news. Thank you for letting me know."

McGregor hung up the phone as Hallie walked back into the lounge. She'd changed into a scandalously small white bikini. Her new pixie haircut styled into dark brown curls displayed her exquisite bone structure. She pushed a large pair of sunglasses into the curls.

"What is it, darling?" she asked, seeing McGregor's expression.

"They've found Hazel."

"Which island?"

"No, they found her dead in her house."

Hallie walked over to the distraught plastic surgeon and wrapped her arms around him. "Oh David, are you okay?"

"I am, I have you."

Hallie's insides melted. What had started as a media stunt, the glamourous actress comforting her distressed celebrity friend through a breakup, had turned into more. Her feelings for the surgeon had crept up on her slowly, and now instead of playing a couple, they actually were a couple.

"What happened?"

"The police think a crazed fan killed her the day after I flew to America."

"Can I do anything?"

McGregor smiled into Hallie's beautiful warm and round breasts. His hands moved from her waist to her pert bottom. "I think I just need to know there's good in the world. That I am alive," he said, moving his lips to the pink nipple poking through the white fabric of her bikini.

Hallie moaned and pushed her hips into McGregor. Her fingers untied her bikini top so it fell to the floor and McGregor's teeth could tease her nipples unhindered.

The Reverend watched the lady stood alone by the unmarked grave. It was always sad when no one attended the dead. A sign of the breakdown of community and the lack of care human beings showed each other in this modern, fast-paced world.

"Did you know the deceased?" he asked, walking towards her.

Rebecca jumped and turned to face the collared

man. "I…" she started. "I worked with his uncle," she finished lamely.

"Will he be joining us?"

"No, he's unable to."

The Reverend wanted to ask more about the nameless man he was about to lead to the Lord, but the lady's expression told him his questions would remain unanswered.

"Was he a Methodist?"

"He was a troubled young man, mixed up in things he couldn't deal with."

"He is with our Lord now. All his troubles are over."

"That's good," Rebecca replied, wishing her troubles were as easily over.

The court case against Trae La Muerte was going badly. Lord Mowbray seemed intent on throwing out every piece of evidence against the cartel, and Patrick Sharp was coming across as a money-grabbing lowlife rather than a respected surgeon. The letter in her pocket from Eloise was her last line of attack, and one she'd decided to keep from her bosses at Scotland Yard. The letter was addressed to Vargas, and the content had surprised even the jaded Rebecca West. Roberta Juan De-Vargas, the third wife of the cartel general, had been born Roberto Juan in Potosi, in 1994. His best friend and lover, Luis Prado, had been abducted by Trae La Muerte and trafficked to the UK a year after Roberto became Roberta thanks to the kindly patronage of one Mr Costa. Luis, now Eloise, had assumed that the love of his life had been killed until encountering her at the NuYu clinic. Eloise's letter was clear revenge on the lover he thought had abandoned him. Yet the ramification for the two generals of Trae La Muerte was far greater. The deception on Costa's part to infiltrate Vargas' inner circle would lead to war within the cartel.

"Does the gentleman have a name, if you know his uncle?" the Reverend asked, interrupting Rebecca's thoughts.

"Robert," Rebecca answered, looking at the small cardboard box of ashes the Reverend was placing into the grave. "I just didn't want him to be buried with no one marking his passing."

The Reverend placed his hand on Rebecca's shoulder kindly.

"You are a good person, my child."

"Am I?"

Chapter 49 – A year since

Rebecca walked down Blow Row, her high heels clipping rhythmically on the pavement. It had been a year since she'd sat in the back of an operations van waiting for the all clear from the raid at the NuYu clinic. Her step slowed as she passed the polished door of the Fitzroy Clinic. She watched a smartly dressed man hesitantly push open the door. A slight nervous sheen on his brow and the briefcase made her wonder if this was his first day at a new job. Maybe he was Robert Sutherland's replacement? This thought made her study his face more intently, the naïve apprehensive smile, the clenched fists as he forced himself to walk through the door. Momentarily, she caught a glimpse inside the building. Elegant ladies sat on plush chairs, flicking through magazines. An elderly gentleman with a bulbous red nose and hearty laugh greeted the young man with a warm handshake.

"You arrived at the perfect time, my boy. My anaesthetist and his new wife, Claire, are on their honeymoon. It's all hands on deck."

The door closed shut, and Rebecca was left standing on the cold street as a black Town Car pulled up and Hallie Robinson stepped out of the passenger side. Rebecca remembered an article in a glossy magazine about Hallie's marriage to David McGregor. McGregor's long term girlfriend had been murder by a fanatical stalker only months before the wedding. The two stars were supposedly 'Happy in Hollywood' but Rebecca doubted this as the actress visited her husband's ex-business partner. Was a divorce on the cards for the celebrity surgeon who now made a fortune making-over the glitterati?

Rebecca stepped out of the way of Hallie Robinson's bodyguards and walked on until she stood in front of the doors of NuYu. The 'For Sale' sign had been plastered over with a 'coming soon' banner for some exclusive designer boutique. The front door was open, and she felt pulled into the building. Her memories led her up the three steps and through the open door. The period features Patrick Sharp had loved so much had been ripped out. The ceiling moulds and deep skirting board lay in a discarded heap. The beautiful oil paintings had been replaced by large ornate mirrors, the flocked wallpaper replaced by smooth, clean whitewashed walls. Rebecca walked with purpose through the empty building to the door of Patrick Sharp's office. She stood in the place where she'd first talked to the man she eventually came to respect. She laughed as she remembered her arrogance that she'd be able to get him to testify, and his certainty that she wouldn't. How wrong she'd been. Rebecca tried to identify the point in time when Patrick had realised his house was made of straw, and that he'd invited the wolf for tea. Layla's baby, Eloise's death or Carole's infidelity? Carole Sharp had been spotted over the last year. She was now a major part of her lover's gambling racket. Shit really did float!

"Can I help you?" a curt voice asked.

Rebecca turned and looked at the man dressed in paint-covered overalls.

"Sorry," she stammered. "The door was open. I used to know the man who had his clinic here."

"The plastic surgeon who was mixed up with the Bolivian mob?"

"Yes," Rebecca said, her voice breaking slightly.

"He left some amazing furniture and stuff. Have you come to collect it?"

"Are you the new owner?"

"My girlfriend is. She used to work as a waitress at Beckwoods while she trained as a designer. I think she knew the man who owned this place."

"Tell her to sell it and put the money in this account. It will reach his estate," she said, reaching into her wallet for the government bank account details that would eventually lead to Layla Arze.

"Should we speak to Mr Sharp first?" the man asked hesitantly.

"Mr Sharp died this morning."

"Do you want to talk about it?" the man asked, hearing the grief in her voice. "You must have been close."

Rebecca shook her head, "I just wanted to see..." she began. She didn't know what she wanted to see, or why she was here. Patrick Sharp had played his part. He was just another witness, wasn't he? Maybe it was the sacrifice he'd made to save those he loved, or maybe she felt guilty about her role in his death. Patrick had known, she realised that now. When he'd made a deal with her, he'd known a lighter sentence wasn't worth arguing for. Five years, ten years, a life sentence. To him, it was all the same. He knew Trae La Muerte would get to him before he served a year.

The case against Costa and Vargas had collapsed a month into the trial. Lord Mowbray had ruled again and again in favour of the cartel. Throwing out critical pieces of testimony on technicalities and eventually reducing the charges against the men due to a lack of evidence. Costa had been found guilty of employing and harbouring illegal immigrants, Vargas with possession with intent to supply. Neither man had served a custodial sentence. Trae La Muerte had won. Rebecca took some comfort in the destruction of their prostitution ring, fifty women and men saved from a life of slavery. Drugs had been seized and destroyed, in total over three million pounds of product. Surely these facts gave Patrick's death some meaning? But as she stared at Patrick's empty office, Rebecca knew the one thing that made Patrick Sharp's death meaningful. The small, dark-haired baby wrapped in a pale pink blanket, safe and sound with her mother in the heart of Ireland. Layla had sent a picture via the official channels in the hope Rebecca would be able to get the photograph to

Patrick. It arrived too late, and instead of providing comfort to a brave man, it sat nestled in Rebecca's wallet. A little piece of something good that came out of the horror.

Being in the building made her think about the other people involved on that fatal night. Gwen and Andrew had been relocated with Gwen's children to Scotland. Andrew worked for the NHS under a new identity while Gwen retrained as a teacher. The children had settled into new schools and forgotten all about the night when armed men collected them from school and shoved them into the back of an unmarked car. Sasha had taken a job offer from Lawless Management as an entertainment executive for their new celebrity nightclub and moved to America.

"When did he die?" the man asked.

"Last night," Rebecca replied, not filling in the details. Pictures of Patrick's dead body had landed on her desk. His throat cut in a deep, diagonal slash and TLM carved into his chest in bloody letters. The coroner's report had stated Patrick hadn't fought his attackers. Either he was asleep or, more likely, knew fighting was pointless.

"Do you want a moment?"

"No, thank you. I just came to get answers."

"Did you find them?"

"Maybe."

The answer, Rebecca had found, was painfully pointless. Nothing changed. No matter what people did or didn't do, life continued. People would always have plastic surgery, wanting to improve their looks and their chances at a better life. People would always start new jobs and new businesses, full of hope and aspirations. Crime would conspire in the darkness until people shined a flicker of light into its depth. People like her would not stop fighting for justice, fighting for the small babies and children who deserved to grow up in a better world.

"Thank you," she said, turning and leaving number 37 Blow Row.

Rebecca walked towards the small red post box on the corner of Blow Row. She took out the letter Andrew had given her. The blood stained envelope was addressed to Vargas, written in Eloise's neat handwriting. Rebecca had read the letter numerous times, waiting for the time when she felt enough loathing for the cartel to act unethically. Now was that time. Without hesitation, Rebecca pushed the explosive letter into the rectangular mouth of the letterbox and walked away from Blow Row. Her phone rang.

"Ma'am," Luke said as she answered, "the enforcer who survived the raid on NuYu has requested a meeting. His name is Riky. He says he has a book."

Printed in Great Britain
by Amazon.co.uk, Ltd.,
Marston Gate.